KADE

THE LAST IN THE FALLEN CREST SERIES

TIJAN

Edited by Jessica Royer Ocken
Beta read by Crystal R Solis, Debra Anastasia, Kelly Fallon Sloane
Proofread by Amy Briggs, Paige Maroney Smith, Crystal Clear Author
Services, Michele Ficht, Chris O'Neil Parece, Amy English, Kimberley Holm

Male model on ebook and paperback is from Regina Wamba.
Special edition illustration by Milena Rives Illustrations.

To Eileen.
Also to all the readers who have loved the Fallen Crest world over the
years,
I am writing thanks to you.

To Eileen.
Also to all the readers who have loved the Fallen Crest world over the years,
I am writing thanks to you.

BREAKING DOWN THE COVER

New covers were created for the Fallen Crest Series. On the front and back page of the paperback, an emblem with different initials are displayed. The individual letters refer to the character(s) on the cover. The individual school(s) are also named that pertain to the story itself. On Kade's cover, Mason (M) and Maddy (M) are displayed. Fallen Crest Academy is the school most regarded within Kade.

A NOTE TO THE READER

Kade is the culmination of the entire Fallen Crest Series.
As I was writing this book, I realized how Mason, Logan, and
Samantha are the glue for the series including the spin-offs.
This means that readers who haven't read the spin-offs in the
Fallen Crest/Roussou Universe, you will see some of these
characters in this book.
You will not get any spoilers about their books. You will just see
where some of these characters are in this timeline, which is
after their books.
Also,
While I did research the legalities of owning a tortoise, I took
some creative license surrounding Harold.

FALLEN CREST TITLES

Books in this series:

Fallen Crest High
Fallen Crest Family
Fallen Crest Public
Fallen Fourth Down
Fallen Crest University
Logan Kade
Fallen Crest Home
Fallen Crest Forever
Kade

Mason is a prequel novella and can be read at any point. For new readers, Fallen Crest High is intended to be the first book read.

PREFACE

Within the first chapter, Mason and Logan witness an event that may not be suitable for all readers. For more information, go here.

1

MASON

My brother and I exchanged a glance when we arrived at our father's company, and it wasn't a good look. No words were needed. We both knew whatever we were walking into would not be welcomed. It was midnight. Our dad's business had morphed into a huge corporation, and his headquarters had grown with it. At this time of night, no one was here.

Logan shut his car door first, and I moved to follow, but as we hit the pavement, I took the lead. He angled himself to cover my back, literally and metaphorically. I hadn't needed him to have my back in so long. A lot had changed in the last few weeks. I retired from the NFL and we recently moved to Fallen Crest, but me and Logan, our dynamic hadn't changed. It never would. He was my brother. We'd been each other's shadows our entire life.

"You feel that itch?" Logan asked once we were inside and waiting for the elevator.

I grunted, not wanting to admit it, but fuck, it was there. "Yeah," I said gruffly, glancing over my shoulder. No one was there.

The elevator arrived. The doors opened. We stepped in, and

Logan said as he hit the button for our dad's floor, "I don't like this."

I nodded. I was right there with him.

The elevator began to rise, and the closer we got to the top floor, impending doom blanketed me. I didn't want to talk. Logan must've felt the same because he was quiet too.

Absolute silence.

I didn't know what we were going to find upstairs.

James sent us a text telling us to see him immediately. Our dad included the location: his office.

He'd been struggling, and before we moved back, we started visiting more often because of this. Analise died six months ago from cancer. His wife was also the mother of my wife, and the reason I'd met Samantha and fell in love with her when I did. I would have met Samantha and fallen in love with her anyway—it was inevitable—but the timing had been all about Sam's mother. She dated my dad and decided to leave her husband.

I still remember when I first saw Sam. It was at a gas station, and she blew me away.

That had never stopped or changed. I was still blown away as she planned our daughter's upcoming eighteenth birthday with Heather Monroe. Her best friend. They'd been laughing like school girls in the media room when I'd popped in to let her know I needed to run out to check on my dad. Sam sobered enough to give me a sharp look, the unspoken question in her eyes if I needed anything. I gave her a short shake of my head, answering without words before I took off. She'd settled back, but I knew she'd be awake and waiting for me when I got home.

She was like that. Fucking amazing.

As we approached James's office, there was a soft glow of light coming from under the door.

Logan cast me another glance as we got to the door, but I opened it, striding inside. I wasn't one to beat around the bush.

Once inside, I stopped and took inventory before saying anything.

The light was coming from Dad's computer screen, but he wasn't in front of it. He was standing at his floor-to-ceiling windows, his back turned to us as he stared out over Fallen Crest. The town had grown steadily over the last few years, becoming a vacation destination for celebrities and the wealthy.

A near-empty bottle of Jack Daniels hung from James's hand.

He always kept himself trim, but the last few months wore on him. His hair was messed. His shirt was wrinkled. There was a defeated slump in how he stood. The proud man he used to be wasn't in this room. I didn't recognize this father of mine anymore.

He waved his empty hand toward the window. "Look at it. Look at that, sons." There was a slight slur to his words.

Logan stepped up to my side with a dark look. I understood how he felt.

It wasn't unusual for us to walk in and find our father trashed. However, after being a horrible husband and a horrible father most of our lives, when his wife had needed him during her mental health struggles, he stepped up.

He became a decent human being.

He was also a good grandfather to my kids, and to Logan's kid. They loved their grandpa, and they'd been heartbroken when Analise passed away—another giant step, because she'd been a truly despicable parent to Samantha. When she'd committed to staying in the hospital until she was stabilized, she also changed as a person.

I wasn't quite sure if I could say I'd gotten a father back after James changed, because I wasn't sure I ever had one to begin with. Samantha felt the same about her mother, but in the end, they'd tried, and they were good to our kids. That was good enough for me.

"What are we doing here, James?" I took the lead, stepping forward.

Logan fell back a step, the usual shift in our dynamic showing itself in our stance, but then he growled. "Taylor's sick and pregnant, and I left her side *to be here*."

James's head lowered, and he stood there a moment as if in contemplation before he took another long drag from the bottle. He turned to us, using the back of his hand to wipe his mouth. He was grief stricken, which I knew. I'd been prepared for that. He'd truly loved Analise, and without her in his life, he was losing himself.

I'd be the same without Sam, I was certain. But enough was enough.

"Dad," I demanded. "Fucking tell us why we're here. Samantha's a wine glass away from being Ninja Sam, and if I time it right, she's going to be glowing and happy when I get her to bed. I like seeing my wife glowing and happy."

"I like holding my wife when she's puking in the toilet because she's about to give us our second kid." Logan glared at James, his words biting.

James swallowed. I could see the usual grief in his eyes, but this felt like more. Utter destruction read on his face. He shook his head. "My grandbabies. Your babies." A single tear slipped down the side of his face. "I'm so proud of you both. What you have become—the way you love your wives. Both of you. I know I had nothing to do with that, except to teach you what not to do, but I'm proud of you. I love you both so much." He whispered the words, grief strangling him.

That impending doom was getting worse in my gut now.

"Dad?" My head lowered. "What's going on?"

He blinked, as if clearing some of the grief away, and he

nodded briskly. "Right. You're taking over for me, son—both of you, but Mason, since you're here and retired from football, I need you to take the helm."

I met Logan's gaze in surprise. He seemed just as shocked.

"What are you talking about?" He moved to stand at my side. His shoulder brushed mine. "Are you stepping down?"

James's eyes flooded again with unshed tears, his hand trembling as he placed the bottle roughly on the desk. He motioned to the computer. "Everything's in your name, Mason. I changed all the passwords to Maddy's birthday." He nodded to his phone. "Logan, your son's birthday is the password on there. You can get into everything through my phone. You'll be at the helm. Logan, you'll be at his side. You were always joined at the hip. That's the way to go through life." He stopped and drew in some air, a wheezy sound rattling from his throat. "There's no other way I can see around this, but with the change in leadership, it'll stall them. He can't run over you the way he can me. Not you both. With your connections. You know how to stand your ground and fight. I know you'll do just as well in the boardroom. I know it. It's the only way."

"Dad." I stepped forward again. "You don't have to retire or step down. Just take time off. I'll step in and run everything. The way you're talking, this is grief clouding your thoughts."

Suddenly, a light shone from his eyes like clouds parting, and I saw some clarity.

I started to relax until he said, "This is the only way." He said to Logan, "You'll need to research them. Know who exactly you're going to be fighting but ask Monroe. He's connected to that world. He knows their true business. He'll know why I did this. He'll understand. I'm so sorry, boys. I would've loved to hold my grandbabies as long as they would let me, but this is for the best."

"Dad," Logan growled. "What are you talking about? *Who*?"

James lowered his head, but then he met my gaze. Seeing

the level of torment in him, I felt punched in the stomach. It was worse than I thought. Way worse than I thought. His voice was raw as he said, "They're trying to move in and take over everything. Don't let them."

He moved in a flash, before I could register what was in his hand.

He raised the gun and placed the barrel under his chin.

Every muscle in my body turned to ice. "DAD! NO—" I started for him.

"Monroe will know him," he said calmly. "Kai Bennett."

He pulled the trigger before I got to him.

2

MASON

Cops were everywhere. I felt like when I closed my eyes, I would see those flashing red and blue lights forever. They were ingrained to the insides of my eyelids.

The police questioned us, together at first, then separately.

Samantha showed up.

When she got out of her vehicle, I hated seeing the lights flashing over her face. My wife should never have to look like that. She was devastated for me.

Fuck.

My dad killed himself, and in front of us.

She rushed to me, opening her arms. Her voice hitched on a sob. "Mason."

I caught her, folding her against me. I needed this. I needed her. I bent my head down, nuzzling her neck and shoulder. "The kids?"

She shivered, raking a hand through my hair. "The twins are asleep, but Taylor's there. She was awake. If Maddy wakes up, she'll be there for her."

Logan's wife.

I nodded. That was good.

We both checked on Logan, where he was standing. He looked like death. My brother usually looked full of life, full of attitude. His brown hair was trimmed. He'd been keeping it cut how I usually kept mine short. His lean and defined build was in shadows tonight, from the overwhelming oppression of what we both witnessed.

I guessed that was appropriate, considering what happened. *Dad.* The image of him flashed in front of me again. The look in his eyes right before he lifted the gun.

How determined he'd been. *Fuck.* How relieved too.

That was going to haunt me.

Another vehicle rolled in, and when it parked, both doors opened. "Sam," someone called. Heather and Channing had arrived.

Heather ran to Sam's side, who kept one arm around me as she reached up to hug her best friend. Channing headed to Logan and gave him a hug. They talked a little before Channing moved back to survey the scene. Heather frowned my way, and I gave her a small nod in return. She was here to support Sam, who was here to support me. And right now, I needed to deal with business. That's what was going to help me.

I stepped to the side, letting go of Sam.

She put a hand to my chest, stopping me. "You okay?" She swore, shaking her head at her own question. "I mean..." She moved closer, cutting everyone else out for a moment. She reached up, catching my face, and tilted my head down to look at her.

I resisted. I couldn't get lost in her. Not yet. I needed to talk to Channing. I had to know who this fucker was that had driven my dad to suicide. But I also needed my wife. I'd always need my wife. "Tonight," I told her, my voice gruff. "I'll lose myself in you later tonight."

She nodded. That's what she'd been looking for. Her hands left my face. "What do you need now?"

God, I loved her. She was my ride-or-die, and right now, she was riding with me. "I need to talk to Channing." I glanced over to Logan. "Take care of Logan. He's worried about Taylor and now this." I shook my head. "I'll handle business, but he's on the edge right now."

She pulled in a breath. Logan and Taylor had lost their first kid. There were problems in the pregnancy, and they'd been told their child wouldn't live. They just didn't know how long they would get with her, or if they'd get any time. They got a day.

The next time Taylor got pregnant again, that little boy came out kicking and screaming.

Now Taylor was pregnant a third time. Things had been iffy, so my brother was already dealing with that stress. He didn't want to lose another child and now this?

Sam turned to go to him, but I caught her pants pocket and pulled her to me again. My hand slid up to her throat in a gentle hold. I tipped her back, speaking into her ear. "He needs to feel his shit. He's pushing too much down, and if he doesn't deal with some of it, he's going to explode."

Sam drew in a shuddering breath. Her pulse fluttered. "Got it."

Another goddamn reason she was my perfect fit. She always knew what I was saying, probably without me even needing to say it. Sam was about to take my brother somewhere, and she was going to piss him the fuck off. We could both see that he was about to take our dad's death and add it to the shit pile inside of him he wasn't dealing with. He was only able to focus on not losing Taylor and not losing their third baby, which made sense, but Taylor was fine right now. If he didn't process some of his emotions, it'd be bad.

"I'll talk to Chan, but call me if you need me," I told her.

She nodded. I felt the movement through my hand.

"Mouth." I growled.

A shudder went through her, and she tipped her head back. I caught the lust swirling in her eyes, but that was for later. That's how I was going to handle my shit. Until then, she met my lips with hers and gave me a taste to get me through.

Then she pulled away from me and motioned for Heather to follow her.

As they approached Logan, Channing moved around to me, grazing Heather's hand as she passed.

"What do you need?" he asked me.

Fuck. This guy. We'd gotten close over the years. We'd always been friends, but the last few years, a tightness had formed between us, and I knew if I needed someone dead, Channing would handle it without blinking.

I didn't answer him. Not yet.

I watched how Heather and Sam had a little brief meeting before they went in separate directions. Sam went to Logan, and Heather broke away to talk to one of the cops.

Channing settled in next to me where I was standing to the side. I was watching everything. He asked me, "Cops already talk to you?"

I nodded. "That same one your wife is talking to now. Tell me about him."

"Ah, that'd be Detective Arroyo." He moved a little closer, lowering his voice so no one could overhear. "He's decent, but I'll be honest, shit wasn't good around the time my sister was in high school. It got better. Now it's bad again. There are other players moving onto the scene, and Fallen Crest is in a tug-of-war between those players. There's one cop I trust for what I need, but I can't tell you who else I'd trust."

"Arroyo?"

Channing shrugged. "Time will tell. I can have someone look into him."

"No." As we continued to watch, Heather broke away from the detective, and he headed toward me as Heather returned to Sam and Logan. I could see the torment in Logan's eyes.

"Fuck." He didn't know what to do. I pulled my phone out and texted him.

Me: Go with Sam. Get drunk. Do what you need to do to let out some of the shit inside of you.

He looked down at his phone and drew in a deep breath. His fingers moved over his phone in a response.

My phone buzzed.

Logan: Got you. Sam will pull me back from the edge if I go over too, but once I let out enough of my shit, I want to be looped in. Got me?

Me: Without a doubt. Go get drunk. Rage. Do what you need to do right now.

He lifted his head. I hated seeing the anguish he now wasn't holding back.

I sent another text.

Me: Go.

His shoulders slumped a little. Sam moved in and took his hand as she walked him with Heather to her car.

"You want me to call Monson?" Channing asked.

That question sucked me dry of every last semblance of... I didn't even know. What Logan and I had just witnessed, what we'd heard, it was life-changing, and I'd been trying to deny some of it. At Channing's question, I couldn't deny it anymore.

Nate Monson was our other best friend. He'd been my first best friend growing up, and the two of us had gotten into too much trouble so his parents took him away for a while. I was too much of a negative influence on him. As soon as he could, he came back, but the dynamics were different. Sam was in our lives and Logan and I had gotten closer.

Eventually, Nate and I got close again. But bottom line? He was family. We were all family.

Lifting my phone, I pulled up his contact. As I hit his name, I put the phone to my ear and said to Channing, "Call Matteo."

Nate answered, alert even though it was either fucking early or fucking late for him, "What's happened?"

Channing was already moving away, his phone at his ear.

Nate knew. I didn't know how, but it shifted something in me.

My voice went gruff. "How'd you know?"

"A gut feeling. I kept getting this bad feeling all night long. I couldn't sleep and I've been driving Quincey nuts. We're already packing our shit up and heading to the airport in twenty minutes."

Jesus. I half laughed, wincing at the sound of my own voice. Hoarse. "You're psychic now?"

His own voice went soft. "Tell me what happened, Mase."

I readied myself, shoving my grief and shock aside so I could get the words out without fucking falling to pieces. The family was circling the wagons. As I told him, a part of me slipped away so I didn't have to witness it all over again. "My dad shot himself tonight."

He drew in a breath. "Fuck. *Fuck.*" He needed a second to process that too.

I waited, hearing his ragged breathing.

"Okay." His voice came back, clearer. "Does Sam need Quincey there?"

I frowned, thinking. "Uh... I don't know, to be honest. She and Heather are handling Logan right now."

"I'll ask her. This is what we'll do. Babe..." His voice moved away. I heard his wife in the background, saying, "What?"

"Change of plans," he told her. "Mason and Logan's dad died tonight."

"What?" she gasped.

It was hard, hearing her shock at the news.

Nate's voice stayed even. "I need you to text Samantha, ask her if she needs you to come now or if you can hold off enough to take care of shit here."

"What are you thinking?" she asked.

"I'm going to fly down tonight. If Sam needs you, you come with me. If we do that, I was thinking your brother could bring the kids down with him."

"Graham?"

"Yeah. Or I can call my sister. She'd fly over to do that for us and drive the kids down."

"No," Quincey replied. "That's too much to ask Aspen to be away from their kids. Graham will do it. He'll bring his kids with him."

Nate's voice came back to the phone, clearer. "Quincey's calling her brother right now, but I'll be heading down. She'll either be with me or if he can't help, she'll bring the kids down in a few days. Are *you* okay?"

No, I wanted to bite out, not at him but because of the question. "He shot himself in front of us. Logan and me. I'm not going to be okay for a long fucking time."

Nate was quiet for a beat, and then his voice wavered. "I'm coming, brother."

That meant a lot. A whole hell of a lot.

I had a hard time swallowing. "Thanks," I rasped out before I ended the call.

There was a wall inside of me. I'd built it the second my dad pulled the trigger, and I was hiding behind it right now to deal with all of this shit. But he was coming. The wagons were circling. I needed them. Logan needed them.

That meant *so much*.

Despite all this, I knew how fucking blessed I was. Logan was always there. Then Nate. Then Logan. Then Logan and Sam. After that, Nate returned. Heather joined. Channing stepped a foot in, and over the years, he'd come all the way in. Matteo joined in college.

I felt the support around me. I needed more of it than usual.

Channing returned when he saw I was done on the phone. He held his own up. "Matteo will be on the first flight. He's in Hawaii with his family right now."

That was good. That was real good.

"What about David and Malinda?" Channing asked.

I shook my head. "Not yet. Maddy will wake up. She'll know something's wrong. I want to wait until the kids are awake tomorrow. We'll have them come over. I'll tell David and Malinda outside before we tell the kids. They can be there for Maddy and the twins."

"Max will want to be there." Channing's son, who was a year younger than Maddy.

That sounded right. "Bring him."

"Your mom?"

Christ. My mom. Would she even care? I shook my head. "I don't want to deal with her bullshit. She'll make everything about her." I'd tell her. I'd have to tell her, but not yet.

Channing looked down at his phone, probably typing out instructions to the rest of the group.

I texted Logan, because he was the only one who might have a different opinion about our mother.

Me: If you want mom to know now, you can tell her. I'm not up to dealing with her on the phone.

His reply was immediate.

Logan: She should know, but that doesn't mean we have to tell her. I think she's in New Zealand anyway. We can have Malinda call her tomorrow.

That was a good idea. Relief flowed through me. One less thing to manage.

"Anyone else we need to notify right now?" Channing asked softly.

I ran through our immediate circle. There was no one else. Everyone else could wait.

It was time to handle business. "I need to know *everything* you know about someone named Kai fucking Bennett."

3

MADDY

Something was wrong.

I woke up and went to the bathroom, and as I was slipping back into bed, light was coming from under my door. I could hear voices. It was the twins. Nolan and Nash were awake. I grabbed my phone and opened the door.

Nash was holding Nolan in his arms, both sitting on the top step. He looked back at me. Nolan didn't. She was crying.

"What is it?" I asked, keeping my voice down.

Someone was talking downstairs. Aunt Taylor. She sounded like she was on the phone?

The uneasiness doubled inside me. I only needed to look at Nolan to know I was right. She was more sensitive than me. She was psychic. I was sure of it. Hell, everyone knew she was psychic. It was just a matter of whether they wanted to admit it to themselves or not.

She wouldn't look at me.

Nash's eyes flashed. "We think something happened to Grandpa."

No. I blinked away immediate tears. We'd just lost

Grandma. I moved to sit behind them, going to the wall and sliding down.

Nash put his arm back around Nolan, and I scooted in, stretching my leg to touch both of them. They moved closer, and Nolan leaned against me. She was shaking so I reached over and brushed some of her blond hair back from her forehead. Where she got it, I had no idea. Both Mom and Dad had black hair, but Nolan's was soft and wispy, with some white strands mixed in with the blond. Nash had darker blond hair too. His looked similar to Aunt Heather and Uncle Channing, but he had the same jawline as Dad's and the same green eyes. Besides the hair, there was no mistaking that Nash was definitely a Kade. Guess I got Mom's genes since I had her same body shape. We were both slender. Plus, I got her hair. Jet black.

It was beautiful. I ran my fingers through it.

She settled more of her weight into me.

"What happened, Nolan?" I whispered.

She stilled before sniffing again. "Grandpa killed himself."

"How do you know that? Did Aunt Taylor say something?"

She only shook her head, and I met Nash's eyes over her head. He was giving me the look, the one that I should know how she knew. Her gift.

But Grandpa... There was no way. Right? *No.* Just, no.

Nolan sniffled again. Nash scooted even closer on her other side, his fingers laced with hers. She lowered her head, whispering something I almost missed. "Something bad is coming too."

More bad stuff? Something else?

No. *No.* No! I couldn't.

This couldn't be happening.

I texted Max: **I need you.**

4

MASON

C hanning paled when I said the fucker's name. That made everything worse.

His normally tanned skin, covered in tattoos, looked washed out. He seemed staggered, his hand grabbing at his dark blond hair before it moved to grab the back of his neck for a short moment.

He blinked a few times, shaking it off before scanning around us. "We can't talk about him here."

He really wasn't making me feel better. I wanted to find this asshole. I wanted to find out why my father was so torn up about this guy, and then I was going to rip his head off. That was my plan for dealing with him. Simple murder.

Channing had connections. He'd help cover it up.

And I wanted to keep Logan out of it, so if anything happened, he could defend me to the best of his ability. His conscience would be clear.

Everything inside me raged right now. Murder might not have been the best answer. In a few days, rational thought would come back to me, and I'd think about Sam. I'd think about my kids. I couldn't put any of them at risk of losing me, but fuck. If someone found this Bennett guy, brought him to me, and handed me a gun? I'd take that gun and pull the trigger so fast. I'd kill him. I'd do it without thinking, with no hesitation.

"Where?" I demanded, scowling. A few people were looking over. I heard someone say my last name, and I didn't know if this was typical scene-of-the-crime attention or if it was because of my football celebrity status.

Goddammit. I hated everything about this. The grief, losing my dad... Later when I was with Sam in the privacy of our room, I'd feel it. Until then, I needed to scramble to find my footing. James laid a pile of shit at our feet and told us to clean it up. I needed to sort the pile of shit before I could even think of how to clean it up.

Frustration jammed my throat.

First fucking thing first. "Where, Channing?" I asked again. "Where can we talk?"

He sighed, looking around again. "I don't want to do this in my office, just in case. Let's go to where we used to have the bonfire for Fallen Crest. You remember where that is?"

The old stomping grounds, where we'd had more than a few Fallen Crest parties during the District Weekend, a tradition among Fallen Crest, Roussou, and Frisco. Each town had an event. "I remember."

"You can follow me if you forgot the way."

I raised my middle finger, to which he barked out a laugh. Each of us broke away to our separate vehicles.

We hadn't gone far before my dashboard started lighting up. My phone had automatically connected, so all the texts were coming through—some from Sam, from Channing. There was a pause, and then some from Nate came through. The last few were from Matteo. And still more from numbers I didn't know. I frowned, hitting *ignore* so they'd stop. I'd need to read through them on my phone, but later. Everything was later.

When we arrived, Channing swung in among the trees, parking.

I slid in next to him, and by the time I got out and rounded the back end of my Escalade, he had a beer waiting for me. I shook my head. "I'll need something stronger when I start doing that."

He nodded but had no other reaction.

I sighed, leaning against the bumper. "I need to know everything."

"Yeah." He didn't sound happy about it.

We looked around us for a moment. We were in the middle of the woods, in a valley before a bunch of hills. Sam used to run around here. *Jesus.* That was so long ago. She'd go for hours, running from all her demons. Everything had been so different, but in a way, we were back there all over again. If someone told me today that I needed to pick up my little brother before we headed to high school, I wouldn't have argued. It felt natural.

Time was a funny bitch. I hated her.

"I gotta know something first." Channing focused on the ground. "Where'd you hear that name?" He lifted his head, his gaze eerily sharp. "It's not a name someone like you would know, and trust me, brother, you don't want to know that name."

"Too fucking late." I told him how James called us, how the whole thing had gone down.

At the end, after I quoted him word for word what my dad said, Channing's mouth hardened. He flinched. "Fuck."

"Tell me I can kill this motherfucker."

He shook his head. "I wish you could. But no." He drew in a deep breath, exhaling as he said, "He's mafia."

I stared at him.

I heard him wrong.

"Say again." It wasn't a request.

Channing's mouth firmed even more. "Mafia, Mason."

"My dad cut all that shady shit a long time ago. He wouldn't have any dealings with the mob, not anymore. Try again, Chan. Who is he? Why can't I kill him?"

He grew wary before flinching all over again. "I can't give you a different answer. He is, quite possibly, one of the most powerful crime lords this side of the world. And he is still growing in power."

Fuck.

Fuck.

I frowned. "I feel like I've heard his name before."

"You remember Quincey's father?"

"Nate's wife? Her dad?"

He nodded. "The one that your dad told you had mob connections, and because of that, there was a conflict of interest for him?"

Anger burned through me. I clenched my jaw. "That was when he was into some questionable business dealings, but he went straight."

"I'm not saying that. I know your dad went straight and has been for a while. I'm saying that's the mob connections to Quincey's dad. I'm sure it was probably some of his minions down the ladder that loaned Quincey's dad money. But, follow that chain of command up and there you go. Same guy. Same name. He's at the very top."

Well, *shit*. "Fucking mafia?"

A look of pity flashed over Channing's face before it hardened. "You need to go through your dad's books. I'm talking go tonight and get them. They'll start an investigation and they'll freeze everything. With his company being as big as it is now, they'll look into it. You might not get out from underneath this."

"You think my dad owed them money?"

"Maybe." He shrugged, his head tilting back. "It's not so

black and white with the Bennetts. It's a family operation. They're from Canada, but they've expanded huge down in the States. The last I heard, they ran most of the Midwest, going all the way to Oklahoma. I don't think they've been able to get a good hold on that state. Red Demons control most of that and Texas. You remember them? The biker gang that operates out of Frisco?"

I nodded. I remembered when he went against them too. They were the one percenters, the real deal criminal motorcycle club gang.

Channing was still saying, "They've also got most of the southwestern states, and a brand new fucking charter moved into Frisco."

I felt my eyes widen. "What?"

"Yep. Same club, but they replaced the old charter. New members. We've had a few run-ins, and they're not that bad, as far as Red Demons go. Brandon's woman is friendly with their president's woman. Shane King. Goes by his biker name Ghost. He's the national VP, last I heard. I think there was a question about whether their national prez was alive or not. I'm not in the know as far as that goes, but it's not a total bad thing to have them so close. They separated from a cartel that'd been pushing up here, and they did it in a big way. We don't have cartel here anymore—or at least not as strong as they were—so it makes sense that Bennett is sniffing around. No doubt the Red Demon turf war got his attention."

"What other areas does he run?"

"Montana. Idaho. Washington. They might've pushed into Oregon. I'm not sure."

"Utah?"

He shook his head. "I don't think so. The Red Demons might have Utah. Maybe. Or they're duking it out. I know the Red Demons have Nevada. I'm not sure about Colorado or Wyoming. Bennetts have Kansas, the Dakotas, Minnesota,

Wisconsin. I'm not sure about Iowa. There's other mafia around there—all of which is none of my business. I'm aware of the players around here and around where my sister lives, but other than that, I keep my head down. It's easier that way. I go in, grab our guys, and we get the fuck out. We touch base with cops in the area to make sure they know we're there and to find out if the way is clear for us. That's the most I'll probe in." He paused to take a breath. "Your dad killed himself because of Bennett?"

"That's what he said." I closed my eyes and saw it all over again.

Bang.

"I'll never fucking get that out of my head."

"I'm sorry, man." He reached over and clasped my shoulder.

"I need the layout on this family. Kai is the one in charge?"

Channing grimaced before nodding. "This is what I know. Again, I try not to get too nosy. They tend to know who's looking into them and don't take kindly to that. Rumor was there used to be a board for all the Canadian mafia families, but I don't know if that's true. Right now the Bennetts are in charge. Kai's the leader. I'm not sure about the other siblings, but there's one other brother who's heavily involved with the business. Tanner Bennett. He spends a lot of time in Kansas." He studied me. "There's another rumor. I don't know the validity of it, but you may know someone connected to Tanner Bennett."

I tensed. "Who?"

"Cutler Ryder."

No fucking way. "The pro NHL hockey player, Cutler Ryder? Kansas City Mustangs?"

He gave me a slow nod.

I shook my head. "No way. Fuck no. No fucking way does Ryder have mob connections."

"I'm not saying he *knows* he has mob connections, but yes, I think he does."

"How?"

Channing heaved a silent sigh. "Look, I don't like knowing this shit. And I don't want my name attached, because this information came from someone connected to my sister, and if she's put at risk, heads will roll. I mean it."

I raised an eyebrow. "I don't even know what you know."

"Bren can't be put at risk. That's what I'm saying. I know you. I give you this information, and with the rage going through you right now, you'll use it to burn down the place. They'll start looking and *will* connect the dots, you get me? My sister *will not* be collateral in this."

I growled. "Jesus Christ. I know your sister. I don't even want to fuck with her, but yes. I promise not to put her at risk."

He was quiet for a moment, considering me before he gave in. "There's a nightclub outside of Kansas City, Bresko's. That club is connected to your friend, right?"

"I'm familiar with it," I clipped out. I did not like where this was going.

"There's a silent partner. The rumor is that it's Tanner Bennett."

I cursed under my breath. Ryder was a stand-up guy. If this was true, he didn't know. There was no way he could know. "This is insane."

"It's a connection."

"What do they do? Specifically. The Bennetts."

"They do almost everything except sex trafficking. That is *not* a rumor. I know as fact that they have a hard line against sex trafficking, but I believe they do everything else. Distribution. Transportation. Guns. Drugs. If this is true and they were coming after your dad, they're likely forcing a hostile takeover with Kade Enterprises. That's my guess. Your dad had to open up a small percentage of shares. If we look, I'd bet whoever bought those is connected to the Bennett family."

I sat with this for a beat. "If this is all true, how do we fight them?"

He shrugged, but he was still studying me. Wary. "You're legit. You're not a criminal. You don't have any shady ties. You're famous. Your name and face alone gives you some protection. It should scare off any hostile takeover attempts, I'd think. Pair your name with Sam's?" He whistled under his breath. "You guys are like one of America's sweethearts. When press finds out what your dad did, it's going to be crazy. All eyes are going to be on you. Your dad—though I don't like what he did, it makes sense in a way. If he was the weak link the Bennetts were using to push in on, he eliminated their way in. What he did will force all that attention your way. But not just you—you and your brother and the entourage that comes with you guys. Me and mine included. Plus, you guys are connected to Brett's new wife. The media is still in a frenzy about her."

I shook my head. "We're not that close to Brett or Billie."

He shrugged again, crossing his arms over his chest. "I'm just saying you have some arsenal in your backyard, if you need it. Brett will step in to help. You know that. Plus the niece as well."

I shot him a look. "We're *not* using our kids."

"His niece is going to your kid's school. Your kid and mine are like glue with each other. I'm just pointing out the connections, that's all."

I shook my head. Maddy and Max. Those two couldn't get enough of each other, and I didn't know if I liked that, but I also knew Maddy got my stubbornness. And there was some extraness in my daughter. Just extra. Extra attitude. Extra grit. Extra...we were still learning, but my daughter was unpredictable and uncontrollable. She was also loveable at the same time. If she was going to rob a place, she'd waltz in, give the cashier the gun, and somehow get them to help her rob the place. Not saying she would do that, but if she did, that's how she would pull it off. There was no telling what she would do. Max was a good kid. If anyone was the bad influence, it was my daughter. As for Brett's niece, Maddy had only mentioned the girl a few times since she'd started at Fallen Crest Academy.

I wouldn't say they were friends.

Hell, I wasn't sure who my daughter's friends were besides Max, and he went to Fallen Crest Public. "Max mentioned Brett's niece?"

Channing shrugged. "Only reason I mentioned them was an added connection. If you needed Broudou, he'd throw his hat in the ring because of his niece."

I shook my head. I didn't want to get to that stage. I'd handle my business. Channing should remember that part of me. If we needed to do something, we'd do it, and I didn't want to owe anyone favors.

My phone buzzed.

Sam: We're all drunk at Manny's.

I snorted, showing Channing my screen. A thin ray of light pushed through the storm clouds. It hurt to feel it, but it was needed. A small pocket of air to a vacuum where all the oxygen had been sucked out.

He chuckled as he grimaced at the same time. I understood that reaction. Now that we were back, it was as if Sam and Heather made it their mission to have daily adventures. They went down town in Fallen Crest for a book club and three hours later, Sam called to tell me she joined a marathon that was running through downtown and won. She was pissed they weren't giving her the title. Their argument, she never registered to run. Her argument, she won. That'd only been *one* of their adventures.

"How do you want to proceed?" Channing was back to considering me.

The slight reprieve was gone. The light was snuffed out and the pressure was back on my shoulders. "I'll call my publicist and have her do damage control as long as possible. Hopefully we can keep it out of the press about how my father died. We'll break it to the kids in the morning. You guys should come over when we do. Maddy will want Max there. The twins will want Natessia there."

"And this business?"

"Family first. We'll tackle the business stuff after. Even if they're going to try to push in, they'll wait to see how everything pans out with Logan and me coming in. We already have shares. Nate too. No matter what, they can't get the majority. We have it."

He grunted, raking a hand down his face. "It ain't good, and I've got a feeling shit's going to get worse."

I had the same feeling.

"Let's go get our wives. I'll check in with Logan, see where his head is. He'll want to know all of this."

Channing led the way after we returned to our cars, turning in the direction of his wife's bar. I followed him but made a call on the way.

My private investigator picked up, her voice wary. "I know whatever you're about to ask me won't be good, not with a call at this hour."

I told her the basics about what had happened.

She was quiet for a long while. "This isn't good, Kade. This is so fucking not good."

I remained silent. She wasn't telling me anything I didn't know.

She sighed. "Okay. I'll find the specifics on what they're doing. We'll go from there. But what I know—apparently more than what Monroe told you—is that Kai Bennett is another animal. He is smart, ruthless, and calculating. If you look up the word *mastermind*, his picture would be next to it. He's not a normal human being."

None of that made me feel better. "Get everything you can. I have to go."

"Hey, Mason?"

I was pulling into Manny's, and as I parked, I held off turning the engine. "Yeah?"

"I'm sorry about your dad."

"Yeah," I said, rougher than I'd intended. "Call when you have information for me."

5

MASON

The next week sucked. There was no good way to explain it, and there was no good way to deal with it. We plowed through. That's all we could do.

Heather and Channing came over and they barely left. The house was big enough so their kids slept over.

Nate and Quincey arrived the next morning, so they were there when we told the kids. I watched my children, all three of them. Not one of them looked surprised when we broke the news. It was as if we were just confirming what they already knew, and once we had, the dam broke. The tears began falling. When Maddy saw my unspoken question, she motioned to Nolan.

Ah, I forgot. She was convinced Nolan was psychic. Maybe she was.

Logan mostly focused on Taylor, and we all understood his concern.

Taylor, on the other hand, was rock steady. This wasn't a surprise either, considering her personal history and how she loved working in the emergency room. She tended to lock

down when there was a threat in the air, and that quality came
in handy during times like this.

Not that she was the only one. All the women banded
together, taking care of everyone and everything. They
managed the kids, and with help from Malinda, they planned
the funeral and everything that came along with that.

Which was a fucking blessing for the rest of us.

Channing called it with the press. They got wind of James's
death almost right away. It might've been a leak from the police,
but however it got out there, it spread fast. Kade Enterprises
had grown in the last decade. It was ranked in the top fifty businesses in the state and considering some of the biggest companies in the world had headquarters in our state, our standing
was saying a lot. When Dad fixed things, he really succeeded.

I was proud of my dad. Proud of the man he became at
the end.

When I went into the office and got a look at all the files, I
choked up, my pride just reaffirmed. And then I almost broke
again because no matter what, he hadn't needed to do what he
did. There would've been a way.

Bitter regret blasted me because why hadn't he called us in
earlier? We were here. I was here. We were coming back more
and more. I would've helped.

I would've done everything—

I had to stop those thoughts.

I laid a foundation down inside of me. It was shaky, but I
was standing on it. It was the way I was getting through this,
being there for my kids. Nolan cried herself to sleep in our bed
last night. When I got up in the morning, I found Nash on the
floor outside of our door, a blanket and pillow with him.

I scooped him up and crawled right back in bed; him
with us.

My foundation trembled when I heard Nolan crying all
night. It shook even more when I found my boy in the morning.

Business. I had to get back to business.

Shoving aside the grief, I made calls next. To my business manager. My agent. My publicist. Along with the PR and marketing team from Kade Enterprises, a statement was drafted and given to the press. It was nice and polite and said nothing at all. A basic bullshit statement to appease assholes who demanded to know what was going on. But it was necessary and would buy us some time before more pressing questions would be asked. At this time, they were given a story about how he'd had a heart attack.

That'd been earlier in the week.

"When are you going to need me?" Sam trailed me into the bedroom. Shutting the door, she crossed the room barefoot, wearing a black lace dress she'd picked out for the day.

The house was bursting with people—our family, Channing's sister, and their entire network of friends, people they considered family. Nate's sister had flown over, but his brother-in-law hadn't been able to get away from his soccer schedule in Europe. Matteo would arrive in the morning. Samantha made room for him in the pool house. He was newly single again, and Sam was likely hoping if he wanted to meet someone, he'd feel comfortable bringing her over for the night. Unfortunately, she was a little blind. We had teenagers in this house. The pool house would be the first place they'd hang out.

There'd be no privacy for Matteo unless he got a hotel room.

But back to my wife's question.

Sam knew there was a threat, but we couldn't move forward until we got further clarification there actually was a war coming. We were in the waiting phase, though Sam wasn't really asking me about that.

I couldn't let myself get lost in her, not fully, not until I knew what else was coming our way.

That hadn't stopped me from *trying* to lose myself in her the couple nights when it was only her and me. I could've fucked her from sunset to sunrise. It was only the fact that we both needed *some* sleep I forced myself not to reach for her for a fourth or fifth round.

When that time came, when I would "need" her, I didn't know how our interaction would go. Would I be fine breaking down, or would I do what Channing worried I'd do, and travel cross country to burn down a certain fucking nightclub.

I was tempted. I was really fucking tempted.

I wanted to ask for forgiveness later, but I couldn't. Two innocent people would be hurt because of my actions.

I needed to wait for more information. I needed to understand who I was fighting before I made any moves, but someone would pay. That vow and my family kept my rocky foundation from shattering to pieces inside of me.

"Mason," Sam murmured softly, moving so she was behind me. She pressed herself against me, resting her forehead to my back. I felt her draw in some air. "You have to break."

I couldn't.

I covered her hand with mine and raised it to my lips. Resting it at the corner of my mouth, I breathed her in deep. One whiff wasn't enough. I needed more of her scent. Of her warmth. "Once I can, I will."

She tipped her head up, meeting my gaze in the mirror. Concern and love flared in her. It was so fucking strong, and my God, I was swept away again because what would my life be like if I'd never found her? My chest ached at the thought. It would've been an empty nightmare of a life if that'd been the case. My hand curled around hers. My chest rose and fell. "Thank fuck I got you."

Her eyes widened in surprise. She blinked away tears and pressed against me. "Goes both ways, buddy."

I raised an eyebrow at her word choice, but I heard the lust.

Tugging her in front of me, I slid my hands down her back, cupping her ass cheeks.

I groaned, tucking my head into her neck. "I really love your ass."

She smothered a laugh. "Mason."

I squeezed her, lifting her from the motion. "Nice. Round. Firm. Some jiggle too. I like seeing it when I'm fucking you from behind."

"Okay." She caught one of my hands and stepped back. A grin was at the corner of her mouth. "We have a house full of guests, and we need to start herding everyone into vehicles so we can get to the wake on time. It's a literal circus down there with kids, dogs, and all the pets. Nova brought her tortoise, insisting it's now Harold the Emotional Support Turtle."

I frowned, moving my head back to see her better. "A turtle?"

"No." She snorted. "It's a tortoise. It's bigger than some of the dogs."

My eyes got big. "And it's in our house? How is that legal?"

"Yes." Her eyes went wide. "Apparently it's a certain kind of tortoise and they had to get a permit to have it, and it's only with them for a short time period before it goes to a rescue sanctuary. Quincey told me all about the legalities of it, but it's still a tortoise."

There was a giant tortoise walking around in my house. Nova was Nate's kid, so he had signed off on it, but the fact that it was in my house meant Samantha had signed off on it too. "Is it in the house all the time?"

"No. They brought a whole trailer of things to build up some sort of encampment outside, but Nova brings it in. Him. She brought him in this morning."

I shook my head. She was right. It was a literal circus downstairs.

I didn't want to deal with a turtle right now. "Fuck it." I lifted her up.

She squeaked, her legs winding around me, and I carried her over to the bed. "Mason!" She gasped. "We seriously can't."

"Is the door locked?" I nuzzled into her neck.

She shivered, running a hand down my back. "I don't know."

Well, fuck that too. I reached for the button on the wall. The lock clicked into place, and after that I was a man on a mission. I slid a hand up her leg, pushing up her dress as I went, and groaned. "We'll be quick."

She laid back, a laugh leaving her on a moan. "Since when are we ever quick?"

She was right. I was going to savor this.

Bending between Sam's legs, I pushed open her knees and bent down, grazing my nose up the inside of her leg.

Her body began trembling. "Mason."

I liked hearing that moan. I needed to hear it again. More.

Moving to her other leg, I feathered kisses all the way to her pussy. Which was mine. Mine to have. Mine to play with. Mine to love.

She was already holding her breath, trembling again because she knew what was coming next.

I pulled her panties aside. Settling more comfortable between her legs, I stretched out, then I licked.

Sam was goddamn delicious.

Her entire body lifted up. "Jesus. Mason." Her legs tightened around my head. I only chuckled, getting off on this, on making her feel good. It was helping to push out the bad that was coming today.

I wanted to escape in my woman. I wanted to *only* hear these sounds from her. I'd keep them in my mind, remembering until I could slide back inside of her again, escaping into my haven.

Another taste.

She sucked in some air.

I licked again, this time using my thumb to rub at her clit. Jesus, I loved doing this shit for Sam.

"*Fuck.*"

Her hands reached down, grabbing hold of the side of my head. She didn't move me out of the way, just anchored me to her.

When I slid my tongue inside, her fingers latched onto my hair, fisting me.

I went as deep as I could taste.

She was bucking under me.

I kept going, making her fall apart underneath my touch. Knowing this was sweet torment. I reveled in that.

In and out. Around. It was all about her, drawing out more of those little gasps and how she writhed over me.

"Fuck! Mason!"

I kept going. I was inhaling her, and *shit*, my dick was so hard. I pressed down on the bed, needing some of my own release. That felt good. God. Everything about Sam made me feel good. I kept moving inside of her, around until I felt her tensing. Her hands clenched, yanking me against her. I kept flicking my tongue up and down, across her nub before dipping back in for another taste.

I needed to do this. It was for her, but it was for me. We could both feel good. Help us forget for a moment in time.

"*Fuuuuck.*"

She was yanking at my hair, grinding down on me at the same time.

She jerked against me, coming in my mouth. I swept it up, lapping at her, and continued tasting until her body stopped trembling. Her hands slid from my hair. I gazed up, feeling half drunk. She gave me a half-grin. She was damn near purring. Satisfied.

She whispered, "You're really good at that."

"Hmmm. Am I?" I crawled up over her, dipping down to meet her mouth with mine.

She would taste herself.

With her eyes closed, she tipped her head up to meet mine, her hands softly holding onto the side of my jaw. *Yes.* I loved the soft kiss of her lips, which was what she was giving me now. A tender little bite. A tease. She moved her mouth over mine.

I pressed against her, needing more pressure against my dick.

She moaned, rocking her hips to meet mine.

I smiled back, my lips grazing hers. A deep groan rumbled from me.

So good. So fucking good.

The pleasure built, like it always did.

I needed to fuck her. I *needed* to be inside of her, right fucking now.

"Babe." I swept my tongue inside of her mouth before pulling away to move down her throat, sucking on her neck. Her carotid artery. That was my spot. I tasted it, needing to mark her. I didn't care how old we were, if we were married, how many kids we had. That mark on her, that was mine, and I hungered for people to see it.

Sam was mine. She belonged to me. I wanted everyone to be reminded.

"Hmmm?" She was replete after her release, but the longer I rubbed against her, the more I tasted her, she began to move underneath me. Her hips were moving, seeking out the beginning of another release.

"I need to fuck you." Now. Right fucking now.

I pressed hard against her.

My hands began to shake. The need to get inside of her was too much.

I hoped this desire, this lust, never went away for us.

Shoving down my pants, I lined up with her.

I looked up, her eyes collided and held onto mine, and right there. That's the connection I needed. I hungered to see inside of her at the same time as I was *in* her. Feeling that link fill me up, I thrust inside of her.

6

MADDY

"Hey," I whispered. "Come here."

We were at my grandfather's wake, and what a joke it was. We couldn't even see him. Closed casket. Grandpa would have hated that. He was a good guy. I knew he hadn't made the right decisions in his life. Man oh man, we heard that same old *all* the time, and hello? Grandma Analise had been a headcase. Those were her words. But they tried to change, and I thought they had. I don't remember them being assholes. They loved me, still did in my books, and anyone who doted on me was good in my books.

I blinked away tears and shoved aside that stupid ball of emotion that kept trying to wedge its way into my chest.

Well, it was already there. It kept trying to move higher up in my throat to choke me, but nope. No way. I had no intention of letting myself submit to—what? Sadness? My emotions? My stupid grief?

I missed them both, and it sucked they were gone, but I'd see them again. They weren't *gone* gone, and I mean, hell, if you believed in the afterlife, they were still around. That weirded me out, because I didn't think either of them would be okay with what I wanted to do, but I also kinda didn't care. If they were around and disapproving, they couldn't tattle on me.

"Sorry, Gram, Gramps," I said. It didn't hurt to cover my bases.

I had this buzzing inside of me. It was in my blood. I knew I should be the good and dutiful daughter and sit by Mom's side, maybe hold her hand. I'm sure she'd want me to help watch the kiddos, but I wasn't doing that.

Max followed me. I led the way to the back of the building, exiting out to the lot behind it. It was more of an alley. There was minimal light. but it was enough to see the two guys waiting by the Ferrari.

"Oh. Whoa. Wait." Max stopped me, touching my wrist. He went rigid, glaring at the guys before turning me around to face him. "What the fuck, Mads?" he hissed under his breath. "Do you know those guys?"

Beltraine Moreaux and Axel Johannson. Yeah, I knew them. They were seniors at my school, and they were the gatekeepers for mostly all the sorts of fun I wanted to do. Tonight, included. "Yeah. Duh. They're why we're here."

"Little Kade." Beltraine spoke up, lifting his chin.

"A second." I held up two fingers, glancing over my shoulder.

Axel smirked, shifting to sit on the Ferrari. Why they brought a Ferrari was beyond me. They had money. I was aware. Everyone was, but they were stupid. Honestly. There were gangs in our town that would boost a car like that. If I were in a gang, and I needed to boost a car, that Ferrari was the first I'd go for. There was usually a GPS tracker installed and another added as a backup, but both were reachable. Yank them out, insert your modifier, which took twelve seconds to replicate the vehicle's fob, and *boom*. Press a button, and that engine would be purring.

I wasn't supposed to know this stuff, but I did. I'd done my research. Every adult in my family had been a hellion growing up. It was in my blood.

"What are you doing with those guys? I don't want anything to do with them."

God. Max. I fought against rolling my eyes, stepping back a little.

I loved Max. I did. We'd grown up together. We were best friends. He was family, though not actually blood, but he was such a smart, careful, don't-get-in-trouble kind of guy. I wouldn't call him lame or a goody two-shoes, because I knew he wasn't either of those. If he needed to lay it down, he would, and when I say that, I meant whatever was needed in any situation. The guy was one of the most adaptable and intelligent guys I'd ever known, which was why I needed him to come with me.

He was my conscience.

If there was fire, I had to get so close to it that I burned. Something in me made me go to the fire. Max would pull me back. He kept me safe even from myself. It wasn't fair to him, but that was our dynamic.

So, I needed him.

I shrugged, moving around him. "They're just our way in. Don't worry. We'll ditch them when we get there."

He groaned. "This is not a good idea, Maddy."

I just grinned. I was going. And if I was going, he'd go too. Seeing the set expression on my face, Beltraine and Axel both straightened from their car. They were the cool guys at my school. Hot. Wealthy. Assholes. Both were tall, lean. Beltraine had dark shaggy hair. Axel had the same hair style, but with dirty blond hair. They were white, came from old money, and were beyond privileged. They both knew it too.

They were smug. They smirked at us, but neither said anything else. They didn't dare. Because while these guys were the top of the top, they weren't what Max and I were.

I was a Kade, and he was a Monroe, and *no one* fucked with our families.

"Boys," I greeted, almost coyly.

Beltraine went to the driver's side.

Axel opened the passenger door and stepped back. "After you."

I climbed in, going to the back.

Max hadn't moved. He stood glowering at the car.

Beltraine got in. "Are we leaving your buddy?"

I rolled my eyes, folded my arms over my chest, and slid down in my seat, getting comfortable. "No. He just needs a minute. He'll come."

Axel leaned down, poking his head into the car. "We can leave him."

"*No,*" I said. "If he doesn't go, I don't either."

The guys shared a look, but in the next moment, it didn't matter.

"Fuuuuuuuck!" Max yelled, his head falling back as he let out another shout. He glared, his hands in fists, and stormed over to climb in next to me. His shoulder nudged against mine as he sat. He hissed under his breath, "You so fucking owe me."

At this point, I'd owe him all the way until it was our coffin at our wake one day. Until then, I was planning on living it up and forcing Max along for the ride. He'd thank me when we were old and had to wear diapers again. You know, when we were fifty.

As we pulled out of the lot, the engine purring fantastically, we went past a line of people going into the funeral home for the wake.

A girl stopped on the sidewalk, watching us drive past. I recognized her. She went by a different last name, but I knew who she really was.

She was a Broudou.

Then we drove past, and it was as if she never existed.

7

MASON

"**D**o you know where your daughter is?" Samantha sidled up to my side.

The wake was over. We'd left the funeral home and congregated across the road, to the patio of a bar. The owner invited us personally. I'd just sat down, after going inside to shake hands with the owner and the staff. They hadn't asked for pictures or autographs, which I was thankful about considering what I'd just left.

Logan, Nate, and Matteo were sitting at a table. Channing was in the back, standing with a bunch of his crew members. They worked as bounty hunters with his company but were still his crew. It was an old system from their school in Roussou, but that dynamic was strong. Catching my glance, he tipped his chin up in question. I texted.

Me: You know where your son is?

Wherever Max was, Maddy would be. They were joined at the hip, and I didn't want to think about them fucking. Though maybe I should. Maddy was seventeen. I'd been having sex for years by the time I got to her age, and for fuck's sake, her mom and I were like rabbits. I didn't want to think of any of that with my little girl. Not with Max. Not with anyone.

Though, once again, I was certain my kid would be the one to push it. Max had every part of Heather and Channing within him. He had an edge, some darkness. I'd witnessed a rough side of him, but for the most part, he had a good head on his shoulders. He liked getting along, which to him meant not getting in trouble. He didn't like disappointing his parents. I couldn't understand why. Channing was still a hellion. He was barely legal with the things he did with his job. He was able to indulge in all things violence and gore.

I was jealous.

He read my text and frowned before hitting a button and lifting the phone to his ear.

"You tried calling Maddy, right?" I asked Sam.

She harrumphed, hitting me in the arm.

The others snickered around the table.

"Of course I did. I haven't seen her for a while, actually. She turned her phone off."

Logan snorted before raising his hand. "We do know a hacker in town." His eyes went to mine. "Just saying."

I scowled. "No fucking way. I'm not inviting that stalker into my inner circle."

Logan cracked up. Nate snickered too.

Matteo glanced around. "What am I missing?"

"Nothing." I gave them a warning look.

Logan kept snickering. "Just what he said. Mason's had a certain stalker from Fallen Crest for a good while. It's cute how worked up he gets about him."

I shot him another look, but Channing came over at that moment. His two giant crew members were behind him. One was Goliath. The other was mini-Goliath, but just as wide. Their crew names were Moose and Congo. They looked like they ate bricks for breakfast with a side of eggs. And their weapons and bulletproof vests were usually out and proud when I saw them. Tonight, if they were wearing them, they were hidden.

Each gave Logan and me a nod, extending their condolences.

"Heather can't get ahold of Max?" Channing asked Sam.

She hesitated before shaking her head.

I reached over, pulling her into my lap. She melted into me. If none of us could find our kids, that meant we'd be going on a hunt. That also meant we'd have a long night ahead. When we found her, we'd deliver a lecture, and when she got home, she'd get another lecture from her mom. I knew my kid. She loathed the lectures from her mom the most. We all adored Sam, and it was hard when you looked in her eyes and saw disappointment there.

But Maddy took after me. She needed to get into trouble.

Sam and I had made sure she grew up without the sort of shit that haunted us. She didn't have a lot of trauma, that we knew of, so I figured her need to get into trouble was genetic. Sometimes it made me wonder if I'd wrongly blamed my father as the reason I did half the shit I did growing up. But no, I just had to take a moment and remember being in the house with him and our mom, taking care of Logan back in the day. They'd been horrific parents.

Sometimes I watched our kids with amazement because they didn't have the deep-seated anger that Logan and I had, or the demons Sam had, and I was always perplexed. How did those kids come from me? They were normal, or sort of normal.

I took my phone out and tried calling Maddy myself. I didn't figure she'd answer, but it was worth a try. It went straight to voicemail. She'd turned the phone off, which meant she hadn't figured out how to disable the tracker I'd put on her phone. She'd bitched and moaned about it, but I didn't care. She was my kid. If someone took her, I *was* coming for her, and I *would* be leaving with their head on a plate.

Brett and his wife got up from their table not far from us, looking like they were leaving, but he stopped by our table.

"Hey, man."

We'd already said hello at the wake. I was surprised they were still here. Billie was a little skittish around the rest of us. She lived hiding from attention, and our group was the opposite. Attention just came our way.

He inclined his head to the rest of the table, holding his wife's hand, but he frowned when he saw Sam's face. "What is it?"

Sam stiffened in my lap. "We can't find a couple of our kids."

He glanced at his wife. "Stevie mentioned seeing Maddy take off with a couple guys from her school."

My eyebrows shot up, and a rumble started in my gut. "What guys?"

He turned away a moment, remembering. "Stevie only mentioned it because Billie asked if she wanted to go find Maddy and Max. She said that was a flat no because she didn't like the guys she saw take off with Maddy."

Suddenly we were all sitting up straighter. Every single one of us.

"Did she give you a name?" Logan asked, bristling. He stared at Brett's wife.

She shook her head.

"Ask her."

His wife jumped, her eyes swinging my way. I grimaced. I hadn't intended to speak so sharply.

Brett spoke up. "Stevie's no narc. She won't say anything unless we trick her, and when she finds out we did that to her, she'll be pissed. We're not fucking up any progress we've made with her."

I didn't like this, not knowing where my daughter was.

Sam leaned back against me, tucked her head to her shoulder, and whispered, "She grew up with Shannon."

Shannon Broudou. Or that's what she went by in high school. I almost forgot about her, but Sam was right. Stevie was her daughter and from what I heard about her, Shannon only got worse as she got older. Well, fuck. I forced the anger to ease out of me and gave Brett a quick nod. "We'll find 'em a different way."

Brett's eyes flashed. He tilted his head to the side. "You know... I might've also noticed the car and the kids driving it, and when Stevie mentioned that, I might've asked a buddy to look up the license plate. You know, because maybe I might want to know what kind of assholes Stevie doesn't like or what kind of assholes your girl is hanging out with." He was enjoying this, and he held his phone up.

A text came through on my phone.

I opened it to find a driver's license for one Beltraine Moreaux, along with the car's owner, Phillip Moreaux, a name I recognized from the board at Kade Enterprises.

I grunted. "Thank you."

"Have fun hunting." Brett gave a wave before leading his wife out.

Sam shot off my lap, hurrying after them. She'd give them her thanks, but she'd also try every card in her arsenal to charm Billie Harm into being her friend. Sam had made the decision she was going to befriend the woman, come hell or high water.

I used social media to look up this punk. When I got to his TikTok, it wasn't private, and I clicked on his last live, which was posted forty-three minutes ago. My blood went cold when I saw they were at some place for underground fighting.

I shoved up from the table.

Everyone took notice. Logan frowned.

I sent him the link, and his eyes flared when he saw what kind of place they were at. "Oh. Those little fucks are ours." He shared his phone with Nate, who passed it to Matteo, and in the meantime, I had a little difficulty curbing my excitement.

I'd been missing the violence that used to be part of our lives.

This was different. Being home was different, being in Fallen Crest.

Outside of this city, I was Mason Kade, NFL Hall of Famer and a retired football star. But here, to an extent, people didn't care. I loved that. I was just Mason Kade, and where this little shit had taken my daughter, I was going to hurt him. And I was going to enjoy every second of it.

"His dad's on the board," Nate remarked, standing with the others.

I grunted, pulling out a wad of bills to cover everyone's tab. I held it out to a passing waitress. "How old are you?" I asked her. "You know where this is?"

She took the money, her eyes widening before she focused on my phone. I had pulled up the kid's live video. "Oh." She tucked a strand of her hair behind her ear, squinting at the phone. "Oh!" She jerked back. "That's out at the old county fairgrounds."

Channing started laughing.

It was the same place Channing used to fight.

Logan laughed with him. "Nice to know some shit doesn't change."

I thanked the girl and nodded to the money. "That's for the owner. If it doesn't cover everyone, he can reach out. I'll come in and pay it off."

"Oh. Uh..." She blushed, trying to hand it back. "He won't take it. He's real proud that the legendary Mason Kade came to his establishment."

I shook my head. "Then use it to cash out as many as possible. Keep thirty percent tip for yourself and whoever else waited on us. We need to take care of something now."

She nodded, speechless, as I pushed past.

Nate and Matteo headed outside.

Moose and Congo were waiting on the sidewalk. Channing cut across the section to talk to Heather, his hand at the small of her back. Sam headed my way, her eyes dark and worried.

Logan intercepted her first, giving her a kiss on the cheek and saying something into her ear before throwing me a wink. He was almost skipping out the door. Like me, violence was in his blood.

Sam finished her walk toward me and glanced at the group of guys now lingering on the sidewalk. "You found her?"

"We know where she is."

Her eyebrows pinched together. "What does that mean?"

"They took her to an underground fighting ring." I didn't mince words. This would give Sam time to decide on the best punishment. Maddy was allowed to hang out with friends, but she was never, under no circumstances, allowed to turn her phone off. And she always had to notify us where she was. She'd broken three rules—the last was roping Max in with her. Because even though Broudou hadn't mentioned him, I was a hundred-percent certain he was with her and she'd gotten him to turn his phone off too.

Our girl was going to be grounded.

The blood drained from Sam's face, and her eyes widened.

Maddy earned a strike for putting that look on her mother's face. I was tempted to take a picture so I could show Maddy later. It would haunt her.

She chewed on her top lip. "Okay. Be safe. Bring her back. Don't kill anyone, hmm?"

I cupped Sam's elbow and stepped in, kissing her forehead before flashing her a grin. "It's like you don't know me. Telling me to be safe." I was teasing.

She caught my hand as I began to pull away and gave me a mock glare. "I do know you so do I need to repeat what I just said?"

I gave her another kiss before giving her a smirk. "Don't worry. No heads will literally roll, and I'll collect our daughter. You can start thinking how to make her next two weeks hell. That should be fun."

She growled as her eyes flashed. A hint of a grin lifted up the side of her mouth. "I love my daughter, but you're right. Instead of worrying about her, I'll channel that into brainstorming. Heather will help."

I winced, now almost feeling sorry for my daughter, but no. I remembered the look on Sam's face only a moment ago. Maddy knew not to turn her phone off. She needed to regret that decision.

I headed out, and Logan fell in step with me. Just as I opened the door, Malinda called our names. She was weaving through the tables, coming our way.

I moved to the sidewalk. Logan was beside me.

Malinda joined us.

The others waited to the side.

I started to ask her what was up, but Malinda shook her head. Tears filled her eyes and she opened her arms. Stepping to us, she pulled both of us in for a hug at the same time. "Nothing. I'm not here for anything. Just—I love you boys. Men. You've both grown into remarkable men. You take good care of your wives and I'm proud of you. I wanted to tell you that. When I fell in love with David, I had no idea that I'd be getting Samantha and the both of you as well."

She tried to squeeze us close before letting go. She swiped at a tear that fell down her cheek.

Malinda stepped in as a mother to all of us, not just Samantha. We were the ones grateful for her. I opened my mouth, intending to tell her that, but the words got choked in my throat. There was a lot of repressed emotion in me at the moment. The words couldn't come out.

She shook her head again, catching my hand and giving it a last squeeze. "You don't have to say anything. I mean it. I just wanted a moment to let you know that I love you both. That's all. David and I love you *both*. We don't need to get anymore mushy, but just know I'm here for you. David too."

Tenderness washed through me. I tugged Malinda in for another hug and said softly, "We know. Trust me, we're the lucky ones here."

"*Oh.*" Her hand flung out and Logan caught it.

She hugged me back, one last time, before waving us on. She was blinking, trying to stop more tears from falling, but they were already trickling down her face. She used the back of her arm to wipe at her face. "Okay. Go on. Do your thing. I need to get myself under control here." The corner of her mouth lifted up. She gave us a wink. "Don't worry. I'll keep an eye on the rest for you." She went back inside, and paused on the other side of the door for a moment. Then, her head snapped up and seeing Sammy running for her, she moved forward to sweep the little guy up.

"Damn," Logan said quietly. "We lucked out getting her in our lives."

I exhaled. "That's the truth."

"Guys." Channing slid his hands in his pockets, waiting with the others. "Shall we do this?"

Yes. Right. Track down Maddy needed to commence.

I tipped my chin up. "Let's go."

Everything else got shoved down, way down inside of me.

We crossed the street, returning to the funeral home where we were parked. He dropped his voice, shoving his hands in his pockets. "If she's fighting..."

My gut tightened. I didn't like hearing that possibility, but it was within the realm of possibility. She was *my* daughter.

I bit out, "Then we're getting her into a training program, and we'll monitor her closely."

He nodded, his shoulders relaxing a little. "She's got the bloodlust. Same as we did growing up."

I gave him a look, raising an eyebrow.

He met my gaze, and the tops of his cheeks flushed before he looked away.

He wasn't going to admit it and I had to wonder about that. Why not? Why wasn't he going to admit it?

Because we *still* had the bloodlust. Maybe it was there to act as a distraction from the last week and what we were going to deal with tomorrow? Maybe I was leaning on it for a slight reprieve from burying my father tomorrow. Either way, our bloodlust was here. Right now. In both Logan and myself. He was every bit as excited as I was to head off into whatever the fuck we were going to find ourselves in. Into the fray? Into the chaos of Fallen Crest? Into what?

I didn't know, but I was buzzing.

I should've been worried about it.

I just wasn't.

8

MASON

When we arrived, it was clear that the place Maddy had gone wasn't just an underground fighting ring for people her age, like it had been back in the day. There were all ages, including adults. The fighting was something entirely different as well.

Weapons were allowed in the ring. The betting was out in the open. I recognized a bunch of gang tattoos.

Channing groaned. "Fuck. I know a good portion of these guys."

I cast him a look, thinking he was referring to the guys he tended to hunt down as a bounty hunter.

A group stood to the side wearing Red Demon cuts and we were walking past a whole line of Harley motorcycles parked in the front. This was all sorts of bad.

Logan moved in close, nudging my elbow. "People are recognizing you." More than a few heads turned our way. I clocked it too.

"If you see a phone, grab it," I told him, as well as Matteo and Nate.

"No." Channing halted us. He held up a device. "If anything

happens, I'll hit this button. It'll jam every cell within three miles. All of my guys have it. We use it when we have a high-risk bounty."

Nate shook his head. "Monroe, fuck. I don't know if that makes you scarier or if we should be comforted."

I grinned, feeling exactly the same. Logan eyed the device like he wanted to eat it.

Matteo was frowning, looking around the place. He hadn't been around for a lot of our escapades in high school, and he hadn't been close enough for a lot of the shit we did in college either. This was new to him.

"Can we talk about some sort of game plan? We're all, uh, not exactly young anymore. Some of us are hitting our forties."

"Pushing forty," Logan clarified, shooting Nate a smirk.

"Settle. You're a year younger."

"Still. Late thirties here. It makes a difference."

Nate looked like he wanted to show Logan how there really wasn't, but he just shook his head. He tried again. "Some of us don't hunt people for a living or work as professional athletes, so maybe we can have a plan for how to operate in there?"

Despite this word of reason, there was dark excitement in Nate's eyes. He was probably looking to cover his ass when questioned by his wife later on. Everyone here had children, except Matteo—that we knew of. I eyed Moose and Congo. I was sure they had kids. Both were married. I grimaced, thinking of their children. Little fucking Goliaths running around, snacking on rocks and hurling logs.

"I'm going to find my daughter and ground her ass. If anyone gets in my way, I have no problem taking heads from bodies." With that, I stalked forward.

Logan began laughing. "There's the brother I love."

"All right then," Channing said wryly. "Potential murder. Check that for the evening."

"We might want to get some cops on our payroll." Nate paused. "Are we into that sort of thing yet?"

"Seems like we are," Matteo answered. "Mason gets intense when he gets to the home turf, huh?"

Nate sighed. "You have no idea."

I stopped listening, moving into the open part of the warehouse where the fighting ring was located. As we drew near, three Red Demon guys blocked us, holding their hands in the air.

One spoke up, "Hey. Whoa. We don't know you..." He trailed off, looking past my shoulder. A sneer of disgust came over his face. "Monroe, you know better. You and your friends aren't welcome here. This is our territory."

I glanced back to see Channing's face darken with anger. Congo and Moose had stayed in the background, but now they pushed forward. The biker took them in, but his sneer didn't fade. The other bikers closed in, and one motioned behind him. Five more headed our way.

What is this? I didn't have patience for this shit. "I don't know what the fuck's going on, but my kid is here. Let us get her, and we'll be out of here." In the mood I was in, I didn't give one shit that these guys were probably killers. Sign me the fuck up.

The guy in charge cocked his head to the side. "You look familiar. How do I know you?" His mood changed, an aggressive scowl crossing his face. "I don't like feeling like I know someone without knowing how I know them. Makes me think you're a snitch and that's how I know you." His eyebrows furrowed together. "You a fucking snitch?"

I matched him scowl for scowl. I didn't know if I wanted him to recognize me. I wasn't sure if that would make things better or worse, but another biker joined us. Tall. Built lean. He had long dark hair that hung down his back. His dark eyes flicked with interest, flaring with recognition on Channing before moving over the rest of the group. He lingered on me. His eyebrows pulled together, just briefly before clearing.

"Go get Stripes," he said. "Let him know some people he might know are here."

"Boise, let us in. We're just here for our kids," Channing said.

The biker he had been talking to turned and pushed past the rest of their group.

Boise moved forward and gave Channing a cool look, shaking his head. "No can do, Monroe. Stripes is the guy in charge here."

Channing's eyes went flat. His nostrils flared. He did not like hearing that. "Is he in charge of the whole charter?"

Boise's eyes grew glacial. "You'd be smart to remember the boundaries. You're in *our* territory here."

Channing's mouth twisted.

Shouting, cursing, and high-pitched laughter sounded from behind our circle as the fight continued in the ring. The people wanted blood. The thirst for it was in the air. It was damn near intoxicating. I knew it was affecting me. Logan too. He was eyeing the ring with a hunger I'd not witnessed in him for a long time.

"When are you going to need me?" Sam's soft and knowing question came back to me.

Past patterns for us were mixing with our recent personal trauma. An old rage had awoken inside of me, and it was growing, turning into a fury that shouldn't feel as comfortable as it did. Like an old friend that wasn't good for me. I'd learned how to curb my anger growing up, but there was some new elements to this anger. There'd been too much change, too much loss.

I was done being a football player. That career forced me to keep myself in check. Marrying Sam and having kids helped reinforce my walls of control, but none of it seemed enough right now. I gritted my teeth as the urge to reach out, take one of the bikers's heads in my hands, and *pull* increased in me.

It wasn't a feeling I wanted, but at the same time, I'd missed it too.

"Monroe," a new voice said.

This must be Stripes. His men all stepped back.

Dark hair. He had a younger looking face, but it was a face that would always look young. His eyes told a different story. They were dark and hardened. Smart. There was an extra sense around him. It made me give him a second look. All the bikers were dangerous and deadly, but this one had more to him. I wasn't sure what I was picking up, but a sixth sense told me to be cautious with him. His eyes lit up when they found Channing, then shifted to share a look with Boise.

I couldn't read whatever they were expressing to each other.

Without saying a word to each other, Boise moved off into the warehouse again.

Stripes faced Channing, a smug smirk on his face, but it was a mask. Saw through it. I just couldn't see what it was covering. He said, "I thought we had an agreement. I stay out of Fallen Crest, and you don't come to our territories. Prez hasn't reached out. There's no warrants for our guys. You got no reason to be here."

Channing growled. "I've adhered to that protocol. We're not here for that."

Stripes's chin rose and his shoulders squared back. "This is my fighting ring. I run it. If you were anyone else, I'd say you'd have to put up or shut up. You hand over your phone and you either fight or put money down. Those are the rules for stepping inside."

My blood boiled. "What are the rules for the ring?"

Logan's gaze swung my way.

I ignored him, focusing on this punk.

He focused on me, and recognition flared. His smirk transformed to a genuine grin. "Well, fuck. The Hall of Famer himself." His voice cooled. "It's been a long time since you ran this area, Kade. You and your brother aren't welcome here either."

Logan sidled up next to me. "He asked about the rules for fighting."

Stripes studied Logan, his face locking down again. "No weapons except your fists. No killing. Winner is declared by knock out or if your opponent can't get up. That's it."

"Done." I was fine with that. In fact, I needed it.

Stripes frowned at me, still assessing. A small bit of surprise was on him.

"What?" Channing held out his hand. "No. We're not here to fight."

I looked over at the ring again. The two current fighters were young. I didn't want to worry about hurting someone my daughter's age. That didn't feel right, but there were others waiting on the sideline. They were closer to my age. I wouldn't feel any sort of guilt about laying into them.

"I don't think they discriminate by age," I noted.

He rolled his eyes, stepping up in front of me to block me. "Our kids are here," he told Stripes. "They're underage. Unless you're cool with having underage teenagers around these parts, just let us in to get them. We'll leave right after. No blood needs to be spilled."

The last statement was for me. I could feel Logan, restless next to me. He wanted to open his mouth and let loose, but Fallen Crest had changed. We had changed. If we were younger, we'd already be throwing fists, but Channing was keeping his head, and he was right. We were here for Maddy and Max. And Jesus, if Maddy saw me take to the ring? That wouldn't be good.

What was I doing? I was losing my head.

"You have a kid here?" Stripes's voice went sharp. His eyes darkened. "Who?"

Channing's eyes narrowed, and the roles reversed. Something shifted between them. Suddenly he was the one being smug and smirking. I didn't know what brought it on.

"My son."

Stripes lifted his chin. The mask fell away, revealing he was all business. He stepped back and motioned for his bikers. Two dispersed immediately.

My gut churned.

Maddy was here. If we'd stayed in Boston or San Diego, this wouldn't have happened. She'd had a more normal life there— the occasional party, movies, a trip to the mall, beach bonfires. It was different here. The shadows around Fallen Crest, where all the wealthy millionaires lived, had grown more dangerous. Maybe as one rose, the other declined? They balanced each other, I supposed. The more wealth, the higher the hoity society in Fallen Crest, the more dangerous the territories around it became. Which meant living here was possibly the worst decision we'd made for the kids.

Channing was a bounty hunter. We all had other businesses, some of them together, so I knew he didn't need to be a bounty hunter for money. It's just what he did, but even he looked surprised at everything happening here. That made me wonder if there were elements around here even he wasn't aware about. Maybe he kept his head down, focusing on what stood in front of him and no longer searched the shadows anymore?

One of the bikers rejoined us. He spoke to Stripes before the latter shifted, looking somewhere further inside. After a moment, he ran a hand over his jaw before giving a small nod. "They're in the back. You and Kade can collect your kids."

We moved forward as a group, but the bikers quickly formed a wall.

"Only the two fathers can go in," Stripes clarified.

Logan growled, his restlessness snapping. "I don't fucking care what you say—"

Every one of us readied ourselves. We all recognized the sound coming from my brother. The need for violence twisted inside of him too.

Neither of us was quite in control.

Stripes showed his teeth, moving to face off against Logan. I checked him, moving faster than him. Stepping into *his* path, I made it look like he'd made the first move, not us.

He noted the positioning and his eyes jerked to mine. He was surprised.

We shared a look in that split second. We both got a read on the other and a week ago, our roles would've been reversed. This was his place of business. His territory. He had more men to back him up. Hell, he had all the power on his side, except I was on edge. I was the unknown in this situation, and I couldn't make myself care that he was a killer.

Everything in me needed to feel someone's blood.

He read that. Just like I read him, that he was aware in the moment, they'd win. He was also aware my name would bring a spotlight to this world that thrived only if it was in the dark.

He eased back, holding up a hand because his guys were about to throw down with ours. He raised his voice, speaking low and calm, but assertively, "We're going to let 'em pass."

"What?" one of the bikers snapped. "Stripes—"

He clipped out, "We don't need to be on the evening news when an NFL Hall of Famer ends up in the hospital, breathing through a tube."

I saw red. I was reacting as if that were a threat made.

A hand caught my arm and jerked me backward. Nate body-checked me, shoving me to the side. "Dude, get yourself under control," he hissed. "We're here to get Maddy. That's fucking it. Got it?"

I rubbed at my forehead, because *fuck*. He was right. I already knew he was right.

Stripes began laughing.

"They're both grieving," Nate snapped at him. "Neither one is thinking clearly right now, but if we threw down, you'd be surprised at the end result. Believe me. I don't know what the dynamic is between you and Channing, but *I don't care*. We're just going to get the kids."

Stripes's eyes were glittering, an eerie image of a cobra rising before an attack flashed in my mind, but he only moved aside. He held up a hand. "Like I said, let 'em through."

As we passed, he'd switched to watching Channing. His gaze never left him.

Jesus fucking Christ. All that work just to step into a warehouse.

A wave of clear thinking doused the fight that'd been boiling inside of me once we moved farther away from the bikers. Nate was right. Get Maddy. Get home. Take my frustrations out at the gym. Keep my head clear. That'd always been the number one rule of surviving Fallen Crest. I half laughed to myself as we prowled through the crowd. *That* hadn't changed.

Heads turned our way. People stopped watching the fight as more recognition swept through the place. I heard my name spoken, along with Matteo's.

Nate was right.

Get Maddy. Get out. Throwing down was not a good idea.

The bloodlust was calming down inside of me.

That was until we got to the other side of the warehouse and a scream ripped through the air.

It was Maddy.

9

SAMANTHA

"Ladies," I said, taking the first bottle of wine and three glasses outside to the table on our patio. I filled the glasses to the absolute brim before Taylor brought out the second bottle, as well as a water for herself. She slid it over as she, Quincey, and Heather all sat.

I sat in my chair, but it felt like I more collapsed. All the kids were asleep. They'd been fed. They were content—for the next five minutes, at least. We needed to make the most of this. I held up my glass.

The others did the same. We shared a smile because damn, this week had sucked, and today was no exception.

"A toast to us motherfucking mothers," I began. "Here's to the men we fuck. To the kids we raise. To the work that goes unseen. We may love our families, but here's to us. Because at the end of the day, we're the queens. No one can fucking do what we do. Here's to you, my sisters. Live. Laugh. Love. But most importantly, we all deserve an award for keeping our sanity."

They all laughed and lifted their glasses a little higher before taking a drink.

"How are you holding up?" Heather asked.

I shrugged, leaning back in my seat. "It's... It is what it is. I don't really know what to say right now."

"How's Mason?" Quincey asked, glancing at Taylor. "And Logan?"

Taylor and I shared a look. We'd talked, but not in detail. There wasn't time. My kids were older. They were less demanding, but their little Sammy was a handful. I'd been trying to help as much I could with the rest of the kids, as well as the animals. Nova's tortoise had an attitude. If he didn't get lettuce, he followed you from room to room, just watching. Staring. Judging you until you gave in and handed it over. He'd figured out that I knew the kitchen the best, and as soon as he was done eating whatever someone had given him, he'd come find me.

He didn't make a sound, but his stare spoke volumes. Who knew tortoises could be so judgmental? Harold felt like a grumpy old man stuffed inside a giant turtle body.

"Logan's... He's hurting," Taylor said after a moment.

"Same with Mason."

"Grief is so hard." Quincey frowned, staring into her drink.

I wondered if there was something more behind her words. Heather met my gaze with the same question. I could only shrug to her.

"The funeral's tomorrow," Heather noted. "The guys are all gone, probably getting into trouble trying to find Maddy and Max. We'll handle it when they get back to us, if there's anything to be worried about, but right now, I'm not."

Taylor sat forward, her eyes shining. "What are you thinking, Heather?"

"I'm thinking we should take advantage of all the fourteen-year-olds we have in the house. Natessia can babysit. Nolan and Nash too. We could go out and have our own fun."

Quincey tilted her head. "What are you thinking?" She looked at Taylor. "Would you be up for doing something?"

Taylor ran a hand over her bump. She looked tired, but smiled. "I'm thinking the guys have been spending a lot of time together. Why can't we?"

"Exactly." Heather's grin grew wicked. "We don't have to do anything crazy. I can make a call and reserve the back room at Manny's. Music. Darts. Drinks. Food."

Oh man. A night at Manny's. Our private room. "I'm down for this. Let's do it."

"Wait." Taylor stopped everyone before we could start getting up. She lifted her water in the air. "One more toast." She waited until everyone raised their glasses with her. "We've met at different times in life. Some of us in high school. Some in college. Some even later than that. But once we met each other, a sisterhood began with all of us. It wove between us, bringing us close, but allowing us to separate as we each went to our homes. Boston. San Diego. Seattle. Fallen Crest. Now we're all in one place. We've been brought together by a tragedy and we're here for each other. Through birthday parties for goats, or campaigning for adult athletes or performing a ballet dance for a parakeet or praying whenever we hear a scream that our child wasn't the one to draw blood, the point is that we're in this together. We understand the crazy moments, the stressful moments, the times we're pulling our hair out, pretending you need the bathroom when you have four paws and ten fingers sticking under the door. We understand the funny times. The reasons each of us fell in love with our partners in life. The joys of the future to come, and also the tragedies that will happen in the future as well. You. Me. Us. You are my sisters in this world, and I am one thankful bitch to have you all in my life. To us."

Hell, yeah.

"To us!"

Taylor ended it with, "Now let's go have some fun and see what version of Drunk Sam emerges."

We toasted. We laughed. I shed a few tears.

We were ready to go out.

10

MASON

W e passed through the warehouse to an area in the back, and I saw them right away. Maddy was standing with a group of guys. Two of them were holding her back—smooth little fucks. I didn't like them—each with a hand on her arm as she lunged toward another group of guys. Those two reeked of elitist pricks while the other group of guys were rougher. If I had to guess, the rough group was Roussou, and the elitist assholes were from Fallen Crest Academy.

Then the Roussou guys shuffled to the side, and behind them were two guys fighting.

I recognized Max and cursed under my breath, picking up my pace. That's why Maddy was trying to get loose.

Channing roared next to me. He'd seen his son as well. We tore over to them, but Max was not the one getting his ass handed to him. He was the one delivering the beatdown, raining hit after hit on the guy. The other kid was trying to dodge and block, but it didn't matter. Max herded him into a corner with the guy's back against a shed. He reached over, took hold of the guy's arm, and held it aside as he delivered a barrage of clean hits straight to his head.

I winced at one particular punch, almost hearing the guy's nose break.

"Okay." Channing waded in, grabbing his son and yanking him backward. He swung him clear. Max didn't register it, still trying to kick at the guy. He landed one last blow before Channing had totally removed him. The guy folded, collapsing to the ground.

"Let me go—" Max screamed.

I winced. Whatever had happened, Max was in a feral place. He wasn't thinking clearly. He was somewhere else, in fight-or-flight mode. There was a haze over his eyes, his pupils dilated but fierce.

I stepped between the two groups, a hand stretched toward Maddy. She'd stopped fighting as soon as she saw us.

Her eyes were wild. There was fear in there too.

What the fuck happened?

"Max! Stop." Channing growled.

I turned back.

Max had gotten free. He was scrambling back to the guy, who was barely conscious. His friends knelt beside him to check on him, and one fell on his ass, trying to get away from Max. I began to head for him, but a hand caught my arm.

Matteo jerked his chin in Maddy's direction and I got his meaning. I needed to focus on my daughter. I dipped my head in a quick response.

He moved in and reached for one of Max's arms. Channing wrapped an entire arm around his son's middle and stood, lifting him. He began to carry him clear all over again.

"Boss." Moose's deep baritone cut through the fray. "Let us."

He and Congo were there.

Matteo shifted out of the way so both Moose and Congo took hold of Max, who was still scrambling to get free.

"*Max!*" Channing got in his face. He blocked his view. Once

Max couldn't see the guy anymore, he blinked rapidly, seeming to come back to himself.

"Dad?" he choked out.

I inwardly flinched. That was the voice of a little boy.

Where had Max gone to just now?

"Dad," Maddy whimpered, pulling my attention back to her. She was reaching for me, and I caught her hand. Yanking her into my arms, I held her tight to my chest. She was fine. She was whole. I had her. No one was going to get to her.

Logan stalked forward. "What the fuck just happened?"

Boots moved over the pavement. The sound of rocks sliding over the cement came from behind us. A few of the bikers had trailed us. One cursed under his breath before slipping away. I had a feeling he was going to get Stripes.

We needed to know what happened before he showed up.

"Start talking. Now." I seared the two elitists with a glare before turning to my daughter. She was trembling and blinking rapidly like Max had before.

Fuck. Fuck. Fuck.

Both seemed still slightly in shock.

She looked almost identical to Sam at her age, but while she had Sam's kindness, everything else inside of my daughter was me. She was a female version of myself, so I knew what was coming next.

Whatever had happened, it had happened fast, and it was all coming to her now. She was processing. As the shock began to seep away, indignant rage swiftly replaced it.

"Mase." Logan was seeing the same thing.

"I got her." I made sure my hold was firm because she was about to blow.

And she did. A guttural and animalistic growl rumbled from her and she began twisting, trying to rip from me. "I'm going to rip *that fucker apart*."

"Maddy. Stop." Logan stepped in, blocking her view.

I grunted, holding onto her, but not trying to bruise her. Christ. Her body was all muscle. She seemed slender. She didn't look ripped, but there was no mistaking it. This girl was unnaturally strong. She almost got out of my arms, so I had to readjust, doing what Channing had for Max. I wrapped my arms around Maddy and picked her up. Her feet flailed in the air. That same animal sound roared from her, "I'm going to tear his insides out and wrap his intestines around his throat to strangle him. You piece of—"

"Maddy!" Logan dodged her feet, shoving them down when they would've gotten him. He got in her face. "Chill out."

Some of the fight started to leave her.

I moved back, carrying her farther away from the group.

Nate and Matteo continued their glares with both groups. They weren't letting anyone leave.

Channing, Congo, and Moose took Max away too, needing space. The two big guys were standing behind him now, and he wasn't trying to get away anymore. His head hung down, resting on his dad's shoulder as Channing had a hand on his shoulder. His head was folded down as he was speaking fiercely to his son. As that was happening, Max's gaze was pinned on Maddy, regret and anguish all over his face.

Logan dropped his voice, moving closer to Maddy. "I need you to tell me right now what happened. Are you hurt? Did someone say something to you? Threaten you?"

Nothing. Nothing. Nothing. There was no reaction from her.

He asked, "Touch you?"

We both heard the slight inhale of air from her.

Horror slammed through me, and I shared a matching look with my brother. That horror quickly morphed into the need to murder someone.

Logan swallowed and cleared his expression as we looked at Max. Seemed like he'd done our job for us.

Maddy stepped away from me a little, enough to place her hand to my chest. I looked down to see her biting her lip. "It's okay, Dad."

Fuck no, it wasn't. "Where?" I seethed. Fuck. Shit. I gentled my tone. "Where did he touch you, Maddy?"

Fear leaped to her eyes. She swallowed nervously. "Dad..." Her hand began shaking against my chest.

I reached up, covering it with mine. She drew in a breath, her shoulders lifting and rolling back. Her mother used to do that as well. When she was drawing in strength, she readied herself like that. Her chin tipped up, and then she'd open her eyes and face whatever was coming at her.

A wave of tender love swept through me, for both Samantha and my daughter. Before she could say anything, I cupped the back of her head and pulled her to my chest once again. "We can talk about it later."

I heard shuffling behind us, and moved to the side, still holding my daughter. Stripes walked through the small crowd that had formed. Apparently this fight had been more entertaining than the one still happening in the ring. Boise joined Stripes as well, but he kept quiet.

"What the ever-loving fuck is happening out here?" Stripes was pissed. His chilly gaze swept over everyone. "You want to fucking fight? You do it in the ring. That's it. There's no violence outside of the ring. You got it?" He frowned as his gaze swept over Maddy before ending on Max.

He took in the guy still on the ground, blood pouring from him. A wheezing sounded from him. He was having a hard time breathing. Stripes cursed under his breath, motioning to one of the bikers. "Call Prez. See if he could bring Kalista with him."

The biker nodded, moving away, already on his phone.

One of the Roussou guys said, "He needs an ambulance."

Stripes turned to him, and he went eerily still before he clipped out, "No ambulances. No cops."

"But..." The guy flung an arm out, pointing at his friend. "He can't breathe."

"Which is why we got a nurse coming here," Stripes barked back. "Stand the fuck down unless you're going to give me a nicely detailed description of what exactly happened here." He waited, his head cocked to the side.

I was struggling. The offended person was my daughter, but this was an illegal fighting ring, and it was run by a one-percenter motorcycle club. We didn't start shit, but we finished it. That old dynamic was strong inside of me, *yearning* to come out.

Closing my eyes, I reached inside for some iron discipline, the same will that had helped me remain competitive as a professional athlete over the last few decades. There it was. It had slipped low, but I began pulling it up. Enough of it so it coated my insides. Once it was locked in place, nice and suppressed, I cleared my throat.

Stripes turned my way.

I was about to speak when one of the elitist dicks burst out, "That fucking dick touched her." He nodded to the guy on the ground and then indicated Maddy. "He cupped her pussy—"

He stopped abruptly, and everyone's eyes came to me and Logan.

It took a second to realize what was happening. We sounded like animals, my rage transformed into sound. The old discipline slipped back down. I was going to murder the kid.

"Who *the fuck* is that kid?" I began stalking him.

Then Maddy was in front of me, stopping me.

I blinked, coming back to myself. She wasn't the only one who had moved between us. Stripes was blocking me. Nate and Matteo had moved closer.

"Okay. Here's what we're going to do," Stripes clipped out,

his jaw clenched. "I don't give a shit what happened, not really. The girl looks like she'll survive. But the girl's big, bad father and uncle are here, and it looks like her honor has been defended so it's a fucking moot point now. If any more justice is to be handed out, do it away from here. We got a family nurse coming in, along with our charter president, so if you all don't want to deal with him, a bigger and badder asshole than me, I'd suggest you *get the fuck* out of here." No one moved. He barked, "*Now!*"

Two of the bikers snapped their fingers to the Roussou guys, who went to pick up their friend. They carried him out, following the bikers to another building off to the side.

The two punks took off. One gave Maddy a look as he went, but I didn't let myself decipher it. If I had, I couldn't promise I wouldn't go after him, rules and bikers be damned. They'd brought her here. They'd exposed her to this world.

Fuck.

"What do you want?" Logan's voice was icy and lethal. His question wasn't for me.

Stripes moved toward us. He ignored my brother, his eyes on Maddy. "Are you okay?"

She drew in a deep breath before she nodded. "I'm fine." Her words were hoarse.

"You don't sound it."

She drew in another breath, stopping her body from shaking and stepped away from me. "I'm fine. Really." Her eyes moved over his shoulder, trained on where Channing and Max were approaching.

Stripes and Channing shared a look before he moved his attention to Max.

"Stop fucking looking at my kid, Ryerson," Channing snapped.

The hint of a grin showed on Stripes's face before he coughed, clearing it away. He lifted his chin toward Max. "With the beatdown I heard you delivered to that kid, I'd say you could pick up a match any day in my ring—"

"Like fuck." Channing stepped forward.

Stripes flicked a cool look at Channing as he said, ignoring him and speaking to Max, "But I know your aunt. I've got a hunch I'd wake up one morning with a knife in my gut. Tell Miss Bren that her nephew and all his friends are banned from this establishment. And she's welcome. No need to call."

Max looked deflated.

"What?" Maddy whispered.

Stripes wasn't done. "But if you find yourself back here and somehow slip through security, let us know if you need anything. You got me?" His head lowered, waiting for his response.

Max gulped before bobbing his head up and down. He didn't look torn up about being banned. He seemed relieved. He looked over at Maddy and pushed away from his dad, clearing his throat. "Can we go?"

"Max—" Maddy started to go to him.

"Now." Max turned his back on her.

He'd been speaking to his dad.

Maddy gasped, rocked by his rejection.

I reached back for her, not understanding the details, only knowing she was hurt by that action. But this was Max. It was Max and Maddy. The dynamic between them was solid. Max was the good kid. Maddy led him into trouble, and Max usually had to clean it up. I wondered again what else had happened to precipitate all of this.

Logan met my gaze and shook his head.

Channing glanced over.

I dipped my head, indicating we should all go.

He nodded back. "Yeah. Okay."

"I want to go home," Max added. "Not to..." He flinched when he saw me.

Not to my house, where my daughter would be. Shit. What had *happened*?

"Max," Maddy whispered again.

Channing coughed. "Yeah, we'll head home."

"We'll give Heather a ride home," I told him as he passed.

He nodded. "Appreciate it." He gave Stripes one last glare before he and Max disappeared into the crowd. Moose and Congo trailed behind.

Maddy whirled to me. "Dad—"

I shook my head, stopping her. "We're going to wait a little bit. Let them get clear before we follow."

Her shoulders fell. She looked utterly dejected. Her head hung down and she mumbled, "He didn't want to come. He told me he knew he'd end up fighting, and he didn't want to go where he knew that would happen. I... He asked me to leave, and I wouldn't go. He's not mad at me about what that guy did, which I hate. I was just standing here and he walked up and put his hand there. He didn't fully cup—you know, make contact. He was close enough, and Max lost it on him. This is all my fault."

"Hey." Logan's voice was sharp. "It's not your fucking fault some guy invaded your boundary. It's called personal space. That's never your fault. I don't care what you're told. We don't blame girls and women for fucking just standing there. You could be naked, and no one's got a right to touch you unless you ask for it—" He grimaced, hearing his words. "You know what I mean. I have a wallet, and if someone sees my wallet, my cash, they don't have any right to take it. Same fucking premise."

She drew in some oxygen, her eyes watering. Seeing her bottom lip trembling, Logan held his arm out. She stepped in, and he folded her against him, holding her. His gaze met mine over her head, heated.

We were both angry at a lot of things.

Stripes returned, almost cordial. "They're clear. You can go now."

We nodded, turning to leave.

"Kade," he called.

Matteo and Nate paused with me.

He lifted his chin toward Maddy, who was walking ahead with Logan. "I'm not going to lie. The fighting ring is popular, especially with the high school and college crowd on the weekends. I'm sure they'll show up again. I'll put them on the banned list, but I'll just be honest. Sometimes it hurts them more not to be able to get into a place their friends are going, and if that's the case, they'll probably be allowed in. You'll get a notice from us when and if they show up."

Fuck's sakes. I didn't know how to take this guy. I just gave him a grunt. "Thanks."

People were looking as we went back through the warehouse. Logan moved in front. I kept Maddy tucked next to me, using one of my hands to shield her face. I knew they had a policy of no phones, but I'd learned people figured ways around rules. Matteo walked on Maddy's other side, and Nate blanketed us from behind.

It wasn't long until we were to the lot and heading for my vehicle.

Once we got inside, Maddy started, "Dad—"

"Don't." I gave her a look in the rearview mirror.

She clammed up, shrinking down in her seat.

I tried to gentle my tone because dammit, there were multiple layers here. I didn't know which one to handle first. I needed to talk to Sam. Get a game plan together. Sam tended to know the best ways of dealing with things. "We'll talk it all out with your mom."

Sam rarely yelled. She rarely lost her head when it came to the children, but she listened to everything. When it was all said and done, she would deliver a clear and precise assessment of everything Maddy had done to put herself in this position. Then she'd deliver an articulate list of all Maddy had learned for the future, which usually seemed to deliver the hardest blow, because that let Maddy know how she'd let her mom down. That's what she really hated hearing. At the end of the night, Sam would open her arms and hug her kid, and she'd cater to however her daughter had been hurt. Sam never missed a beat. Maddy would leave that discussion feeling like she'd been put through a tornado of emotions.

Maddy closed her eyes, falling back in her seat. "*Fuck.*"

I held back a laugh because she was right. She *was* fucked.

11

MASON

Turned out, Sam wouldn't be taking point.

Logan got a text as we neared Fallen Crest and began laughing. "The women are at Manny's and they're wasted."

Nate groaned. "Quincey tends to want to check on all of Nova's animals when she's had a couple too many drinks. She gets all weepy about how wonderful each of them is. We brought five of Nova's animals with us this time. *Five.* That damn fucking tortoise. She's going to try to bring Harold into our bed."

"Harold?" Matteo laughed. "What?"

"The tortoise. She's going to bring a stepladder into the room so he can climb into the bed. Goddammit. I'm not sharing my bed with a giant turtle."

I snickered, at least until Logan got another text. His gaze met mine in the rearview mirror.

My grin fell fast. "What?"

He grimaced. "We don't get Ninja Sam tonight. We get Dinosaur Sam."

I frowned. *The fuck?*

When we got to the house, I sent Maddy to bed, saying sternly, "We'll talk tomorrow."

"We have the funeral tomorrow."

"We'll talk when we can—maybe the day after. Go to bed. I mean it, Maddy." I raised my voice as she started up the stairs.

Matteo and Nate didn't stick around. Both headed to their respective areas of the house, or outside to the pool house, in Matteo's case. Logan disappeared into the kitchen, and I waited, checking my phone to see if Channing sent a follow-up text. He hadn't.

Ten minutes later, I found out what Dinosaur Sam meant.

Taylor walked inside first. She was sober, biting back a grin. Her shoulders shook with laughter. "I can't—I just can't. They're...good luck." She looked around. "Where's my husband? Husband!"

"Wife!" Logan walked from the kitchen, a plate of warmed-up pizza slices in his hand. He beamed at his wife. "My Taco."

She flushed. "Logan."

He chuckled, pulling her in for a kiss. He held up the plate of pizza. "Hungry?"

She moaned. "God, yes. I shouldn't. I might be up all night, but..." She stared at the plate.

He took a slice and pushed it into her hand. "Eat. I'll hold your hair if it doesn't agree with you."

I frowned. "Shouldn't you be out of the morning-sickness stage?"

Taylor groaned, shaking her head. "I wish. I still never know when something is going to not agree with me, but I'm starving."

Raucous sounds came from outside. Taylor chuckled, nabbing a second slice and kissing Logan on the cheek. "And that's my cue. Have fun." She snorted, disappearing down the hallway to the wing where they always stayed.

Logan and I turned in time to see the door kicked open. I

had to blink a few times to make sure I was seeing what I was seeing, but I was. Sam was in the doorway, her arms up and bent outward, and her knees bent in a squat.

"What the—"

"KER-BAHHHHHHHHHP!" She leaned forward and her mouth opened as she made the sound, then clamped together as her head moved backward. Her legs and arms moved forward, her knees still bent. She looked like a crab trying to walk forward as it stood up. She only went another few feet before there was a repeat performance.

Head out.

Mouth open.

"KER-BAHHHHHHHHHHHHHPP! KER-KER-BAHHHHP-BAHPP-BAHPP!" Her mouth snapped open on each word like her lips were a beak.

Her head returned to its normal position and onward the crab-walk continued until another repeat.

Heather couldn't walk behind her. She was on the ground, hugging her sides as she laughed so hard she couldn't breathe.

"What the—" Logan started to say.

"KER-BAHHHHHHHHP! BAHHHHHHHHHP!" Snap. Crab-walk. Crab-walk.

This was Dinosaur Sam?

She was going to wake the kids. Or some of the kids.

I moved toward her, getting ready to pick her up, but the sliding door from the back of the kitchen opened. Soon after, we heard Quincey saying, "Shoo. Shoo. Come on. You can do it. Let's go."

Logan backed up a bunch of steps until he had a clear view of the kitchen. He cursed, his eyebrows shooting up his forehead. He snorted, laughing as Sam let loose with another, "KER-BAHP BAHP BAHPPP! KER KER KER!"

He almost dropped the pizza, and he had to sit in the

nearest chair, looking back and forth from whatever the fuck Quincey was doing in the kitchen to Dinosaur Sam.

"Come on. Yeah. Good job, Harold," Quincey cooed. The patio door slid shut.

I took three steps and plucked my wife up in one arm.

"KER-BA—Oh!" She squeaked. "Mason."

I carried her into the kitchen to see with my own eyes as Nate's wife led Harold into the house. She was bribing him, holding out lettuce. He moved forward, reaching for the food. She kept pedaling backward, holding more leaves for him. He kept following.

Sam blinked away some wetness in her eyes. Heather had moved into the house, but only made it far enough to lean heavily against the wall, bent over with laughter.

When she saw Harold, she lost it all over again.

Sam started laughing with her.

Soon both were howling so loud that for a second I blanked on how to handle this situation. I looked to my brother, but he was no help. He'd abandoned the pizza and was out of his chair, his knees almost touching the ground as he wiped a hand over his face. He couldn't stop laughing.

Hearing those three, Quincey looked around and began trying to hold her laughter in.

She failed.

Logan looked over at me, trying to get ahold of himself. "Nate called it," he said.

I had no idea how to wrangle these women when they decided to indulge and have a good time. Though, I was glad this was the problem I got. Back on the team, other players's wives would sometimes get drunk. Loneliness, sadness, maybe basic selfishness came out. They'd want attention so they'd do what they needed to get it. Flirting with other men. Having affairs. It happened. It was more common than some of the guys wanted to admit. I was aware some of those same husbands were also cheating, so what came first? The chicken or the egg. It was that same sort of question. Or maybe it was that like attracted like.

Not my wife. Not her friends.

They got drunk and came back impersonating dinosaurs and trying to bribe a giant turtle to cuddle up for the night. I chuckled. I had no idea why Sam chose me, but I would *never* stop thanking the stars for her.

I pulled her close and pressed a kiss to her forehead.

She blinked a few times, and a soft, gooey look melted over her. "Oh, husband. I love you too." She reached up, trying to cup my face. Her hand landed over my nose, and she pressed a kiss to my earlobe, sighing into it. "Take me to bed, husband. Fuck me good. I promise I won't fall asleep. I'll hold my legs up for you."

Logan lost it all over again, wiping tears from his face. "That's just what every husband wants to hear. 'I promise I won't fall asleep'—this time."

"Oh!" We all turned to Heather. "My husband and child aren't here. They went home?"

Sam scrambled out of my hold. I didn't trust her. I didn't know what she would do. She might go to Heather or start keeping pace with the fucking turtle to 'motivate him.'

Also I enjoyed feeling her in my arms so I pulled her back.

She struggled until I slid a hand into her pants pocket, finding a hole and moving my finger over her panties. She melted back into me. "Oh," she breathed.

Heather was trying to make sense of her phone. "Wait. What happened? Natessia and Crew are here?"

I nodded. "I checked on them, both are sleeping. Max wanted to go to your place. Things were tense when we found them. There was an altercation."

"An altercation?" She straightened. All the laughter melted away.

"Everyone's fine. Max is fine. I think..." I didn't want to throw Maddy under the bus.

"He and Mads had a little disagreement," Logan explained. "You know how they are. They'll be fine tomorrow, but he needed a breather for the night. Probably just wanted to clear his head. Sleep in his own bed. That sort of thing."

She nodded, but still seemed worried. "I should..." She looked up the stairs, toward where her kids were resting.

"I can give you a ride home," Logan told her. "Nat and Crew will be fine. We'll bring them to the church tomorrow. Feed 'em even." He winked, standing and reaching for his keys.

"No." I shook my head at Heather and Logan. "I'll drive her."

"Are you sure?" Logan's gaze went to Samantha.

Quincey was bringing that damn turtle past us, and I knew my wife was going to forget what was happening and would want to join the fun. Wanting to avoid all of that, I hoisted Sam up and over my shoulder.

She gasped. "Mason!"

I spoke over her to Logan. "Yes, I'm sure." I smacked her on the ass. "I'm bringing this one with me."

"Ah—Mason!"

I ignored her, turning to Heather. "You ready to roll out? Need the bathroom or anything?"

Heather looked a little dazed. "No. I'm good."

Logan trailed after us. "What do you want me to do with this one?" He indicated Quincey over his shoulder with his thumb. She and Harold were moving past the entryway.

I shook my head. "Not my wife. Not my problem."

12

MASON

Heather asked a few questions on the car ride to her place, but we didn't really get into it. When I pulled up to their house, their front door opened. Channing came out, shirtless and wearing sweatpants. He ran a hand through his hair before scratching down his chest, yawning.

"Oh God." Heather reached for the door handle. She swallowed. "He waited up for me. That's not good."

She opened the door, but I called out, "Jax."

She looked back.

"Your kid's fine. He's a good kid. A good head on his shoulders. It's not something to lose sleep over."

Seemed those were the right words to say. Some of her panic faded, and she let out a deep breath. "Right. Thanks. That—yeah. Thanks, Mason."

She slipped out, shutting the door.

I waited until she went up to their patio.

Channing reached for her, pulling her in for a hug. He nodded to me, then pulled his wife inside their house.

I glanced to the backseat, where Sam had quickly decided she was going to lie down. She was too out of it to make sense of what was going on, and I pulled my phone out to snap a quick picture of her—arms crossed over her chest, torso twisted halfway to me, drool pooling on the Escalade floor. Her legs were bent the other way, one of them slipping between her chair and the door.

That was my wife. Adorable in any awkward position.

I backed out of their place and headed home, content to listen to Sam's snoring. She didn't wake as I carried her inside and moved through the house. Logan must've shut everything down, because all the usual lights were off. With Sam still in my arms, I moved her so I could maneuver a free hand. Checking the security panel, all the doors were locked. Windows too. The house was locked down.

I took Sam to our room, and once I eased her down to the bed, she began to wake up. "Wha—Heather? What..."

I smoothed a hand over her forehead and tucked some of her hair behind her ear. "It's all okay. Go to sleep, babe."

"But, Mase..." She began to sit up.

I studied her and decided she'd feel better if we did the whole routine for bed. "Okay. Up you go." I plucked her off the bed and carried her to the bathroom counter, sitting her next to the sink.

Her eyes were so drowsy, heavy bags beneath them, but she held a hand to my shoulder. She'd sobered up enough to know what I was doing.

I handed her the toothbrush and toothpaste. She took them and brushed her teeth without comment. After that, we switched. I gave her some makeup wipes, a warm cloth. Once that was done, she was okay enough to wiggle down.

I handled my own shit, then ducked into the closet to grab what we wore for bed. Having a house full of kids meant neither of us could sleep naked, which was always my preferred way of being in bed with my wife.

The toilet flushed. She used the sink again before shuffling over to me, taking the clothes I held out to her. She dropped them on the bed.

Mumbling something, she removed her pants and pulled her shirt up and over her head. I had to help, but once it was clear of her head, she tossed it to the side. Her bra followed.

Ignoring the clothes on the bed, she reached for my shirt and began tugging it off me. I didn't help with that, enjoying the attention. She grunted, biting her lip and arched up on her tiptoes until it lifted from my head. She pulled it over hers.

After that, she patted my chest and crawled onto the bed, stopping once to nudge the other clothes to the floor.

"Sam?"

She grunted, crawling the rest of the way to our pillows, where she dropped down on her stomach. She burrowed into her pillow. I waited a second. Soft little snores came from her almost immediately.

I sighed, taking her in. I didn't move. I wanted to savor this memory, sear it into my brain alongside all those other moments before it and knowing so many more would come after. I never thought I could love her more, but little moments like this taught me that I could because I did. I was *wrecked* for this partner of mine.

Climbing into bed, I started to reach for Sam, but she was already moving. She crawled to me and curled into a ball, mostly on top of me. I knew she wouldn't move again until one of our alarms went off or if one of the kids woke us up.

I held her tight as I went to sleep.

Night, Dad.

13

MADDY

I messed up. I *really* messed up.

    I couldn't sleep.

I had so seriously messed up.

Throwing my blankets off, I tiptoed over to my desk for my phone. There were no messages from Max.

I checked my social media. There were some private messages from Beltraine and Axel.

I frowned, seeing a notification that Stevie Broudou had left me a message.

I wasn't going to click on it. I still wasn't sure how I felt about her. She was also new at FCA with me. We'd been in the same orientation meeting with the principal, and of course I knew her uncle. Brett Broudou was awesome. His niece, though, was a different story. She was weird, but I didn't know if it was a cool weird, a stay away from weird, or just *weird* weird.

I swallowed my disappointment. There weren't *any* messages from Max on *any* of my social media accounts. My eyes watered as I clicked out of everything, plugging my phone into the charger.

He was really mad at me. I'd so seriously and completely fucked up.

I sniffled, crawling back into bed and rolled over. Hugging the pillow, I buried my head in it and used it to quiet my tears.

I couldn't lose Max. I just couldn't.

I'd make it right tomorrow.

14

MASON

People like to say the funeral service was beautiful. I heard it enough times as people came up, shaking my hand, kissing Sam's cheek, hugging my kids. But I hated hearing that phrase. It wasn't true. The funeral sucked. My dad was not supposed to go out that way. It was bullshit and wrong and a tragedy. He should've died in his sleep, from old age, needing a handheld urinal to piss. He should've been surrounded by his grandkids.

Or fuck, I didn't know. Just longer. He had more years in him.

Why the fuck couldn't he have brought us in earlier? We would've helped. We would've done fucking anything to stop this. He was a Kade. Anyone messing with him messed with us. Fuck the business side of it.

He was one of us.

No one fucked with us.

But it had happened and we'd had one week to process.

One. Week.

That ended when people began arriving for the funeral, because it quickly became a who's who. CEOs of global companies arrived in droves, celebrity athletes came for me, Olympic medal winners showed up to support Samantha. Channing's sister and her entire crew arrived. Nate's sister showed up, along with my stalker and another girl Heather pulled in for a tight hug. Quincey's half brother traveled down with his family. I was hoping to talk him into taking the giant tortoise back with him.

Then there were the board members. Their families. Shareholders. Any investor and wannabe investor. Fallen Crest's town council. The mayor. Roussou's mayor. The chief of police.

The church couldn't hold any more, so we had to get security. Of course, that was around the time pictures started hitting the internet, and I knew the press would soon show up. A few cameras had been there from the beginning, but by the time the service actually started, the cameras doubled.

Once again, the casket was closed. The minister said his piece. Music played. There were a couple solos and at the end, we took our places at the casket to carry it out. Logan and I were in the front. Nate and Channing behind us, and Matteo and Max were next. Two of our cousins were last. We all wore matching white boutonnieres. Sam had been crying when she helped pin mine to my jacket.

I hated every fucking second of the day.

I cursed every step we took to carry my dad's casket outside. When it lowered into the ground, I wanted to light it on fire. Fuck throwing in the dirt. Sure, it was symbolic. I knew there was a respect and a sacredness about it, our last goodbye and returning him to the ground. It was the cycle of life.

I loathed everything that happened today.

Fuck my dad for deciding to go out this way. Fuck him. Fuck the Bennetts. But also, fuck that sadness in him, because a part of him *wanted* out. He wanted to join Analise.

Also, fuck how much I was going to miss him.

We had food and beverages afterward for people at my

dad's place. We'd never sold it, though we'd talked about it enough times. He and Analise would move out. Then they'd move back in. There was a revolving door on that house. I wanted to sell the place, but someone always changed their mind at the last minute. Today it was a good place to host the after-party. I'm sure there was a better, more appropriate word, but that's what it was. An after-fucking party for putting a dead guy in the ground.

The mayor came around again. The board members. Most of them wanted to know what was happening with the company and when the next meeting would be. All the faces started to blur together. I escaped to my dad's back office, and Jesus, as soon as I stepped inside, I felt his ghost.

"Took you long enough," Logan said from the corner. He was slumped in a chair in the shadows.

I grunted and moved to the desk. "What are you doing in here?"

"Same as you. Hiding from all the ass-kissers."

"We're leaving our wives out there?"

Logan laughed, the sound bitter, and he raised a bottle of bourbon for a swig. "They'll be fine. They all move in a herd anyway, and Sam's hung over. No one's going to mess with her when she's hung over." He shuddered. "Plus, Channing's sister is out there. She's protecting *everyone* in our group."

His sister was even more antisocial than me. Her entire group could form a literal wall to protect the kids. They'd step in if Sam or Taylor needed anything.

Logan took another swig, and the liquid swished in the bottle. "Nate and Channing are out there."

I went over to the chair beside him, taking the bourbon and drinking too. "Matteo?"

Logan grinned, darkly, snatching the bottle again. "I'm pretty sure he took someone to the pool house. Doubt we'll see him until tomorrow."

I raised my eyebrows. "Who?"

He shrugged. "Don't know. Just saw the back of her hair." He changed the subject. "What'd Sam say about last night? Maddy's avoiding everyone today."

"Yeah." I sighed, reaching for the bourbon. "We'll deal with that tomorrow, but I told Sam about it this morning. She wasn't happy, and she was pissed that Maddy didn't listen to Max. I'm fairly certain she's going to rope Heather in with a plan for how to destroy that kid's life—the one who disrespected Maddy. If they don't, we will."

"I'll drink to that." He held his hand out for the bottle.

I handed it over. "You already are."

"Yeah."

"Your base is still in Boston. What are you going to do?"

He raised his eyebrows. "What do you mean?"

"I'm going into the office tomorrow, to start looking at the accounts."

He shook his head, his mouth tipping up.

"What?"

"Just use the kid. He'll get you into everything. He's a computer-hacking genius."

I scowled. "He's not a kid anymore. And no." He was talking about my stalker.

He laughed. "You were his idol growing up. He's one of my clients. I've gotten to know him. He's not that bad." He winced, adding, "Anymore."

Zeke Allen. From the little I knew about him, he'd started out as a douchebag and a bully. That had changed to being just a douchebag, and somehow he'd ended up as what? A good guy? I didn't buy it. I'd been told he kept pictures of me in his locker in high school. I'd dealt with stalkers. Women and men. They were dangerous. It was bad enough that he had access to my family. I would not bring him into this business with my dad.

I wanted nothing to do with the guy.

"I'm just saying. He's a resource we could use. He'd help you out in a heartbeat."

"No."

He sighed, finishing the bourbon. "Fine. Did Moreaux corner you yet?"

He was one of the board members, the pushiest one of them. "At the church *and* when we were leaving the cemetery. He tried again in the kitchen too."

"Fuck that guy. We're burying our dad today."

I agreed with him, but I also knew narcissistic assholes tended to only think about themselves. I hadn't been expecting hugs and cookies from the guy. "I'll start going through everything." It was worth repeating.

Logan frowned at me. "On a Sunday?"

I nodded, eyeing the empty bottle.

Logan laughed and pulled out his phone.

"What are you doing?"

"Texting Nate to bring us another bottle."

"Good thinking. And yes, I'm going in on a Sunday. No one should be there. His office was cleaned on Thursday."

Logan didn't say anything for a minute. "Mom's not here."

My gut tightened. We had called her and she did what she did. It became about her.

"Good riddance."

Logan's gaze sharpened on me. "You don't care that she's not here?"

"You do? She loathed Dad, and she barely remembers she has sons, much less grandchildren. Good fucking riddance to her. We have bigger things to deal with besides wondering where our fucking mother is."

I'd stopped caring long ago. Helen had been decent enough when she was married to James, but she chose to hide in a wine bottle. There'd been a couple stints in rehab, but nothing stuck. The last time she left one of the treatment centers, she'd gone to an all-day brunch and woke up the next morning with some young stud boyfriend. She hadn't looked back since. "She's probably on some yacht with who the fuck knows."

Logan snorted.

Maddy was the only one who remembered her with fondness. Nash and Nolan were too uncomfortable around her. They didn't have good memories with her. It was ridiculous. Anyway, they had four sets of grandparents, or they once did. Helen was a lost cause. James and Analise had passed now. The last two worth anything were Malinda and David, who were fucking godsends.

Logan must've been on the same wavelength because he scowled. "Where the fuck is Garrett? That fucker's not been around for ages."

I had to grit my teeth. "He's another lost cause."

Sam's biological father had tried coming around for a few years, but it wasn't long after Maddy was born when that began to fade. He and his wife moved to Europe. The estrangement was on their end, not Sam's. She reached out. It was never reciprocated. She didn't talk about it much, but I knew it bothered her. There was no relationship with her two half-siblings.

I knew that killed her.

"When was the last time he was even around?"

I frowned. "Fucking forever."

He grunted.

The door opened, and Logan burst out, "Took you goddamn long enough."

Nate entered with a grin. I half expected him to have brought a slew of guys with him, but he nudged the door shut before heading our way. He handed Logan the bourbon and sank down in a nearby chair with a beer in hand. "What are you dipshits doing in here? You're hiding from everyone."

Logan glowered as he opened the bottle. "We are not. We're commiserating."

He didn't respond to Logan, though, instead giving me a slight nod. "What were you talking about?"

"About how Sam's bio dad is a fucking piece of shit," Logan said.

Nate's eyebrows shot up. "Say it like you mean it. Say it from the chest."

Logan frowned, but he didn't seem to care enough to decipher that Nate was messing with him. "How was cuddling with Harold last night? Do tortoises get wood?"

I stifled a laugh.

Nate scowled. "Thanks for all the help with deterring my wife from luring that turtle into our bedroom. Heard all about the audience who thought it was hilarious. Quincey was laughing about it this morning."

Logan shared a look with me before he smirked. "Not my wife, not my problem."

Nate growled.

Logan snickered before gesturing to me. "We're talking about our piece-of-shit parents who are also piece-of-shit grandparents. James and Analise are the exception—" He winced, paling. "*Were* the exception. Helen's pathetic, and Brickshire's been a ghost. Does Maddy even remember him?"

I shook my head. "I honestly don't know. I think he's been in contact with Sam over the last five years, but it's been sporadic and nothing substantial. He sent her a postcard once."

"A postcard?" Nate shook his head. "I forgot those things exist."

Samantha's half sister had been six the last time she saw her. There'd been another kid, but I couldn't remember his name. I'd questioned Sam one time about it, asking if it bothered her that Garrett was absent from our life. She'd shrugged. "*He doesn't have the excuse this time of not knowing about me.*" She hadn't wanted to talk about it anymore and rolled over, taking the blanket with her. I'd considered asking my private investigator to look into him, but when I brought it up a few days later, Sam shook her head. Her shoulders tensed and her jaw got tight. *"You will not. It's his decision not to be in my life. I chase no one. If this is how he's chosen to be as my father, I don't want him in our kids's life as a grandparent. They've got two sets who love them tenfold what he might've. Let's focus on the ones who are here."*

We'd dropped it after that, but I knew Sam kept tabs on her little sister somehow.

"That's sad," Nate remarked.

I tilted my head to the side. "It's life. We have blessings in other ways."

"Yeah. Focus on the silver-lining shit." Logan took another swig, thrusting his free hand in the air. He coughed a few times before rasping out, "Let's go fuck 'em up. What's his number? I want to find out where he is. We got a whole list by now, Mase. It's like we never left."

I raised my eyebrows at him. "We never left? You move here in the last day and I didn't catch when that happened?"

He glowered. "You know what I mean."

I did. I was a little salty about it. Now that I was here, now that we were going to war, I wanted my brother by my side. I took the bottle away from him, capping it and putting it on the floor on my other side. "He's in Europe, and no, we're not."

"Hey," Logan protested

I glared at him. "You've had enough. You can't keep getting drunk and leaving your wife to deal with Sammy. That kid is a handful, and she's pregnant."

He rolled his eyes. "I got drunk one night. Tonight's the second. Don't insinuate I'm a selfish husband." He scowled at me.

We were glaring at each other as Nate laughed, missing the actual anger bristling between us. "I still think it's fucking hilarious that you named your son Sammy," he said. "And even more hilarious that Taylor was okay with it. You basically named your kid after your sister-in-law."

I grinned, remembering when he delivered the news. Sam had been horrified.

Logan laughed too, the tension easing. "It started as a joke, but we were so sad after losing our girl that we wanted to take our time naming him. Then Taylor's dad had a heart attack and well, time took off. The little guy just became Sammy."

Nate was still laughing, shaking his head. "And his nickname is Sam. That's the funniest part of it."

Logan snickered, and then closed his eyes, going still.

Nate lost his grin, casting me an inquisitive look.

This was dark Logan.

We were in Fallen Crest. We'd lost our dad. He remembered how shitty some of the other grandparents were, and he'd been reminded about his daughter.

Logan and Taylor were shattered when they lost her.

Two years later, Sammy came along, and it was as if he'd gotten his soul, plus his older sister's soul as well. His personality burst out of him, and sometimes, they could only contain him enough to keep him safe. He was *a lot.*

He'd been staying with Malinda and David this last week. Taylor had been able to sleep, which she said every day she was thankful about. That usually came up around the time she was readying herself for when they'd come to the house.

The front door would burst open and Sammy would tear into the house. *"Mommy!"*

It was the same entrance every morning. No walking. No skipping. No jogging. A full-on sprint. He'd barrel right at her.

He'd grasp her hips for a quick hug, and then he was off, looking for his next victim. Thank God his cousins all doted on him, as that kid was nuts. I was his godparent. I should've been nicer about him, but nope. The kid was nuts. Funny, but nuts.

I loved catching his arrivals whenever I could. Malinda didn't understand why I asked her to alert me when they were on the way over, but I never wanted to miss the moment Sammy entered the household.

I couldn't wait to see what he was like as he got older. Logan was fucked.

The door burst open again. It was Channing this time. He gave us all a look, jerking his chin. "Stop hiding. Kids are crying, and your wives need time off. Let's go." He didn't wait around, striding off.

There was a momentary pause before Nate began laughing.

Logan exhaled, grinning slightly. "What the fuck was that?"

Nate stood up, grinning at the two of us. "I feel like we got caught sneaking booze by our dad. I'm suddenly fourteen again."

Logan looked down at his lap. "I feel like I just got caught watching porn, and not the good kind. The raunchy shit."

"Dude," I said.

Nate went for the door. "I don't even want to understand where that came from. I'm out."

"That's because your daughters are angels," I called. "They do nothing wrong, and they want to save animals and the planet."

Nate tipped his head back before he disappeared into the hallway. "Not Lilac. She's focused on gymnastics already. I think she's going to be an athlete. See you out there."

Logan tilted his head to the side. "Can't she be both?" He looked my way for the answer.

"Fuck if I know. They're not my daughters."

His scowl was immediate. "You're supposed to know everything." He walked around me, bent down, and picked up the bourbon.

I whisked it out of his hands. "I know enough to know that

if you keep drinking this shit, you'll be sleeping instead of going on a little mission I want to take tonight."

"Mission?" he asked.

I ignored him, leaving.

"Mason!" he called after me. "What mission?"

"Stop fucking drinking and you'll find out," I tossed over my shoulder.

"*You've* been drinking."

I didn't enjoy getting buzzed or drunk, and he knew that.

When I got to the main floor, I heard someone screaming at the top of their lungs. "IF YOU DON'T PUT THAT SNAKE DOWN RIGHT NOW, I'M GOING TO BRING OUT MY PYTHON. SNAKES SHOULD NOT BE AROUND LITTLE KIDS."

For fuck's sakes. Who brought snakes to this house?

I made an amendment to our mission tonight. First order of business was finding all the snakes and getting them the fuck out of my house.

Someone else screamed, "IT'S GOING FOR HAROLD!"

15

SAMANTHA

The guys had taken over caring for the kids once we got back from the funeral, which had been great. Mason and Logan were hurting, and when they hurt, everyone felt it. The kids too. They had needed that time with their fathers. When the guys showed up and *stayed*, it gave the group a sense of peace they'd been needing. That had spread to the wives as well.

It had done nothing to ease Mason's pain.

I knew that, and I felt it when I walked into our bedroom that night. He wasn't going to do a goddamn thing about it. He was just shouldering it all right now. He walked out of the closet, dressed all in black. Black henley. Black jeans. Black boots.

I frowned. "Where are you going?"

He paused. Dark desire pulsed in his eyes, and his jaw clenched. He raked a hand over his face. "Logan's about to combust."

I sighed. "Taylor said the same thing."

"She did?"

I nodded, sitting on the edge of the bed. All the kids were in bed. Not sure if they were sleeping—that was a different issue to tackle—but we'd gotten the last one put away. The girls were planning on sitting around the back patio, maybe having a few drinks tonight, but nothing like last night at Manny's. "He's not putting it on her because of her pregnancy. Taylor's tough. But he's in—"

Mason nodded. "He's in overprotective mode. I know. Listen, I need a favor tonight."

I tipped my chin up. "What is it?"

"I know the guys have been doing our own thing a lot lately, but I need to take them tonight again. Or just Logan and Nate. We'll keep it smaller tonight."

"Not Channing or Matteo?"

He hesitated but shook his head. "Matteo doesn't understand this side of us. I could see it last night."

"He was around in college."

"Cain wasn't the same, not quite."

"Channing?"

He hesitated again. "He's—there's a connection between him and where we're going. I don't want to mess with that. Plus, I might need..." He shrugged. "I don't want to say anything now, but there's a reason for it."

I frowned. I didn't like this, but I trusted him. "What's the favor?"

"Handle the girls when we come back." He held my gaze. "We might not be as pretty returning."

"Mason." My chest tightened. "What are you planning to do?"

"Logan needs to deal with shit, so I'm going to make him."

"He's not the only one."

He paused, his eyes grew bleak for a moment. "I will. I promise I will, but Logan and Taylor are going back to Boston soon. I need to make sure I've done what I can to help him before he leaves."

"You can't make someone deal with their grief in one night."

"I can try," he shot back. His tone softened. "It's this fucking place. This town. He–I—old shit's coming up in us. It's not good."

"He'll feel better when he goes back to Boston. When it's just him and Taylor."

"I know." He exhaled deeply.

Logan carried the burden for everyone in the family when we were younger, whether we asked him to do that or not. Until Taylor. When she came into his life, he leaned on her. He gave her everything inside him. They were opposites. Logan was tough on the outside, soft inside. Taylor was soft on the outside, tough inside. She was exactly what he needed.

"I still want to do this tonight," Mason murmured.

I narrowed my eyes. "On one condition."

His lips pursed together. "What?"

"I get *you* after this. We go away. You drop the wall."

He hadn't given all of himself to me. We'd been together, obviously, but what I was asking for was different. I'd been waiting since I saw him standing, his eyes haunted, with flashing red and blue lights all around him. My stomach rolled, remembering that night.

He nodded, his eyes holding mine. "Deal."

He cupped my face with both his hands, tilting me up to him. His thumbs smoothed over my cheeks. "I have thought how much I love you no less than three times every fucking day since I lost my father." He rested his forehead on mine. "Not that I didn't have those thoughts before, but this week, I..." His voice cracked.

I reached up, circling his wrists with my hands. I felt his anguish. His pulse pounded into mine. I wanted to take all of it from him—his demons, his pain, his hurt. I wanted to push in all the good to take its place. But I couldn't. "Why do I feel like we're on the precipice of something devastating?"

His chest rose suddenly, filling with air, and he held me to him.

We could've talked about how Maddy had been the dutiful daughter and older sister today, or how Max had kept his distance, but while he didn't stray from his dad's side for long, he couldn't stop looking at our daughter. All of that could wait.

"I love you," I whispered.

He angled his head back to see me. His voice dropped low. "How the fuck did I get to have you as mine?"

My heart skipped a beat. I clung to his arms and I *yearned*.

I yearned for him.

16

MASON

Logan jerked forward, seeing where I'd driven us. "What the fuck?" He looked my way. "Why are we here?"

I brought him back to where the underground fighting ring was located.

Unlike the night before, the venue was closed, and the only vehicle out front was ours. I assumed there were some Harley motorcycles parked behind.

Nate kept quiet in the back except his eyes met mine briefly. His mouth flattened.

I cut the engine and thrust open my door, not answering him. "Let's go."

Logan scrambled out next to me. I could feel his excitement. He was almost skipping beside me, like a serial killer who'd been told he could have his pick of prey to hunt. I felt every day of my age, but him? He was giddy like a teenager. It's why we were here tonight—among other things. I knew we couldn't make someone deal with their grief. It had to be on their timeline, but I knew my brother. He needed a nudge to get some of it out. He could deal with his grief on his own schedule, but I wanted him just to start feeling something. This was also for me.

There weren't a lot of great ways to deal with the pressure building inside of us in a legal way. So organized violence it was going to be.

Stripes met us just outside the warehouse door. He straightened, his foot falling to the ground as we approached. He scanned over us, his gaze dead. Unemotional. "Ready for this?"

I handed over the money. "Rules?"

He tucked the money away and shrugged. "Rules are what we talked about. No permanent damage. No killing, obviously. Just some good, old-fashioned violence between strangers. I ran it past the club, and we got a nice selection of guys to face you. No weapons except your fists in there."

I grunted. "Sounds good. Give us a minute."

He tilted his head down and slipped inside.

"What the fuck, Mason?" Nate's nostrils flared.

I shot him a look. "You don't have to do shit, but I am."

Logan bounced on his heels. "I am *so* down for this. Fuck yeah."

"These guys have a history with Channing," Nate noted.

"Which is why he's not here," I countered.

Nate bit back his next words, his eyes flicking upward. He stepped away from us. "I'm not okay with this."

"Then leave," I retorted coolly.

Logan stopped bouncing, his gaze skirting between us. "What's your issue?"

"This—Channing won't be okay with this. It's like you're going behind his back."

"Look." I moved to face him directly. "I need this. Logan needs this. If you can't be here, fine. Go. But they run the only underground fighting ring in the area now. There are no others."

"You could've set this up with Channing's crew. Those guys would fight us."

"They would've held back."

Nate looked away. He knew it was the truth.

I motioned with my head toward the warehouse behind us. "These guys don't give a fuck about us. They're from a different world. They're also businessmen, and I paid a good amount for this to happen tonight. If you can't see why we might need this, you can go. For real."

"It's not that," Nate said, his mouth twisting. "It feels too much like back in the day. You cut out Channing. And the violence. Some of us have ended up in the hospital. I just don't like it."

That was valid. Nate had tended to be collateral damage for people going after Logan or myself. "I'm sorry about that, but we have a war coming our way, whether you're here or not. And you need to trust me. I'll talk to Channing about this later, but right now, there's another reason we're here. Are you in or not?"

Nate expelled some air. "I'm not agreeing with this, but I'm not leaving you guys either. I don't have the same need to spill blood you savages do."

Logan grinned. He puffed his chest up, cocky. "Fuck yeah we do. And I'm first."

He turned and headed inside.

I held back, waiting for Nate to meet my gaze. He did, giving me a small nod. I nodded back, some of the pressure leaving me, but a different tension took its place.

A whole host of bikers waited inside—leaning against the walls, lounging. Some were at the ring, talking in groups of two or three, but when Nate and I joined them, their conversations quieted. I scanned the inside, wondering if their president was here. Channing hadn't wanted to talk about the Red Demons's Frisco charter. The other reason I was here was because they were my best link to real information about Kai Bennett. Channing was a bounty hunter, so he had some connections to that world, but it wasn't enough. He hadn't been able to give me enough information. I needed a more sustainable link, so I had to go around him.

My family was on the line.

My private investigator hadn't gotten back to me, and with the funeral finished, handling my dad's business and this mafia threat was next on the docket. I was stepping into a whole new world, and I was already in last fucking place.

Nate looked around and cursed under his breath.

I felt that. These guys were the real deal. Big. Muscular. Tattooed. Real criminals and real killers. Logan was already warming up in the corner. A biker was taping Logan's hands and talking to him. My brother nodded, listening to him. He was getting himself focused for the match.

Stripes headed my way, stopping a few feet away to look at Nate. "This one all uppity?"

Nate stiffened. He turned cold eyes on the biker. "Mason doesn't know who you are. I do."

Stripes paused, his head cocking. His eyes narrowed.

"Cross Shaw's brother is my brother-in-law."

Stripes cursed, and his eyes turned mean. "That was a long time ago. I went to prison, and I've been a Red Demon ever since. You got issues with me, you can take a hike." He motioned beyond the warehouse.

There was no other option with him. His tone said to shut up or leave.

Nate was still glaring, but he gestured to me. "I'm with them. If I leave, I'll be calling Monroe for backup."

The biker's gaze shifted to a whole new level of chilliness. "We have a fucking tentative peace with the New Kings crew. That's your buddy's crew, by the way. They may be all legit with their bounty-hunting business, but they're still a crew—just like Shaw, just like Bren. If you want to blow that up, make it so we're not friendly anymore, *you* do that. Let me remind you of where you are. This is *our* warehouse. Our territory. And the reason your friend here reached out to us is because we don't give two fucks who you are, what family you come from, or if you're famous or not. We eat, breathe, fuck, and live the biker world. Shove your attitude somewhere else, because I'll let you know right now, my guys won't stand for it. One of them will step up and shove it down your throat for you." He paused a moment. "We good?"

Nate seethed beside me, a rattlesnake coiling up, ready to strike, but I knew he wouldn't. "We're here for some good old-fashioned fighting," I assured Stripes. "That's it."

He was still eyeing Nate, but he spoke to me. "We're a betting bunch. You want to throw in on that too?"

I took out some more money and handed it over. "On my brother and myself." I gestured to Nate. "He won't be fighting."

The biker took the money. "Shocker." He looked over and got a nod from the guy in my brother's ear. "Looks like we're ready to go."

As soon as he was gone, Nate hissed, "Mason."

I moved away. "I don't want to hear it. You're not seeing the big picture. Until you do, keep your mouth shut."

Logan climbed into the ring, and I went to talk to him. They'd gotten him ready. His hands and feet were taped. He'd lost his shirt and now wore only a snug pair of shorts. He bounced up and down, swinging his arms to warm up. He gave me a crooked grin, a slightly maniacal look in his eyes. "Nate's still having a hissy fit?"

I declined to answer. I rested a hand on one of the ropes and leaned in. "You ready for this? You're okay with this?"

His eyes flared, his arms moved back and forth in front of him. "You kidding? This is my kind of candy store." He winced a little. "I'm not sure how I'm going to explain this to Taylor, but..."

"Sam's going to handle the girls."

Logan stopped bouncing, stopped swinging his arms. "What do you mean?" He was suddenly all serious.

"I told her enough about tonight, asked if she'd run interference with Taylor and Quincey, if we need it."

Logan's eyes flicked to Nate before the corner of his mouth tugged up. "Don't think she'll need to worry about Quincey, but she'll have to debrief Taylor before we get back because I don't want my face to give her a heart attack."

He turned toward the middle of the ring as two guys climbed inside.

"Hey."

He looked back down to me, an eyebrow raised.

"This is for us tonight. You hear me?" I said gruffly. "When you've had your fill, you can tap out. You don't have to win if—"

He snorted. "Get the fuck out of here. I've not had a decent fight in decades. I'm fucking *salivating* for this."

"Yeah, but..." Nate was right. The rules said no permanent damage and no death, but these weren't sanctioned fights. Shit could go sideways.

"Mase." Logan stopped everything—the attitude, the unhinged look in his eyes. His voice and face were all Logan again, the brother who had been at my side when we walked into our dad's office a week ago. "I *know*."

Jesus Christ, I'd missed my brother. I hadn't fully had him with me this last week, but he was here now. He was thinking clearly. I drew in some of the comfort I always felt when he was at my side and nodded to him before stepping back. "Got it."

He held my eyes another moment before he blinked and the maniacal Logan was back. Maybe he needed to slip into his old role in order to deal with everything. I understood that.

Fuck. Maybe I should start doing the same.

The bell rang, and the fight was on.

17

MASON

The guy fighting Logan was big. He had a good twenty extra pounds of muscle on my brother, and I didn't like the look on his face. He was looking at Logan as if he were about to steal candy from a child, then eat it in front of the kid.

He was going to enjoy this fight. Or so he thought.

The guy went in fast, with brute force.

Logan dodged him easily, not even moving, just ducking his head. There was no hint of anything light or unhinged or surface level with my brother right now. He was all serious, and he was all dark. It was as if all this had been festering inside of him—building, rising—and the second the guy charged him, Logan gave himself permission to peel back the layer he used to face the rest of the world. *This* was the real Logan. As the big guy turned and went at him again, delivering an uppercut, Logan stopped it. He fucking reached out, stopped it, and then he leaped and pounded down with his other fist. It was a pretty move, and once that happened, a different wave of energy entered the warehouse.

This was what I'd known coming in. They thought we were

pretty boys. We were famous. We were wealthy. We were civilians.

Yes, we were all that, but in our heart of hearts, we were like them. And as I looked over to where Nate was standing, I knew another truth. Logan and I were not like him. We had these monsters inside of us, and mine had been hiding. The moment I committed to the NFL, I tucked that beast away. I locked him up and tossed the key. My years of playing football had been some of the best in my life.

I had my children. Dinners with my colleagues. Fancy fundraisers. We'd been to a few movie premieres. To the White House. Played in the Super Bowl. Won a couple rings. I had lived life, and one could argue that I'd lived life to the fullest.

We'd been normal.

The difference between Nate and Logan and me was the life I had before my dad killed himself, that life would've made Nate content. Being normal. He would've been at peace. Happy.

But for Logan and me, that life was our mask. It's what was expected of us. So we went the normal route. I did it because I loved playing football, but I also did it because I didn't want to work in my father's company. Taking that road would've led here a lot sooner. In this warehouse full of criminal bikers, at a fighting ring where my brother was dominating a guy twenty pounds bigger than him, and I was buzzing with anticipation. This felt altogether too comfortable.

I'd barely kept myself in control growing up, and now that I was back in Fallen Crest, here I was anyway. A part of me loved this. My soul thirsted for this, and Logan was the same. I could see the sick delight on his face.

His opponent had gotten a few hits in. Blood streamed down the front of Logan's face, but his eyes were alive. They were dancing.

I glanced back to Nate, wondering what he saw when he looked at my brother.

I knew they had their own dynamic.

Stripes came over to me. "You could've told me he was a ringer."

I grinned at him, not hiding it. "A ringer? My brother's a lawyer."

He still glared. "You know what I mean."

"Not my fault you didn't do your homework. There's a documentary about us."

He scoffed, but I caught a hint of a grin before he left again, ambling over to some of the other bikers.

"What'd he want?" Nate asked, reappearing at my side.

I told him.

Nate snorted. "He should've done his research."

I searched Nate for derision in his face or in his voice, but there wasn't any. He was tense, on guard, but he wasn't judging us, not the way he had earlier.

"You're okay with this now?" I asked, keeping my voice low.

A wariness came over Nate's face, and he seemed to be choosing his words. "I...I hate this shit. This..." He waved toward Logan, nodding at the rest of the warehouse. "I think you're better than this. I think we're better than this. But I see your point. Logan needed this. I can see that now. You were right to bring him here." He hesitated. "And whatever other reason you're doing this for, I'm sure it's valid."

I waited to see if there was more.

After a moment, he gave a short laugh. "Being a dad now, I can understand why my parents pulled me out of here." His eyes sparkled, until he saw me.

I wasn't amused.

His laughter fell away. He cleared his throat. "I was referring to you being a bad influence on me, so they sent me to that school."

"I remember." I still wasn't amused.

He frowned, looking away.

Stripes stalked back over. "Your boy is playing with him. That shit's going to get old real fucking fast."

I shrugged. "What do you want me to do about it?" I gestured to the ring. "Get another guy in there and get that one out. And if Logan starts playing with that one, do it again. I paid for this."

He huffed. "Yeah, we can do that. We'll consider this one a win for your boy." He whistled sharply and motioned. "Get in there. Core, you're out."

"What?" the guy started protesting.

"He's playin—" Stripes had his hand in the air.

Wham!

Stripes stopped talking because Logan rounded on the guy and hit him so hard in the face the guy's entire body flew in the air. When he landed, no one was surprised that he was knocked out.

Logan stood in the ring, heaving, blood and sweat streaked over his entire body. After a moment he came to the edge. "I want to go again."

Stripes gave in. "Roadie, it's your turn. Let's see if you stay pretty for all those girls."

Some of the bikers laughed, whistling as the next guy climbed in. He eyed Logan with a bit more wariness than the first guy.

The second fight wasn't won as easily. Logan eked it out, but just barely.

After that, it was my turn.

Logan passed me as he climbed out of the ring. His hand slipped, but Nate was there to catch him. Logan patted my back. "Kick ass, Mase."

I watched as Nate eased him to the ground. He threw an arm around Logan's shoulders and took him over to a corner. A biker was there with a first aid kit ready to go. The two bikers Logan had fought were already there. The first one was lying back on a bed, beer in hand. He saw me looking and held his beer up. "Good luck. Hope you're half as good as your little brother."

I held his gaze, seeing he meant what he said. He was being good natured about it. Scanning the rest of the room, none of the bikers seemed pissed. This was what? Normal life to them? All in good fun, that sort of thing?

And Nate was back there, helping my brother out. My chest rose, but not with jealousy. With... I don't know, but it was something good. It hit me all over again, just how much we'd evolved since we'd grown up. I wasn't the leader anymore. I was just one corner of the square box our fearsome foursome made. I liked that, even if I couldn't completely understand it.

I climbed the rest of the way into the ring.

I recognized the guy who climbed in across from me. Boise. I didn't get a big motherfucker. He was my height. Slender. His long black hair was loose, but as he stood across from me, he reached back to pull his hair up. Since he was shirtless and in similar shorts, I could see some of his tattoos. They looked Native American. A buffalo. A headdress spread out over his chest. A set of wolf paws. He turned to talk to someone behind him, showing me the giant tomahawk that ran down the middle of his back, right between a set of two red demons. When he caught my gaze, I knew this guy wasn't going to be a normal fighter.

He'd be fast, and he'd be good. I felt it in my bones.

I closed my eyes, breathing out harshly. I needed to wake up. Warm up.

"You ready?" Stripes called from the sidelines.

I looked at the other guy again. He shifted, and I saw the guy he'd been talking to. He was tall, well over six feet. Lean. Muscled. Tan and tattooed all over. That was their president. The guy Channing said was also the National VP for the entire Red Demons club.

He was here for the fight. He turned to look at me, and there was a knowing in his gaze. I had a hunch he knew the second reason we were here.

Nate was taking care of Logan. Samantha had the family. No one else was here that I needed to be responsible for. Just myself. I let out a deep breath, feeling a lot of the fucking weight come off my shoulders, and I reached up and plucked off my shirt. I kicked off my jeans, standing now in shorts like the others. I'd done my research. This is what they wore.

"Fuck," a guy spat, lunging and climbing up into the ring. He strode over to me with a toothpick in his mouth. "He ain't taped. WE NEED SOME TAPE OVER HERE." He shook his head at Stripes. "What the fuck you thinking? About to ring the bell when he's not taped and ready. You should know better, bo—"

Stripes was up on the ring in the next instant, a savage growl roaring from his throat. He grabbed the guy's shirt and yanked him hard. "You fucking want to finish that sentence?"

The grizzled biker in front of me looked like he did, but he did not. He closed his mouth. Stripes nudged him back with his elbow as a sharp whistle sounded. He looked over and raised his hand in the air to catch the tape.

Or he would've. I caught it first.

He blinked, surprised. He hadn't even seen me move for it.

I blinked too, because I hadn't thought about it. I'd just caught it. I handed it to him. "Habit," I explained. "Something's thrown my way, I catch it."

"Hell yeah, he does." The other biker was done getting patched up and strolled over to us, grinning. Roadie. "That's why he's got two Super Bowl rings. You couldn't have stayed another year? Helped the Orcas get their Lombardi?"

I chuckled. "They're still a new team."

He scoffed. "You got 'em to the game in the first year. You kept getting us there. If it wasn't for the Kings, we would've had it. They had to go and sign fucking Broudou, man. Their team's stacked. Or was, I guess."

Stripes motioned for me to sit, and I looked back to find a stool had been put behind me. Once I did, he knelt and began taping my feet.

Logan and Nate came over. Logan was holding a bag of ice to his head, his knuckles already black and blue. "We're still talking?"

Roadie grinned at him. Apparently he held no ill will against my brother. "Shit, man, we're bonding now, but the real bonding's about to start." He motioned around the room. "A lot of these guys are new. They don't know about you around these parts. But I do."

"You're from around here?" Nate asked.

"Fuck no, but I listen."

Another biker grunted. "More like he's got TV."

Roadie threw him a dark look. "I watch shit."

"You watch porn and sports. That's it."

"No!" he said hotly. "There's a documentary out, but I hear things too."

A couple guys made some slurping sounds. Another guffawed.

Roadie grinned. "Nothing wrong with liking the sound of pussy—"

"Roadie."

One word. That's all it took. Everyone stopped for a second. It was Ghost, their president. Shane King. He leaned his arms over the ropes, giving Roadie a bored expression. "Get to the point."

The biker nodded. "Yeah. Well, even Stripes isn't privy to this, but I'm just saying, I know the reputation of these two." He motioned to me. "Especially him." He reached into his pocket and pulled out a wad of money. He handed it to Stripes before stepping away. "My money's on Kade. Sorry, Boise. Any other guy, it'd be you."

Their president gave me an assessing look before he stood. "Let's get to it then." He gave Stripes a nod. "Let's fight."

Stripes didn't ask me again. He hit the bell and backed away from the ring.

My turn.

18

MADDY

My computer dinged.

I'd gone to bed and should've been asleep an hour ago, but I couldn't get there. My mind wouldn't stop. It'd been Grandpa's funeral today, and that sucked. Max would barely look at me. That made it worse. Mom was pissed that I'd lied and didn't tell anyone where we went last night, so she grounded me. I lost my phone privileges too.

Another ding came through.

I slid out of bed, padding barefoot to my desk to nudge my mouse a little. The screen lit up. I'd gotten two messages from Beltraine.

I'd been checking my Snapchat. I shouldn't have been. I barely had any friends anymore. A lot of my friends from Boston said they'd keep in contact, but they didn't. They were busy. Then we were in San Diego for just a few years. The girls at that school were cliquey, so it'd been hard to make any friends. Now we were in Fallen Crest, and it'd only been a few weeks.

I clicked on the message.

Beltraine: Party at my house tonight. What are you doing?

LoganMaddy: I'm grounded. Can't.

Beltraine: Fuck that. Sneak out.

Beltraine: Don't tell me you don't know how to do that. Girl like you.

LoganMaddy: Girl like me? Wtf

Beltraine: Don't mean anything bad by that. Just that you seem like you do what you want. That's all. My boy's back. Steele. I want you to meet him. He just got back from across seas. He had to go see his parents there last week.

LoganMaddy: I know who Steele is.

Beltraine: Right. Lol. He's my cousin. I forget people know him at school.

This guy was... I sat back, frowning at the screen. Beltraine and Axel were the two most popular guys in the senior class. But they weren't alone at the top, because Beltraine's cousin Steele was right up there with them. Any girl who attended FCA for just a day would know all three of those guys. Beltraine had been friendly with me over the last couple weeks, but honestly, I figured it was because of my dad. Mason Kade tended to have that effect on guys. But Traine hadn't seemed too tongue-tied when my dad and uncle showed up last night. He seemed more annoyed.

Then again, he hadn't liked that I forced Max to come with us.

I chewed on my bottom lip, going over everything. I'd never really been in the popular crowd, which I didn't care about. I was too confrontational for most girls. They didn't know how to fight me, and I didn't put up with the jealous catty remarks. The guys were scared to try anything with me. One guy in San Diego got too handsy with me, and I impaled his hand with a spoon. That got around real quick, and no guy even looked at me for a year. Not that it mattered to me. The only guy I had ever looked at in any way was Max. The only guy I'd ever felt any sort of way for was Max, and he was barely talking to me.

Pain sliced through my chest.

I hated this, being on the outs with him. I'd tried to talk to him today, but he just gave me a polite smile and said he needed a couple days. A couple days for what? Not like I wasn't going to see him tomorrow. Our moms were best friends, and our dads were super tight. He was family. They were family.

A tear leaked out.

I hated this.

Ding.

Beltraine: We're not far from your place. I can swing around and pick you up.

Screw it.

LoganMaddy: Pick me up a block over. Go to the house with the red door. I'll be there in fifteen.

My computer dinged again, but I shut it down.

This was stupid of me. I knew that. I also didn't care.

Being sad sucked.

19

MASON

I tried being quiet when I crawled into bed, but the second the mattress pitched to the side, my body tipped and my ribs felt like they were trying to rip out of my body. I groaned, unable to hold it in.

Sam yelped, jerking up and throwing a hand out toward me.

It hit my face, which made me groan again.

"Wha—?" She reached over and turned on the lamp, then gasped when she saw me. "What the fuck happened to you? Oh my God, Mason." She lunged for me, but stopped, looking too scared to touch me. She lifted the sheets and gulped, seeing the rest of me.

I finished crawling in and collapsed on the bed, mumbling, "My legs shouldn't be too bad. Some bruises. The fucker got some good kicks in."

She went still. "The fucker *got some good kicks in*? What are you talking about?"

I rolled to my back, still groaning and reached for Sam. I patted her on the waist, my other arm over my eyes. That light was killing me. "Let me sleep, babe. I'll be better in the morning." I wouldn't groan, not in front of the kids. Or Logan. Or Nate. Or anyone else. But it was just me and Sam here. I could be the baby I wanted to be right now.

"Mason," Sam said softly, touching my skin cautiously. She sucked in a breath when I hissed from the pain. "This is insane. What did you guys do?"

"Can I sleep first?"

"No," she said firmly. "Now."

I heaved a deep sigh, ready to start talking, but Sam touched my arm gently. "Hold on. I can't handle seeing you like this. I want to grab Taylor and let her be a nurse for you, but I'm assuming Logan doesn't look much different. Nate too? They're leaving early in the morning." She slipped from the bed, padding over to the bathroom where she began rummaging through the cupboards.

I waited to talk, wanting to rest anything and everything until she could hear me clearly. She brought over a couple washcloths, antibiotic ointment, and dressings. When she crawled back on the bed, kneeling over me, she gave me the nod. "Okay. Start explaining." She began cleaning me up as I did, pulling away the dressings the biker had put on me after the third fight.

"Logan needed to let off steam, so that's what we did. Him and I. Nate didn't—"

"Get beat up? Like you and Logan needed to?" She wasn't mad. She sounded more resigned but frustrated. "What are you into, Mason? It's time to loop me in."

I'd been keeping everything to myself. I wanted to get through the funeral, and I knew she'd be torn between trying to help me and taking care of the kids. But I had to admit I didn't like it. I'd been doing my thing, and she was doing hers. We weren't a unit right now.

"I know," I told her. I started talking, telling her everything that happened from the beginning as she recleaned my wounds and put new bandages on me. I'd just finished when she climbed off the bed.

Pausing, she gave me an inscrutable look before sighing. "Stay here. I'm going to get you some ice packs." She returned with some pain relievers and extra water as well, putting them on the bedside stand. "Okay. Sit up."

I leaned forward.

She placed the ice packs around my arm and began taping them in place. She'd done this for me for the last two decades. She did both of my arms, since I'd fought with both. Though, fuck, I couldn't move much now.

She held out two pain relievers. "Open."

I opened my mouth. She dropped the pills in and brought the water to my mouth. After I swallowed them down, she got back into bed and settled in. She handed me one of the last ice packs so I could hold it against my face and put the other over my ribs.

I hissed at all of the cold contact. "I should've just done an ice bath."

She raised an eyebrow, her lips pursed. "Next time."

I looked over at her. "You're not happy with me?"

She dropped the mask and let me see how unhappy she was. "I get that you needed to work off steam. But you didn't have to do three fights. Jesus, Mason. Three?"

I flashed her a grin, which hurt. "It felt good to be fighting again."

"That isn't a statement I enjoy hearing from you."

"Sam."

She sighed again. "I get it. I remember how I was when I met you and Logan for the first time. Of course I get it, but what's the point of the excessive amount of fighting?"

"Respect."

She quieted. "What do you mean?"

"I may need a resource in that world. Their information

could be helpful, and they aren't going to give it if they don't respect me."

"You couldn't do any of that through Channing?"

"The history's too raw between them. And I don't even know all the history. But this new charter isn't the same group that was here previously. I could see that myself. I met some of the previous charter. These guys were different."

"Does it matter?" She chewed her bottom lip and moved her gaze over my face, like she was trying to feel the answer before I told her.

"It matters. I wouldn't have approached the last charter. These guys, I need them to respect me. Logan too."

"It doesn't feel right that you're going around Channing."

"I know. I'll handle that." I grimaced. "Channing will be pissed, but he'll understand. I had to go without telling him. He'll get that too. Once I'm healed a bit more, I'll tell him. Chan's a good fucking fighter too."

"So you did all of this. Is it going to be worth it? Will they talk to you about this Bennett family?"

"I don't know."

Her mouth went flat. "Mason."

"I mean, I don't know their charter, but I feel like I fought some of their best fighters. The first guy, Boise. He was good. Like, really good. I barely won against him. The second guy was a little easier, but he was still fucking brutal. Then the last guy," I held Sam's gaze. "He was their president."

She sat up a little higher. "What?" Her eyes rounded.

"Their prez climbed into the ring. That has to mean something."

Her mouth turned down. "He's the one who beat you?"

I snorted, then grunted from the fucking pain. *Shit.* "I was worn down, which the fucker knew. But, God. He hit hard. Precise. He knew exactly where to hit the hardest."

"I don't like it. I don't like any of this."

I needed Sam on board. Reaching for her hand, I tugged her closer. "Everyone is leaving soon. It'll be just you and me soon."

"And Heather and Channing."

"Channing will be pissed, but he'll understand. My PI's not getting back to me. I can't even get a hold of her. I had to make this move. I need to get a feel for who the fuck I'm going against."

"You could make a call to Kansas City."

"I don't know if that's the right call. I can't edge into this world blindly. If I make one wrong move, someone could get dead. I can't mess up."

I waited. She was still thinking.

And then, she gave in. She didn't look any different, but I felt it. The air lightened around us. The pressure on my chest eased. She traced her hand over my leg. "You and Logan struggle when you're here."

"What?"

"What you said...that you noticed how you and Logan are different than Nate is. Nate doesn't have the darkness in him that you and Logan do." She hesitated before adding, "I have it too. Heather and Channing, they have it in them as well. But you're right. Nate doesn't. That doesn't mean anything's wrong with you or with him. It's just a difference. He's one of your best friends. He's family. He'll always be family."

"I hadn't realized that until tonight. I didn't have a lot of insight when I was young, you know? And then we were out of here. We were normal, like him."

"You and me. Logan too. We're able to be here, but we can be not here too. Heather and Channing aren't like that."

I nodded. I knew what she meant.

"This whole area—Fallen Crest, Roussou—it's too much in their blood. They wouldn't be able to function anywhere else."

A tenderness came over me. She understood it so seamlessly. She understood me. "I really love you."

A coy grin tugged at her mouth. "Really?" She chewed on her bottom lip. "I *really* want to ride you, but you went and got yourself all fucked up."

She lifted her hand away from my leg, but I caught it. "I'm always up for an offer like that."

"Mason." She shook her head.

I leaned into her, closing my eyes, and nuzzled her neck and shoulder. "I was in a couple fights, not a car wreck. Climb me, baby." Feeling her shiver, hearing her breath quicken, I didn't wait. Ignoring the pain, I lifted her on top of me and fit her right where she belonged. On my dick. My hands went to her hips, beginning to knead them. Her body melted on top of mine, settling in, but when she didn't touch me, I moved my head back. "What's wrong? I'm fine. I've been worse and we've fucked."

"I don't know about that, if you've been worse before." She snorted. "But that's not..." She was back to biting her bottom lip.

I groaned. "I don't like how you keep chewing that mouth of yours. It's mine to chew."

She stopped, blinking as if she hadn't realized.

I nudged her gently. "What is it?"

She swallowed, her eyes lowering, and she looked away.

I caught her face, bringing her back to me. "Same page, Sam."

She flushed before closing her eyes, but I caught the flash of pain there. Her hands curled into fists on my lap. I felt her pain before she even said a word. "I thought he would've called. I sent him a message."

He.

Shit.

I caught one of her hands in mine and laced our fingers. "Your dad?"

"Garrett, yeah."

I tugged her down and curled my hand around her, anchoring her to me. "I'm sorry."

Her body shuddered. She twisted her fingers into my shirt and tugged hard. "It's stupid. It's so fucking stupid. He—he decided he didn't want to be part of my life after all. I thought..." She turned away, her chin trembling. Her voice grew hoarse. "I don't need him. I know that. And I know what he said, that he needed to prioritize his family and then he'd be in touch, but it's bullshit. Yes, I had Analise. Yes, I have David and Malinda. But fuck. *Fuck.* He's my dad. He was starting to actually become like a dad to me. I have room for two dads. Why couldn't he have room for two daughters?" She whispered the last sentence.

He'd broken her heart.

"Sam," I murmured, sliding my hand up into her hair. I angled her head to meet my eyes. She resisted, closing her eyes, but when I didn't let go, she groaned and relented. Her eyes opened.

There. The pain swam right there, on the surface. It was too much for her to push down. Tears welled up in her eyes and she tried blinking to stop them. She wasn't fast enough.

"I'm sorry," I told her.

She blinked again, but more tears appeared. She couldn't hold them back. "She's here." Her voice was rough.

"What?"

"My sister. She's three hours away, Mase. She's going to college in Cain. What's wrong with me? He doesn't want to know me, fine. Fuck him. But did he have to keep her away too? She's my half sister. And I have a brother. I don't even know what he looks like anymore."

"How'd you know she's at Cain?"

She hung her head, pressing her forehead to my chest.

"Tell me." I lifted her chin, tipping her head up. When Garrett took himself out of Sam's life, Maddy had been young. The reason he gave was a lie, saying it was too hard for him to raise his family. He needed to give all of his attention and love to his new daughter and son; he was being pulled in two separate directions. Sam was an adult. She'd been loved growing up. She was thriving now. He hadn't had a hand in that, and since he hadn't, it was easier to step away from her than it was his other two children. Sam never understood his reasoning. I hadn't either.

If he'd owned up to being a piece-of-shit dad, that'd be different. Sam didn't need him, not in a literal way. But she'd loved him, and I hated him for turning his back on her. I wanted to destroy him. Sam asked me not to. She pulled me back. But the thought reappeared in my head.

"I think Sharon made him choose," Sam said.

I could barely handle it. I'd give anything to take away her pain.

She let out a deep breath, both of her hands now fisting my waistband. "I don't know why. She said she was fine with me, but she could've changed her mind. Or she was lying from the start, not really okay with him having a daughter that wasn't hers. If that's the case, I..." She tucked her chin down and looked away, so fucking defeated. "I've been cyberstalking my sister's social media. I know I shouldn't. It's like I'm torturing myself. I don't check it all the time, but once a month. I'd do the same for my brother if he had social media. I don't think he does." Another tear rolled down her cheek. "I don't even know what he looks like anymore. She doesn't put up pictures of him. Why is that? That's weird, right? Or she does, and I can't see them. Is that a thing?"

"I could have my PI look into him."

"You have your PI looking into this other thing. She's probably busy." She shook her head. "And no. I said no back then. Garrett chose not to be a part of my life, so *fuck* him."

"My PI has a team. She could get one of her colleagues to look into your siblings."

Sam's eyes glazed over, the pain completely taking her until she squeezed them shut. She swallowed and shook her head. "No," she choked out. "No." She said it again, more clearly. "I'll wait until they're adults."

"Your sister is an adult."

"I know. I mean after college. Let them finish their schooling and get into their careers. They'll be more on their own feet. I'll approach them then. Garrett and Sharon won't have such a hold over their decisions. I'll tell them who I am, if they don't know me, and I'll ask if they'd like to...I don't know? Get to know their sister?" Her chin was back to trembling.

I caught her hands in mine, disentangling them from my shirt, and tugged her to me. Making a decision, I removed the ice packs. Realizing my intent, she protested, growing tense. I smoothed a hand down her back, lifting her completely onto me. Her legs. Her feet. Her thighs. I pressed her head to my chest. I wanted all of her weight on me.

"I'm going to say this to you and you're going to listen," I said, assertive.

She tensed, but I wouldn't let her move. Not even an inch.

I gritted my teeth. "Your biological father's decision is bullshit. He's the problem, Sam. He is. Whatever the fuck his reason was, it was wrong. You know that. You are not the problem, and normally I'd never even think to say those words to you, but I know there's a part of you that can't help but wonder. It's not you. It's *him*. It's *his wife*. It's whoever the fuck else made the decision Garrett would not be in your life. He is goddamn lucky to be sharing genes with you. And it is entirely *his loss* not to have you in his life. He's the defect. You are perfect. You came from him, and you came out *better* than him. Your sister and brother, when you decide to approach them, they're lucky to be sharing blood with you. This connection gives them an opportunity to know you, and I cannot for the life of me make sense why someone would choose not to know you." I lifted her head so she could see me and how strongly I felt about this. "Unless they are fucked up. You got that? Your sister might be fucked up too—"

Her lower lip was shaking. "She doesn't look fucked up. She looks beautiful."

"Then she will be blessed to get to know her older sister, and she'll probably be all sorts of pissed off at her mom and dad. That's their problem. It's not yours. You have so much love to give, and anyone decent would recognize the gift of having you in their life. That's all you have to think about. Nothing else. You hear me?"

A few tears slid free until she wiped them away, but I'd gotten through. I could see her strength shining back at me. She was the Samantha I loved and held every chance I got.

She bent forward to graze her lips against mine. "Thank you."

The kiss started light, but it didn't stay there. Everything else melted away.

I needed my woman, but more importantly I needed to make her forget.

I rolled on top of her, moving over her, but I just kissed her. I wanted to push out all those thoughts and doubts he'd left in her mind. Garrett didn't fucking deserve Sam as a daughter. There'd come a day when he'd return. He'd realize his mistake and he'd panic because she would be gone. He wouldn't be able to get her.

I was going to relish that day because the fucker deserved to be punished every day of his life. Anyone who hurt Sam, who caused her even one sliver of pain did.

I tasted her mouth, and she gasped, her back arching up to meet me.

My tongue moved inside of her, commanding, but thoroughly letting her know that she was mine. All fucking mine. And I was hers. I was here. I wasn't going anywhere. She could let go of the pain, any pain that was inside of her.

I wanted to fuck her so hard she stopped breathing, stopped thinking.

As I kept tasting her, I moved my hand down her side, moving her underwear and sleep shorts down. Then I rolled up, put my foot in them, and shoved them down at the same time I returned to her body.

I hissed as my dick came into contact between her legs.

That was my heaven. My paradise.

I rolled against her, pushing up. Moving.

She gasped, her hand sliding down my neck and shoulders. She rose, pushing half of her body up and against mine, angling her head for a deeper kiss. I moaned against her lips. A fucking saint sent here for me. My sanctuary. My salvation. That was Sam. That was every piece of love she'd given me over the years. All the smiles. The sighs. The tremors.

As her kiss grew more frantic, more desperate, and she scraped her nails down my back.

Shit. I trembled, loving the pain she gave me. My dick jerk against her, but he couldn't get harder than he was. He was a goddamn rocket, and as I moved up over her body, he saluted her, slapping against my stomach.

I reached down and stroked myself, just a little, to ease some of the pressure.

"You going to put that thing inside of me?" She panted, a glow coming to her cheeks. There was light in her eyes. My cold and dead monstrous heart preened at knowing I helped put the spark back in her gaze. I was beginning to think I was put on this earth for the job, to coax out those little panting sounds and make her forget every fucking time one of her parents hurt her.

"You in a hurry or something?" My grin was wicked.

Her eyes lit up. "You—" She sat up, a determined expression coming over her. She shoved me back, hard enough that I went with it. I wanted to see where this was going. When Sam got all demanding in bed, fuck yeah. I loved when she was rough. She could slam herself down on my dick any day and all day long. I could still go.

I sat beside her, and she rose up over me.

Those golden fucking strong thighs came down on each side of me, straddling me. She settled right over me, rubbing herself over my dick. Up and down.

Shit. I hissed. She felt so good. The pleasure was going to make me blind. The edges of my vision began lighting up.

I grasped her waist. My fingers dug in. "Sam."

"Shut up." Her head fell back. "This is for me. Fuck. That feels so good."

I concurred. My dick too. He kept trying to sit up and slip inside of her as she rubbed over me.

I moved my hand down, watching her. She seemed into this, but uh...I wanted inside of my wife. As her hips sped up, bearing down harder, I moved my thumb to meet her clit.

"Fuck," she said, breathless.

She was beginning to seize up.

She was going to release.

"Sam," I said, sitting up. I caught her and yanked her against me, but she kept moving over me. She was lost, totally in her own trance. "Mason," she whimpered. Her hand went to my hair and fisted it.

"Agh."

That was me because she yanked my head back, and in one swift motion, she rose up, grabbed my cock, and slid down over me.

Holy. Fuck.

It felt insanely amazing.

"Shit," I half growled and half shouted.

Jesus. She was fucking me, rising up and slamming down.

My dick was loving this. I was loving this.

I needed a second to catch up and adjust myself, but only a second. Then I was good and I let the sensations start to roll through me.

She moved over me, rolling her hips in that seamless way when she rode me, like everything was for her enjoyment. Like I was here for her. Like my dick was her personal joy stick. Like no matter what, this touch from me was something no one else could do, and a savage rumble bore out of me at those thoughts because it was true.

My woman. My pussy.

The other part of me to make her feel loved and wanted and desired and to deliver every day I was breathing.

Half laughing, half sounding drunk, she picked up her pace. She tensed, her legs clamping down on me, and as a shiver wrought through her, I yanked her to me right as she tilted her mouth down on my throat too. Her teeth sank into me, and a choked grunt slipped from me at the feel of my skin breaking.

She made me bleed.

I got off on that shit.

Then she exploded, and her teeth sank even further into me.

I waited, holding off, gritting my teeth as she kept moving through her climax. She caught her breath a few times, her whole body shaking in my arms, but once she came back to herself, I moved my head back so I could see her. "You good?"

She laughed again, her body melting against me. "Oh fuck yeah. Just don't ask me to go anywhere."

I raised an eyebrow. "You ready for me?"

She stared at me, her eyes blank. "Wha—"

I flipped her back over.

I could've gone inside her from behind. Sideways. Sam didn't care. We'd always been into exploring new shit, but maybe I was showing my age because I wanted face to face. I wanted my whole body pressed and rubbing against hers, and I wanted my mouth on hers as I shoved inside of her so we went missionary.

I did all of that. I caught her gasps and her cries, and her whines, and I fucked her through all of it. When she began crying out because another release was building, I really began stroking inside of her. I was banging her and only when she screamed into my mouth, did I let myself join her, spilling inside of her.

Her walls grabbed onto me, and I moaned all over again from that sensation.

After she fell asleep, I stayed awake just a little longer— long enough to know my hatred was now divided. Kai Bennett had some of it, but so did Garrett Brickshire.

He'd hurt Samantha, made her feel the way she used to when I first met her.

Garrett's name was added to my list.

I was going to destroy him.

20

MASON

Ngone of this made sense. Not one bit of it. I'd been sitting in my dad's office all day, going through his business accounts. Granted, my head was a little slow since last night had been brutal (but needed), and I'd been here since this morning. I couldn't find any reason he should have been scared for his life.

The numbers were good. They were better than good. A solid profit had been coming in for years, and based on the projections, it didn't look like it was going to stop any time soon. Why the hell had my dad been scared enough to take his life?

I shook my head and reached for my phone. I needed answers from my P.I.

Me: I need an update.

Lael: I know. There's a reason for the silence. I'm still digging.

Me: Look into the shareholders. See if anyone is having problems and needs to sell.

Lael: On it. I'll have Ben start looking tonight. You think someone is trying to buy shares secretly?

Me: Maybe.

Lael: That should be easier to find out. Looking into the Bennetts has proven a challenge. I'll need to update you in person.

That surprised me. Lael was usually too in-demand to travel for a debrief in person. Whatever she'd found had to be significant.

I didn't reply, and the desk phone rang a moment later.

It was the guard at the front gate. The offices were closed. They'd been closed the whole week, though we'd kept a full detail of security guards still on staff around the clock. When I came in, I'd told them not to disturb me.

I pressed the button for the speaker. "Yeah?"

"Sir, your daughter is at the gate."

Whoa. What? I switched the feed to bring up the front camera, and sure enough, Maddy was behind the wheel of one of the cars we let her use. She was still grounded and shouldn't have been away from home, but I could see how tightly she was gripping the wheel. She'd picked up her mom's nervous habit of chewing her bottom lip.

"Send her through. Let Rich know as well." Rich was the front desk guard. He'd buzz her in before she reached the door.

"Will do, sir."

When she walked in carrying a latte, I had to suppress a grin. She paused, uncertain. "What?"

I shook my head. "Nothing. You just look more and more like your mom."

"Oh." She went to the chair in front of the desk and sat. She put the coffee on the edge of the desk before sitting back, hugging her knees to her chest. "Pumpkin spice. Don't hate me. It's pumpkin season."

I didn't care. I was just happy to see her. I'd drink anything she brought me. Which she knew.

I waited, but she didn't say anything else for a few moments. She only watched me, her eyebrows pulling together.

I leaned back. "What's up, kiddo?"

She bit her lip, her eyes widening before they fell to my arm. Her face cleared, and she leaned forward. "You got another tattoo?"

I glanced down. I'd almost forgotten, but she was right. The guys all got matching skull tattoos after I officially retired from the NFL. Myself. Logan. Nate. Channing. Matteo. But Logan wanted something just for him and me.

I ran my thumb over it. "It's a tribal tat. Me and Logan. Not real original, but Logan liked the look of it."

"A lot of guys have tribal tattoos." She looked over the rest of my arm. "Tell me about the others."

I half-grinned. She was stalling before getting to the reason she was here, but I knew she liked to hear about some of the rest of my tats. I had a few before football, but had been indulging myself once I joined the Orcas team. I pointed to the orca tattoo, starting there. "I got this one because of my time on their team, but also because orcas stand for family, longevity, protection, and community. Which to me, stands for you all. My family."

She grinned, softly.

I pointed to the small butterfly tattoo on the side of my finger. "Because of your mother." I held up the finger where I had the other butterfly tattooed under my wedding ring, then moved to another under the orca. "The astrological sign for Gemini, which stands for the twins. I wanted it small, but looking half-carved into me because when Nash and Nolan are older, I'll get another tattoo for each of them. Their choosing. Then there's yours."

Her grin widened, her eyes shining.

"A lion." My chest filled with emotion at the same time her chest seemed to puff up. "It's what you chose."

She added, almost under her breath, "It was my favorite animal when I was little."

"Which never surprised me. You're ferocious. You're fierce, and kid, you have so much power. No matter where you stand, *no one* can take that away from you."

Her eyes glistened.

I felt a pull in my chest because I meant it. This kid of mine was an apex predator. I only hoped she wouldn't realize the extent of how strong she was until she could handle it in a responsible way, but she was everything a lion represented.

I had more, but it was time to get to other business. "Okay. Out with it, Maddy. What's the reason you're bringing me your favorite latte?"

Her gaze averted away, and she slouched a little. "Oh."

She drew in a breath.

A moment later, Maddy mumbled something under her breath, sitting up straight, but still keeping her one knee propped in front of her on the chair. She began picking at her jeans, *not* looking at me. "So..." she began, her eyes lifting. "I need to ask you something, but when I ask, you're going to want to know where I heard about this, and that means I'll need to..." With a big breath, she rushed out, "IhavetocomecleanaboutsomethingIwenttoapartylastnightI'msorryDaddy."

I took a minute to decipher that and leaned forward. "Sorry. What did you say?"

She frowned. "Huh?"

"Say it again. Slowly. With spaces between your words."

She gulped, closing her eyes for a moment before she took a deep breath. Putting her own coffee aside, she pulled up her knee again and hugged both to her chest. Her eyes dipped. "I have to come clean about something. I went to a party last night, and I'm really sorry." She lifted those eyes back to me. Pleading. "I'm sorry, Dad. I snuck out again."

I sat back in my ch—my dad's chair—and swept that wave

of grief aside, focusing on my daughter. I knew her well. She was here for a reason. She just outed herself, which meant something more pertinent was coming on its heels.

I knew the signals. Maddy was not one to come clean so her conscience was cleansed. She didn't work that way. I blamed myself because I wasn't like that either. All of this was spelling more trouble was brewing and Maddy was about to deliver it at my front doorstep.

She certainly didn't get this side of her from her mom, who was a saint after she got everything healed inside of her. I was a different matter, and the raging monster that had come out of me last night confirmed that. I'd passed this fucking gene, whatever it was, to my daughter. *Jesus*. I hoped Nolan and Nash hadn't gotten it.

I extended a hand toward her. "I'm sorry."

She stuck her bottom lip out. "Huh?"

I gave her a smile that wasn't a smile. It was a warning, and she read it correctly, her eyes going wide.

I said, "I'm apologizing to you because I must need to have my hearing checked. What I thought I heard come out of your mouth is that you went to a party last night. And I know my daughter. She couldn't have, because she's grounded for breaking the rules *already*." My tone hardened, and I leaned forward, letting her know how much trouble she was in. "You know the rules are that we know where you are, and you take your phone with you if you leave."

Her mouth snapped shut as she flushed, rolling her eyes. "That defeats the point of going to a party. You can track my phone. Then you'd know where I was! What's the point of sneaking out?"

"The point is that you're alive!"

"I'm—"

"Who do you think you are?"

That stumped her. She blinked at me, dazed, not having a goddamn clue. I would've laughed if she hadn't been my kid.

Her mouth turned down and she spoke slowly, a finger touching her chest. "I'm...Maddy...Kade?" She said it like she wasn't sure anymore.

I wasn't amused, and I didn't have the patience to decipher whether she was truly confused or being a smartass. "Your dad's a Hall of Famer. Your mom is an Olympic star. We recently moved back to this town, and your grandfather, who runs a multi-billion dollar company—"

"Used to run," she muttered.

"What?"

"Used to run." Her eyes lifted back to mine, bright with tears. "You said he runs, Dad. As in present tense. He doesn't run it anymore. You do."

Fuck my life. She was right.

I'd be taking over.

I knew that. I'd thought it, reminded myself of it, but feeling it in my bones and my body, looking into the future and figuring out how to keep this company running was a whole different issue. She'd just reminded me of how much our lives had changed, would change more.

I lost some of my steam, sitting back in the chair. This desk. It had been his, but it would be mine. My desk. I shook my head. I couldn't get used to that. It was his. It would always be his. This office too.

I glanced around. "I'm going to take a different office."

"What?"

I looked up at her and waved my hand. "Never mind. Keep digging that grave for yourself. You already 'fessed up. Come out with the rest of it."

She flushed again. "Jeeez, Dad! Different terminology, please. We just buried Grandpa yesterday."

"And not even ten hours later you were violating your grounding? Sneaking out. Leaving your phone—"

Her nose wrinkled. She hugged her knees to her chest again. "I took my phone with me. I just didn't turn it on."

I glared at her. "That's not helping."

"Come on, Dad! I came here to ask you a serious question. Serious enough that I'm getting myself in more trouble to do it."

I eyed her, knowing bullshit when I heard it. "You're coming clean because it benefits you to come clean." I didn't have a great feeling about what else my daughter was about to tell me. "Your mom and I still need to talk about Friday night. Good thing we waited, huh? We'll just tack this on as well."

Her mouth fell open. "Dad—"

"Logan Malinda Kade."

She quieted.

"I love you, but my patience is wearing thin. Get to the point of why you're here." Seeing hurt in her eyes, I held a hand up and softened my tone. "I love that you sought me out. I love that you wanted to spend some time with your old man, especially because you're here now, so after we get through this conversation, you're in for the long haul. You're staying the rest of the day."

Her eyes bugged. She hadn't considered that.

I lowered my hand. "But back to what brought you here in the first place."

Her eyes lowered to her lap. "Did Grandpa kill himself because the company's going bankrupt? Was Grandpa James doing something illegal, and he would've gone to prison and that's why he...you know."

Alarm shot through me. I knew I wasn't going to like this conversation, but I hadn't expected *those* words to come out of her mouth.

My forehead furrowed. "We never told you how your grandfather died. Where did you hear that?"

Her mouth opened again. She'd been caught once more. The party line had been that he had a heart attack. We'd kept everything under wraps. I knew there was a chance of a leak, a good chance, but so far, no press had found out how my father died. When we told the kids, we were specific in our wording. We'd told them his heart gave out.

Jesus. "Did you hear that at the party?"

Her eyebrows jerked up. "No! No. No, but Aurelia Avoy said the timing was suspect, that James Kade died when his company was on the verge of going down."

Who the fuck is Aurelia Avoy? I scowled. "What exactly were her words?"

Maddy heaved a sigh and shrugged. "She said it's too bad I moved to town when my family's legacy was going into the shitter. She said her dad is going to buy Kade Enterprises and change the name to Avoy Enterprises, and it's too bad we'll have to move away because we're, like, poor again."

Maddy scowled and I blinked, seeing my scowl on her face. I adjusted mine to an annoyed glare. "Poor again?"

"Apparently." She rolled her eyes, letting her legs stretch across the distance until her heels were on the edge of the desk. "Between you and me, Aurelia's such an HBOTC."

Christ. I was going to regret this. "What's an HB..."

"HBOTC." She growled, sneering. "Head Bitch of the Cunts."

"Maddy!"

"What?" She shrugged. "She is. Think of all the evil popular girls in every movie you've ever seen and roll them into one. Then put her in a ginormous house. That's Aurelia Avoy. I hate her." A smug smirk gleamed. "But I know she hates me because she thinks Beltraine and his friends like me. It's why I was invited to Traine's party in the first place." Her voice evened out.

"They're the popular guys in the senior class. They've been nice."

Her eyes cast down, and she frowned slightly.

I didn't like that look. Why was she frowning at that statement? *Fuck.* I had so many questions I wanted to ask, but even though we had a good relationship, Maddy was still a teen. She'd shut down if I started grilling.

Fatherhood was rewarding. I needed to keep thinking that. Rewarding, but it was the fastest way to drain me of any patience I had. I coughed, clearing my throat. Right. Be... casual? "So. Uh..."

Maddy looked up at me, and the corner of her mouth lifted. "I'm not interested in any of those guys, Dad. You don't have to worry about me. No one tells me what to do. Pressuring me doesn't work on me. I don't go to my knees for anyone."

Fuck. She was me. Which I knew, but seeing it in a female body was something else.

She added, "Except maybe for Max, but that'd be different."

Jesus Christ. "Maddy!"

She blushed, grinning. "Sorry. I just didn't want to say something and do the opposite, like, later. You know. Moving on because we don't need to have that conversation yet."

She was giving me heart palpitations.

She waved her hand to the side, dismissing. "The normal girl stuff doesn't work on me either—like the catty stuff, you know. Rumors. Cyberbullying. Things like that. I mean, no one would ever cyberbully me. They go online and see who my parents are and change their minds *real fucking fast.* I get trolls sometimes, but that's because of you guys, and I don't take any of it to heart. Half the trolls are people from another country trying to mess with us anyway."

"Can you stop swearing?"

"Dad," she scoffed.

I felt my face grow hot. "I'm aware of my propensity, but...

for the sake of me being your father right now and you being the underage child, can we pretend I'm a good role model? Cut the swearing."

"Fine." She huffed.

This kid. She was so nonchalant about all of this.

She reached forward to grab a stapler but kept speaking. "So anyway. Yeah. The prissy girls, that's what I call them—"

"Unless they're the HB..."

"HBOTC and yeah, unless they earn that title, but so far, only Aurelia Avoy has earned it. Trust me, she's even worse than you think. I'm pretty sure she's going to bully that Stevie girl —"

"What?"

She ignored me, messing with the stapler. "But the guys don't really know how to deal with me either. They can't sexualize me. That's what they do to most of the girls. They try to pressure them in group chats and demand nudes. They don't do that with me because, *hello*." She motioned to me. "And also, like, I'm too athletic for them. Do you know what I mean? I'm almost like a boy, but I'm not. I'm a girl. I have a girl's body, but my athleticism is as good as a guy's. I know, I know." Another eye roll. "I'm you, Dad, in like, Mom's body, and that's so weird to say, but I watched the documentary on you guys. It's true. It's so weird. Can you imagine?"

She pulled the bottom of the stapler down, turned it around and began pressing on it. Staples flew out, landing on the floor.

"So anyway." She kept clipping the stapler, using it like it was a gun. "It also helps that Uncle Logan taught me how to throw a punch, but—"

This was going nowhere except raising my blood pressure. "Put the stapler down."

She paused, eyeing me.

"Can we circle back to the whole thing about your grandfather?"

She stopped and stared at me, owl-eyed, lowering the stapler. She'd forgotten the whole reason she came here. "Right. Yeah. So that's what Aurelia—"

"Yes. The HBI—"

Eye roll. "HBOTC, Dad. It's not head bitch in charge. She ain't in charge of me." Her head rolled with the last statement, some sass coming from her.

"Maddy," I groaned. "The cursing."

"Right. Sorry." She cleared her throat. "But technically the B word isn't a swear word. It's a female dog, which is so offensive to women. Errr. Maybe not. Is it? I don't know. Okay. Anyway, like, I don't like what Grandpa did, but this isn't me trying to process those feelings. I know you and Mom are big on those conversations, or Mom is. You do it if you have to because you're a good dad, and that's what good dads do if they have to, but again, Dad. You're like me. You'd rather come across a two-hundred-fifty-pound lineman than talk about your feelings, if you had a choice."

I suppressed a groan. She wasn't wrong, but there was no controlling her thoughts. She'd get back to the point...someday. I sat back and waited her out.

Maddy talked for a while about Uncle Matteo. I have no idea how she landed there. That progressed to the difference between horses used for therapy and those who raced. Somehow that led to the migration of orcas and how they're the bullies of the sea.

That went back to football.

Which went to running.

Then to her cousin Sammy.

She came back around. "That makes me want to know if the company's going to be sold to Aurelia Avoy's dad. I just want a heads-up. Because, like, if that's going to happen, I need to prepare for war. I'll have to cyberstalk her and find out any dirt I can because I'm not letting that HBOTC hold it over me that her dad's taken over my grandfather's empire. Hel—I mean, no way." She stopped a moment. "So, is it? Are we going to be poor again?"

I'd lost the context for *everything* in the last hour she'd been talking, except a few things stuck out. One, was high school like this now? Were they worried about whose father was going to buy whose grandfather's company? Two, had it been like that when I was her age? We only cared about business in terms of whether we had money or not, but the way she was talking about going to war, that was familiar.

Also, we'd never been poor.

"Honey," I started, speaking softly.

She drew in a breath.

"Where did you hear that your grandfather shot himself?"

She sucked in some air, her eyes bulging. "He shot himself? That's how he did it?"

Fuck. "No. I—"

Tears began streaming down her face.

I'd made it worse. "Maddy—"

"Nolan."

"What?"

"Nolan. She knew, Dad. She knew. She told us the night it happened. We knew before you even got home."

I stared at her, not wanting to accept that, but I couldn't dispute it. Nolan knew things when the only way was intuition. But they'd known? This whole time? "I'm so sorry, Maddy." *Fuck.*

More tears slipped down, and she sniffled, trying to clear the emotion away. "I just need a heads-up. Are you going to sell Grandpa's company?"

I shook my head. "No."

She held onto my eyes and swallowed. "Really?"

"Really."

She sniffled. "Promise me?"

I inclined my head, wishing again for the ability to take pain away from the people I loved. All I could do was be honest. "I don't need to. The company's fine. We're not going to sell it."

"But then..." She looked away, hugging her knees again. "Why?" Finally her full question came out, choked, "Why did he do it?"

My heart broke as my little girl slid open a door and let me see the pain she was enduring. It was a gift, though it shattered me at the same time. I wanted to pull her into my arms, but Maddy didn't work that way. If she wanted comfort, she went to her mom. From me, she wanted truth.

"We don't know. I—what I can tell you is that your grandfather said some words to me that suggested he felt he was under threat. He said he knew I'd be able to protect the company."

"So the company *is* going under?"

I shook my head quickly as panic rose in her gaze. "No. I haven't gone through all the accounts. It's too much for that to happen in one day, but I've seen enough to know that the company is fine. It's more than fine. It's doing good, which I'm not surprised about. Your grandfather was a phenomenal businessman over the last twelve years. He built a strong empire. It's not going anywhere, not that I can see."

"Then why?" Her voice broke again.

Staring at her, seeing her pain, I had to remind myself that right now all I could do was love her. "I don't know, but we're going to find out. *That* I can promise you. We will find out."

She shook her head, looking away. "I don't think it'll ever make sense, but if someone made him do it, that'll make some sort of sense. Right? And if someone did make him do it, that's who'll pay."

When she said those last words, with a promise of vengeance, I didn't know what to say. If someone hurt you, you hurt them back. I used to live by that mantra. Apparently it was genetic.

I hadn't thought that way since college, but here it was again. Coming from my daughter.

I didn't know the right way to handle this. "I love you, Logan Malinda Kade."

Some of her anger melted, and she rested her chin against her knees. "I love you, too, Dad."

I coughed. "Don't tell Mom about the HB—about that terminology. Or your siblings."

She rolled her eyes and scoffed. "No kidding."

21

MASON

W hen it was time to leave that night, I had Maddy go first.

There were separate entry and exit gates, and as the exiting gate opened for her to pass, the entry gate began opening as well. Maddy leaving shouldn't have done anything to open that gate, but as she went through and paused on the other side, four black SUVs raced through the entry gate and whipped around to circle me.

I wanted to gun the acceleration, but I couldn't. Maddy blocked me without realizing it. If the gate swung closed, it would've come down on me. I considered ditching my vehicle and running for hers, but another SUV drove in, wedging its way sideways so it was between myself and Maddy.

I was effectively blocked in.

Her brake lights were going off and on. I cursed. She probably didn't know what was going on or what to do. My phone began ringing through my dashboard. It was Maddy. I hit accept and ordered, "Go!"

"But Dad—"

"GO! Now." I laid on the horn.

She took off. "What do you want me to do? Where do I go?"

"Go home."

"But—"

A man got out of one of the SUVs and leaned back against his door. He did nothing except stand there. Everything dried up in me because I recognized his face. Kai Bennett. He was here, and right now, he was waiting for me. His hands were folded over each other. I didn't know if this was certain death or something else. I closed my eyes, for one second, and sent a prayer that it wouldn't be the last time I talked to my daughter.

"Maddy."

"Dad—Daddy?"

"I want you to go home. Call Uncle Channing."

"Uncle Channing? Why? Are you okay?"

"I'm fine, honey. Just tell Uncle Channing that KB made contact. He'll know what that means. He'll take it from there."

"KB? Who's KB?"

"I love you, Maddy." I reached forward and ended the call. *Fuck.* My heart raced.

Kai Bennett was waiting for me, standing outside his SUV. I'd Googled this fucker, and there should've been way more images of him online than there were. He also should have been in his sixties, not just a few years older than me. He had dark features. Short black hair. He was powerful and feared. He was mafia, the real deal. There was a real possibility I could die at the end of this talk with him. And unlike the other enemies I'd faced against, this time, his men *would* shoot and they *would* kill me. I'd be just another execution to them.

The phone started ringing. Logan. Maddy had called him before Channing.

I declined the call, leaning forward to see if I could glimpse the guard at the gate. We had four guards. Where the fuck were they?

Knock, knock.

One of Kai's guards was at my window, and seeing he'd gotten my attention, he stepped back, folding his hands in front of him. I put my vehicle in park and opened the door. Broad. The guy had more muscle than I did, and he was an inch taller. Clad in a business suit, wearing leather gloves, and I could see bulges under his jacket. Those were guns. More than one.

"Turn your vehicle off, please, Mr. Kade."

So fucking polite. I hesitated, though, meeting Kai Bennett's dark gaze before swinging around to the front. The entry gate had closed now, and it was supposed to be reinforced so no one could break through it. They weren't flimsy gates. My dad hadn't been messing around, but the guards were another thing.

Kai Bennett watched me with an impassive curiosity as his eyebrows furrowed just slightly. He didn't make a move. He didn't look alarmed either, just the slightest bit impatient as he continued to wait for me. As I reached over to turn the engine off, I heard doors opening.

Men got out of the other SUVs, all wearing the same uniform. Business suits. Tall. Broad. Fit. And with bulges under their jackets from their guns. But no one moved closer. Some fanned out, spreading through the parking lot, walking in the opposite direction.

"Let's go." The first guard moved to grab my arm.

"I wouldn't, Thomas."

We both froze, hearing Kai Bennett speak. His eyes were on his guard's hand, which was two inches from making contact. His voice was a warning, but not an urgent one. It was as if he were here to cross an item off his to-do list.

"He's a professional athlete, and if my research is correct, skilled enough with fighting that you'd be surprised at his reaction. I never told you to strong-arm him, so don't." His gaze shifted to me. "Kade, I'm here as a respectful formality." He thought a moment. "That's the best way I can put it. I mean you no harm, nor your daughter, which is why we waited to move in until she was in the clear. I hope you take that into consideration with the decision that's weighing on you right now."

I grunted, not liking this fucker. "What decision is that?"

"Whether to disarm my man, jump into your vehicle, and take your chances with my men out there or give in and have this meeting with me. You're weighing the options because you know who I am. You know what I do. You know there's just as much of a chance of you walking away from here alive as having a bullet lodged in your brain." He gave a small nod. "Like I said, I am here as a respectful formality. Nothing else. I wish to have a conversation, to inform you of a few misconceptions you have about me, and then we'll be on our way. I'm hoping that'll be the end of this, but I suppose that depends on what you decide to do in the next few moments. So, Kade. What will we be doing today?"

I really, really did not like this guy. Way too smart. Way too smooth. Way too fucking arrogant. I ground my teeth against each other because he also could back everything up, and we both knew that.

I reached in and pulled out the keys.

"Hand them to Thomas, please."

I'd started toward him but paused at his order. I positively loathed this guy. I handed them off.

As soon as Thomas had the keys, he moved behind me, shutting my door and nudging me forward. "Just walk to him."

I held my hands out. "I have no weapons on me."

Kai Bennett lifted his chin. "We know."

I frowned at that, because how? Once I was closer, he stepped away from his vehicle and motioned with his head. "Let's walk around the parking lot. I've been flying a lot lately and could stretch my legs."

There was nothing about this guy that would've prepared me to meet him. This was the reason my father killed himself?

The threat of this guy coming after us? No matter what the books said, I supposed I could see it. I'd known dangerous men in my life. Rapists. Murderers. None of them could touch this guy. It was his intelligence. There was a cold aura to him, a way of thinking that had made him a mastermind. That's what made him more lethal than the other bad men I'd known—Budd Broudou, Park Sebastian, Jared Caldron. All of them were criminals, and all of them were imprisoned because of me.

Those guys were nothing compared to this guy.

"Come. Let's walk." He started off, watching until I fell in step, a few yards separating us. He continued to study me until there was a little distance between us and his guards, enough space to give us a modicum of privacy.

"You killed my father and you feel safe enough to walk with me?" I exhaled sharply. "I don't know if that makes you foolish or just arrogant."

His gaze never left me, and his mouth turned down at my words. "The reason I'm here... Your private investigator was the first to catch my attention, her digging into me. She's not as discreet as she thinks she is, but she wouldn't have been a problem. We gave her enough information to bait her. She'll find out soon that the trail we left for her leads to a dead end. She's gotten information on me. I'll give her that, but not enough that she feels confident. When you meet with her, her file will be a lot thinner than you or she will want."

Okay. That was annoying. "You killed my father. You don't think I'm going to send a PI after you? You're my enemy. I need to find out everything I can about you." I stopped to face him. Enough with the walking bullshit. We weren't friends out for a stroll.

He faced me, regarding me coolly. "That's the second time you've brought up your father's death. What would lead you to the idea that I killed your father?"

I was going to kill this guy. One day, somehow I would.

"Other than the fact that he told me you were coming after him? My father is my source, you smug prick. Right before he shot himself."

There was no reaction in his gaze. Nothing. Not even a blink. "Until six days ago, I had no idea who James Kade was. So no, Mason Kade, I am not the reason your father shot himself."

That statement hit me in the sternum. That didn't make sense.

"You're lying."

"I'm not."

All the air left me. I didn't want to believe him, but why seek me out?

There was a ring of truth to his words.

"It would be safer for me to not believe you. Someone coming after my father would probably tell me that—"

"Do you know who I am?" he cut me off, an edge of impatience in his voice. His eyes flared. "I am not looking for you to stroke my ego. But I'm not sure if you're aware that I don't need to waste time with bullshit manipulations like a meeting as this if I were coming after your father's company. I'm assuming that's why you think I killed your father? I didn't know the man so there's no other reason I could fathom I'd want him dead."

I studied him, listening to him. There was truth in what he was saying.

"A man like me, if he were going to forcibly take over your father's company, I would kill all the shareholders in one night. I'd have lawyers ready for them to transfer their shares to me, and they would sign them away because if they didn't, I would kill their families. I would have all the official employees already in my pocket so when each one of them were killed, I would be able to walk into your company the next day knowing it was mine. That's how I would take over your father's company if I chose. So trust me, I'm not the villain in this particular instance."

"Something tells me you're always the villain in any instance."

His eyes flashed, now showing some anger. "To be quite frank, I'm annoyed that I had to come here and have this conversation with you. *Again*. I have no interest in Kade Enterprises. I looked into your family a little bit after we became aware of your private investigator. I looked into you. Your father. Your mother. Your wife. Your brother. Your friends. I hope you don't take offense to this, but there's nothing you have that I would want. Kade Enterprises is a good business. It's doing well. The other part of my scenario is that the way I would force my way into your company or your father's company. It's a losing situation for me. This company is too public. You are too public. I don't like media coverage about my family. I do everything I can to stop it, but if your name was attached, your wife's, all the plethora of other little celebrities in your group, I wouldn't be able to contain that press storm.

"That would be my downfall, which you would eventually realize. That's why I'm assuming your father chose to go the route he did. With the first leak in the press, I have no doubt that your government would leap at the chance to step in. They would think of it as a way to take my family down. Now, that battle, I would win, but all you need to know is that any fight to take over your father's company would not be worth it for me in the long run. It would be a pain in my ass, to be frank. By the time I beat your government, the company would be useless to me. I'd have to declare bankruptcy on it and then I would have to tear it apart. That would be the only financial gain I might acquire at the end. The ends would not justify the means. Not to me. Not in this case."

I frowned. "You've put a lot of thought into that." I was a

little bowled over by everything he laid out. None of it had crossed my mind.

He laughed and shook his head. "No, I didn't. I knew all of that within five minutes of looking into your father's company and into you."

"It was enough to warrant a personal visit from you."

"You're mistaken again." An edge returned to his voice. "A phone call would've been adequate to let you know your father had been misled, that I'm not the enemy you're looking for. But it was your *other* interested party who really got our attention—not just mine, but my brother's. Both of my brothers. You don't know my brothers, but generally they're happy if I leave them to manage their own personal lives."

My frown deepened. "I only sent my PI. I don't know who else—"

"Your little hacker." His words clipped out with bite. "Your PI's been snooping around for six days. Your hacker took one day to *royally* piss off my brothers. He or she hacked into their personal accounts—theirs and their significant others. He couldn't get into mine, and if he had tried getting into my wife's, I wouldn't be coming to you about him. He would already have a bullet in his head. Or her head, whoever your hacker is." The impassive bullshit was gone. He'd dropped the mask and let me see how serious he was. His eyes narrowed, very much promising death. "I saw the look in your eye. You know who I'm talking about. Right now, your hacker's been immobilized, unable to dig any deeper, but that hold on them will only last another day. They will be able to break free by tomorrow morning, and I'm telling you that if they continue going where they *should not* be going, we will have them executed within the day."

Fuck.

"And if you think we won't be able to find out who your hacker is, that will be a mistake. I came here to see for myself if you were aware of this person, and you are. We have two options now. I'm assuming you won't willingly give up this person's identity, so either we torture you for their identity or we let you handle it from here. What is your choice, Mr. Kade?"

Holy shit. If I could murder this guy right here and now, that would be my choice. No brainer. I'd pull the trigger in a heartbeat, but that was the difference between him and me. He'd chosen to pull a trigger. I still hadn't. That had kept me on the path that led me here, where I would win in a fight if we went to the press.

A shudder worked its way through me, but I suppressed it. I might have a monster inside of me, but this guy was a stark reminder of why I wouldn't let that monster take over, not fully. Sam was right. I needed both sides. The normal side, but also the side that thirsted for violence when I was here.

"Consider it done," I told him.

His eyes narrowed, and then he nodded. "Good." He started back to his vehicle.

I let him get two steps before I said, "I know Cutler Ryder."

He turned to frown at me, his head cocked to the side.

"He's a good man. I know there's some sort of connection to your brother, but I don't think Cutler knows who your brother really is."

His nostrils flared. "The hockey player. In Kansas City." I could see him calculating before his eyes went blank. "You could tell him, but I'll lay out what will happen. That is my brother Tanner you'd be pissing off. He also likes your friend being his friend, but you're correct. I don't believe Cutler Ryder knows about Tanner's family business."

"And if I educate my friend?"

"You'd be killed."

I sucked in some air, not expecting that. "My brother thinks less than I do," he continued in the same careless tone. "He would react, and he'd be wrong to do so, but he would kill you and he wouldn't care about the fall-out. While I wouldn't agree with him, I would back him up, because that's what we do for each other. I believe it's the same in your family." He paused a moment. "Do not make a trip to Kansas City or even a phone call." A hint of a smirk showed. "After all, I do what I do, and you do what you do. One of us has no problem with murder. Now." He nodded toward the pocket where my phone was. "I've no doubt you should call your family and let them know you're safe."

God. I didn't think I could hate this guy any more...

He began walking away.

I took out my phone, and a flood of calls and texts were coming in. I hadn't silenced it, so that meant he had a cell jammer on him.

"Mason," he said.

I looked up.

His eyes were dark with promise. "I will find out who used my name to force your father into that position." Another layer slid away, another mask, and I could see the killer inside of him, the monster who had conquered the mafia world. "When I do, I'll handle my own retribution."

"Is that a promise or a threat?"

"It's just what I'll do. *No one* uses my name as a manipulation."

He returned to his vehicle. Within seconds, all five SUVs were gone.

My phone began ringing.

22

MASON

Sam's call came through first, and I hit accept. "I'm fine."

"What?" she asked.

I stopped walking. "You're calling to make sure I'm okay, right?"

"No, but now I'm wondering why I would've been doing that. *Are* you okay? What happened?" She made a frustrated sound. "Never mind. You need to come home."

I picked up my pace again. "That's where I was heading. What's going on?"

As soon as I got into the Escalade and the phone transferred over, I could hear noises in the background. "Is that—is someone yelling?" I drove through the gate and looked over. There was no guard. I made a mental note to have someone look into all four of those guards—and fire them if they were still breathing somewhere. Actually, that seemed imperative, so I pulled over and sent Channing a text to see if he could look around the place.

Sam huffed. "I don't even know what I'm seeing."

Channing: What am I looking for? Aren't you there?

"Try to explain," I clipped out, typing on my phone at the same time.

Me: Four bodyguards. Did my daughter not contact you?

Channing: She called, but I couldn't answer. She didn't leave a message.

Channing: Like their *bodies*?

"So you know Mark and Cass broke up last summer?" Sam was saying.

"I didn't." My phone buzzed again.

Channing: Mason. Wtf?

Me: Emergency at the house. I'm still trying to figure it out. Lmk.

I tossed the phone and gunned the engine.

Sam had quieted. It took me a full block to realize that. "Sam?"

"Sorry. I got distracted. This is—I can't really believe this, but I think it's happening for real this time."

"What is happening?"

"Mark and Cass are breaking up."

Who the fuck are... It took me a second. *Mark.* Sam's stepbrother. Malinda's biological son. And Cass. I wished I could forget about her again. "They're still together?"

Sam snorted, lowering her voice, "Well, you know things have been rocky for the last few years. Cass was really trying to win over Mama Malinda, and we thought Mark would pull out a ring. I mean, he's like bachelor age at this point—"

"Sam." I had whiplash from all this—and *what happened to Maddy?* "Is Maddy home?"

"Maddy?"

"Yeah. She left the office a little while ago. Is she okay?"

Sam quieted for a beat. "Why are you asking if our daughter is okay?" Her voice rose. "Did she do something again? We *just* grounded her a day ago."

I huffed out a laugh. "She's home?"

"Yeah. She got here about twenty minutes ago, said you had to stay back to talk to some KB person. She said he was a shareholder, and that's when Mark showed up with his bags. He announced he was moving in for a while—"

I groaned. "No. No more people."

"—like this house isn't built as a hotel. It'll be fine."

"He'll bring his shit to our house. Like what's her name."

"Cass."

"What?"

"You asked what her name was."

"No," I bit out. She was distracted, and I was trying to come down from having a goddamn threatening heart-to-heart with a fucking crime lord. Not a good combo. "It was a phrase— never mind. Maddy is okay? That's my whole point."

"She's fine. Mark came in, dropped his hockey bag, which reeks, and went straight to the liquor cabinet. Your daughter immediately began popping popcorn. No joke. Mark was here for five minutes before Cass showed up. They've been going back and forth, and they do not care that we're here. Apparently Cass is done with waiting for a ring and wants to get pregnant. I'll be honest. Cass is our age. I'm shocked she's waited this long. I'm kinda Team Cass right now, but also, what the fuck? Why didn't she leave him if she wanted a ring and kids? Has she met my stepbrother?"

I...had no idea what to say to that or if I fucking cared.

"Okay. I'm going to break this down for you. Mark apparently has commitment issues. Although, there could be an argument that maybe it's Cass. She's never been a nice person, but moving on from that, they had a pregnancy scare last summer. I did not know that." Her voice dropped to a whisper. "Mark panicked. Cass wanted to keep it, and she seems destroyed about it."

I heard from the background, "Not helping, Sam!"

She moved away from the phone. "Sorry, Mark. Mason's on the phone. He wanted to know what was going on."

I shook my head. "I might argue with that statement."

She snorted and returned to whispering again. "Okay, and now they're—oh! They broke up last summer. Cass dated someone else. Wait. Did Mark?"

"Really not helping, Sam!" That was Mark again.

I heard shuffling movements. A slight squeak. The yelling quieted a little.

I frowned. "You're hiding in the pantry?"

"Shh. I want them to forget I'm here."

"Where is Maddy?"

"She's at the kitchen counter. She and Logan are eating the popcorn, and they're transfixed."

"What about Taylor and Sammy?"

"Sammy's with David and Malinda, and Taylor is upstairs packing."

"Matteo left this morning?"

"Oh my God! That was what started this whole thing." Her voice hitched. My senses were scrambled. I couldn't tell if she was excited, horrified, or whatever else she could be feeling. "My whole thing with putting Matteo in the pool house backfired. He did hook up with someone, but guess who?"

I had decided. I officially didn't care about any of this. "I'm guessing it wasn't Mark."

"It was Cass! He doesn't know her the way we know her. And Mark's not always around, you know? Anyway, during their break, she got with Matteo. They met randomly at a bar in town. It was during one of his visits here. Then she told him."

"Matteo?"

"No. Mark. She told Mark that she'd hooked up with Matteo. She didn't think Mark knew who Matteo was, but how could he not? Then again, you and him had a weird thing going for a while and Matteo wasn't around in high school. Mark was never around in college. Plus, he doesn't hang out with us that much. But Matteo and Cass saw each other at the funeral yesterday and well, now this is happening. Hold on. They're talking again."

Her phone buzzed.

"Why is Heather asking why Channing has to go look for *bodies* where you are?" She gave up whispering, going straight to high-pitched and not happy.

I turned on to the road that led into our neighborhood. "It's nothing to talk about right now. I'll be home in five minutes."

"Are you sure?"

"Did Cass murder Mark yet? Do I need to send Channing to our house to look for a couple more bodies?"

"Har har. You're so funny."

"I'm a riot."

"I think they should both cut their losses."

"Channing or the bodies?"

"What?" she hissed. "What's with the bodies talk? And no. Cass and Mark. I mean, I don't think she and Matteo are a love match. I don't think Matteo will hook up with her again, but it's time to move on. Meet someone else. Marry. I wonder if Cass froze her eggs? Probably not if they had a pregnancy scare last summer."

I really did not care, but I was at our gate and hit the button to open it. We had a large courtyard, and most of the time we could easily park six vehicles. Tonight we had a couple more, but the last white Vespa was parked diagonally, so I couldn't get around it. I growled. That likely wasn't Mark's car.

Slamming my Escalade to a stop, I left it where it was and stalked for the house. As I got to the door, I could hear the shouting. It got decidedly louder when I opened it, and I took a second to scan where everyone was.

Sam came out of the pantry, and Logan smirked at me.

Maddy met my gaze and smiled. She held a hand up to hide

her mouth and pointed at Cass. "She's an HBOTC." Her eyebrows went up and held for dramatic effect.

I scowled. "Way to be real worried about me."

Her grin fell flat. "What?"

"Nothing."

"Wait. Dad. *What?* You said you were okay?"

She was right. I had.

Logan was now eating his popcorn slower, and his eyes were volleying between my daughter and me. Mark and Cass had momentarily paused in their fighting.

"What happened?" Logan asked, his frown deepening.

I shook my head, deciding that I needed a drink. "Nothing."

Maddy was chewing her bottom lip.

I crossed to her and brushed some hair from her forehead. Giving her a kiss there, I said, "I'm sorry. I'm all good. I'm glad you came to the office today."

"Are you sure, Dad?" She twisted around to look up at me from her chair.

I nodded. "I'm sure, sweetie."

Sam was continuing to frown at me, but I ignored her and Logan for a moment. I kept scanning, finding Nolan and Nash at the top of the stairs. When confrontations happened, they could always be found on the stairs. It had been their perch since they were three.

I headed for them. As I did, Taylor was coming from behind them.

Mark and Cass picked up their fighting, but I tuned them out except I heard Mark huff, "Don't bring my mother into this."

I watched in real time as Taylor clued into the drama. She gripped the stair rail and stopped behind my twins. Nash scooted over for her, but she met my gaze, seemed to consider her options, and then sat down beside him. Immediately, he melted into her side.

Nolan, though, was fighting back tears. As soon as our gazes met, she flew down the stairs and launched herself at me. "Dad!"

I caught her. She was all gangly legs and skinny arms. She shuddered in my arms. "What's wrong?" I asked.

She shook her head, unfolding her legs and slid down to stand on the ground. She kept her arms wrapped around my waist, her face pressed into me.

Sam came over to join us, running a hand down her hair. "Honey? What's wrong?" She whispered to me, "What happened earlier with you?"

Nolan just hugged me tighter, but she looked up, her eyes bouncing between us.

I met Sam's gaze over her head, but I couldn't answer. Not here.

"Nolan, honey." I bent down and nudged her a little. "You need to give us a clue what's going on or your mom and I are going to have a heart attack—"

Sam slapped my shoulder, and she glared at me. "Are you kidding me? You pick that choice of words?"

She was under the impression the kids thought their grandpa died from a heart attack. I took her hand in mine and whispered, "They know."

"What?" Sam went rigid.

I nodded. "They've known since before we told them anything. Nolan knew."

Sam sucked in her breath, comprehension dawning. Then remorse. "Oh, honey."

Nolan detached completely from me and wrapped her arms around her mother.

"Sweetie. Is this about that—"

Nolan looked up at Sam and then me. "I just had a bad dream. I was napping."

Movement caught our attention from the stairs.

Nash came down with Taylor behind him.

I frowned. "Wha—"

She reached out, touching my chin. "What did you do to yourself? You and your brother."

Sam winced. "I tried my best."

My bruises. Sam had bandaged me up last night. Taylor did that for a living.

I was a bit slow with everything going on. "I'm fine," I said.

She ignored me, turning to Sam. "You did great work. It would still be a good idea to go in. A couple of these could do with a stitch." She reached up to my face.

I swatted her away. "No one touches me except my wife and my children."

Taylor didn't care. She pressed her finger into one of the cuts.

I grimaced. That hurt.

She rolled her eyes. "You don't scare me anymore. I don't think you ever did."

I shot her a dark look. *The fuck?*

Sam was still holding Nolan and rubbing a hand over her back, but she started laughing.

Mark and Cass continued arguing, but Logan meandered over to us, holding one of the bowls of popcorn. He held it out to me. "Hungry?"

I growled.

He snatched it back, shooting me a look. "Fine. No popcorn for you. I'm never offering you popcorn again, big brother."

Nash grinned. He idolized his uncle. "I'll have some popcorn."

Logan immediately turned the bowl toward him. "Of course, anything for my favorite godson and nephew."

Nolan giggled as Sam ran a hand over her forehead. "He's your only nephew, Uncle Logan."

Logan grinned at both of them, his adoration evident.

"That's true. Don't tell the other kids who think they're my nephews."

Taylor looked over to Cass and Mark, still yelling. "Do I want to ask?"

Logan opened his mouth.

Sam's hand shot out, clamping on his arm. "Please. Let me." She gave him a meaningful look. He nodded, giving her the floor. "You, me, and Heather need to have girls's night tonight," she told Taylor.

"Again?" Taylor asked, but her smile said she was down for it.

There was a moment of peace from the other room, and I used the quiet to regroup. Kai Bennett was not the threat that took away my dad. I believed him. I had no idea why Logan had called me earlier, but we only had the night to handle the hacker because there was no way I was going to deal with him by myself. *Fuck.* That meant I had to relay everything to Logan and Sam, and all of the sudden, I was really fucking tired.

Nolan chose that moment to tell me, "The bad guy left, Dad. You *cannot* let him come back."

23

MADDY

Me: I messed up. I was supposed to call your dad and give him a message from my dad.

Max: Why didn't you?

Me: I did call, but got distracted. I feel bad. I keep messing up.

Max: You want me to tell him now? I don't think he's here.

Me: No. My dad came home from talking to that KB guy.

Max: I have no idea what you're talking about.

Me: You want to come over? We have live and in-person entertainment. Uncle Mark just broke up with his live-in girlfriend. Actually, I think they broke up three times since they walked into the house. Or since she followed him here.

Max: We have school tomorrow.

Me: So?

Max: I can't.

Me: You're still mad at me?

Max: IT HAPPENED TWO NIGHTS AGO! You ignored my request and made me *go there*. It's not even been a full forty-eight hours. Leave me alone.

I tried blinking back my tears. Forget him then. He wanted me to leave him alone?

Me: Message received.

Everyone was standing in front of the stairs so I went the other way down to the basement and crawled onto one of the couches. I let some tears fall. I hated crying so I'd just let a few fall. After that I was stopping.

I wasn't that kind of girl.

24

MASON

"How do you know this kid is a hacker?" I asked.

Logan groaned, sitting next to me in my Escalade. "I already told you."

We were sitting outside the house of my stalker. Zeke Allen. Who was also a hacker, according to Logan, which was a big fucking surprise considering nothing about him on the outside said computer nerd. Douchebag. Wealthy. Prick. Fraternity A-hole. That's what everything about him yelled to anyone who gave him a look, but Logan insisted there were layers. I'd done what I could to keep him away from my life and my family over the years, but he was best friends with Nate's brother-in-law, so that boundary could only go so far. And in fairness, the kid hadn't pushed for anything except to be friendly with me.

I'd had other stalkers over the years. Most of them were women, and a few were arrested when they tried to break into our home. These days, only this guy and one woman were left. I was out of the spotlight for football now, so I was hoping that kind of attention would fade.

"Tell me again." I stared hard at my brother. "He drew the attention of a crime lord to our front doorstep. I need to know there's no way we're wrong. Because if we do what we're about to do once we step inside his house, we can't be wrong."

Logan sighed. "Like I said before, I can't tell you how I know. I just know."

"He's a client?"

Logan didn't reply, not because he couldn't tell me that, but because he already had. I needed to make sure. He hadn't been the one who had Kai Bennett cut me off behind my daughter. If that had been Logan and Maddy had been Sammy, I don't think he would've reacted the same way.

"He's not a kid, Mason," Logan added after a moment.

"What?"

He shook his head. "We need to remember that he's in his thirties. He's married. They have children. He's not a kid."

We couldn't hurt him. Logan swore by this guy. Others did too, but I still wasn't sure. After a few phone calls, though, it seemed I was the only one. Nate had stood up for him, saying Zeke Allen was a good guy now. He was someone we wanted on our side.

Our side. Christ. We didn't even know who the other side was anymore. We'd had a name before, Kai Bennett. Now we had no name. Our enemy was faceless and nameless. How did we fight someone like that? A wave of exhaustion crashed over me. Why was there always a battle? An enemy?

When we didn't live here, we didn't have this.

But now we were back, and here we were once again. Sitting outside a house, preparing to break in and do what we needed to do. In that past, that meant blackmail, violence, maybe arson.

We'd had so many enemies. So many battles.

My father.

Sam's mother.

Budd Broudou.

Park Sebastian.

A fucking secret society.

Logan dealt with Rankin

Jared Caldron.

Adam Quinn.

The last battle had been with ourselves, with our own uncertainty until we got our act together. Since then, there'd been challenges, but normal life struggles. We'd been blessed.

"We need to change things."

Logan looked my way, raising an eyebrow.

"Look at us." I motioned to Allen's house. "What we're going to do. This is the old us. We got out, and not once did I need to contemplate violence. If my family is going to stay here in Fallen Crest, we need to make changes."

"What are you saying?"

I shook my head. "I don't know. I just—Maddy talked to me about needing to gear up for war. That's how we used to talk. It's how I used to think. I don't want Maddy to grow up like that."

Logan frowned. "Some of that is normal. I can't think that high school is much different than any other place."

"Yeah, but we're adults, and we're still here. I don't want Maddy to be fighting like this when she's an adult. Or in college. Nash. Nolan. They're normal kids."

"Nolan's not quite normal," he said lightly. "Neither is Maddy."

I amended my statement. "They have an innocence that we didn't at their age. I don't want them to lose that. Maddy's already losing it."

"I love my goddaughter, but you're wrong about her." Logan inclined his head, holding my gaze. "Maddy's coming alive since you've been here."

"What do..." I stopped, though, because I knew. I knew what he was going to say.

"It's the same for us," he continued. "Fallen Crest is like a

fire. Normal people learn to stay away from it, to circle it with
caution. But not us. You. Me. Sam. Maddy has it too. The fire
draws us closer. It demands that we change, morph into who
we need to be—not to survive, but to thrive. Maddy doesn't
know she's changing, but she is. You can't snuff out that fire
because it's already gotten inside of her. The same thing is
going to happen to the twins. If Taylor and I move back, it'll
happen to Sammy. And my next kid, I'm sure." He grunted.
"You saw Max. It's in Heather and Channing. Their kids. Max
knows it's in him. I think that's why he tries to be a good kid.
You saw him fight the other night. He became who we are when
he fought."

That grim feeling deepened in me. "He has his own
monster inside."

"No. I don't think it's a monster. It's like a bloodlust not to
submit, not to just survive, but to become who we need to be so
no one rules over us."

I shrugged. Maybe. Maybe not. I didn't know what it was,
but something affected all of us. And maybe we were normal
after all, this would change anyone...

Just then a truck pulled into Zeke Allen's driveway. He was
home.

As he drove into his garage, Logan and I moved as one,
pulling black ski-masks over our faces. Getting out of the
Escalade, we darted across the road.

Everything had been planned to the last detail.

Zeke's wife was invited out with Heather and Taylor. The
kids were offered to be babysat by Malinda and David since
they were already watching the other kids. And for Zeke, Nate
called him for a job—a request to look into Quincey's father's
files because Nate wanted to make sure her father couldn't
make trouble for them again.

It was a lie, but it would get Allen where we needed him.
Home and alone.

We'd considered questioning Allen as ourselves, Mason and Logan Kade. Logan was for that. I wasn't. Zeke Allen put me up on a pedestal. He didn't see me as a person. He saw something else. That meant I wouldn't get the version of Zeke Allen everyone else got. And if we were going to do this—question him, blackmail, threaten, whatever we would end up needing to do—I wanted to meet the Zeke Allen everyone else knew.

I wanted the real Zeke Allen. So that meant we'd do this as strangers.

He was already inside as Logan and I rolled under his garage door, right before it clicked into place.

A weird sense of déjà vu settled over me, and I saw it in Logan as well. It was that part of us that rose up when we were in Fallen Crest, that needed to do things like this. The fire to thrive, how Logan had put it.

No matter what I thought before, this wasn't normal. We weren't normal.

Logan and I both rose to our feet and started for the door, about to slip into our old ways.

Nothing about this that should feel right, but it did.

25

MASON

We waited inside the garage. The lights went out, and still we waited a little longer. I figured if Zeke was coming back to hack, he'd need to do some things to get situated. Food. Drinks. His favorite clothing. I didn't know, but within ten minutes, it grew silent on the other side of the door.

I nudged the door open. People didn't typically lock the door between their house and garage. Some did, but most didn't. It was a calculated risk. If he came home, thought he was secure, we could sneak in.

I turned the handle, holding my breath, and it went all the way.

The door opened.

No alarm sounded.

I eased inside with Logan moving silently behind me.

We moved like breaking and entering was something we did on the daily. It wasn't, and we were committing a crime, but my heart had no idea. My pulse was calm and steady. My mind was focused. I'd been more nervous before a professional football game.

Only a single light was on over the stove. The living room

was dark. Kitchen. Dining room. We could see enough to know when to step over the kid's toys. As we worked our way through the house, clearing the first floor before heading to the second level, I went over what I'd been told about this guy.

Fallen Crest born and bred. His dad had been on the Kade Enterprises's board for a few years before something happened and he sold his shares. He and his wife began traveling after that. I wasn't sure of the timing or the reason, but I wondered if something had happened with their kid? There were quite a few reports of his run-ins with Channing's sister. He went to school in the same timeframe. Then Zeke Allen did a one-eighty. There were no notes about what happened or why, but suddenly he was considered a good guy.

What was so good about him?

There'd been no mention of his hacking skills in the file my PI had one of her colleagues send my way. None at all. He'd joined the same fraternity as Park Sebastian had, and that right there told me everything I needed to know about him.

We got through the second floor, and still nothing.

There was no third floor. I doubted he would have a computer system in the attic, so that left the basement.

Logan fell into step behind me. We moved down the stairs and circled, looking for the basement entrance.

I began to move into the kitchen, then backtracked when I noticed the door with a sliver of a light underneath it.

I tested the handle. It opened, leading to their pantry.

What the fuck?

I began to turn around again. While their pantry was big enough for three of us to comfortably stand inside, there was no point—until a light flashed from the floor.

I paused, kneeling down to inspect it. It flashed again, like a flashlight moving below. I blinked in surprise. It was a hidden door. I touched the shelf, and it moved. Logan stepped in close, looking just as perplexed.

I pushed the door open wider. It moved, revealing carpeted stairs leading into their basement.

Jackpot.

I glanced at my brother, who nodded. He stepped aside to let me lead, and as we crept down, he pulled the door shut behind us. The only light downstairs came from underneath another closed door.

When we got to the bottom, we framed the door where the light was shining. I surveyed the room behind us. There were two more doors. A larger room behind us. All the lights were off. I stepped back, wanting to clear the rest of the basement.

When Logan saw what I was doing, he went with me. We moved fast and were soon back in position. I waited, meeting his gaze. Was he ready for this?

He gave me a nod.

All right then. Here we go.

I turned the knob, letting the door swing open.

Zeke's desk spanned the entire wall. There were multiple computer screens. A plastic mat covered the floor, and as he worked, he cursed, then wheeled his chair over to type away on a different computer screen.

I'd never witnessed hacking. I had no frame of reference, but this wasn't what I expected to see. Zeke Allen had been a jock in high school. Baseball, I thought... He frowned in concentration. A couple of energy drinks sat next to him, along with a bowl of candy. He was shirtless with sweats. There were barbells on the floor beside the desk. A kitchenette was in the corner of the room with a microwave and a small refrigerator. He'd pulled out some water and a beer, leaving them on the counter beside the sink. A Keurig machine sat in the corner.

"Fuck...shit," he muttered. "Not today, asshole. Not. Today." He hit a button and froze. Then he shot out of his chair and whooped, throwing his arms in the air. "Fuck yeah! Take that. I got you, you little piece of—" He shoved the chair away and bent down to keep typing, but when he looked back to see where his chair had gone, he saw us instead.

Fear flashed. It took a second before he understood what was happening. He sprang, going for his desk. His hand reached for something under it.

We jumped first. I launched myself at him, tackling him, and I rolled him all the way away from his desk and chair. I didn't know what he was reaching for, but I wanted to be safe in case there was a gun stashed underneath.

During the roll, he started fighting.

I kept my grip on him tight and shifted my leg to block his kicks.

He tried to get to his feet. Logan was there, but I grabbed his ankle and yanked. Hard.

He fell flat on his face.

He roared and was in the air in the next second, red in the face and swinging. The fight was quiet, but it was violent. We didn't goad him. Instead we were silent, calm. He was desperate to get away from us, and he knew he was going to lose. His eyes were dilated, panicked. He just hit and hit and hit. For the most part, Logan and I continued to block his hits until he began to tire out. Once that began to happen, Logan raised his eyes to me.

I nodded.

We rushed him again, taking him to the ground. I reared up, coming down with one last punch to knock him out. His body slumped. He was unconscious.

We worked quickly to clean any evidence of our struggle. When we were done, the room didn't look as if a struggle had happened. We took his phone, wallet, and keys. Everything went with us, including his truck. A note was left behind that he needed to run an errand. His computer was still unlocked so we searched for the security cameras, erasing us. Logan was still at his computer when I returned after carrying Allen to his truck and loading him in the backseat.

"Look at this." He gestured to the computer.

I saw the file he had open, titled *Bennett family*. Inside there were additional folders for Kai Bennett, Tanner, Jonah, Brooke, Cord, Riley, and others. Logan looked at me. "Is that their whole family? Zeke's looking into all of them?"

I shook my head. "I don't know. Kai mentioned his brothers and their partners. He mentioned Tanner by name." I motioned to Tanner's folder. "Click on his."

It contained a multitude of photographs taken with a long lens. In one he was walking with Cutler Ryder. Others showed him with a different guy, and in one Tanner had him backed against the wall, gripping the guy's hair.

Logan clicked on a few other files inside of Tanner's folder. Bank statements. Building layouts. There was too much for us to take in at this moment. I tapped his shoulder. "Make a copy."

"I didn't bring a USB—" He stopped talking because I had. He took it from my fingers, a wry grin on his face. "It's like condoms. You came prepared."

"Speak for yourself. Some of us weren't man whores growing up." I scoffed, heading for the door. "Hurry. I'm going to take his truck and leave."

"Okay. Wait."

I waited.

"Security system. We don't know how to arm it."

Fuck. He was right. "Finish with the copies. I'll go upstairs and see what I can figure out."

He nodded but didn't say anything.

Studying the security panel when I got there, I realized I had no clue what I was doing. There was no button that said *push me to arm*. I didn't recognize this security system, and I'd been around my fair share of security systems.

I weighed the odds.

If his wife came home and the system wasn't on? If we weren't done with him by then? She'd know right away something was wrong. Cops would get called.

We didn't intend to harm Zeke, not any more than we already had, but I wanted to scare him.

The most logical person to call would be Channing, because of his profession. He might know this system or a way to get around it. But my gut wasn't telling me to call Channing. I grimaced but called Nate.

He answered on the third ring, growling into the phone. "I'm going to murder you, Mase. You better be in the hospital or the police station or—" He cursed. "God. Sorry. I didn't think. I'm hoping you're not in either."

"That's Mason?" I could hear Quincey in the background.

There was rustling. "Yeah." He said to me, "Hold on."

More rustling. A door shut. He groaned. "Fuck. I'm tired. Why are you calling me at—seriously? It's... What? That doesn't make sense."

I rolled my eyes. "You're being dramatic. It's not even midnight."

"I'm in Pacific Standard Time."

"We're in the same time zone."

"Still fucking tired," he mumbled. "What's up, though?" His voice grew more alert. "Please tell me you're not in the hospital."

"Uh, no."

He was quiet for a beat before he cursed. "What'd you do?"

There was no way around this one. I just said it, "There wouldn't be any reason you might know how to re-arm Zeke Allen's security system?"

There was silence on his end.

I tucked my chin down. "You know, since you're practically family with him."

"I'm not family with him. And *what the fuck are you talking about?*"

Yeah. He wasn't happy about this call.

"Why *the fuck* are you asking how to arm his security system?"

I laughed a little. "Maybe I decided to turn the tables on him for once? See how he feels being stalked."

"Cut the shit. What's going on? Why can't you ask Zeke himself?"

I sighed. "It's better if you don't know. I thought maybe you'd dropped by his house or something over the years and maybe he rearmed it in front of you, but I can see I was wrong—"

"No. Wait."

He went silent again, but I waited.

I knew what he was thinking. I was in Allen's house, and I couldn't ask Allen himself. Everything about this call indicated I was doing something illegal. Highly illegal. I'd called him for information because I trusted him, and I was asking him to choose which side he was on.

He wasn't like us, as I'd been reminded the other night with the bikers at the warehouse. I'd been hurt at first, thinking he was judging us. But I'd realized Sam was right. I needed Nate because he balanced out whatever was inside of us that surfaced when we were in Fallen Crest. If I didn't have friends like Nate and Matteo, and if we stayed too long in Fallen Crest, I didn't know who I might become.

I didn't want to think about that.

He sighed. "Goddamn you, Mason."

I straightened, my voice going cold. "Forget it."

"*Wait.*" He cursed again, but I heard more rustling sounds on his end. "My sister goes over there all the time."

I closed my eyes. He was going to ask his sister how to arm the system. I knew Nate well enough to know that if she asked the reason, he would lie for us. A part of me regretted asking, but another part of me didn't. I needed to know. That was the ruthless side of me. The same side that had chosen to call Nate, because it would put him in this exact spot.

I needed to know nothing had changed since he'd learned Logan and I still had our dark sides.

Bottom line, I liked knowing my best friend still was my best friend, and I didn't care how I found that out. Not right now. Everything would be smoothed over later, but Nate didn't know that.

I heard a beep, and he spoke into the phone. "She said there's a button on the right side. A tiny button. You have to look at it squarely or you won't see it. It's supposed to blend in with the panel. She doesn't know the code, but if you hit that button, you'll have thirty seconds to get out of the house."

His phone beeped.

He cursed, his voice tightening. "She didn't ask why, Mason. Fuck you, man. That's my sister. So goddamn good, and she never even questioned me why I was asking that shit from her."

Logan was coming up the stairs. He raised his chin in question.

"It'll be fine," I told Nate.

"I fucking hope so. If she mentions this to Blaise, he's going to ask why, and when he doesn't believe my lie or when he checks out my lie, he's going to raise hell. You don't know that side of my brother-in-law."

"They're in Europe. You have time to evade."

"You'd never lie to Logan for me—"

"I'd lie to Taylor for you."

Logan punched my arm, glaring. I shrugged. It was true. I'd lie to her if Nate asked me to. Now, if Sam or Logan himself asked me about it, I wouldn't lie to them. Maybe it wasn't quite fair, but I also didn't care.

"That's not the same," Nate countered.

"I have to go. We can fight about this later." I ended the call before he could say anything more.

"You go first. I know how to arm it."

Logan's eyes were narrowed into slits, but he didn't linger. I heard the garage door go up, and Allen's truck started. He backed out. The garage door began to lower. I waited until it was on the ground before hitting the little button and taking off, leaving through the side door. That would lock behind me too.

Logan was almost to the street when I ran past him.

I crossed the street to my Escalade, climbed in and followed after him.

The first phase was complete.

26

MASON

There was a soundproofed room inside an empty Kade Enterprises warehouse. I had every intention of looking into why it had been soundproofed, but until I had time, we were going to make use of it.

Once we had Zeke strung up so he wasn't going to hurt himself, it was time. Logan and I kept our masks on, and I trained the spotlight on him. "Wake him up."

The room was warm and it smelled weird, but it'd do for what we were about to do. This was not going to be pleasant. Logan picked up the smelling salts and put them under Allen's nose.

He jerked awake with a cough and a deep groan.

Logan stepped back, disappearing into the shadows with me. We waited until Zeke got his bearings.

After a moment, his eyes squinted against the light. He tried to move, but his arms and legs were both tied in place. Only then did panic start to hit him. He tried to see us, but the light hurt too much. He flinched, twisting and trying to move away. "What the fuck? *What the fuck?!*" He struggled against his bindings. "Let me go." He took a deep breath, fighting again. "LET ME GO! *NOW!*"

Logan started laughing, trying to be quiet.

Zeke froze, glaring at us. "You think this is funny? You fucking sick psychos. You twisted, fucking sick psychos. Who are you? When I get out of this—"

I was suddenly not in the mood to hear any threats. "Shut up."

He did, but only briefly. His eyes narrowed, and his lip curled in an ugly snarl. "Or what? You're going to break into my house and kidnap—" His eyes widened, and he froze. "My wife. My kids." He strained toward us, eyes blazing. "My family, are they okay? If you did anything to the—"

More threats.

His fear was valid, but this wasn't about his family. This was about mine, and he had put them in danger. A primal-sounding roar escaped me. He shut up for a moment, but still he strained to get free, pushing his body as far toward us as his bindings would let him.

Logan moved to my side. "That's a good strategy." He looked up to check on where we'd anchored the chains. It looked solid. "If we needed to keep him here longer than a day, he'd get free."

My eyes fell to the anchor at his feet. He wasn't focused on that, but he should've been. That was the weak point. I nodded at it, getting Logan's attention. If Zeke was thinking, he'd twist his body as far forward as possible, taking the pain, because that anchor on the floor wouldn't hold. It would loosen, and it'd pop out of the floor.

Good lesson if we ever did this again.

We let him struggle for a while, tiring himself out.

When I'd had enough, I stepped forward. "You've been looking into the Bennett family. Why?"

He went still, his chest heaving. Sweat trickled down his

face, wetting his shirt. His eyes narrowed. "That's what this is about?"

Logan growled. "Answer the fucking question. Why are you looking into them?"

Zeke scanned around the room, as if looking for other people before his eyes returned to us. "Can you respect my right to privacy?" he taunted.

Logan started for him.

Zeke laughed, sucking in his breath as Logan neared. He watched my brother walk over to a table where he had some weapons laid out. "Kai Bennett is a bad fucking guy. He's..."

Logan picked up the knuckle rings, sliding them on and flexing his hand.

Zeke's voice faltered. "What are you going to do?" He tried leaning away but couldn't. "Look, man. I don't know—obviously you know who I am, but I've got people who are going to be pissed that you're doing this. They'll fuck you up. Trust me. My best friend is..." He stopped, swallowing.

Logan shook his head, stepping around to inspect him, probably trying to decide on the first place to hit him. "We have you strung up, and you're letting us know about the first threat to take out once we're done with you? Thank you in advance." An ugly chuckle came from Logan's mouth.

Zeke tried watching him as Logan circled around to his back. "What do you want? I'm not going to tell you shit. You work for the Bennetts? Is that what this is? They're pissed at me or something? It was just a little hacking. Nothing serious. I didn't do anything. I was only looking for information."

I stepped forward. "What information?"

He twisted back to me, his eyes widening. He'd forgotten I was here.

Zeke swallowed again. He closed his eyes, readying himself. "I—just information on them. Nothing incriminating. I... Who the fuck are you guys? I don't know shit. Okay? *Okay?* They're messing with people I know and I'm—I was just trying to help. That's it. Fuck's sakes. That's it. I'll stop."

Logan stepped back so we could share a look.

Zeke looked between us. He licked his lips. "Seriously. I'll stop. Don't..." Suddenly, the fight drained from him. His body slumped. His arms strained with his weight, strung above his head. "Whatever. I can't tell you shit, and I'm not going to. Fuck me up. Just... Leave my family alone. Okay?"

Logan tapped the knuckles against his other hand, but Zeke seemed to tune him out. He was waiting for the torture to start, which put us in a bind because we didn't actually want to torture him. Scare him? Yes. Put some pressure on him and see how he handled it? Absolutely. But making him bleed... Well, I couldn't deny that something about that held some appeal for me, but Zeke wasn't the real enemy.

"You've given up already?" Logan picked up a knife and tapped it against Zeke's forehead.

Zeke shook his head, trying to flip him away.

That same ugly chuckle left my brother again as he stepped around in front of Zeke, trailing the tip of the blade over Zeke's chest.

Zeke just waited. His chest and stomach trembled under the knife's point.

Logan was enjoying this, and he angled the knife higher, so only the tip touched Zeke's stomach. He grabbed hold of it with both hands and moved in, pushing it further. It cut through Zeke's shirt and he grimaced as the tip pierced his skin.

I waited. This was new for us. We'd not done this type of interrogation, usually resorting to blackmail or straight up violence in the past. A writhing ball of emotion twisted in my stomach. I liked doing this. How fucked up was that?

Logan pushed the knife farther.

Zeke grunted, panting. "Fuck. Fuck! Stop."

I moved to the side, checking to see how far the knife had gone. It wasn't that far, just a little past the tip. But it was enough to make him feel searing pain and bring some blood seeping out. It looked bad, but in the end, he'd only need a stitch or two.

Zeke went pale, struggling again. "What do you want? You still haven't told me shit."

"We want information," I barked. "Why were you looking into Kai Bennett and his family?"

His eyes flicked my way but returned immediately to Logan. That knife was still there. Zeke was moving around, making it worse. "I—" His voice broke before he yelled, his tone strangled. "What are you going to do? Cut me up? Just do it! Do it, assholes. Slide that shit deeper. *Come on.*" Zeke began straining toward Logan, pushing the knife deeper.

Logan didn't move back, just looked my way to see what I wanted to do.

"Stop." Grabbing Zeke's shoulder, I held him in place.

He strained against my hold, driving the knife deeper. He'd snapped or something. There was a wild look in his eyes, and I reached up, tugging on the chains to release his body. He dropped.

Logan removed the knife, so it didn't do more damage, but as soon Zeke was down, we were on him. I knelt on his shoulders as Logan knelt on his legs, still gripping the knife.

Well, I had my answer. This guy was certifiably crazy.

He was also like us.

"Get off me! Get off—" He was twisting so much that Logan had to let go of the knife.

I'd seen and heard enough. This guy was—I didn't know what his endgame was. But this wasn't getting us anywhere. I stepped up and delivered a punch straight to his head. As it landed, his body thumped against the floor. He was unconscious again.

Logan stepped back, peeling off his mask. He was shaken, a little pale too. "Holy shit." He ran his hands down his face.

I peeled off my own mask, knowing I looked the same. I stared down at the kid, who—I know, I know, wasn't a kid, but I'd first found out about him when he was in high school. Now he'd chosen to hurt himself over telling us anything.

I respected him for that. "We need to take him to the hospital."

"I can call Taylor," Logan said. "She can stitch him up. He'll be fine." He shook his head, standing. "The dude's crazy."

I grunted. "He's more solid than I thought."

Logan lifted laughing eyes to me. "He's like us, Mase. I never would've thought that."

I shook my head, reaching for my phone. "He took a risk. If we actually were from the Bennetts, he'd be dead. And they would've used his family against him, no qualms about it."

"Yeah." Logan sighed, sounding exhausted. "Fuck, man. *Fuck.*" He took a staggering step back, still not totally steady.

I crossed the room to pull out the first aid kit. I'd do what I could until Taylor got here. I motioned to Logan. "Call your wife. Don't let her tell anyone where she's going."

Logan cursed, his head tipping back. He dug out his phone, hit a couple buttons, and lifted it to his ear as he turned and moved away. "Hey, babe?..."

I regarded Zeke at my feet.

He'd surprised me. Not a lot of people did that anymore. But when he woke up, we'd have to start all over again because I still wanted to know why he was looking into Kai Bennett.

27

MADDY

Rap music blared when I got to Traine's mansion. I hadn't called ahead, but I knew he had people over. He'd texted earlier today to see if I wanted to come. I hadn't responded. I'd been focused on whether I should talk to my dad about what Aurelia had said the night before. Then we'd had our chat, and there was the weirdness leaving his office, and then when I got to the house, Uncle Mark's chaos had spilled over. I thought Mom would call me when we were having dinner, but no one said anything. When I came up from the basement two hours later, everyone was gone.

I'd texted Mom and Dad, but neither responded.

Nash had finally let me know that Grandma and Grandpa took everyone to get ice cream, and then they were going to the movies.

My phone buzzed.

Mom: Honey! I'm so sorry. I thought you were with David and Malinda. Did you eat? I'm at Manny's, but I can leave early. Do you want me to bring food back for you?

Me: Where's dad?

Mom: He's doing some business stuff with Logan. He

won't be home for a while. What do you want to do for dinner? I can come get you. You can hang out with us.

I rolled my eyes, because *pass*. Not that hanging out with my mom and her friends wasn't fun. They actually were great, and I worshipped Aunt Heather, but... Mom wouldn't let me slip booze, and they'd start 'coding' everything they said, and that's annoying. Like I couldn't handle whatever they're talking about. I'll be eighteen soon. I'm in high school. The shit we see? My mom would have a heart attack just knowing half the stuff I hear and see on social media during any given day. Oh well. I'd protect my parents from their heart attacks. I wouldn't want them to worry, but that meant a night in the house by myself.

Hard pass on that too. The place was huge, and it was never a good idea for me to be by myself when I had all these feelings I was trying not to feel. I tried numbing myself to the grief, but I couldn't. Every time I tried, it went bad. I kept getting myself into more trouble, so it seemed staying busy and distracted was the best option for me.

I considered texting Max to see if he wanted to hang out, but he was still on that 'space' kick. I figured I'd wait another day before tracking him down and tackling him. It was Max. He couldn't stay mad at me forever.

Until then, I decided my best bet was to reconsider Traine's offer. So here I was.

I let myself in. The music got louder. It was coming from the back.

I'd never asked what Beltraine's deal was with his parents, if they were around and active or if he was a kid who basically operated on his own. My mom and dad gave me freedom, but there were rules. *Structure*, as they called it.

I paused, remembering that I was grounded. Here I was, violating that again. I shrugged. I was already here. Might as well indulge. Have as much fun as possible. They hadn't known where I was last night. Of course Dad knew now because I told him, but the day had been weird. So much odd shit happened. My dad would remember, but for some reason, it wasn't the first thing on his mind.

I frowned, wondering if I should be hurt by that.

Nah. Dad loved me. He was just distracted. His attention would come back to me. He and Mom would have a whole *talk* about me, and they'd descend on my ass until I was pleading for freedom.

I needed to enjoy this while it lasted.

I moved into the kitchen as a guy entered from the side hallway. Tall. Lean. Jet black hair. Dark brown eyes. He was shirtless and wearing swim trunks. Barefoot. He paused when he saw me. "Who are you?"

I snorted and turned to peruse the counter of drinks instead. It didn't hurt my feelings that he didn't know who I was, but I mean, come on. That was his loss, really. Once he found out who I was, he'd never forget. That was just a fact. Right now I'd enjoy this little bit of mystery.

He moved to the side, watching as I poured myself a strong drink. "You seem oddly at home in my bro's house. Traine know you're here?"

"Traine's not your brother."

"I don't mean it in a literal sense."

I made a noncommittal sound, reaching for another bottle. I had no idea what I was mixing. I operated under the rule that if it smelled good to me, I'd see how it tasted. Some whiskey went in there, but all the other liquids were sweet. I wasn't worried. To top it all off, a good amount of rum joined.

"What's up, man? You coming out or..." Traine trailed off, stepping inside and seeing me. "Hey! You came."

I glanced over, grunting a greeting, and closed my eyes as I tried out my drink. It was...not bad. My nose wrinkled. It was a little too sweet. What could I do to balance that out? I grabbed some stuff from a green bottle and poured it in, taking another sip.

Both guys watched me.

The new guy was scowling.

Beltraine was grinning. He crossed his arms over his chest. "Experimenting tonight?"

It needed more of the green-bottle stuff. Once I got it just right, I took a good drag. *Damn.* That tasted good. I smiled broadly at the guys. "My feelings are hurt, Moreaux."

His eyebrows shot up. "About what?"

I indicated the guy next to him. "Your cousin had no idea who I was. Where's the love?"

Steele Manning was the last member of the male trio at the top of the social hierarchy at Fallen Crest Academy. I was under no illusions. They'd been nice to me so far, but of course they would be. Who'd fuck with me? I had no problem handling bullies. I enjoyed it. A stand-off made me feel alive. So, I guess, in a way, if people catered to me, that was disappointing.

That's why I enjoyed Max so much.

Ugh. Just thinking about him, I remembered his text. He'd been shoxting me. Shouting at me through text. I hated it because I'd rather he shouted at me in person. That'd be more fun.

The guys were watching me.

Beltraine snorted. "You're a trip, Kade."

Steele's head jerked toward him. "Kade?"

Beltraine stepped up to grab my drink. "Maddy Kade. Or, wait. What's your first name? Everyone calls you Maddy, but it's something else, isn't it?"

He was about to take a sip of my drink when I said, "It's drugged."

He froze, his eyes latching to mine.

I stepped forward and plucked it from his hands. "Just kidding." I laughed, taking another long drag and moving toward the patio. "And don't worry yourself about my name. You boys can just call me Kade. Right, Moreaux?" I taunted as I stepped outside.

Gathered around a table by the pool was the rest of Moreaux's friend group—Axel, Aurelia Avoy, and her two best friends, Nea Kyoto and Amber Spiel.

I took a deep breath for patience.

Nea and Amber were okay. Aurelia, though, was a different thing.

Axel grinned when he saw me, laughing to himself as he launched himself into the pool, pulling off an impressive backflip.

I glared at Aurelia. "You."

Nea and Amber's mouths dropped open silently.

Aurelia's face twisted. "*You*. What are you doing here?"

I took a seat at their table. "Traine mentioned it."

"He didn't tell us you were coming." She sat stiffly, her eyebrows permanently stuck halfway up her forehead. It was a weird expression.

I had another sip. This drink was *good*. "Why? Wouldn't have come if you knew I was here? Scared?"

Her face got red and she gripped the table. "As if. You don't scare me, Maddy Kade. Your grandpa's—" She choked on her words because my hand was at her throat.

There was a beat of quiet. No one expected me to grab her throat. It would take a minute before their brains could make sense of what they were seeing. I was going to make the most of their shock.

"You're going to stop lying," I told her, squeezing.

She began choking, trying to stand up.

I was strong. Like, really strong, and I kept her in place. I know, I know. Girls aren't supposed to be that strong, but what could I say? When she tried to stand up, it was easy to keep her in place.

Then she forgot about trying to stand up and began tugging at my hand. Her nails scraped my skin, but I took a beat to have another sip of my drink.

Really good stuff.

Also, I wasn't hurting her that much. She wouldn't have bruises or anything.

Nea and Amber finally comprehended that I was choking their friend and they shoved to their feet, yelling at me, but they didn't come over to me. They were too scared, and honestly, if I wasn't myself, I'd be scared of me too. Or at least nervous.

This wasn't a normal girl move. But again, story of my life.

Aurelia gasped for air.

A part of me, deep in the back of my mind, couldn't help but note that maybe this was wrong of me to do. Of course this wasn't right, but I wasn't really thinking about it in those terms. I was more evaluating myself. Why did this feel so natural? Like it was in my DNA.

It wasn't normal.

Was I a psychopath? A sociopath? I didn't feel anything about doing this to Aurelia. She was annoying, and she was a liar, and she was a problem. I was just shutting her up. Literally. She'd think twice before shooting her mouth off about my family in the future.

That's why I was doing this.

Huh.

She kept trying to dig her nails into my hands, trying to get me to let her go. Nea and Amber were crying now. I heard a splash of water and then, "What the fuck?"

There was a pounding of feet from behind me.

My fun was about to end so I gave her a last squeeze. Her eyes bulged out, but I was ripped away. A pair of arms encircled me, lifted me up and carried me away from the table. Beltraine was at Aurelia's side, patting her back as she slumped forward, gasping for breath. He soothed her, but his gaze was locked on me.

Everyone was watching me, different expressions on all of their faces. The girls looked terrified of me. The guys... I couldn't make out their thoughts. Traine gave me a look as if I just turned green in front of him.

I frowned to myself, feeling like I should feel something about that. Satisfaction? Regret? I felt nothing.

Whoever pulled me off Aurelia continued to carry me a good distance away before setting me down. It was Axel, I realized when he moved to stand in front of me, a hand on my arm like he needed to hold me back. Steele moved to stand between me and the girls, blocking my view. He scowled at me.

What was his problem? "What? Is she your girlfriend? You don't want me to harm a hair on her head?" I rolled my eyes, lifting my drink back to my mouth. Satisfaction pulsed through me because *hell yeah.* I'd kept hold of my cup. That seemed like something to be impressed about.

"She's not my girlfriend." Steele moved toward me a step. "I don't give a fuck if you stab the bitch. Choke her out all you want."

A ripple moved through me, and I frowned, not totally recognizing what that ripple was. "Then what's your problem?"

He didn't reply.

Axel cleared his throat, letting go of me.

That's when Aurelia decided to finally say something. "You bitch!" She shrieked. She flew at me, but the guys caught her.

Excitement raced through me. "Let her go."

The guys's mouths dropped.

I laughed, tipping my head to finish the rest of my drink. I flashed Traine a grin. "You're right. This is fun." I didn't catch his reaction, but I eyed Aurelia's neck. There was no mark from me. My mouth turned down.

I wish there was, just a little.

That was... Interesting.

I considered Max, the thought of leaving a mark on him and him wearing that around—holy fuck. I was drenched between my legs. Throbbing.

Yeah. I liked that idea a lot.

Maybe I was going to be into BDSM?

I had so much new stuff to Google about myself.

Aurelia was still shrieking, getting louder. She was sobbing, half clinging to Axel. "I should call the police! That was assault. You fucking whor—"

I took a step closer. "I wouldn't."

She stopped talking. Nea and Amber jumped at my movement. They hid behind Beltraine. His head was cocked to the side, his gaze dark. A corner of Traine's mouth curved up. Axel and Steele shared a look. Axel's lips twitched.

"What? Rethinking your invitation now that you've realized I'm a different kind of animal?" I said to him. "Found yourself in the wrong circus?"

The other end of his mouth lifted in a slow grin. "Nah. Thinking I like this circus a lot more than I thought."

I couldn't help myself. His grin was contagious.

Axel laughed, shaking his head.

"That's it!" Aurelia seethed. "I'm going to call my father."

"To do what?"

Her mouth opened and closed, but she said nothing.

I rolled my eyes. "What? You lied about my grandfather. The business is just fine."

She got red all over again and huffed. "My dad—"

"Your dad's saying a lot of shit that's false. You need to shut the fuck up. I can't stand liars, and that's what you are. Just another fucking liar." I gave her a onceover. "Ugh. Girls like you. Fake. Insecure. Needing to lie to make yourself feel better. You have to do that because you've got no substance. Nothing good. Just...*fake*. All fake."

Nea and Amber had gone still.

Axel slowly dropped his hand from Aurelia. He was no longer shielding her.

Her shoulders hunched as she continued rubbing at her throat. "That was assault. I *can* press charges against you."

I snorted. "Please. My godfather has his own law firm. Besides, you press charges against me and guess what that makes you look like?" I didn't even need to finish, because she only needed to look at the guys. It was in their eyes, all three of them. Only one word would come to their minds, to everyone's mind when she got to school the next day.

Snitch.

It's what everyone would whisper in the hallway. She paled as she realized it too. I watched as the fight drained out of her. It happened so fast. She succumbed because being popular was what Aurelia cared about. She didn't care about standing on her own. She should go to the police. I had assaulted her, but I hadn't really hurt her. That's what everyone would talk about. Just what I did. It would be a different story if I had actually hurt her. More people would rally around her. I never understood that. Why people only cared if there was physical evidence of harm? The emotional harm was done. That was the worst part. That's the injury that would linger. The physical would heal and go away. Not the psychological. That's what I wanted to inflict on her. I mean, yeah. I wish I could've left evidence on her neck, but I wasn't altogether so rash that I didn't think it through.

No mark. No evidence. The point went to me.

I'd done more than just violate her personal space. I showed her who would fight for her. No one. Her friends were too scared to approach me. The guys separated us, but that was it. They were amused by me. I surprised them. Guys like Traine, Axel, and Steele were catered to all their life. The same girls climbed into their bed. Cried. Whined when they were kicked out. I watched them in school, how the teachers catered to them there.

I wasn't that type of girl. I was different.

I won. Plain and simple.

Her shoulders folded down. Her arms hugged herself. She stifled, turned away, but this battle was done. She'd come at me again, after she licked her wounds and probably in school. I had no doubt she'd try to bully me through other girls. Maybe spread rumors about me?

I couldn't wait.

Maybe moving to Fallen Crest hadn't been such a bad thing. I missed Max.

28

MASON

I sat and waited for my stalker to wake up. He'd started to move around while Taylor was working on him, so we'd used some medication to knock him out.

My phone buzzed.

Sam: Nash is home. Nolan is here. Maddy is not.

I frowned, standing to call her. When she picked up, I asked, "She's gone?"

"Yeah." There was some rustling on Sam's end before her voice came back clearer. "She texted earlier asking where everyone was. She got left behind when Malinda and David took the kids to the movies. I asked if she wanted to hang out with us at Manny's, but she said no. I've not heard from her since."

"Did you check her phone?" I was going to lose my shit on my daughter real soon. She'd been grounded for two days. She'd violated it both days. If she'd left without her phone, she was on my last nerve.

"It says... That's weird."

"It's not in the house?" I asked.

"No. I think it's with her, but I don't know this address."

Zeke was starting to stir, finally. "Text me the address. I have to finish something up, then I'll go get her."

"Okay."

I frowned, hearing an edge in her voice. "What is it?"

She sighed. "I—I just don't know if I should be worried, annoyed, or ready to murder her. This week's been a lot. She's grieving, and she's doing it in her way, but this is the second time she's slipped out without telling us."

Well, fuck. "Third time."

"What?"

I coughed, now seeing Zeke's eyes open. "She snuck out last night too."

"What?" she clipped out. "How do you know this? When did you know this?"

"She came to the office earlier today and came clean, but only because she had to explain something she needed to ask me about."

"What did she need to ask you about?"

I turned away and lowered my voice. "Let's talk about this when I get home. When we're done here, I'll get her."

"How long is that going to be?" There was still an edge to her voice.

I winced. My wife was not happy, and I wasn't sure if waiting for our homecoming would calm her down or work her up.

Zeke was sitting up now, and he had a hand to his head, grimacing in pain.

Logan returned after walking Taylor back outside. She'd not been happy with us. I saw him process the situation in one second. An indifferent mask fell into place, and he moved around to sit across from Zeke, a mocking smirk on his face. I knew my brother. He was still hoping for some fun to be had. Our weird torture earlier hadn't been enough to quench his thirst for destruction.

"I don't know," I told Sam. "Just..." I let out a breath. "Go to sleep if you can. We'll tackle this tomorrow."

"Fine," she bit out before ending the call. She didn't say goodbye.

I frowned at the phone.

"She's pissed?" Logan asked.

I pocketed the phone, approaching him with a grim look.

He flinched. "Sorry."

"Thinking your doghouse isn't too far from mine."

He snorted before leaning forward in his seat. He cocked his head to the side. "How's your head?" His voice rose. "Does it hurt? I'm hoping it hurts. Along with your stomach, you *crazy motherfucker*."

Zeke winced, leaning away from Logan's intensity. "Jesus. Lower your voice. I'm in pain here. What happened?"

Logan shook his head. "Don't play fucking dumb." His restlessness was back. He was pissed, and he was about to unleash on Zeke Allen.

I leaned back against the wall, getting comfortable.

Zeke looked around the room, but his eyes never strayed far from me. An unfocused and blank expression filled his gaze every time he saw me, as if he was making sure I wasn't an apparition. He blinked a few times, then rubbed his eyes.

When he saw the discarded ski-masks on the ground, some of the confusion left him. "What the fuck?" he ground out. His eyes hardened. "You guys did that shit to me? *What the fuck*?"

If he hadn't been in so much pain, I would've been waiting for him to swing at us.

Logan shoved to his feet and began pacing. "Oh, fuck off, you piece of shit." He rotated back and leaned down in Zeke's face. "You're hacking? Are you serious? *Hacking*? Do you know whose shit you were hacking into? Did you stop to research the fucking maniac whose private accounts you accessed? Whose family's accounts you accessed? A killing maniac who would have no problem letting you continue to impale yourself on a fucking knife. They would have no problem nabbing your wife and kids and using them as collateral against you. You're *fucking stupid*."

Zeke tried leaning away from Logan, but he was stuck.

"You want to know how we know? Because Kai Bennett came and told Mason himself."

Zeke froze, his eyes shooting my way. "He did?" His face drained of color again.

I studied my brother, checking to see if he was legit losing his cool or what he was doing. He started pacing again, his jaw tense. Okay. It was my turn. Logan was truly pissed at this guy.

I spoke up, raising my chin. "He came to the office today."

Unlike Logan, I was going to make sure everything I said to him hit home. I waited until those words registered. He blinked again, losing a bit more color.

"My daughter had come to see me at the office," I continued. "My daughter. She was there. We were leaving, and he waited for her to leave first in her car. Once she cleared the gate, his SUVs drove in and circled me. Another one got between Maddy's vehicle and mine. Pinned me in. Mighty nice of him. Letting *my daughter* leave." I gritted my teeth. "Don't you think? You brought that here. You brought that to my daughter. Different guy, different family and my kid might not be alive. You getting that?"

Zeke swayed on the couch. "Holy fuck," he whispered, his head hanging down.

"Guess what he had to say?" Logan snarled. "Spoiler: it was about *you*."

Zeke gulped, still swaying on the couch.

I cursed. He was about to keel over. "Logan." Two steps and I caught Zeke just as he was about to go down.

"What?" Logan snapped. "This little fucking hacker. Kai Bennett is in the *mafia*." He yelled the last word at Zeke, who clutched my hand before giving me a nod, assuring me he was okay to sit by himself again.

I waited another beat, but he gave one more nod, so I moved away.

"The fucking mafia, Zeke. You hacked into his brothers's accounts. Into their partners's accounts."

My eyebrows rose. I'd not expected this from Logan. He'd been annoyed. I knew that much, but he was pissed about what Zeke had done to himself. I had no idea Logan cared for this guy this much.

"Tell him what he said to you. The other part." Logan turned swiftly, glaring at me. "The part about what would've happened if he'd gotten into Kai Bennett's accounts."

Zeke had slumped over again, a hand on his stomach. He grimaced, trying to sit up straighter. "You can tell me."

No.

Fuck.

No.

I shook my head. We'd done enough to him. It could wait.

"No! No, Mason. Fuck no." Logan thrust a hand at me. "You fucking tell him."

I hesitated, but Christ, Zeke looked about two more shouts away from passing out. I shook my head.

Logan growled. "Come on!"

I narrowed my eyes. "Look at him. He's going to fall over. We still need to take him to the hospital."

"Taylor looked at him." He resumed his pacing, muttering, "He's fine."

"He's not."

"Uh..." Zeke tried lifting his hand.

"Taylor checked him out with the assumption we'd be taking him to the hospital," I noted.

"No, she didn't."

"Logan!" I barked.

He stopped mid-pace.

"Look at him. Fucking really look at him," I demanded. "He's normally a smartass douchebag."

"Hey."

That proved my point, because that was weak coming from Zeke.

Logan stared at him, and some understanding finally dawned, some of the haze began clearing. "Goddammit."

I grunted. "We need to shelve this."

Logan glared at Zeke as I pulled out his phone, tossing it to the hacker.

"You will not breathe a word of this to anyone," Logan warned. "In case you know anyone with telepathy, you won't *think* a word of this to anyone. You won't write a word of this. You won't learn morse code. You won't text a word of this. Use your computer—"

Zeke's face was twisted in pain as I went over to help him stand. He put an arm around my shoulder, the other over his stomach. "I got it. I have selective amnesia for all of this. Got it. Fuck, Kade."

Logan growled, but he didn't reply. He also didn't move to help us.

I'd expected to be the one laying into Zeke, and Logan would have to call me off. But he'd gotten so up his ass that there was no room for both of us. I was kinda pissed at Logan for that.

As we walked slowly outside, Zeke groaned. "I went a little crazy, huh? Did this to myself."

He tried giving me a slight grin, but I didn't respond. There was nothing to say.

We'd broken into his house. Assaulted him. Kidnapped him. Strung him up. Logan brought the knife out, and Zeke went into a frenzy. Then again, if he hadn't been hacking into Kai Bennett's family, none of this would've happened.

Zeke swallowed, his hand clenching my shirt.

I unlocked my Escalade and helped get him up in the back-seat. "Go ahead and lie down."

He didn't, but he did lean his head against the headrest and close his eyes. Fresh sweat beaded on his forehead.

I didn't think any of that was a good sign.

Logan was just coming out as I rounded to the driver's side.

He'd locked up the warehouse. I held off before opening my door. "You lost it in there."

He shrugged. "Just pissed about the whole thing. If he'd pushed harder and gotten through, he'd be dead. What then? His wife would be burying her husband. His kids would be without a dad." He cursed again, savagely, looking away.

A heaviness came down over me. I reached up, resting my hand on his shoulder. "I need to get him in. I think maybe that knife wound is infected. I..." I hesitated, not knowing what to say. Get Zeke to the hospital, stick around and hope for a decent prognosis, and then collect Maddy. It was going to be a long night.

It had *already* been a long night.

"I'll meet you at the hospital."

"You sure?"

Logan nodded, his eyes shooting behind me again. "Yeah. I'm his lawyer. I'll come up with a better lie than you will."

He was right about that. I'd forgotten that we'd have to explain the knife wound when we dropped him off. The hospital might call the police. I looked over my shoulder to the hacker again, who seemed focused solely on breathing and sitting upright, still holding his stomach. "Let's hope he took your warning to heart."

29

MASON

I was tired. Like, tired to the bone.

The last week was wearing on me. Logan stayed with me while we got Zeke to the hospital, and he was right. He lied better than me. I never would've considered telling them that Zeke got that knife wound from a long-winded story that centered around golfing and trying to cut an avocado on hole nine, but the nurse barely blinked. Of course, once he said he was Zeke's lawyer, everything became official. No one questioned why a lawyer would be at his client's hospital bedside. The police station made sense. A hospital, not so much. But regardless, Logan had everyone running around at his command within seconds.

It was impressive.

A minute ago, the doctor let us know that Zeke had a minor reaction, but they were already pumping him full of antibiotics. He was going to be okay. He was passed out and would be for the rest of the night

At that point, we left. Logan fell in step beside me on the way out. "I need a ride."

He'd driven Zeke's truck here. "You left his keys with him?"

He nodded, stuffing his hands in his jacket pockets. "Along with his phone and wallet."

I didn't remember that we'd grabbed his wallet and gave my brother the side-eye. He cared for the guy. Legit cared. Why hadn't he mentioned that to me? A few people recognized me as we were leaving. We'd gotten attention from some of the nurses, and one of the doctors, but only one person recognized me from the NFL. But as we entered the waiting room to leave, some guys were there and scrambled. A couple of them approached for autographs.

It was then that I saw ESPN was on the television. The commentators were talking about the Orcas's chances for the Lombardi and I saw my name scrolling across the bottom. We were still somewhat new into the season. It was my first year of being retired. My name and face would be up there for a while.

When we left, I checked Maddy's phone tracker and saw she was still at the address Sam had given me. I sighed on the inside because what was this going to be? Another fight? Different sort of fight? I never truly knew.

Logan didn't question me until I turned down a street that was not in our neighborhood. "What the—where are we going?" He became more alert.

I pulled up to the gate at the entrance to the subdivision, rolling my window down. I ignored Logan and when the gate guard asked for my code, I told him, "My daughter's at one of the houses. I need to go in and get her."

Logan cursed under his breath.

The guard didn't seem inclined to let us through until he got a good look at my face. "Hey! You're Mason Kade." After that, his inner fan came out and this fan couldn't be more helpful. We were not only allowed access, but he gave us directions and offered to escort us to the home.

I gave him a wave as we pulled through. "We're good from here. Thank you. Appreciate it."

"Is this new?" Logan asked. "Maddy's just ignoring that she's grounded?"

I grunted, that tired feeling spreading through me again. "Fuck if I know."

I felt my brother studying me. "What are you going to do? You don't seem too pissed right now."

Coming to the next street, I made the turn and it was easy to locate the house, even without the address. It was situated at the end of a cul-de-sac, and it was twice the size of all the other houses. Two giant columns framed the front entrance, along with a circle drive currently littered with vehicles. All fancy cars too. Logan whistled under his breath. "Remember when Sam used to drive that old Corolla?"

I grunted, remembering it fondly as I parked. "Good times."

He got out and strolled next to me. "Simple times." We passed a Ferrari. "Jesus. No teenager should be driving a vehicle like that."

"You wouldn't have said that when you were a teenager." But I didn't disagree. "I think I'm too tired to be pissed right now. That'll probably change once we get inside, depending on what kind of reception Maddy gives us."

"I hear you."

We got to the door, and I could hear the music inside. It was muted, but I expected it to blast us once this door opened.

Logan glanced my way. "What are you thinking?"

"What kind of trouble could I get in if we just walk in?"

Logan's grin was wolfish. "Well, I mean, a reasonable argument could be made that we were concerned for the welfare of your daughter, who's underage." He reached out, barely tapping the door. His grin turned wicked. "Look at that. We knocked and no one answered."

"So you're saying there's a good chance we *won't* get in trouble."

He held my gaze, a spark now lit. "Chances are good. I mean, you showed up with your lawyer."

I scoffed but opened the door with no problem. "Comes in handy, your law degree."

He snorted, following me inside.

I half expected to hear an alarm pierce the air, but I was wrong about that, and I was also wrong about the music. It remained muted, coming from somewhere below. Logan whistled as we walked through the kitchen. "Drink, anyone?" he remarked, perusing the very large supply of alcohol. He picked up a few bottles and whistled again before putting them back. "It's a school night—or school morning—and Mr. Moreaux's parents are very much not in attendance. What would the PTA say about this? Hell, what would our board say about this?" He was being sarcastic, but he had a point.

I motioned to him. "Step back." I raised my phone, taking a few snaps.

"What are you doing?"

I took a video, starting on the booze and circled around, turning it off right before I got to my brother. I pocketed my phone. "Evidence."

His eyebrows shot up. "For the board? I was joking. All those guys are the same. They won't blink at their kids throwing a party or even getting arrested."

I shrugged as I walked back out to the main hallway and looked around. "You never know. Moreaux is the next-biggest shareholder after us and Nate. What other incriminating shit might we see here?" I cocked an eyebrow at him. We were here to get my daughter, but before we did that...

Logan's grin turned wolfish once again. He rubbed his hands together. "You're ruining my hard-on to go back east. All this fun we're having? I'm never going to want to leave again."

"Maybe it's time you moved back."

He didn't reply to that, instead pursing his lips and led the way down the hall on the first floor. "Wanna bet the office is down here?"

"No bet. It's always on the first floor."

We found it, and while the music raged beneath our feet, we went through Phillip Moreaux's office. Logan was on the computer, searching around.

"You got in?"

He lifted the mousepad. "Dumbass tapes his password here."

"Right." I studied the screen, noting all the files on there.

"You got any more USBs handy?" he asked.

I snorted but handed over the one from earlier. "I bet there's still space on there."

He took it. "Search upstairs. Keep your phone handy. I'll do this and do a search for any security cameras, just in case."

"The Moreauxs won't have cameras in here."

"You don't think?"

"No way. And if they do, they aren't on. His kid is throwing a party with that amount of booze out there? Phillip Moreaux won't want evidence of that shit. Or anything else that might happen in this house. We haven't even gone downstairs yet." A dark look passed between us. "Should we go down there first?" Logan asked.

I went out into the hallway. "No. Maddy is fine. If we have to worry about anything, it's what she might be doing to the other kids. We won't get this chance again, and you never know when it might come in handy. I'll be fast upstairs."

"Fast, but thorough," he called after me.

I darted up the stairs and started my walk-through. Most of what was up here were guest bedrooms—nothing in there except the usual things. Beds. Towels. Televisions. I checked the primary bedroom, taking my time going through the drawers, the medicine cabinet in the bathroom, the closet. There were a couple safes, but I left them alone because both were locked.

This might be the beginning of a new criminal career and I'd advanced fast, but not enough to have the skill to get into a safe.

There was nothing significant about the primary bedroom. No personal items. There wasn't a lot of clothes either. There was no makeup or jewelry on the dresser or in the bathroom. The parents didn't stay here.

One of the guest bedrooms was being used and I went through that room too, but there wasn't much to find. Clothes. Toiletries spread out over the counter. Another laptop on the desk. A few framed pictures.

The kid's bedroom was last.

The door was open, which meant he was likely downstairs with the rest at the party. At first glance it was obvious that the kid lived here. His room was full of his things. A gaming system was in the corner. Two chairs on the floor. Snacks stashed everywhere. His school homework was tossed to the side. His closet was full of clothes.

There was a good amount of drugs in a hidden drawer. The kid wasn't too smart. The fake bottom was too high up. Anyone would've lifted it to see what was underneath, if they were looking.

I took more pictures and a video to make sure there was no doubt where I was. There were more pills in the bathroom. I gave his backpack a quick toss. The only thing I wanted to search thoroughly was his laptop, but I didn't move it. It would be password protected, and this kid wasn't going to keep his password under a mousepad. He was a lot more high-tech than his father. Though, I was a little thankful I'd been the one to find the laptop. Logan might've just stolen it.

I snapped pictures of everything.

Logan was coming up the stairs when I finished. "I did another search through the kitchen and pantry," he said. "There was some odd lingerie in the laundry."

"What do you mean?"

He shrugged. "Just a feeling. I want to get a quick look at the missus's closet. See if she's the type to wear the lingerie I saw down there."

"They don't stay here."

"What do you mean?"

I lifted my chin in the direction of the primary bedroom. "Their room is like a hotel's. No way are the parents living here. The kid is. A friend maybe too." I eyed my brother. "You're thinking this is where Moreaux brings a mistress?"

"The kid uses it for parties. Dad uses it when he's cheating."

"Kid's living here."

He stopped. "What? You mean the kid's here without the parent's? Like full-time."

I nodded. "I think so. Yeah."

His mouth went flat. "I don't like that."

I didn't like it either. If Maddy didn't live with Sam and me? No. I didn't like that one bit. When we went back to the main floor, I gestured out the patio door. "Did you look out there?"

Logan paused. "No." He opened the sliding door, stuck his head out. "No one's out here, but hold on. I'll do a quick walk-through with my phone."

It didn't take him long.

He stepped back inside and we moved to the basement door.

Who knew what we'd come across down there. "Let's get this done."

Showtime.

30

MADDY

I was still at Traine's house, sitting on the couch in the corner of the room.

Coming here hadn't been the smartest move. I needed to head home. I needed to stop drinking, but I was still sitting here. And I was *still* holding a glass I'd filled with my personal concoction. It was highly alcoholic and highly delicious.

Aurelia had gone hours ago, but others replaced her. Now I wasn't sure who was here. I stopped paying attention. Phone in my hand, I was going through Max's social media like a good little stalker.

Steele also sat on the couch, but there was a wide space between us. He'd been weird since finding out who my dad was —well, and maybe since my interaction with Aurelia. He'd been giving me long looks all night. What was his deal? Aurelia's two friends stayed when she left. Amber tried hitting on him, but he ignored her. When we moved to the basement, she tried sitting on his lap. He'd rolled his eyes and shoved her off. *"Go fuck the others,"* he'd told her.

So, she had.

She was in the other room, servicing Traine, Axel, and

another guy who showed up after Aurelia left. The door was wide open. Anyone and everyone could see. Things were different here, including the sexual activity. No one even blinked at Amber on her knees with Axel thrusting into her from behind, Beltraine's dick in her mouth, and the other guy getting a hand job from her. They'd already switched places a couple times.

Nea had disappeared into one of the back bedrooms with a guy. They'd reappeared a few minutes ago with Nea giggling as she wiped the back of her hand over her mouth. The guy was zipping up his pants.

There were a few other girls here, but they were in the back, dancing and grinding against whoever else was back there. The only person I wanted to grind on wasn't here, so I'd been chilling on the couch.

Steele landed next to me, and we'd been sitting like this, not saying a word, for the last hour.

I should really go home, but first, I asked him, "What's your deal?"

He looked my way, his face impassive. "What?"

"Why are you sitting here?"

He didn't blink. "Why are you here?"

"Because I'm too drunk to drive home." Oh yeah. That's why I was still here.

He raised an eyebrow.

I rolled my eyes. "You're not drunk. You've only had water. I watched."

He smirked. "You watched, huh?"

"You wouldn't be sitting here, not doing anything, not saying anything, if I weren't here. Why are you sitting with me like this?"

"Maybe I like you." He looked at me, long and hard.

There was no interest in his gaze. I'd considered that

option, but there was no way he was interested in me like that. I shook my head. "I don't like liars. They're scum to me."

"Scum?" He laughed. "Is it so hard to believe I might be into you?"

"Yes." I didn't say that because I was insecure and needed a guy to say all the pretty things to me. It was the truth. Guys were either intrigued by me, scared of me, or *really* into me. There were guys like Beltraine, who thought I was cool and treaded carefully around me. I'm sure if an opportunity happened where he could slide inside me, he'd take it, but he had no interest in anything more. Axel, on the other hand, was nervous around me. Not in the way where he liked me and was self-conscious. It was in the way of 'I'm nervous about this creature that I don't know what she is' kind of nervous. He didn't know how to operate around me.

And Steele... I'd asked because I couldn't figure him out. He didn't land in any of the previous groups. He wasn't insecure enough to be intrigued by me, only to find out he couldn't dominate me and get mad. Those were usually the guys intrigued by me. The guys who were really into me were worse than I was—like, real criminal types. They thought they found Bonnie to their Clyde. Maybe I'd fall for one of those guys in another life, but in this life, I knew who it was for me: Max.

I got him because I'd wear him down. I knew it was going to happen, and so did he. I liked to think we were in the pre-negotiation stage, before we started the real negotiating, that was going to end tomorrow. I already had a plan.

I said, "You're not interested in me. I know the look. You don't have it."

Steele laughed. "It's not you that I find interesting. Let's just leave it at that."

I frowned, not liking that answer.

But I got distracted because I was having a hallucination. I began laughing because my first hallucination ever was seeing my dad and uncle coming into the basement as if this were their house. My dad's eyes found mine and locked on. He was not happy. His jaw clenched.

Uncle Logan glared at me too, but his eyebrow shot up as he caught sight of the four-way happening in the other room. He said something under his breath.

I continued to watch them, curious to see what else was going to happen. Maybe Max would stroll in behind them. I watched, eager to see if it would happen.

"Ho—" Steele jumped to his feet. "Put that camera away! Who the fuck are you?"

A few people screamed. Some guys shouted.

Beltraine and Axel scrambled to put their dicks away. Amber was still in a haze. The other guy's head was back and his eyes closed, fully entranced in the hand job.

A few of the others tried making a run for the basement door, but Uncle Logan blocked them. He was the one with his phone up, and while there was an evil grin on his face, his eyes did not match it. He was pissed. "Thanks for putting your dicks away, gentlemen. Wouldn't want to get that on my video. Before anyone is allowed to leave, you will be handing over your names, your parents's names, and their contact info, because we'll be calling each and every one of them." He smirked. "Yes, children. We are those types of assholes. Since we're now the adults on the premises, the responsibility falls to our shoulders." He smiled, not batting an eyelash as protests rose. "Now, now, children. Don't piss me off or I can make things go badly, very badly for you. Then again, if you don't believe me, call my bluff. Please. I get off on this type of shit."

"Fucking with teenagers?" a guy sneered.

Uncle Logan swung his phone to aim right at the guy, who now paled and seemed to be rethinking his comment. "No. I get off on ruining people's days, and it's a two-for-one situation here. I get to ruin yours *and* your parents's. It's just up to you how bad my destruction gets."

My dad came to stand in front of me, scowling darkly down.

I blinked up at him a moment, still trying to decide if he was real, before I registered the looks on the others's faces. Amber was blushing and checking my dad out. The guys were pissed, but there was also fan adoration in their gazes.

Oh. This was real. This wasn't a result of too much alcohol or stress or grief. I couldn't help my smile. "Thank God. I was getting disappointed in my first hallucination. I would've hoped for something more fun like a grizzly trying to eat the four way that was happening. Can you imagine the terror and bloodshed?" My dad and uncle had totally crashed this party. I sighed at the look of murder in my dad's eyes. "Guess I'm still grounded."

My dad opened his mouth but couldn't speak. That's how mad he was.

Uncle Logan snorted, taking down information. "Niece of mine, you are so grounded you'll be lucky if you get the tracker taken out of your hip by the time your last prom gets here."

"I don't have a tracker in my hip."

He lifted his head, his gaze finding mine. "Not yet." He smiled.

I sank down on the couch and looked back at my dad. There could've been steam coming out of his ears.

"You, me, and your mother are going to have a very, *very* long discussion in the morning."

Well, that sealed my prison sentence.

He was bringing Mom into it.

31

SAMANTHA

I woke up hot, sweaty, and *pulsing* with need. Mason was between my legs. His tongue licked me, about sending me off the bed.

So good. I panted. "Wha—what time is it?"

He lifted his head, just barely, before crawling up my body. "Fuck early in the morning, but I need you." He positioned himself, his dick hard and ready. He used his knees to push my legs farther apart. Taking hold of his cock, he rubbed it over my folds, pushing up and back down before he leaned forward. A deep groan left him as he slid inside, holding himself upright with a hand on the bed beside me. We both moaned as he pushed all the way in.

"You feel so good," he said hoarsely, his eyes closing a second. "Holy fuck. I needed you."

The pleasure was immediate.

He waited until I adjusted to him, which I only needed a second. As our eyes met, he began thrusting, using long and strong strokes. He didn't go fast, instead letting both of us savor the sensations. Letting it build.

Grow.

I raised my arms, one curling around him, and glanced over to see the time. Five in the morning.

God. This felt good.

He'd just gotten in? I wondered what he'd done last night, but also didn't want to know quite yet.

He cursed under his breath, grabbed my legs, and moved farther under me to get a deeper angle. He looked down, holding my gaze as he powered into me, quickening his pace.

My mouth watered. The pressure rose. I felt it pooling, but I didn't want to come this fast. Not yet. Not when I could see Mason was going to hold off and make me come more than once. He'd keep thrusting through my climax. Sometimes I loved that. Sometimes it drove me crazy. He was relentless, but I could see there was something more in him. Something dark. Hungry. A torment that was different from the way he'd been looking at me this last week.

I smoothed a hand over his forehead, traced his eyes, his cheek, his very square jawline. Up over his mouth, where he opened and sucked me in.

My heart sped up. He felt so good. Pushing in and holding. He rotated his hips.

I grunted. "Mase." I couldn't say more. I gritted my teeth, still trying to stave off my release, but he pushed back inside on another deep stroke. One hand went to my clit. He rubbed in long, circular motions.

We kept moving together.

I was losing track of time. My eyelids lowered.

I could do this all day. Feel this pleasure. It was intoxicating.

Was it normal? To feel like this with him? I hungered for him as much as I had in high school. I needed him even more. There were times I was exasperated with him, but this primal desperation for him that I felt inside of me, that never went away. It only increased over the years.

He cursed, arching more over me, and his hips began slamming into me.

My breath shortened. *Jesus.*

The pressure exploded. I gasped, grabbing for his wrist, and squeezing as I clenched around him. My climax ripped through me, the waves spreading all over, and I just lay there a moment as my entire body felt like a volcano had gone off inside of me.

When I came back down, my pulse steadying, Mason was still fucking me. I moved my hips with him, but he pinned me down, growling. "No." He watched where he was sliding in and out of me, his fingers rubbing my clit.

I reached for his hand, wanting to pull him off me, but he put both my wrists together. Pinning them against the bed with one hand, he stretched himself over me. One hand continued to rub my clit, and his hips powered into me. Hard.

Brutal.

His eyes turned, meeting mine. I saw the need in him. He was angry. Something had happened. It had brought out the anguish he'd buried so deep inside. It had come to the surface, and he needed an outlet.

That was me.

He needed to dominate me. A shudder racked through me. He was going to bring me to climax over and over again—until he'd exhausted himself.

Fuck.

I relaxed my body, sinking into the bed. He released my wrists, delivering one word. "Stay." When I closed my eyes, his hand curled around my throat. He held me there instead, his thumb resting over my artery so he could feel my pulse.

I succumbed to him, surrendering. Over the next hour and a half, he brought me to four more toe-curling releases. Finally I broke down, tears sliding free. "Mason, please." I reached for his wrist and pulled his hand away from my clit. "I can't take any more." I was drained from all the sensations and emotions. He'd wreaked havoc on my body.

His eyes met mine. So stark. Hollow. He wasn't fully here. He had hidden away inside of himself, seeking solace in the pleasure between us.

I cupped his face. "Come back to me." I smoothed a thumb over his cheek again.

A primal growl rumbled from him. "You are mine."

He pulled out, moved back, and flipped me over. His hands went to my hips. His cock thrust inside, and he yanked me up against him, my back to his chest as we both kneeled upright on the bed. His hand circled my throat again. The other slid down my stomach to rub me again. He panted into my ear, "Mine to please. Mine to take. Mine to fuck. My cunt."

I tensed because *fuck him*. He was destroying me. "Mason."

His hips hit me faster.

"Mason!"

His body jerked. His hand trembled at my throat. "Sam?"

Relief washed over me. My knees shook. He'd come back to me. I spoke, my throat moving against his hand. "I can't take anymore. Fucking come, baby. The kids will be up soon."

He cursed and let go of my throat. He fanned light kisses over my neck and eased me to the bed. He guided me down gently and groaned. His hands gripped my hips and I sighed as he drove into me a few more times and finally, *fucking finally*, he released into me.

My pussy squeezed him hard. I couldn't help myself. It was a reflex. Another low rumble came from his chest as he collapsed on me.

We were both replete. Except I couldn't catch my breath.

I—*what is happening?*

I waited until we were both once again in our bodies to look over my shoulder at him.

He avoided my gaze, slipping out of me, running a hand

down my side. "Shit. I'm sorry, Sam." He peppered those soft kisses again to my shoulder. "Jesus. Did I hurt you?"

I rolled over to lie on my back and wiped my hair from my forehead. "I mean, five times. You didn't hurt me, but you drained everything out of me. Five times." I tried to glare at him, but in all honesty, I'd been waiting for this. He'd been holding so much back. He'd told me what was going on, but him *feeling* it was different. I didn't think this was all of it. I was just grateful for the start.

I ran a hand down the side of his face and let it fall to his chest. He laid beside me and raised my hand to his mouth, pressing a kiss there.

"What happened last night?" I asked.

He tensed, stilling before he let out a soft curse.

My eyebrows shot up. "That's not good."

He cast me a look, regretful, before he shook his head. "I'll tell you after we get everyone going this morning."

He swung his legs down to sit on the side of the bed. I caught his arm. "You've not slept at all?"

He didn't answer, which was the answer.

I got out of bed and rounded to his side. "You stay. *Sleep.* I'll handle everything."

He pulled me to stand between his legs. "If Maddy's not drunk, she needs to go to school. It's the consequence for staying up all night partying."

The air in my lungs left me in a whoosh. "Maddy might be drunk? She might *still* be drunk?" A ball of fury formed in my stomach. Oh, child. Child of mine.

My jaw hardened, and I turned. I needed to shower, get myself dressed, and began plotting Mom vengeance. Maddy was screwed. She was so very screwed. *Still* drunk. My child was still drunk? Never again, my sweet little girl. She was going to rue this day.

I closed my eyes, already anticipating the look in her eyes when she saw me coming.

Mason caught my hand.

I gritted my teeth. "Mason." But I curled my fingers around his, because how could I not? "Let me go handle her."

He didn't let go.

I looked back to him, but readied myself so I would not melt inside. I loved our daughter, but she tended to be daddy's little girl. Mason went easy on her when he shouldn't. The hard-ass parenting fell to me.

His eyes were soft, and when he spoke, I realized they were soft for me. He stood and cupped my face with one of his hands. "I was going to carry you to the bathroom, run you a bath, and while you were getting dressed, I want to get you coffee and breakfast." His hands went to my waist, his lips grazing over mine.

I winced slightly, because they were a little swollen.

He withdrew. "Shit. I'm sorry." He lifted a hand to touch my mouth.

I caught it, kissing it instead. "No. God, five climaxes, Mason. Five. You rode me until my bones melted into the mattress, but fuck. As a way to wake up, I'm not complaining."

I still saw regret in his eyes. I pulled away, shaking my head. "Stop it. You're the one that needs to sleep. Get to it. Don't worry about Maddy. Me, her, and her hangover. The three of us are going to have *fun* this morning." I didn't let him argue, slipping away into the bathroom. After I'd showered, I found him back in bed.

He lay on his side, his muscled arms holding the pillow beneath his head. The sheet had slipped down so I got a good view of his muscular back, the angles and cuts of his lean hips, and a tantalizing tease of the beginning of his ass.

God, I loved him. I loved all of him. My man who shouldered so much of our world.

But this time, I would shoulder some of the weight for him, starting with our seventeen-year-old daughter. I got dressed and grabbed my phone, and the first text stopped me in my tracks.

Heather: Zeke Allen spent the night in the hospital because he's got a freaking knife wound to the stomach. Wtf?? You wanted us to keep his wife busy last night. Tell me we did not have something to do with this.

32

MADDY

I was in a twisted version of Groundhog's Day. I *kept* messing up.

Me: I messed up SO BAD last night.

I know I'm supposed to leave you alone for another day, but Max. MAX! I'm drowning here.

I'm hungover. I'm not really drowning. I did it to myself, but you weren't there. Where were you?

Obviously I know where you were. But still, where *were* you? You're my conscience. I can't handle this silence. I've already gotten into so much trouble. If you'd been talking to me, I would've stayed home and hung out with you. Mom and Dad would've been fine with me having you over, and you wouldn't have wanted to go, so I never would've gone. That makes this your fault in my head. I need you.

It's not your fault. Obviously it's mine.

Why are you not answering me?

Oh. Wait. I forgot to hit send.

Send.

Me: OH. LOLOL

Max: What
Max: The
Max: *FUCK?*
Me: I think I'm still drunk.

33

MASON

I had to look again, but the reports weren't wrong. My father's business was doing just fine. Fuck. Fuck. *Fuck!* That meant he was fed a bunch of bullshit. He killed himself because of some bullshit fucking lie. I was inclined to believe Kai Bennett, which meant we had an enemy with no face and no name, and right now, I had no idea the reason for why this all happened.

I sent a text to my private investigator.

Me: I need you to pivot in whatever you're finding or not finding on Kai Bennett. He came to me himself, told me he's not trying to force his way into this company. I'm inclined to believe him.

Lael: What the hell???? You have time for a call?

Me: No. Send whatever you do or don't have. I don't want our time wasted looking one way when we should be looking somewhere else. My dad believed that Kai Bennett was coming after him. We need to find out why he believed that.

Lael: That means I'll need to investigate your father.

Me: Do it.

Lael: Okay. I'll send one of my colleagues with the Bennett file. What I do have, I only trust that it'll get to you in person. I'll change my focus.

Lael: Are you okay? I've seen Kai Bennett in person. He's... Just, are you okay?

Me: I'm fine. I'll be better when I know who killed my dad.

Lael: Got it. On it.

My phone buzzed a second later. It was the main lobby receptionist.

"A Zeke Allen is here to see you," she said when I answered. "He does not have an appointment, but he's insisting that you'll see him. Should I send him up?"

I wasn't even surprised. That's what I would've done in his position. "Send him up."

"Yes, Mr. Kade."

Mr. Kade. I'd been called that a few times, mostly by Maddy's friends. News reporters used my first name. Coaches called me Kade or Mason. Mr. Kade, though, that was my father.

I swallowed tightly at the memories.

Logan: Heads up, Taylor and I talked. It feels too chaotic for me to leave, so I'm staying. She postponed our flight. Sammy's going to stay here since he's attached to David's hip. Taylor's due a ton of vacation, so she's going to take it early, extend it hopefully to when she's due, and then she can switch to maternity leave. Hoping we'll have things figured out by then on the home front.

Me: What about your firm?

Logan: I booted some of my cases to associates. Everything else I can do here. Just feels right staying.

Me: Thanks, brother.

Logan: Don't need to thank me. You've done it for me. Love you, brother.

Channing: We need to have a serious talk. It's getting hard to cover your back when I'm getting questions from all over and I don't know what to say. Why are you setting up a fight night with the Red Demons's Frisco charter? Do you know anything about Zeke Allen suffering a knife wound to the gut and looking like he was tortured? Samantha asked Heather to keep Zeke's wife out with them last night. Ava's a sweet girl, but she's not someone Sam usually seeks out. Optics don't look good. What the fuck are you doing?

Channing: I don't think I need to remind you that Allen is close to Nate's brother-in-law, whose bloodline is connected to my sister's husband. Are you following the dots here? That's a lot of family connections there. You need to loop me in on what's going on.

Channing: I found your security guards. They were knocked out and tied up, left behind the west wall of Kade Enterprises. All were fine when we dropped them off at the hospital.

Channing: Fucking call me back, Mason.

There was a slight knock on the door, and I looked up as it opened. So many things depended on the man coming to see me in person.

I motioned to him. "Come in."

He moved slowly, one arm held across his stomach. He was pale, but his shoulders were set with determination. I studied him, and the previous times I'd seen him came to mind. He'd written letters to me since he began seventh grade. Only later did I attach those letters to a name, to a face, to someone who knew other people in my life. The letters became messages on my social media. There'd been nothing crazy or worrisome in them, just contact from a fan who declared his appreciation for my endeavors. He wasn't a stalker until he started dropping by the house.

He followed Samantha and me around town a few times.

He'd been at the grocery store, the coffee shop, at a table all alone at Manny's. Always there. Always watching.

He'd approached my father.

He'd approached Analise.

When he approached Maddy, I had enough. We got an order of protection against him so he'd stay away from my immediate family. Other people in our lives knew him, but they didn't know about those visits. That was kept to ourselves.

He always had an odd look in his eyes when I saw him in person, as if he wasn't really seeing me in front of him—more like a poster that had come to life. That look was gone today. He could see me.

"You probably should've stayed in the hospital another day," I noted.

He laughed, which ended in a wince as he lowered himself into the chair across from my desk. "Right. Well, Logan's avocado-related accidental self-stabbing story wasn't holding up. The longer I stayed, the more questions I got. A few of the nurses weren't buying how it happened when we were drunk, on a golf course, and why the fuck would we be trying to cut open an avocado? I had to check out. Out of sight, out of mind. That sort of thing."

"Logan said the story was so preposterous that it would have to be true."

He laughed, and immediately paled. "Oh. I regret that." He coughed, readjusted himself again. "So, uh, you and your brother tortured me. I want to know why. Was it just for information?"

I frowned. "Do you not remember?"

He grimaced, his face going pale. "No, I do. Though I wish I didn't. I know you."

I gritted my teeth. He didn't fucking know me.

Zeke dropped his gaze. "I know you don't want me to know

you. You probably think that I don't know you. I get that in the past I've crossed a line, but..." His eyes lifted to mine. "None of those times were malicious."

"You followed me and Sam around town."

"I happened to be in a few of the same places at the same time."

"Multiple times," I bit out.

"Yeah. I mean, what do you want me to say? You're my idol." His eyes fell. "Were my idol."

"My father? What's your excuse with approaching him?"

"I wanted to introduce myself. Before his death, we were in similar social groups here. The elite business world of Fallen Crest isn't that big."

"Analise?"

"Ah..." He frowned, his head folding down. "You won't believe me, but I only approached her once and it was because she looked upset. She was walking on the sidewalk. I just wanted to make sure she'd be okay."

He had a goddamn excuse for every time.

Last one. Worst one. "My daughter?"

He coughed, tugging at his shirt. "Would you believe me if I said—"

"No," I barked. "One time. I would believe you if it happened one fucking time. Not multiple times. Not with the letters. Not with the private messages. No one in your little social group knows the extent of it. They're all telling me you're safe. You're cool. We can trust you." I shot forward in my seat. "No, I goddamn can't. You approached my kid—"

"She—there were some guys. It looked like they were messing with her—"

"—in fucking San Diego! You approached her in another city. You weren't there by coincidence. You looked for her. You found her. You approached her. I want nothing to do with you.

Nothing. But after last night, we have a problem because it seems like my brother cares about you. Go fucking figure on that one."

He fell quiet until he mumbled, "Guessing the torture had more to do with this than the hacking, huh?"

I stared at him. It was all I could do in this moment because all my grief, all my anger, all my frustration, everything that had been accumulating over the last week, all of it had a target. He was sitting in front of me, but fuck him very much. I couldn't do what I wanted to do with him because Logan cared about the guy.

I shook my head, needing to let some of my anger go. A small trickle of it. "I'm a celebrity. I get that. Because of what I earned playing a game I loved, a lot of people think that makes me theirs. Theirs to inspect. Theirs to tear apart. Theirs to objectify, hate, project all their own shit onto. It comes with the territory, and yes, stalkers happen. But you are *here*. You are local. You are connected inside my circle, and you are fucking weird. I didn't know you. I didn't want to know you, and after you approached my daughter, I loathed you. We tortured you because you were hacking into Kai Bennett's family's accounts, and you brought that motherfucker to my front door." I leaned forward again, my eyes hard. "*Why?*"

He opened his mouth but then shrugged, leaning back in his seat.

"I know I didn't read you in on my situation. I can't believe the few who knew would've done that." I asked a different question. "How did you know to look into Kai Bennett?"

He frowned, looking away. "I got a text alert."

"You got a text alert? What does that mean?"

He shifted in his seat, perspiration coming to his forehead. Tugging at his shirt collar, he coughed. "I—oh fuck. You can't say anything..."

"I'm not promising you shit. You stalked my family."

"I know. I know." He held up a hand. "I'm—things are starting to look different to me since you and your brother strung me up. But look, Channing sent a text to the Brenster—"

This fucker could somehow read text messages from Channing to his sister.

"The Brenster?" I asked.

"Bren. Channing's sister." He sighed. "I call her the Brenster since she said I couldn't call her Brentress—like the Huntress. Bren's kick ass. It's, like, literally what she does for a living. She's more badass than her brother—"

I growled.

He changed his tone. "Right. What was I saying? Text alert. Yeah. The Chanster texted the Brenster and asked if she'd heard anything about Kai Bennett operating in the area, specifically Fallen Crest. I thought it was weird. Bren said she didn't know anything. When she offered to look into it, the Chanster shut her down right away. That set off my alarms too, so I did some digging. And..." He trailed off, but after a bit he focused on me. "Once I started digging, I couldn't stop. Are you aware of who they are?"

"Yes," I said dryly. "So you didn't know about their connection to me?"

He shook his head. "No. I about pissed myself when I woke up and saw you standing there. I can't figure out the connection. Channing asked about Kai Bennett. That made me start looking into him. He visited you, told you to get me to stop? That sent you and your brother to me, but I'm not understanding how Kai Bennett is connected..." He trailed off. His eyes got wide. Bright. He shoved up in chair and cursed right away. "Fuck. That hurts. But—" his gaze latched onto me. "Did Kai Bennett have anything to do with your dad's death? That's the only..." He trailed off again, seeing my face.

He gulped. "You're not happy."

"What is wrong with you?"

He blinked. "What?"

"You look excited just now. Like you're *thrilled*. You're not comprehending the magnitude of this situation."

Zeke gulped again. His hands curled around the chair's armrests. "Uh..."

He had no clue. No goddamn clue. I snapped, exploding out of my seat. With one arm, I swept everything off my desk, moving the computer to the edge. All the papers went flying, the stapler Maddy had played with, my phone, paper clips. And I didn't see any of it.

All I saw was red.

Zeke jumped up, backing away from me. "Hey, man—"

"You have no fucking idea what you're messing with!" I thundered. "They're *the mafia*."

Zeke's eyes widened. He took another step, missed the floor, and crumpled.

I didn't care to help him, not one fucking bit. I stood over him. "Stop fucking hacking into Kai Bennett and his family. He came to me, dipshit. If he'd gone to you, *you'd already be dead!*" I bellowed.

Zeke winced, making no attempt to stand up again.

"The connection is me, dumbass. Someone told my father a lie, and that lie had to do with Kai Bennett. He came to me within a day of you hacking into his family's business. One fucking day, Allen. He told me flat-out that if you'd gotten into his account or his wife's, you'd have a bullet in your forehead."

Zeke began breathing hard, raking a hand over his face. He was visibly shaken, and his eyes took on an unfocused glaze. He wasn't here in this room with me anymore. I didn't know where the fuck he was, or what kind of thoughts were going through his mind.

I stepped away, giving him some space. He didn't seem to notice.

"You have to stop hacking."

He looked my way, his eyes flaring. "Like fuck I'm stopping." He climbed to his feet, a storm on his face. "Fuck you, Kade. Hacking is—I hack. I've done it all my life. No one's caught me—"

"Until now."

He stopped, blinking, as my words hit him. "Well, yeah. I'll just be smarter."

I shook my head, knowing a lost cause when I heard one. "You'll stop looking into Kai Bennett and his family—"

"I'll be smarter."

I'd planned to follow that up with a threat, but the way he said those words—so earnest, so determined—I swallowed it instead. He was going to do it anyway. I pointed to the door. "Get the fuck out." Once he got himself there and opened it, I added, "When he kills you, I've had my funeral quota. I'm not going to another. And if you violate my goddamn privacy, my family's privacy, my kids, my brother, his family, anyone I love, I'll come back for you. I won't be bringing my brother."

He stared at me, long and hard. His jaw clenched. A myriad of expressions crossed his face, but none of them were good.

He was pissed. How dare I take away his passion. That's what he was thinking. I didn't know him. I didn't know how good he was. Maybe I didn't, but I did know how easily it'd been for Kai Bennett to get between my daughter and myself.

That shook me.

Once he was gone, I made a few calls. Security was told to make sure Zeke Allen was escorted off the premises and put on the banned list.

Next I called Channing Monroe.

"Are we going for a beer tonight?" he said in greeting. "I figure I'll need a few to have the conversation I'm owed."

"Logan and I needed to blow off steam," I told him, getting the business talk done first. "I reached out to the Red Demons thinking they could help with that. I was looking at a potential war against an adversary in a world that I knew nothing about, and I thought I might need more than one alliance. I don't believe I'll need that anymore, because Kai Bennett himself showed up. I'm not sorry that I made the call to reach out to the Red Demons. I can't. It was for my family. They have a bigger footstep in the same world that also has Kai Bennett, bigger than yours. But I am sorry that in making that decision, I needed to cut you out. I hope you can understand my reasoning, but I'll understand if you can't.

"Incidentally, Kai Bennett is also the reason I had you check for my security guards at my place. His men disposed of them to ensure he and I could have a private conversation, and by private I mean that he got between Maddy's vehicle and mine, and went on a walk with me and eight of his own men patrolling with their guns.

"The topic of that conversation was that he had nothing to do with my father's death. I've looked into things a bit more since then, and I'm inclined to believe him."

"Mason."

"I'm not done." I was absolutely done giving Zeke Allen any leeway. "Check your phone because Zeke Allen just informed me he picked up a text you sent your sister, one where you asked her about Kai Bennett. You do what you want with that information."

Channing was quiet for a long moment. "What *the fuck* are you talking about?"

Channing was going to filet Allen alive, and if he didn't, his sister would. Despite him giving her some cute nickname, people did not mess with Channing's sister. Zeke knew this. He dug his own grave.

He spoke slowly as he was still processing all that I said, "Shit, Mason. When you unload, you really unload."

"We can have that beer, but I'm figuring you got things to do now?"

"It seems I do. I'll reach out later."

The kid wasn't going to stop hacking.

He'd face the consequences.

34

MADDY

I was leaving school when I heard the loud bass blaring from Beltraine's car in the lot. As was typical, a group of people had congregated around his vehicle—or now vehicles because he and Axel and Steele all parked together. They were in the back of the lot, and no one else parked there or ventured over unless they were invited.

"Hey, Maddy." A girl approached me, sounding out of breath as she adjusted her backpack, smiling widely.

She was a little shorter than me, curvy with fitted high-waisted jeans. They were the trendy kind that faded at the hem and were ripped over the knees. She had glossy black hair, in tight curls. Dark eyes. Eyelashes even I could admire, so either she knew what she was doing with makeup or they were fake. She wore white sneakers and a white V-neck tee that showed off her black bra underneath, and she'd layered a black and white flannel over the top.

I knew her. We had a couple classes together. She'd been trying to befriend me. Her efforts hadn't been very fruitful.

"Lucia."

She preened. "You can just call me Luce. That's cool. I mean, we're already on nicknames."

"Everyone calls me Maddy."

She stopped laughing. "Oh. I assumed it was short for Madison."

"It's not." I moved forward, a bout of impatience swirling through me.

I used to have friends. In Boston. In San Diego. I didn't know what was wrong with me now. I used to want to have friends. They were fun to laugh with, gossip with, do girl things like sleepovers or manicures. I'd gotten my ears pierced with my best friend from Boston. I frowned, thinking of her now, as we hadn't done very well keeping in touch when I moved to San Diego. Eventually, my Boston friends stopped making an effort.

I hadn't even tried keeping up with my San Diego friends.

I suppose a part of me assumed they'd be the same as my Boston friends. Why make an effort when they'd stop talking to me too? Since coming to Fallen Crest, I'd focused on Max, but he chose not to go to this school. He went to Public.

Stevie Broudou swept past us, her head down, hugging her bag to her chest. I watched to see which vehicle she'd get into.

Lucia stopped with me. "She's new, too. Do you know her?"

"No." But that wasn't totally true. Stevie was connected to people who were connected to my parents. I knew my mom had a mission to befriend Stevie's uncle and his wife. My mom had asked a few times what I thought of Stevie, and she'd brought up inviting her to the house. She wanted us to be friends. That was obvious.

I rolled my eyes. The person in charge of forming that friendship wasn't me. Stevie seemed to be even more antisocial than I did. She talked to no one, hung out with no one.

"She only hangs out with the moody group," Lucia said, whining.

I frowned at her. Guess I was wrong about Stevie. "Who?"

"You know." She gestured to the car Stevie approached.

The door opened and a guy stepped out. Stevie ducked into the backseat. That must be the moody group—the guy was lean, tattooed, and pierced.

"Caleb Cieran and his friends."

I heard the wistfulness in Lucia's voice. Beltraine, Axel, and Steele were popular, but Caleb Cieran and his group were maybe just as much. Caleb was seriously hot. So was his best friend, Josh—I didn't know his last name. There were a few others in the group too, and I'd heard they "weren't privileged" like most other students here. I had no clue what that meant. They had less money than the rest? Or they didn't make a big deal of how much money their families had?

"Who is *that*?" Lucia drew in a sharp breath.

I pulled my gaze away from Cieran's car, and immediately, everything in my world was covered in a nice warm blanket. The cloudy, overcast sky moved apart to let the sun shine through as Max pulled up to park in front of me in his truck.

Those guys had nothing on Max. No one was even in his stratosphere.

Max with his golden tan skin, dark blond and messily rumpled hair, dark blue eyes that turned gray when he was either mad or something else, and that deliciously square jaw. He was shorter than me until last summer. That's when he shot past me, now standing at six four. He'd also spent the summer honing his physique in the gym. Max never cared about his looks. He always had them. But his pretty-boy face had also transformed into something more ruggedly handsome. Delicious fucking lips. His round cheeks were now chiseled, and his dad let him start getting tattoos. He told me he was keeping those to a minimum. He didn't want to go overboard like his dad, whose body was almost covered in tattoos.

He leaned over and pushed open his passenger door. He jerked his chin to me. "Get in."

I moved forward, reaching for the door and paused to look at him. His jeans were the real kind of faded, not like Lucia's, and all the rips in them were from being worn. They looked good on him. He was also wearing a Fallen Crest Public shirt. It fit nicely over his chest and stomach, and I could see him draw in a breath, waiting for me.

"Are you getting in or not?"

My smile only widened. He was annoyed, but I caught the flash of affection too. He'd so totally missed me.

And he was checking me out. I moved slowly, drawing this out as I climbed up and settled in, letting him get a view of my bra and stomach.

He drew in some air. "Fuck's sakes, Mads."

I chuckled, handing him my bag.

He tossed it in the backseat as I closed the door.

Lucia still stood on the sidewalk, her jaw on the floor.

I flashed her a grin.

"Hey, man."

What? I turned at the sound of a voice.

I had missed it, but as I was taking my time getting in Max's truck, Caleb Cieran had gotten out of his and walked over to stand on the other side of Max's door.

I frowned, not sure how I felt about this. Max was mine. He didn't need to know people. Then again, everyone loved Max. If you knew him, you loved him. The universe deemed it a rule when Max was born. I hadn't met someone who didn't think Max hung the moon.

"What's up?" Max asked.

Cieran looked over to me.

I glared at him.

He started laughing. "Your girl's not happy."

Max frowned at me, but he didn't respond. "What's going on?"

"There's a party out on Bombshell this Friday."

"That abandoned building?"

"Yeah. Wanted to see if you're in." He wagged his eyebrows up and down. "I know you're a killer in that arena. You want in?"

Max's eyebrows pinched together. "Are you setting it up?"

I had no idea what they were talking about. As if Max could sense my frustration, he cut me a look. We'd discuss this once we had some privacy.

"Nah. It's sanctioned by the same people who organize the other fighting ring."

"Why the different location?"

Cieran shrugged, propping his arm on Max's door. "Who knows? But it works out for you, doesn't it? Word's out that you got banned from the last place."

A fighting ring.

The Red Demons.

This kid was asking Max if he wanted to fight, and I was officially pissed off. Max had shit out a Hulk-sized dump because he went to the fighting ring last Friday and lost his marbles. Now Cieran was asking if he wanted to fight?

As if sensing my anger, Max reached over. His hand went to my leg.

My hand covered his, and I began digging my nails in. I wanted to break skin, motherfucker.

He hissed, glaring at me before extracting his hand. Or he tried because I wouldn't let him. I kept digging in.

"Ouch! Fuck, Maddy." He pulled his hand away.

Cieran frowned.

"You know what?" Max flashed Cieran a hard smile. "When's the party again?"

"This Friday." Cieran's smile was wide and filled with sinister promise.

I didn't like him. I looked over at his car where Stevie was pressed in the backseat between another guy and a girl. I also decided she was too good for this guy. Too good to be his friend. Too good for anything else.

I wasn't going to allow it.

Max let out a soft sigh and shook his head. "Sounds good. Let me know the details and rules. I'll be there."

"Yeah?" Cieran's eyebrows shot up. He stepped back from the truck and held up a fist. "Right on. This will be awesome."

Max's mouth pressed in a firm line, but he hit Cieran's fist with one of his own. As the guy strolled back over to his car and got in, I seethed.

Max turned to me. "Do—" *Knock! Knock!*

Max stopped talking as someone pounded on my window.

This time it was Beltraine. I rolled it down. Axel and Steele had also come over. They were looking in the direction Cieran had driven.

Traine lifted his chin up. "What was that about?"

"Nothing." Max's tone was cool.

He didn't like these guys. Well, I didn't like Cieran and his group. So there.

I smiled. "Max just got invited to fight again, except this time it's at a different location. And guess what? He's going to do it. This will be so much fun." I kept my face blank, looking back at Max.

He rolled his eyes, reaching forward and starting his engine. "Can you be more dramatic?"

"Yes."

He shook his head.

Steele stepped closer to the truck. "You're fighting?" His words were for Max.

"I said I would." Max's eyebrows drew together. He didn't know Steele.

Steele stepped back, sharing a look with Traine and Axel.

Max looked at me, and I shrugged. "I'm not on their tele-pathic mind wave. You, yes. Them, no."

He closed his eyes, his jaw going rigid. "Do you have to say everything you think?"

"No, and I don't. There's a lot you have no idea I think about."

Example number one, I was back to being certain I was a sociopath. Or I had sociopathic tendencies. I didn't plan enough to be a psychopath. And I functioned a little more normally than a psychopath. I wasn't acting. I just didn't have fear or emotions about a lot of people.

I turned back to Traine. "We done here? Monroe and I need to go fight, and afterward, I'm going to climb on his lap. The longer you take, the less likely I'll get the happy ending I'm hoping for."

The guys started laughing.

"*Fuck*, Maddy," came Max's voice behind me.

Exactly.

I gave Traine a meaningful look, and still laughing, he held his hands up, taking a dramatic step away. "Not holding you back. Let's catch up later, Kade. Yeah?"

I rolled my window back up, and Max drove away.

My phone buzzed.

Traine: Your car is still here.

Me: I'll get it later.

Traine: Steele's sister is coming to hang out this weekend. He wants to know if you want to meet her. She's cool.

Unknown Number: I can ask her myself. You don't have to be our spokesperson for everything.

Oh. This was a group chat. Scrolling up, I confirmed it.

Traine was there. Me. I changed the unknown number to Steele. There were two other numbers.

Me: Who else is in here?

Unknown: Me! Axel.

Me: Got you. Who's the other one?

Traine: It's Aurelia.

I scrolled back up and removed her from the group chat.

Axel: LOLOLOLOLOLOLOL

Traine: Uh...

Me: It's me or her. I'm not going to deal with her in a text chat too. School and the few times I hang out with you guys is more than enough.

Traine: We'll make a new chat with her.

Axel: Got a feeling this one will be way more interesting.

Me: I don't sext.

Axel: Maybe not.

Steele: Gross, dude.

Traine: Uh...

Axel: Haha, Traine. Steele, wtf?

I was done with this conversation and wanted to get back to Max.

Me: More than likely I'll be grounded again because I'm going to sneak out for that fight. So...probably no (on the hangout with Steele's sister).

Traine: Haha. Okay. Hope you didn't get into too much trouble? We didn't catch up.

Me: The sentencing hasn't happened. My parents were busy this morning.

Traine: Busy... *busy* busy? ** suggestive wink emoji **

Steele: Seriously? Those are her *parents*.

Axel: Her mom's extra hot. You don't got eyes, dude? We might be enjoying Maddy's personality, but I mean, come on. She looks like her mom. I see no problem here.

Steele: STOP TALKING ABOUT HER PARENTS

Traine: Yeah, dude. Respect. Say it to her face.

I snorted, grinning.

Axel: Um. Okay. I'm confused about what's going on here.

Traine: Steele, put your phone away.

Traine: No clue what's up his ass, but let's hang out. If you're too grounded to sneak out, find us for lunch. You're cool people, Kade.

Axel: And easy to look at too. Hot. **meant in a respectful but truthful way, because well... you are. Hot. And I'm a dude. And a teenager.** Hottie.

I snorted again. Max kept looking my way, but I ignored him. Once we got to wherever he was taking us for our talk, he'd get my attention.

Me: Meant to ask today, did you guys get in trouble?

Axel: You mean when your dad and uncle crashed our party and called all of our parents? Because that awesome ride was not one I want to find myself on again.

Axel: Kidding. I'm fine. My dad was annoyed more than anything. None of us got in trouble. Some of the others did. Some of the girls. And a few of the other guys, but the three of us were fine.

Traine: One of the benefits of having parentals who don't give a shit.

Me: What about Steele?

They didn't answer so I put my phone away, sliding it into my pocket as Max parked. I guess we were here, wherever here was.

My phone buzzed, but I ignored it. "Where are we?"

It was a clearing off the road. He opened his door and got out. "Come on. The river's not far. We can have our fight and then go swimming."

I scrambled out the door. I didn't know what I was more excited about.

Fighting or skinny-dipping.

35

MASON

We were at a standstill.
I didn't like it.

Two weeks passed, and my irritation had been growing steadily. It was quiet, too quiet. So quiet that Logan decided to return to Boston with Sammy. If something happened here, he'd be back. In the meantime, I went over the folder my PI got to me. Bennett was right. It was thin, extremely thin, and there was nothing in there that gave me a better feel on him. It was everything I already knew, except for how much he loathed any press talking about his family. He went to extreme lengths to keep his name out of the media.

There was nothing to connect Kai Bennett with a hostile takeover. Instead, she found meetings, photos, and calls going back and forth between Phillip Moreaux and a handful of other Kade Enterprises shareholders.

She kept sending more information on other shareholders daily.

I looked into how many shares Avoy had, remembering what Maddy had mentioned his daughter was saying. Avoy had the least amount of the shares. If he was running his mouth, it was just that. He was running his mouth. I asked my PI to look into him as well. But with the rest, the math made sense. If someone was in any place to push for a majority, it would be Moreaux. If each of those shareholders sold to Moreaux, he'd be close—except he didn't know that Nate also had a stake in the company. When one of the previous shareholders wanted out, we'd gotten there first. It'd been a calculated move early on in case of this exact scenario.

A decision was made to look closer into Moreaux, see if he was going to make a move and when that might happen. And keep trying to figure out who told my father that Kai Bennett was coming after him.

Until then, life went on. It just felt like it was moving at a fucking snail's pace.

I handled Kade Enterprises. Sam returned to consulting and mentored her clients. Maddy was still grounded. Sam had rained down with Thor's hammer. And Maddy seemed to be making an effort to return to being the normal teenager we'd known before losing my father.

Either that or she was getting smarter about sneaking out. Her blasé attitude seemed to be thawing. She'd asked to go to a friend's house to do homework a few times. She'd been allowed to hang out there last weekend as well. If it had to do with school, or if Max was with her, we let her go. I knew Sam was curious about her friends, but Maddy flat-out told Sam it was too early for the friend inquisition. She said she wasn't sure if she even liked the girl—apparently there was a sister who visited on the weekends? I wasn't sure if I got all the correct information—but she did bring over a girl named Lucia and introduced her to Sam.

These flashes of the old Maddy warmed her old pop's heart, and when she asked if we'd come to the football game this weekend, that was an easy yes.

I loved my kids. I'd move heaven and hell for them. A high school football game? Not a problem.

"Maddy's at her friend's again," Sam announced, coming down the stairs. "She's going to meet us at the game." She kept talking, but sorry, wife, I was gone.

With a light sweater that fell past her waist a little, she wore leggings and sneakers.

She looked fucking edible.

She went over to pick up her purse, still talking, and I knew what she was going to do. She didn't enjoy carrying her purse around, and our kids were old enough that she didn't need it as much, so she often downsized. Her wallet, phone, and lipstick were pulled out. She handed the wallet to me, because my jean pockets were bigger. Her lipstick went into her front pocket, and she'd keep her phone on her as well, though she'd pull it out within a few seconds to check for texts from the kids. The purse went back on the counter.

She finally looked at me, her eyes widening on my shirt before she met my gaze. They widened even more because there was no doubt she was able to read how much I wanted to fuck her. Right now. Right here. Up against the wall. And I'd do it fucking ruthlessly.

She shivered, her eyes darkening. "We don't have time."

I grunted. "I'm thinking we do."

She groaned. "Mason."

Fuck the game. I stalked toward her. "We got time. Trust me." Moving in behind her, I fitted myself to her back, and smoothed a hand down her front, sliding slowly, enjoying how her body was already trembling, already getting ready for me. Going to her clit, I rubbed her.

Her chest lifted up in a ragged breath, and she rested her head against my shoulder.

I pressed a hand to her chin so I could have her mouth. As

soon as I did, I slid my hand further. Her whole body surged up in my arms.

God, I loved that. She was so fucking responsive. My finger slid inside, another joined. As I worked her over, my fingers went deep and began rubbing, I kept kissing her. *Fuck.* I groaned, needing more. Just more.

I made quick work here because I hadn't lied. I wanted to get my dick wet. Soon Sam gripped my arm, her nails sinking in. I fucking loved when she did that. If she broke skin, I loved the pain. My woman did that. God, yes. Just thinking about that, my dick ached, pushing against my jeans.

"Mason," Sam gasped, tearing her mouth away.

I growled. I wanted to taste her when I got her off. My hand left her clit. I was going to catch her face and turn it back to me, but she caught my hand and shoved it back to her clit. Okay then. I went back to rubbing, a third finger thrusting in, and she almost levitated in my arms. Her knees came up, and I caught her, lifting her and carrying her to the nearest wall. I pushed her up against it, my fingers still sliding inside of her. She cried out as her release flooded her. Her hands flattened against the wall, holding her weight. She was panting, her head turned sideways to me.

Fuck. I liked that look on her face. Dazed. Blitzed. She gave me a sloppy grin, which made my dick throb even harder.

She moaned, as her climax continued to roll through her.

"Love you," she said, breathless.

I was stupid gone over this woman.

I leaned in and nipped at her bottom lip, my lips grazing hers as I said back, "So fucking much."

She moaned all over again, her eyes darkening.

When her legs were able to hold her again, I rolled her leggings down, shoving them and her thong out of the way. Unzipping myself, I pulled my dick out and rubbed it against her ass.

"Mason," she warned, her eyes dark and heavy as she watched me.

I smirked. "Don't worry, but fuck, Sam. I miss your ass."

Her eyes closed, and I had to kiss her again. I tipped her hips back and ran my cock through her folds, *fuuuuuuuuuuck.* I'd just meant to rub against her entrance, but her slickness sucked me in.

Goddamn.

I loved this woman. I loved everything about her.

My woman.

I shoved all the way in, both of us groaning. She was already primed for me, and I went fast and hard. I drove into her with powerful strokes, and it wasn't long until she cried out again, another release was building.

I loved being able to bring her back up, and up, and up again.

I pounded in, gritting my teeth because she felt so good. She always did, but I held off, panting. Seeing her hands turn into fists and the way she clenched her jaw, I cursed. "Come."

She was fighting it.

I leaned in and whispered, "I want to feel you quake around my dick, baby. I need your pussy to squeeze me hard and hold me in that cement fucking grip you got in your cunt because I love it when you punish me. Do it. Come for me again." Her body was rigid and shaking. I slid my hand over her hip, pausing over her stomach before sliding down. Once I made contact with her nub, she cursed and her walls clamped down on my dick. It was heaven on this earth. I swore once and released into her.

"Ah!" she screamed, her head slammed back to my shoulder. I wrapped my arm around her waist and held her in place. We were both shaking, the waves still rocking through us. I recovered a little faster and panted, just holding her until her body stopped jerking.

I moved my hand over hers, rubbing my butterfly tattoo over hers.

"Fucking, fuck, fuck. Mason. Fuck." She laughed softly.

I was pumped, my body primed.

I could take on the world right now.

When I set her back down, easing her down, her knees buckled.

I swooped in to catch her, but she shoved me off. "I got this."

I laughed, but I didn't step back. I stayed right there, my chest pressed against her back. "Don't get pissed that I'm *thorough*."

She rolled her eyes, trying to pull up her leggings, but her body was still trembling. She had to let go of the leggings to grab the counter beside her.

I *tsk*ed her and pulled her to rest against my chest. Pulling my shirt off, I used it to clean both of us up. Tossing it to the floor, I made a mental note to grab it when we got back or one of the dogs would tear into it. I helped to dress her, pulling up her panties and leggings. I smoothed a hand over them, feeling her lipstick in one of the pockets and running around to stroke her ass. I lingered there. I really, really loved her ass. She'd put on a little weight so she had more for me to hold on to back there.

My bulge was back, and I rubbed it against her. "God, I love when this moves."

She made a mewling sound before she shoved me back again, but she was grinning. "You're so..."

I couldn't take my eyes off her ass. Leggings were such sweet torment. I knew she could see the hunger still in me. It was always going to be there. I'd never be able to appease it, not fully. I didn't know if this was normal. But I never wanted to find out.

As long as Sam loved me, I would die before losing her.

A surge of protective and possessive need swept through

me, and I pulled her into my arms, kissing her forehead. The world could fall down around us, and I wouldn't notice if I had her in my arms and my kids close. Afterward there'd be paralyzing fear, because I'd need to make sure Maddy hadn't been the cause of it. And Nolan and Nash would probably know it was going to happen, so they'd already be by us.

My family. I grinned. We were a force of nature, all of us. Together. Separately.

Fuck anyone who tried to hurt us again.

"What are you thinking?" Sam tipped her head back, her eyebrows up.

I pressed one last kiss to her forehead. "Nothing, just thinking about us and our kids."

Her eyes widened. "Oh God. We're going to be late. I need to call Nolan and Nash. We were supposed to pick them up on the way."

I stepped back, letting her panic and run to the bathroom to make sure she was presentable. Checking my phone, I found a text that made me smile.

Nash: Some of my teammates are getting pizza before the game. Nolan's with me. We'll meet you at the game. Don't worry. We got cash to get in. Love you, Dad.

Nolan: Love you, Dad.

My family was pretty fucking great.

And I needed to grab a new shirt.

36

SAMANTHA

It'd been a long time since I'd attended an event at Fallen Crest Academy. My old school. We came in for a meeting with the administration when we enrolled Maddy and had a quick tour. They had built a brand new school, with an Olympic-sized pool and state-of-the-art facilities. A new track. A new football field. Tennis courts. A soccer field. The school resembled a small university now, and they charged for it. The place was impressive, but I missed the old school. Somewhat.

When we paid and stepped inside the football stadium, the looks and whispers began almost immediately. People pulled their phones out to take pictures. This was always what it was like going to anything football-related with Mason.

He stepped close to me, his chest brushing the back of my shoulder. "I'll grab stuff at the concessions if you want to make sure our children are alive and also not killing anyone else's children?"

I shot him a glare.

He only smiled, moving off. He looked too fucking good in the henley he grabbed on the way out of the door. Then again, Mason always looked good. He only seemed to get better looking as he aged. It wasn't fair. His broad chest. Chiseled jawline. Slim hips. Those big muscled shoulders. And those green eyes.

He was all mine.

What had he said?

Right. I needed to make sure our children hadn't killed anyone.

Maddy had let us know during our discussion about why she violated her grounding three times, that she believed she was a sociopath. At first she'd been wavering between psychopath or sociopath, but she'd watched a video on YouTube and drawn her conclusion. She was a sociopath. She promised me one night that she'd use her abilities for good. Like *Dexter*, without the sibling stuff.

I'd not watched *Dexter*, so I didn't know what she meant, and I made a note never to watch it. Though I was sure it was a lovely sitcom.

"Sam?" A woman was coming over.

She looked familiar. Brown hair past her shoulders. She was wearing a Fallen Crest Academy sweatshirt, with their new colors. White and gold. I remember Malinda telling me they'd voted to change their colors. Fallen Crest Public did theirs, and a month later, FCA was doing the same thing.

Lydia. That was her name. She used to be a good friend, until I learned she never had really been a good friend. Her and Jessica. When I dated Jeff. Shit. The memories.

I struggled not to show my surprise. She looked good. A little heavier, but we were all older. Age happened. It was biology. The extra weight looked good on her. She was almost glowing. A button was pinned to her sweatshirt. It was an FCA football player, kneeling and smiling widely.

"Hi, Lydia. Wow. Hello. How are you?"

"I'm good. Wonderful, actually." She saw I was looking at

her pin and beamed, gesturing to it. "My son's on the team. Number twelve. Patrick Heimler."

"Mom!"

Hearing Nolan's voice, I turned to find her darting my way. Her eyes were big, a little dilated, but she got like that when she was having fun. Her cheeks were red and as she hit my side, her hand caught mine. It was clammy.

"Hi, hi, hi, hi, hi, hi." She tipped her head back, an adorable impish smile on her face.

"Hey, honey." I hugged her to me before checking her temperature, just to be sure. She felt fine. I ran my hand through her hair, trying to calm it down. It was all frizzy, though Nolan never seemed to care. "Where is your brother and sister?"

She rested the side of her face against my arm, tucking into my side. "I don't know. They're here somewhere." She looked back up, rising to her tiptoes. "You don't need to worry about them," she whispered. "Worry about Dad tonight."

I frowned. She was like this sometimes. My little girl who saw things we didn't and knew things no one was supposed to. She rested against me again. I threaded my fingers through her hair.

"This is one of yours?" Lydia was smiling at her.

Nolan narrowed her eyes, tilted her head to the side, and her face went blank. She shuffled around, giving Lydia her back. "Mom. I need to show you something." She pushed me in the direction she'd just come from—where the concessions were and judging by the wave of gold and white, where the FCA people sat.

I held up a hand to Lydia. "It was nice seeing you again."

"You too!" She bobbed her head up and down, a hand in the air. "Let's catch up another time. I'd love to hear how you're doing."

"Mom!" Nolan whined, taking my hand, and switching sides to pull me along. "Let's go. Hurry."

"Uh..." I looked between her and Lydia. "Sure. Yeah."

"Homecoming!" Lydia shouted, just as we were swallowed by a group of people. As soon as we were out of sight, Nolan stopped dragging me. "Oh thank God."

"What?"

She was peering behind me, a fierce frown on her face. I looked too, not seeing anything in particular. "Honey." I stepped close to her, smoothing my hands down the sides of her face. "What was it that you needed to show me?"

"Oh. Nothing." She dropped my hand and wrapped her arms around my waist. "I just didn't want you around that woman. She's not good people."

"What? Lydia?"

Nolan shrugged. "I don't know her name, just know she's not good people. She's one of those people who say one thing, but mean something else, and the something else is always not good for you. Steer clear of her and people like her." Her body tightened, and she tipped her head back again. "Don't worry, Mom. She keeps her not-nice side hidden, but I'll teach you how to see that. You can still learn." She ripped herself away from me, running off. "Dad!"

I shook my head and checked to make sure Nolan was at her dad's side. He was heading my way with two beers and some food.

Nolan was jumping around him, poking at him. When he gave her a nod, she reached into his pocket and pulled out a bag of candy.

I scowled.

He met my gaze and smirked. *Smartass.* But I couldn't stop from grinning. He was not the disciplinarian parent. Every one of the kids knew to go to him if they wanted something. He was the softie.

Another arm moved around my waist, and I jolted before recognizing my son. He hugged me the way his twin had been moments before, scooting under my arm, watching Mason and Nolan heading our way.

"Word's out, I see," he mumbled.

I looked down. How did my eighth-grade son sound so world weary and tired. I hugged him to me. "You okay, sweetie?"

He watched as a few kids ran up to Mason, asking for autographs.

Mason indulged. He generally tried to be accommodating until we needed to find our seats for the game. He was good at drawing a boundary. He'd learned how to handle his fans long ago. The kids sometimes got tired of it, but Mason was a good dad.

Still, I'd not heard this from Nash before. I tipped his head up to look at me. "What's wrong?"

He shook his head. "Nothing."

"Nash," I warned.

He blinked and his gaze cleared. He smiled up at me, looking genuine. "I'm good, Mom."

"Will you tell me later?"

He searched my gaze, probably seeing that I wasn't going to let this go.

He sighed and nodded. "Yeah."

I held up my pinkie. "Promise?"

He snorted, but grinned. He wrapped his pinkie with mine and we shook. "Promise." He stepped aside, looking back at Mason and Nolan. One of his hands went to his hip. "It's not a big deal, Mom. Just...there's a lot of kids who are talking about him."

"What are they saying?"

He shook his head, and his usual excitement gleamed back at me. He loved football. Loved playing it.

I tugged on his Fallen Crest Academy football shirt. "How was your practice?" He'd made the junior varsity, which was early for someone in his grade. They hadn't had a game today.

"It was good." He yawned, looking around. "Oh!" His eyes rounded. "My coach wants to talk to you and Dad after the game tonight."

My eyebrows furrowed. "What'd you do?"

A ghost of a smile flashed over his face. "Mom."

I grinned back. He was like me in some ways, but if you pissed him off, he turned Mason in zero-point-two seconds. People thought he was easy going, and mostly he was. He and Nolan were good kids, but I knew my son had a vicious streak. I'd witnessed it. The other kids didn't seem wary of him so far, but it would happen. That's how it had been before. The other boys learned not to mess with Nash. It started happening as early as second grade. I'd been tense as he grew up, worried about whether I should say something or step in, because I didn't want him to hurt another kid. But no parent ever came to me about it. Then one night Nolan had whispered in my ear that I didn't need to worry about it. *"He only does something if someone is trying to mess with me or him,"* she'd said. *"And he's smart, Mom. He's better at handling bullies than Maddy is."* She had rolled her eyes. *"We both are."*

I'd been surprised, a little relieved, and then worried. Because how many bullies did they deal with? Her comment about Maddy also concerned me, until I'd discovered what she was talking about when I was called to Maddy's school. A group of girls had been trying to bully my daughter. Maddy turned the tide and ended up bullying them, or so they claimed. When the girls wouldn't say what exactly Maddy had done to them, the meeting was dismissed, but I laid down the law when I got home. Maddy spilled the details. A girl tried to cyberbully her, so Maddy had befriended a hacker who got into the girl's phone and shared all of her private messages publicly.

I'd blanched when I heard that. Another girl tossed something in Maddy's locker, and it destroyed some of her books. Maddy got even by going to that girl's house, pretending she was a friend, and hooking up a hose in the nearest bathroom. She soaked the girl's entire room.

To this day, I had no idea why that girl's parents never said anything. We should've been on the hook to pay for the damage, but Maddy laughed when I shared that concern.

"*She wouldn't dare open that window,*" she'd said. "*Once the parents are involved, she knows I can get more dirt I'll spill to her parents. She'd be so grounded she'd never see her friends until she was fifty. These kids nowadays, Mom. They aren't all saints, not like they were when you grew up.*"

"*Maddy, I'm not that old,*" I'd told her.

She'd rolled her eyes. "*Yeah. Okay. But you're so old, you can read a map that's on paper.*"

I stopped bringing up our ages after that conversation.

Nash shrugged at me now. "It's nothing. I think they want me to start dressing for the varsity games." At that moment some of his friends ran past. Nash yelled to them, giving me a rushed kiss on the cheek. "Love you, Mom. I'm going to sit with the guys. See you after!" He tore after them, and I was left with a strange wave of nostalgia.

He was so tiny. Or he should've been.

My little boy.

Now he was going to start dressing with the varsity team? I had a feeling he wasn't going to be dressing and standing on the sidelines. They wouldn't need to talk to us about that. They were going to start playing him.

My baby.

They grew up fast, too fast.

37

MASON

"Mason."

After the game, I waited on the side of the field, near an exit that was off the path of everyone else. I was staying out of the way because a crowd started to form around me whenever I left my seat. It was only because it was my first time at a varsity game. It'd die down over time, but tonight, I caught the looks on my kids's faces. They didn't want pro-athlete dad. They wanted *their* dad tonight. Sam needed to stick around and talk to David and Malinda. Nolan kept insisting her and Nash needed to go with the grandparents for the night and weekend so I made myself scarce. We were flexible. We generally let them. The only time we wouldn't was if they got in trouble, but that rarely happened with the twins.

Sam's stepbrother was heading my way as the teams filtered past. Mark had his hands stuffed in the pockets of his jeans, his shoulders hunched forward.

I moved farther to the side, ducking my head as a few of the visiting team's players seemed to notice me. A couple recognized me, cursed, and shot forward into their locker room.

I wasn't close to Mark.

It just never happened over the years, and I wasn't sure why. He'd stuck around in the area, getting his real estate license a while back. Turns out, he was good at selling houses. He'd helped us with ours. He also owned and managed a few apartments in Fallen Crest and another town south of here.

He and Cass ended their relationship, and it looked more and more like it was going to be official this time. Evidently he'd been drowning himself in alcohol, and he'd been taking home a string of one-night stands.

"You're sober?"

He stopped abruptly a few yards away. "What'd you say?"

"You heard me. I keep getting reports every night you stumble home." I shook my head. "Sam's worried about you."

"Oh." The fight left him as he rubbed his forehead, wincing. "I didn't think about that. I'll be fine. Just the usual post break-up thing. And yes, I'm sober."

The crunch of footsteps came from behind us. Mark shifted to the side, revealing a giant fucking NFL offensive lineman that I'd always thanked my stars that I personally didn't go head to head against Brett Broudou. I ran far and wide for the most part, and he liked to try to make my quarterback eat grass.

"Surprised to see you here tonight." I spoke first, holding out my hand.

He gave Mark a nod and met my hand with his as he joined us. He gestured to the guest bleachers. "Stevie asked Billie to come, so we sat over there."

That's right. His niece attended the same school as Maddy. "Billie's staying incognito?" She must've been. Brett and I both had celebrity status, but if he showed up with his wife, there was no contest. She got all the attention. People were obsessed with serial killers, and Billie's story was still a hot topic.

Brett winced, the movement twisting his giant neck. "Like I said, she wanted to be here for Stevie. All this attention will go away."

I understood what he was saying. Some of the attention his wife received wasn't positive, which wasn't anything she deserved. She seemed shy, skittish. Brett was crazy about her.

Mark snorted. "People are..." He trailed off as the Fallen Crest Academy team left the field, moving past us. The coaches were heading our way as well.

Sam had mentioned that Nash's coach wanted to talk to me, but when the varsity head coach saw me, he came right for me. "Kade." He held his hand out, looking harried, a little distracted. The team had lost by a field goal, and they shouldn't have. They were better than the other team. But it had come down to a few plays that went the other team's way.

David used to coach this team, back when we were teens. When he retired, from what I knew, the head coach position went to this guy.

I shook his hand. "Coach Ravenry. Tough game tonight."

He just grunted in response. He shook Brett's hand and Mark's. "Mark, always good to see you. Patricia wouldn't be happy with me if I didn't pass along that she's got a couple friends she'd like to introduce to you, when you're ready."

Mark's head jerked back. "Ah. Yeah. Sorry, Coach. I—well, we'll see. It's new. We were together a long time."

Coach Ravenry nodded. "There's one or two teachers here a guy would be lucky to get a shot with. When you're ready, let me know. My wife would love to host a get-together at the house. She's used to cooking to feed an entire football team, so we'd have plenty of food. She likes wine and boardgames. Her latest obsession is playing Sequence. You say the word. She's looking for an excuse to throw a party." He turned to Brett and me. "You'll both be invited, with your significant others as well."

Brett nodded. "Thanks, Coach. I'll keep it in mind."

"You do that." His focus turned to me. "Coach Billersman is wanting to talk with you, but since you're here, I thought I'd tackle this head-on right now. You got a worry if we pull your boy to dress for varsity?"

I raised my eyebrows. "Asking a JV player to dress on the side isn't all that unusual. What are you really planning for him?"

He gave me a long consideration, his eyes narrowing before he spoke. "Not going to bullshit around it. Your boy's good. Real good. We've been eyeing him since he started, but he's in eighth grade. If I start playing your boy on varsity, other parents are going to have a say."

I nodded. Nash would be taking playing time a senior wanted, or a junior, or sophomore, or fuck, even a freshman. I got it. Politics of high school football unfolded off the field more than on it and often involved parents, not the kids.

More players were leaving the field. Most continued past us, but a few slowed to a stop.

"I don't have a personal thought. He'd love to play. We're proud of him. If you're worried about someone's negative opinion, I don't care about that. But it's my boy. His mom and I will have a conversation with him, see if he's got a particular opinion one way or another."

Coach raised his chin, giving me another long look. "I won't hold back. I wouldn't be starting him, but he'd see a lot of playing time. He's got speed that will be an asset to our team. There's no way around that."

I looked back at a group of players lingering. They were some of the guys who'd been in Moreaux's basement when we crashed their party. Two of them held their helmets but one, Manning, kept his on. Steele Manning. He'd been sitting on the couch with Maddy. I also noticed him looking at us a few times during the game. He might've been looking at someone else in the bleachers around us, but I had the feeling we were the focus of his attention.

Coach Ravenry noticed them too and dipped his chin to

me. "Let me know. We can have another conversation about it, if you'd like. Boys!" He motioned to them with his clipboard. "Get in the locker room. Let's go. We're not out here having a gossip session."

Another man joined the players, clapping a hand on Beltraine Moreaux's shoulder.

Well... Shit. It was Phillip Moreaux, Beltraine's father.

He ignored what their coach just said, grabbing the front of Manning's helmet and jerking him around.

Phillip Moreaux was a few years on the other side of fifty, but the older he aged, the younger he cheated. He was loud, pompous, and had an ego that was going to be a problem.

He'd come to Dad's funeral, and I'd met him again at a few of our follow-up meetings. The board members needed to be reassured I could step into my dad's place and the company would be fine. The company *was* fine, except for whoever had lied to my dad and Moreaux's recent movements. Because as I was staring at him now, the hunch he was going to make a play for the company was coming back to me.

"Hey, boys!" He jerked the Steele kid forward, shaking him before letting him go. He laughed loudly, pounding on Axel Johannson's shoulder pads, then another kid's before focusing on his son. "How are you feeling about that loss? Huh?" He shoved him back. As Beltraine stumbled, his dad advanced. He shoved him again, taunting, "Think you should be proud of that game? You lost. There ain't nothing for you to be proud about." His voice took on a menacing note as he shoved his kid a third time.

This time, Beltraine fell.

He stayed down.

The kid and his friends did nothing. They were taking it.

Brett glanced my way. I was aware of Mark watching me too.

The coach wasn't doing anything.

"Get up. We aren't losers in this family. And you." He

rounded on Manning, grabbing his helmet's cage. "You're staying at my place. Your sister is there on the weekends. You want to keep staying, you're going to start earning your keep. You hear me? Starting with tonight. You lost tonight. That means no party. You and the others are going to meet me behind the shed. You can learn how my old man conditioned me never to lose a game. I'm going to whip you boys into shape."

He jerked the kid again, and I was done.

I moved in a flash.

He began to shake that Steele kid again.

I warned, "You don't let go of that kid *right now*, I'm going to remove your hand for you."

He paused.

The others went rigid, and a tense silence fell over the group.

"Excuse me?" He looked my way, letting go of the helmet.

"Boys," their coach said gruffly. "Get in the locker room."

Phillip looked the coach's way. "They aren't moving. I'm not done with them."

"You're done for the night, Phil," Coach Ravenry replied. "You've been drinking. We don't want a repeat of our last loss. Word has a way of getting around."

Phillip Moreaux took an intimidating step forward. "You threatening me, Conrad?"

First name basis here. I was noting that.

Sometimes I detested small towns. Being a big fish in a small pond gave some guys an ego they wouldn't have if they were a small fish in a big pond.

When Ravenry gave me a look, I knew this was one of those parents who'd have an opinion about Nash playing varsity.

The boys were still standing around. I motioned to them. "Go inside. Listen to your coach."

They took off. Moreaux's kid only looked back once.

Ravenry stayed.

"You too, Coach," I told him. "Moreaux and I have some other business to discuss."

With a nod, he left, but he moved at a normal pace. He didn't hurry, which made me wonder how the past interactions tended to go down between him and Moreaux.

Moreaux made a move to follow them.

I held up a hand and he hit it, bouncing back. "Not you."

I turned back to see that Brett and Mark moved in, circling him.

He looked around, scoffing. "What do you think you're going to do to me? You're new here, boy. You've been off. Playing under the big lights, but you don't know how things are handled here."

"I know you're not going to lay a hand on any of those kids again, not how you just did."

He scoffed again, a wildness in his eyes that he was having a hard time hiding. "And here I thought we were going to be friendly. I welcomed you to town. Came to your father's funeral. Introduced you to the other board members. How do you repay me for my kindness?" His eyes went mean. "You think you can get between me and my kid?"

"When it's to hurt, not help, fuck yeah I am." I moved toward him. "Not a hardship on my end. Every time I see you, I tend to want to punch you. You going to give me that excuse now?"

That mean glint grew before it shifted to calculating. He smirked, shifting back on his feet. "You know, I've heard a rumor that Kade Enterprises is struggling."

Fine. We could go that direction. "You heard wrong."

"Our stock plummeted the day after your daddy kille—" He choked and stopped speaking, his voice strangled because I had a grip on his shoulder, a painful grip, and I walked him into the side of the equipment shed. I hadn't meant to accelerate things to this point so quickly, but he was about to talk about my dad.

I glanced at Brett. "I think he needs help standing."

He grunted, staring down at Moreaux. "He was stumbling all over the place. Intoxicated at a public event. Good thing he has us. To help him out."

I deadpanned, tightening my grip on him. "That's us. Regular saints here."

With the grip I had on him, he couldn't use one entire side of his body. As he was still registering that he couldn't lift his arm or move his leg, I caught the shadows of Brett and Mark blocking us from view.

"He needs to stand a little, Mase," Mark pointed out.

I eased up my grip, just a bit. "Our stock bounced back the next day, you dumb fuck. You're going to shut your mouth about the company."

Moreaux glared at me, but he remained still. He looked at me as if I'd offended him. I knew his kind. They'd been at the top of the hierarchy all their lives.

Here I come—a name he knows, but I'm new money. I'm an athlete. I've got fame and power, but in his mind, I can't match him. Can't equal him. No. I'm just a football player.

"You think you're top dog, huh? No one messes with you. Poker with the district attorney. That sort of thing."

"I think I got friends in places that you have no idea about." He lifted his chin up.

My grin, if that's what it could be called, was cold. His eyebrows pulled together.

"You think I'm not aware of the calls and meetings you've been having with the other shareholders?"

His sneer faltered, slightly.

"You think I don't know the shit you have on those members? That I don't have that information as well? The photos. The blackmail material."

His sneer faded entirely.

"Or that I don't know about the secret meeting you're going to call early Monday morning with the agenda of finalizing those shares and making a move to force me and my brother from the company?"

His smarmy tanned skin went pale underneath, but then it started to get red. That color spread.

I lifted a thumb, seeing a white print there.

"You don't know shit. And even if you did, it's too late—"

"You're so wrong that you look stupid." This guy was coming for my family. He was going to regret that.

He stopped struggling, but he still seethed. "You don't kno —" He couldn't get out anymore.

I tightened my hold and he dropped down a couple inches. He was folding under my grip.

"Does Johannson know you're fucking his wife?" Axel's dad was also a shareholder.

He went still. "You're bluffing."

"I could tell him I know what sort of lingerie she wears, that I bet she hasn't worn it for him in a while. Course, maybe she's got more than one set, but I'm betting he'll go straight home to look through her drawers himself. He'd be so angry. He won't stop to consider that he's cheating too. Or that he probably cheated first. He'll just care that his wife is fucking you, and moments earlier you had the balls to blackmail *him*."

"You're lying. This is all a massive bluff."

"I got pictures." I smirked. "None of the sales have gone through. You think he'll still sell after I show him those pictures?"

He scowled at me. "I don't think you know what you're doing. This is the big leagues. We don't play around with empty threats. We deal with lawyers and—"

I stepped back, a part of me wishing I could put bruises all over this guy. "Yeah, yeah. You give the cops a good annual donation. You golf with a local judge who's interested in running for public office, and you've promised him a nice sum of money for his campaign. Christ, you're annoying. You think I don't know all of that?"

He fell quiet. Finally.

I glanced around. We'd drawn a fair amount of attention, but Brett and Mark hadn't moved. Sam had come over, but she stood to the side, her back to us. She was keeping watch on who might be recording us or paying attention to us that shouldn't be.

"I was going to wait until Monday to crash your party. I was going to release all the shit I know, and I was going to keep it at the office. But then you swagger up to me, acting like we're bros at my dad's funeral. You come over here, putting hands on kids." I looked at him a moment. "Here's what we can do. You withdraw everything. And you're going to sell *your* shares. I want you out of the company. You do that, and I won't destroy you. There's my offer. And in the meantime, you're not going to shove your kid around, or any kid. You're not going to grab a player by his helmet and use that to jerk him around—not unless you're okay with someone like Broudou doing it back to you."

Brett lifted his chin up, interjecting, "I'd love to do that."

I kept on, "I don't think you'd want the shareholders to hear about a board member's ethical violation. We do have that pesky morals clause in every contract."

He glared at me, pressed against the shed and rubbing his shoulder. He was having a hard time even standing. But I didn't see the fear that should've been there. I sighed. None of this penetrated him. He was going to go home, drink some more, rage, and probably plan to hurt someone. I was looking at the face of a guy that would hire muscled men to find me in a dark parking lot.

Shit. Had it been me that brought us to this point? I had put hands on him.

Then again, when he shoved his kid and jerked Manning around by his helmet, I saw red. If he was doing that in front of witnesses, what was he doing behind closed doors?

Those were the kids that he—what did he say? He wanted them to meet him behind the shed?

What did that mean?

But I had another thought.

"Kai Bennett says hello," I told him, watching intently.

He frowned. "Who?"

There'd been no flash of recognition. Nothing. No fear. No reaction at all. He didn't know him. That meant he wasn't the one who killed my dad.

He just jumped on an opening he saw to take advantage.

Still, for that alone, I was going to destroy him.

38

MADDY

M addy: Max! You need to come over here.

Max: What? Why? R u okay?

Maddy: Shit is going doooooooooowwwwwwwnnnnn. sorrybutnowayImsorry because something is happening.

Max: Fuck, Mads. I'm with the guys. It'll take me a bit to get out of here. I thought we were meeting up later?

Maddy: Can't. This is happening now. I have no idea what went down at the game, but something went down. My mom told me to stay by a different gate and wait for them.

Max: Let me guess. You didn't.

Maddy: No way. I could see something was happening by the players's entrance. By the time I got over there, Traine's dad was glaring at my dad. My dad was glaring at Traine's dad.

Max: Something happened between your dad and Moreaux's dad?

Maddy: See? Right there. Why don't you use his nickname? He told you to use it. Traine. It's not hard to say.

Max: Haha. Tell me what else happened. I'm almost out of here.

Maddy: You're at the fighting shed?

Max: No. House party in Roussou. Fighting shed got axed tonight. Don't know why.

Maddy: I forget you know people there.

Max: Maddy! Keep telling me what's going on.

Maddy: I will if you promise to start using Traine's nick-name. I thought you were okay with them.

Max: I'm never going to be okay with three guys you hang out with at school when I'm not there. And don't think they wouldn't fuck you if you gave them a nod. But yeah, for guys, they're not that bad.

Maddy: That's so confusing.

Max: Don't worry about it, my little sociopath.

Maddy: You certainly know how to talk to me.

Max: FFS. Finish the other stuff. Also, where am I going to get you?

Maddy: I'm at the house. We got back after the game and it was weird. Really weird. My dad—I've heard stories about him. I know he and Mom did things back in the day, with Uncle Logan. Like, crazy things, but they've all just been stories. They weren't real because my dad is my dad. He's a softie. NOT TONIGHT!

Max: what happened???? You're driving me nuts. Your dad didn't hurt you, did he?

Maddy: OH MY GOD, NO! GROSS. DISGUSTING. WHO ARE YOU? DO YOU NOT EVEN KNOW ME?

Max: Maddy. You're scaring me. I *have* seen that side of your dad. I see that side of my own dad all the time. They did crazy and illegal shit back in the day. I fully believe it. I don't know why you don't.

Maddy: Well, excuuuuuuuse me, Mr. my dad is a bounty hunter and guns down criminals every day. He wears a gun. Yeah. You've seen more, but my dad wears tights and a helmet for a living. Or used to.

Max: Thinking a football uniform is not exactly the same thing as tights. And my dad doesn't gun down criminals. They use tasers.

Maddy: He still wears a gun. Every day. And close enough. Like any daughter wants to see that? Whoever's thinking up the football uniform doesn't consider the daughters's POV.

Max: Thinking they are, just not the daughters of the players. Get back to the story. What happened when you got home? I'm in the truck. Heading to Fallen Crest.

Maddy: Thank God. They're almost out of here.

Max: Who is?

Maddy: Anyway, so we got back and my dad started asking me all these questions about Traine, Axe, and Steele. And he was not looking happy.

Max: What was he asking about?

Maddy: What do I know about them? Have I been hanging out with them since my dad crashed their party? Has Traine mentioned anything about his dad? If I was at the house, was I ever there when his dad was around? But it's not really what he was saying, it was how he was saying it.

Max: How was he saying it?

I stared at the last text, but I couldn't answer. I couldn't explain. It was a feeling and a look in his eyes. The way my dad was my normal doting dad, but there was an undercurrent. Like an aftertaste. Remembering it, I shivered, my stomach clenching.

My phone rang.

Future Husband Calling.

I snickered. It went back to Max's normal name in the missed calls and when I texted him, so if he ever looked at my phone, he wouldn't get mad. The first time I'd changed his name in my phone, he'd gotten all huffy and lectured me for an

hour about how we were too young for such a serious relationship.

I'd just planned our honeymoon as he kept babbling.

"Hey," I said when I answered the phone.

"Why didn't you answer me? How was he saying it?" Max
asked.

I shrugged, lying down on my bed. "I don't know how to
explain it. Just a feeling. Like, I believed it. All the stories I've
heard. My dad's capable of hurting someone, like for real. I
never thought he could. He rescues and releases flies in the
house, even when Nolan *isn't* here. Mom, though. She's another
thing. My mom could stare someone down until they start slapping the shit out of themselves. She's got powers. She's tough."

Max sighed, but I heard amusement in his voice. "Your
mom is badass. It's why she's friends with my mom."

I groaned. "I forgot you used to have a crush on my mom.
That's so weird."

"I did not! That's disgusting. You thought I had a crush on
your mom?"

I sat up, frowning. "You don't?"

"I've never. That's your mom, Mads. You and me—I've
always thought we might—you know. No fucking way would I
ever have perved on your mom. I mean, she's beautiful. I have
eyes, but you know."

I smirked, lying back down. "I know. Your dad's a total
hottie."

He made a choking sound. "I don't want to re-touch this
conversation. Ever."

I snickered. "You said re-touch."

"Maddy."

Okay, okay. I got serious, and I shrugged, even though he
couldn't see. "I—it's just a feeling. Something happened after
the game. My dad was asking me all these questions. It was
weird. I don't have a good feeling about it."

"They didn't ask anything about Brinna?"

Brinna was Steele's sister, and she was cool. I didn't think a lot of people knew about her. She only visited on the weekends and went to school somewhere else. Steele said she was embarrassed and it was a whole thing with their family. Traine and Axel hinted that I shouldn't ask a lot of questions about her so whatever. I didn't.

"No."

My parents didn't know how much I hung out with those guys. My mom liked to know my friends. I got the reason, but they wouldn't understand these guys. Lucia was my friend beard. Though, she wasn't that bad. My mom believed Lucia was my friend and that Lucia's friends were the rest of my friends so I'd look more normal.

The guys were graduating this year. I'd need to figure something out for next year. Maybe I could transfer to Fallen Crest Public and make Max my official boyfriend.

Hmmm... That had promise.

"Okay. I'm not far from the edge of town. How am I approaching?"

I got up and checked outside. They hadn't left yet, but I knew they would. They'd said goodnight. They'd said they loved me. They'd done all the normal routine signifying that they were going to bed for the rest of the night, but I knew they were lying.

Maybe Nolan wasn't the only one with some intuition? Wait a minute. Could I have that and also be a sociopath? Another question for Google. Maybe I could meet some sociopaths in real life, interview them to see if they lacked intuition or maybe it was heightened... That was also an idea.

Just then a set of headlights pulled up to the gate. "That's not you, is it?" I asked.

"What?"

"At our gate?"

"No. Who is it?"

I stopped answering, watching as the lights turned off. The gate opened, and the truck rolled forward into our courtyard. It pulled up to our front door, and I watched as my dad went out and got inside. He was dressed all in black. When he opened the door, no inside light turned on. It'd already been dismantled. That was creepy.

"Maddy!" Max demanded.

"Just pull up outside the gate. I'll come out to you."

"Got it. I'll be there in five. I forgot they're doing construction on Eighth."

"Just hurry, and cut your headlights when you get close." I ended the call.

I shifted my attention to getting ready. If my dad was going somewhere all in black, I'd be remiss if I didn't follow the dress code as well. I didn't want to go out the front door and risk setting off the motion detector, which sent alerts to my mom's phone, so I slipped out through the garage and keyed in the code to lock everything back up. I was coming around the side when another vehicle pulled up to the gate, its headlights shining.

I growled, cursing. I'd told Max I'd come to him, but the gate opened and the SUV pulled forward.

It wasn't Max.

What the...

It was Heather. Or Aunt Heather, but after I crawled into Max's lap one time, I changed her name back to Heather. Felt weird the other way. She swung her car into the same place Max's dad's just been. My mom darted out, also wearing all black.

What is going on?

Gah. No. I knew what they were going to do. They were doing what I was doing. My mom and-Heather were going to follow the dads. They were going to spy, just like me.

I was annoyed. They got there first. That meant we'd have to be extra cautious because now we were the third vehicle in this trailing line-up. I mean, they could've been going out for drinks or doing a girl's night, but no. No way. My mom would've told me she was going out. She didn't hide that stuff, and I mean, they had their fair share of girl's nights when the whole group was here for the funeral. They were kinda over it now.

They were going to follow my dad and Max's dad. I would bet money that's what they were doing.

As soon as my mom was in the vehicle, Heather cut the lights, like the guys had done.

I was so right.

I was almost sweating from the stress. When was Max going to pull up? If he got here before they left, there'd be questions. Then no one would be following anyone.

My knees almost buckled from relief when they pulled away from the house.

I darted through the gate, and seriously, thirty seconds later, Max pulled up. Headlights off.

I got all swirly and light-headed at that. He'd listened to me.

Hurrying to the passenger side, I jumped in and hissed, "Go! Follow them."

He looked ahead, frowning, until taillights turned on down the hill. He eased forward. "Who are we following?"

My head was spinning. And I was horny, like really horny. I wanted to jump Max and fit his gearstick between my legs.

"*Everyone.*"

39

MASON

"You have a plan?" Channing asked as we left my house.

"Right now, you're driving so I don't do something stupid, like follow him to his house and beat the shit out of him." I glanced his way. "Did you put the tracker on them?"

Channing raised an eyebrow, looking relaxed as he drove, but I knew he wasn't. After my confrontation with Phillip Moreaux, I'd left the school knowing I'd find whatever this shed was that he'd mentioned to those kids.

Channing hit the turn signal, pulling up to a new neighborhood, and he paused outside the first gate. He put in the code Broudou had given us, and we pulled through, going on up to his house.

Brett had fallen in step with me when we left. "*I know you're going to do something,*" he'd said. "*I'm in.*"

"Your intel said Moreaux tends to be the driver," Channing told me. "So I put it under his very sweet vehicle."

"There's like twenty vehicles at that house."

Shortly after we stopped, Brett came out, also wearing all black.

The door opened, and Brett started to get in, but stopped.

There wasn't enough room.

Channing hid a grin. "In the back, buddy."

Brett fixed him with a look but grunted before closing the door and jumping into the back.

Channing whistled. "You two. Both fucking athletic freaks."

Brett knocked on the window with his knuckles.

Channing reached back to slide it open as he pulled out of the driveway. "How is it back there? All comfy?"

Brett glowered. "Don't tempt me to stomp you into the ground, Monroe."

Channing laughed. He swung the wheel around, and once the gate lifted, we were out of that neighborhood. "Not my fault you're a giant motherfucker."

Brett shook his head.

"Also," Channing said to me. "I saw all the vehicles, and I put trackers on *all* of them." He handed over his phone with his tracking app open. "We're going to follow the dot that moves."

"Thanks, genius."

Brett started laughing.

The sound was shocking, but infectious at the same time.

I hid a grin while Channing quipped, "You have a sense of humor, Broudou? Learn new shit every day, huh?"

The laughing stopped. "Be a smart idea for you not to forget the newest member of my family," Brett countered. Then he smiled. Widely.

Channing swore under his breath.

I started laughing. That was funny.

One of the dots was on the move, and I relayed the directions to Channing. As we were leaving town, my phone started ringing. Pulling it out, I cursed. My brother. This time of night, he was calling for a reason, but I couldn't talk. I slid my thumb over the screen, accepting the call and put him on speaker, "It's not a good time right now. Everything okay with you?"

He was quiet for a beat. "What?"

I sighed. "You're on speaker. Channing and Brett are here. We're following those kids that had the party we crashed."

"*What?*"

Channing shook his head as Brett started chuckling in the back.

"Why are you calling?" I asked. "It's late—really late where you are."

"Are you seriously going to not fill me in on whatever the fuck you're doing?"

"Logan," I grated. "Why are you calling?"

"But—"

"You first."

"Fine," he grumbled. "I'm calling to let you know I got the call. You're right. Moreaux is making a move, but he's not waiting for Monday morning. He's making it tonight."

"Tonight?" I snarled into the phone.

"Meeting is set for five a.m. your time. I booked a flight."

A feminine voice spoke in the background. Logan paused to reply to her, then returned to the phone. "Taylor's taking me to the airport now. It'll be tight. You'll need to stall at the meeting. Now, fill me in on your end."

This fucking guy. After I told Logan about our showdown at the football game, he cursed. "You're following him now?"

"We're following his kid."

"You think he's still going to do whatever he does to these kids tonight?"

I remembered the burning rage in Moreaux's eyes before we parted ways. "I think he's going to need a target for his anger. There's no way I'm going to let this go. If he's hurting these kids, I might kill him."

I felt the attention from the other guys. Channing glanced over, but this wasn't surprising to him. Brett, though. I was letting him see the real me. Looking in the rearview mirror, I met his gaze and saw the surprise, but there was also a deeper and darker emotion there. Understanding. And if I was reading him correctly, he was right there with me.

"No one let my brother kill this piece of shit," Logan snarled into the phone. "At least not until I get there. I can set him up better than you would. Or at the least, connect him with someone who does this type of bad shit on a regular basis, you know? Could we direct your new friend whose name rhymes with bye and whose last name rhymes with Senate after him?"

Brett motioned to the phone. "They're slowing down."

We were coming up to a gravel road in the country. Channing turned, hitting his lights.

I held my phone closer. "We gotta go. Get your ass here."

"Will do. I mean that on the murdering front. *Don't*. Okay? Other than that, be safe and smart. Love you."

"Love you." I ended the call.

"They stopped," Channing said quietly.

We were rolling up to a giant warehouse, but there were no vehicles parked out front.

"Okay. Phones on silent," Channing ordered. "Not vibrate. Silent. Keep them in your pockets just in case. Mason."

"What?"

He motioned to my feet. "There's a bag of ski-masks. Pull them out. Put them on. Do you both want a gun?"

He thought we'd need them? I shared a look with Broudou but shook my head. "I can't. I don't trust myself. If I go after Moreaux, it'll be with my fists. That way, you'll have time to pull me off if needed."

I felt their gazes again, but I couldn't focus on that. When Maddy told me more about these three boys, I kept track of what she was saying and what she wasn't saying. I picked up things my little girl wasn't noticing, like that I'd been right in my first assessment. This kid lived in a giant fucking house by himself. There was no other place they hung out. It was that house and only that house, and the father was never there. It was worse than I thought. I assumed there was contact between the kid and his dad, but there was nothing. There was no check-in. No visits. No phone calls from the mom or the dad. The way she was talking, the only time Beltraine saw his dad was when he "messed up." That was the wording she used, which meant that was the wording he used. Which meant this kid was only punished when he saw his dad.

The kid was neglected and there was abuse.

She talked about his cousin, the Manning kid, and his sister. She didn't know where the sister went to school and had been told not to ask, which made me think a whole host of bad things. Axel's parents were a little more involved with his life. They were shareholders, but I didn't have any other context to get a read on that couple. They were quiet in the meetings. Moreaux sat next to the wife, and I had no idea if the father had a clue about their affair. Everything I'd told Phillip Moreaux was verified information from my private investigator. But if I didn't get to them before the meeting, Moreaux could pull it off. No doubt he rescheduled the meeting because of my threat.

Logan and my PI had combed through the video we took of inside that house. The computer files were what Lael had been the most interested in, but she said it wasn't likely he would keep anything super damning on that computer. The worst we had on him were the drugs at the party. Logan hadn't wanted to catch the sexual acts on his phone so he pointed it at their feet. That was useless.

The PI suggested a route we could take, considering the ages of the kids in that basement, but that would fuck up their lives. I wasn't going to do that.

According to Maddy, Beltraine wasn't that bad of a guy. His friends either.

I was *not* a father like mine had been. If I knew a kid was being neglected or hurt, I was wading in. I didn't give a fuck about the blowback. I'd take it all.

Sorry, Dad. You made things okay at the end, but I learned what not to be from you.

Channing rolled the truck to a stop farther down, by a field. It'd be missed at first glance.

"You guys ready?" he asked.

Brett and I both nodded. Ski-masks on.

Let's do this.

40
_____

MASON

We found two vehicles parked in the back, but no one was outside. Heading for the back door, Channing plastered himself against the wall. I was behind him, followed by Brett. As we waited, Channing turned and gave us a bunch of hand signals.

Awesome.

Neither of us spoke that language.

He waited for us to either respond, but we stayed put. I raised my eyebrows. Brett leaned out behind me and shook his head slowly, holding up a hand. We were clueless, not his normal bounty hunter crew. He groaned softly, giving us an exasperated look.

I frowned and edged around him, because if he was going to act like that, I had no problem going in and kicking ass without him. Brett followed, but Channing grabbed my arm just before I touched the door. He pulled me back, shaking his head.

We could hear voices from inside, and Channing didn't like this door for some reason. He edged backward. Once we were far enough away, I asked, "Why don't we all try a different door?"

He shook his head. "No. We might need backup."

I fixed him with a look. "I'm willing to risk it."

Channing was still frowning. "I don't know. This whole place feels wrong. I've heard chatter that there's a new fighting ring, besides the one the Red Demons run. If that's this place, and if Moreaux is behind it, he's got backing from someone else."

"We're not your usual crew," I told Channing. "You can't treat us like Moose or Congo."

Brett smacked his fist into his palm.

Channing and I looked at him.

"What?" He lowered his hands.

"Okay. Let's spread out," Channing said. "Find an entry point and move in. Keep hidden. Mason, this is your show. We'll wait for you to move first."

I had no problem with that. "Got it."

Channing grunted. "Move out."

If Logan were here, he would've done his own version of hand signals right now just to play around. *He's coming,* I reminded myself. Channing went back to the original door while Brett and I separated. He went to the east side of the building. I headed for the front.

We ended up meeting in the middle.

He scoffed at me, whispering, "Good plan."

"Shut up." I waited for him to get to my side and reached forward, testing the doorknob. It opened with a click. I held the door and slowly opened it, inch by inch, until I could get a better look inside.

Phillip Moreaux was yelling.

I edged the door open enough that I could slip inside, into what seemed like a coat room of some sort—a small room with another doorway without a door.

"You're nothing but a failure," Moreaux shouted.

There were sounds of running and panting, some cursing from the next room. "You think you tried your best tonight? *You did nothing. You are nothing,*" he continued, his voice was hoarse. "You're going to keep going until I tell you to stop. You hear me, you piece of shit?"

Brett stopped. His eyes went dead, and every part of him was rigid. I moved ahead to look around the corner. It was another fighting ring. A cage had been set up in the middle with metal walls that went high in the air. Old sweat, dirt, and the smell of blood lingered in the air. Two boys were in the cage. Shirtless. Their hands and feet taped. They only wore shorts. Their chests heaved and sweat and blood trickled down their faces. Axel and Steele.

The younger Moreaux was running back and forth on the side of the cage. He tagged down and sprinted back. Fuck. This place was hot, and Phillip was making his kid do shuttle runs?

I pulled my phone out, half of me going numb, the other half becoming bloodthirsty. I angled it in front of me and hit record.

"You're going to keep fucking running until I tell you to stop!" he screamed. Then he turned toward the others. "*Keep fucking hitting each other!* You think you're getting off easy? You hit until you're red and raw."

Axel glared at him, his hands jerking up before he stopped himself.

"What?" Phillip stomped over to him. "What, Axe?! You think you're going to fucking tattle to your daddy? You think he gives a fuck about you? You want to stay friends with my son? Come to my house? Eat my food? Drink my liquor? You don't think I'm aware that you basically live at my house, and I'm just going to be okay with it? You fucking hit that kid or you're losing all privileges. And you," he spat as he focused on Steele. "You want to keep living at my place, using my address, letting my family name cover for your lies, and your sister's, then you get fucking swinging too. The one who knocks the other one out won't have to do shuttle runs with this piece of loser shit my sperm brought into the world. As of now, your efforts are pathetic. You're nothing. Why the fuck are you even here? You fucking little boys can't do a goddamn thing for yourselves. Parasites. Every goddamn one of you. Burdens. You're at my house because your parents don't give a fuck where you are. If they did, you wouldn't be here. Well, you're going to earn your keep tonight. *Keep fucking running*! You hear me?" An ugly laugh burst from his chest. His face twisted in a smile that wasn't a smile. It was soulless. "You're going to keep going *until I tell you to stop*! At this rate, we'll be here all fucking night." Another sick-sounding laugh chortled from him.

The boys started swinging at each other again.

His kid kept running. Head down. Sweat dripping.

If they kept at this for even another hour, they were going to pass out. All three of them played nearly the entire football game earlier.

Brett started rumbling next to me.

Right there with you, buddy.

"No!" Moreaux was screaming again. His feet scraped over the dirt that was packed on the floor. "That's not how you swing —" He cut himself off, swearing viciously. "Get out. Get the fuck out. I'll show you how to fucking hit."

Oh, hell no. I'd heard enough.

He got in the cage, and instead of taping his hands like he'd had the boys do, he put on boxing gloves. Boxing. Gloves.

Axel remained in the cage and Steele climbed out, but he stood by the steps, not going far. He saw us first, and he gulped, paling, but he didn't move. Beltraine collapsed on the ground, his chest heaving as he seemed unable to get enough air. Brett went to his side when the kid started wheezing.

I remained locked on where Phillip was snarling at Axel,

and I hated to do this, but I raised my phone. The camera was on, still recording. Steele jerked himself out of frame.

"This is how you do it!" Phillip roared. "Bend your knees. Come on. Bend your fucking knees." He swung.

Axel dodged, and in that moment, he saw what was happening. I felt bad, and I raised an eyebrow at him. Was he okay with this? The kid was smart. He gave me a slight nod and bounced to the side, making Phillip Moreaux move so his back was to me.

Thank you, buddy. I moved closer, getting everything.

He swung. This time, Axel couldn't dodge fast enough.

I felt the anger rising. That darkness in me, the one that helped me survive Fallen Crest, came to the surface, and I was *livid*. Still, I forced myself to wait. I needed a little more. He'd get heat for the verbal abuse. But he could say things got out of control. That he was only trying to help get them into better condition.

He could say that he went in the cage to help him out. Show him better form. It was just a little sparring. Some boxing. Right?

So yeah because I wasn't going to let him get away with this. We either used this recording and go the legit route to punish Moreaux, or I'd be dishing out my own personal punishment. If we went that way, that'd be a risk for myself and my family. Remembering Logan's words, I held back because I needed enough to bury him.

Just a little more.

Phillip roared and he began raining blow after blow, pushing Axel into the corner. His shout was savage. "I'll show you how to take a hit, you little fuck. All you little fucks. I'm going to ream your assholes open. You're going to—"

Axel's knees gave out, and he slumped to the ground. *Fuck.* Phillip was going to stop... No, he wasn't. He knelt down, spreading his knees to give himself a better base and raised his hand again—*No!* I snarled. I was there in a flash. Using the side, I gripped it and launched myself over the ropes, right into the cage.

He froze at the sound, but it was too fucking late.

I took him down. As soon as he was clear, Axel scrambled away.

He tried fighting me, rolling, but I just smiled. Grabbing hold of his arms, I yanked them backward and twisted them. Something snapped as I twisted his body, and threw him into the far side of the cage. He stayed, the wind was knocked out of him.

My phone hit the ground.

I glanced at Axel behind me as Channing ran in. He threw himself into the cage and, giving me a cursory look, went straight to Axel. He scooped him up, carrying him out of the cage. "You okay?" he shouted at Steele.

Steele gaped at me, his eyes just blinking. Wide. His jaw slacked.

"Kid!" Channing snapped his fingers in front of his face.

It did nothing.

"His name is Steele," I said.

Channing twisted around. "Steele! Wake up, kid." He had to get in his face before he registered him. As he did, Steele jumped backward, cursing.

"What the hell is going on here?" Phillip growled, wincing as he used the chain-link of the cage to pull himself up. Some blood trickled down his face. He reached up, touching his forehead. Pulling his hand away, there was a blank look in his eyes, as if he didn't understand what he was seeing. He was gone. I saw it now. The anger was too much. The guy wasn't in the room. He'd let his monster out too.

Difference was that his monster hurt kids. Mine hurt monsters like him.

Punishment. Well-intentioned discipline. Training. I had no doubt he would use those words to excuse his behavior. All would be a lie.

"Mase," Channing barked.

I whipped around, seeing Axel bent over and vomiting. Steele looked back at me, too stunned to do anything more.

Channing jerked his hand toward Moreaux. "KO that piece of shit."

"You were going to show that kid how to take a punch," I taunted, my voice cold. "Let me help you out with that." I didn't give any more warning before bringing my fist down. I got him clear across the cheekbone, through his nose, and his body swung all the way around before falling to the cage floor.

Thud.

He was out.

I stared at him, wishing he'd open his eyes again. Round two. I was game, but nope. He was unconscious. Turning, I bent down and swept up my phone, seeing the recording stopped at some point. I looked down at it and decided to send it to Logan. It'd be an early gift for when he arrived in LA. He'd have all sorts of ideas what to do with it when—a *thunk* sounded.

My head whipped up.

Something fell from the rafters in the ceiling, a whishing sound.

It took a second for it to register, but it was a blanket. Blankets. Plural. Someone was... Was I actually seeing this? Someone was using them to slide to the ground. I looked up. Where had they come from? There were some rafters above, but this person came from the ceiling. What the—they landed with an *oomph* and a grunt.

She fell to her knees, but quickly got up, throwing her arms in the air. "I'm good. I'm here."

A second person slid down after her, and this one ended on her feet. She was also wearing cowboy boots.

The first person grabbed her, steadying her.

The first person was my wife. "That was so good," she gushed, clutching onto the second arrival.

My wife was here.

My. *Wife.*

I was going to explode.

She brushed off her leggings and blew out a breath, pushing some of her hair off her forehead. She'd been grinning, almost stupidly grinning, until she saw the look on my face.

She coughed and stepped back. Her mouth pursed. "Uh..."

"*Heather?*" Channing growled, wrapping his wife in his arms. She was the second person to have made a dramatic entrance from the ceiling.

From. The. Ceiling.

I glared at Sam. How the fuck had they gotten up there? Was there anyone else up there?

"Um..." Sam glanced at Steele before doing a double-take and giving him a longer frown.

Then we heard a shout from outside, something snapped, and the warehouse's main door that was used for trucks, shot up.

Two people stood in the middle of the opening.

I recognized these two as well.

So did Sam as she froze.

Maddy stepped forward, her arms crossed over her chest, her chin raised. She looked too fucking cool for school. Max was with her. He was a lot more wary and a lot more checked into reality as he saw his mom, who was now motionless in his dad's arms. He winced, closing his eyes and pressing a hand to his forehead.

My daughter, on the other hand, smirked. Her eyes were alive, her body was practically vibrating. "I don't know what we're doing, but this is the most exciting night of my life. If we're becoming a real life family of vigilantes, *I am in.*"

41

MADDY

I was so horny. Like, truly horny. I felt like I was an omega in one of those omegaverse books, and I was in heat. This wasn't healthy. It couldn't be. I felt ready to come, which sounded weird and disgusting because my parents were here, and so were Max's, but it wasn't about that. Or them. It was because this was the action I'd been missing all my life.

I *loved* Fallen Crest.

I'd never felt so alive. It was like I was drunk, but I'd never been this blissed out from alcohol. It was like I was on speed. Or how I imagined that would be. The only drug (besides allergy medication and antibiotics) I'd done was a bit of marijuana, and I hadn't liked it. It made me chatty, and I tended to tell people about some of the twisted shit in my head. I usually wasn't invited back for another smoke.

But this? With my dad sneaking out, then my mom, then Max and me? We'd heard some yelling, and the violence in the air was *palpable*. And the smells in here...

Blood.

Violence.

Adrenaline.

Ahem—violence. It bore a repeat.

Purpose.

Violence.

My heart pumped so fast. I was tripping out.

"Logan Malinda Kade!" My dad lunged out of the cage and stalked toward me.

Oh. That wasn't good. My full name, from my dad.

I swallowed my excitement. I needed to tone this down. I blinked a few times, trying to get some fear into my eyes, but fuck. I couldn't. This night was already amazing. I was *so on* for this shit.

"Mason." My mom ran over, touching my arm before Dad could get to me.

I frowned her way. Dad wouldn't do anything. He was all show. He'd stomp over to me, glare like he was going to yell at me, which he might actually do, but Dad was a softie.

Mom was trying to block him, but I sidestepped her. "Dad," I breathed.

Shit. I couldn't hide my high. I'd found my calling. I was going to be a professional vigilante. I breezed over to him, walking on air. "Is this what it was like when you grew up here?" I took hold of his arm.

He turned to stone under my hand.

"Maddy," my mom warned.

I waved a hand to dismiss her concern. I was going to fly away. Giddy. "This is amazing. What are you doing?" I looked around him to see who was in the cage. They were lying on the ground, not moving an inch. My dad had totally knocked that guy out.

So. Fucking. Cool.

"Maddy," my dad murmured.

I danced around him, knowing he'd be fine in a second. I

was the switch. He could never stay mad when I was around. Especially not when I'd reverted back to my ballerina days. Pirouette here. Arch my back. Extend my arm. And then I switched into another pirouette.

I couldn't stop moving.

He sighed. His hand closed around my arm.

"Mason." My mom drew in a sharp breath.

"What do you think I'm going to do?" he asked. "She's my daughter."

"No. I know. It's not that. She's..." She moved closer. "She's on something."

He snorted, pulling me to his front so I was forced to stop dancing. I'd been in the middle of a fouetté and gave him an annoyed frown. "Rude much? That was the best form of my life."

"See?" Dad said to Mom.

Mom huffed, rolling her eyes. "Mads, you quit ballet in third grade. You said the other dancers were too delicate for your vibe."

"I would never say that. I loved ballet."

She said dryly, "You threatened to burn your leotard."

I frowned. "I did?"

"And the leotards of every single girl in your class."

"Ah. Yeah. That sounds like me." I grinned. "I was funny back then, huh?"

My dad put a hand on Mom's back. "That's a conversation for later."

I didn't think he was referring to my ballet days. His gaze returned to the cage. The body was still laying there.

My mom snapped to attention, scanning the room. She looked closely at Axel and Steele, then swallowed when she looked past them to where the big dude was holding Traine. That was Stevie's uncle.

Traine was not looking good.

My mom clapped her hands, taking charge. "Okay. I'm not sure what we missed before we got in, but we are leaving *now*."

I recognized that tone and that look in her eyes.

General Mom was back.

42

SAMANTHA

This was an all-hands-on-deck situation.

Maddy was safe. She was physically fine. That had been my first concern, but she and Max were both fine. They'd showed up late to whatever had been happening in that warehouse, thank God. I'd seen enough to have my stomach curdling and my mama instincts coming out strong.

These boys needed to feel safe, and whatever they'd gone through, it was not going to happen again. Not on my watch.

So until I could make sure they were safe, we were taking in three teenage boys. Thank goodness that Nash and Nolan had gone to David and Malinda's for the weekend, but if these boys stayed longer...I'd have to talk through it with the twins. Make sure they understood.

For now, though, I had these boys in my house.

Before we left, Mason took me aside and told me what had been happening before we got there. My blood boiled.

He stayed behind after that, and I pointedly did not ask what he was going to do. I would ask when he got home, but for now, he'd handle what he needed to handle and I'd handle the kids. The first order of business was the hospital. Beltraine was getting checked out while we were in the waiting lounge.

Channing was outside on his phone, and Heather and I were in our investigator roles. I was going to get all the information about all of these boys and I was going to do it so thoroughly I'd be convinced I could become an FBI profiler by the time I was done.

First boy up: Axel Johannson.

His parents were Briar and Emily Johannson. Briar was another prominent businessman in the area and a shareholder with Kade Enterprises. I made a note to ask Mason about him. Based on this guy's social media, he was smarmy. His hands were too low when he posed with women who were not his wife.

When I told Axel that I was going to contact her, he sneered. "Don't bother. I'm eighteen. Turned adult last month, but I'm already more adult than she is."

My heart broke at the bitterness in his tone and the dead look in his eyes. I wanted to take that from him, but I couldn't. I couldn't take all that away in one night. "What about your dad?"

He shook his head, his eyes going bleak. "I don't want him to know. Please." Fear flashed in his eyes. "I—you don't get it. My parents don't care. You've got no idea what that's like—"

All he had were his friends. A crack tore through my middle.

I said, quietly, "I do, actually."

His eyebrows pinched together, and whatever he read in me, some of the bitterness faded. He blinked a few times before looking away. "Yeah. Okay. Whatever. Just... I'm eighteen. I'm asking you not to contact them. Trust me. I've been living at Bell's for a reason. Phillip's an abusive fuckface, but it's still better than dealing with my parents."

Okay. Noted. We'd be looking into his parents.

I turned to the last one, Steele Manning.

He'd been skittish around me, but Maddy had snorted, calling him out. "*Dude, stop gawking at my mom. You're totally fanboying.*"

He'd gotten red in the face and jerked his eyes away. He paled now as he saw me heading his way. He shoved out of his chair, indicating behind me. "They're done."

He was right.

Brett had returned with Beltraine. A nurse had come with him and she looked around the room.

"I need to talk to Samantha Kade?" she said.

I started her way. Beltraine stood with her, an arm wrapped tight around his middle. He held a bag in his other hand.

"He requested for your name to be put on his medical file," the nurse told me. "He also removed his parents's names."

He raised his chin. "I'm eighteen. I can do that shit."

Her eyes flared. "Either way, he's insistent this was all just an extra physical training session after their football game. For the most part, he's severely dehydrated. He needs rest. A lot of rest. We hooked him up to an IV to start replenishing some of his nutrients, but going forward I'd recommend a service where they bring an IV to your home." She paused, studying the other boys. Her eyes narrowed on Maddy, who beamed at her, then returned to me. She gestured to Axel. "That one looks like he could see a doctor."

Axel shook his head, faking a yawn while somehow smirking at the same time. "I'm all good. Nothing a few bags of frozen peas can't fix."

His eyes moved to me. He had a mask in place. How many times had he shown that to an adult? How many times had no one looked past it?

I saw through it, and his eyes narrowed, staying on me.

The nurse sighed. "He has a right to refuse medical care, but it would be a good idea to get him checked out." As she spoke, the hospital's doors slid open and Channing walked in. The nurse's eyes widened, and comprehension clicked.

"It's like you know who my husband is," Heather said dryly.

The nurse's mouth lifted in a slight grin. "Maybe. Or I might know the wife of one of his employees." The two shared a look before the nurse got back to business. "Beltraine instructed me that if I needed to talk to an adult besides him, you were that person."

Axel held up a hand. "I'd like to make that change too."

She let out a soft sigh. "Why am I not surprised?" She eyed Steele. "And you?"

He straightened up but shook his head. "I'm good."

"Well, okay then," the nurse said. "Then they're all yours."

Beltraine swaggered past us, going over to Axel and Steele. Max and Maddy also sat in that part of the waiting area. Brett was by me. He glanced down at his phone, a heavy frown on his face. "What's your plan?"

I thought he was speaking to the phone for a minute until his eyes lifted to me.

"I'm taking 'em home," I said immediately. Without question.

His eyebrows rose. "All of them?"

I nodded. "Except Max, but yes. Those three. I don't trust the adults in their lives. At this point, they'll have to go through me to get to their kids."

"Has Mason checked in with you?"

I shook my head. "He knew we were heading here first. I'll give him a call when we go to the house."

His gaze moved to Maddy. "Are you worried about them being there with her?"

"Are you..." I cocked my head to the side, sharpening my focus on him. "Are you offering to take them into your place?"

Surprise flashed over his face before he shook his head. "No. No, I—the media is still crazy about Billie. It wouldn't be a relaxed environment. Billie would love it, though. Each kid would have his own pet chicken within a week, and if they did anything to harm them..." He trailed off.

I suppressed a smile. "I'm not worried about Maddy," I assured him. In between smiling around the entire room, Maddy kept checking in on Max. He hadn't moved from the five seconds before she looked at him, but she was still making sure. "She's, uh, pretty focused on someone already."

"So you're *not* worried about them being there with your girl?"

"Let's put it this way. My daughter... Yes, with most daughters, I would worry. But Maddy..." It was the opposite. If the boys did anything to Maddy, I would have to protect them from her. "She'll be fine," I told him.

"If you're sure." He motioned to the door, looking at his phone. "I'm going to head out. Billie's here to pick me up. Let your man know that if he needs anything, just reach out. I'd like to think if I needed help with Stevie, he'd be there for me."

"He would, Brett. We both would." I gave his arm a squeeze before he said his goodbyes and headed out.

Heather came over. "Channing has a guy who's going to look into these kids's situations, but he said Mason probably already has a handle on it. There's some business stuff going on too. Something that has to do with Kade Enterprises. Have you heard from him?"

I checked my phone, shaking my head. "He's not called, but he will. We're both supposed to check in when we're on the move. I'll call him when we leave here."

She nodded and turned to look at the kids. She understood. She really did. I moved closer so my arm brushed hers. My best friend. I'd missed her, and I was grateful she was with me in this. Some people would look at these boys and see their wealth and entitlement. I got that. I saw it too. It was easy to see they were the popular boys, probably the bad boys. But

I also saw the absence of their parents and the absence of love.

I wanted to gut Phillip Moreaux.

Feeling choked up, I whispered, "Thank you for being here."

Heather looked my way.

I held her gaze, letting her see the storm inside of me, the magnitude of it.

She pulled me in for a hug. "Back at you, Sam," she murmured.

43

MASON

I had two hours to deal with this prick, but I'd lost the bloodlust when Maddy showed up—well, Sam and Maddy. Things had started to shift when Sam slid in like the Rapunzel of bedsheets, but I'd really had to stomp that shit down when my daughter made her entrance.

Everyone left so it was just me and this abusive waste of space now.

I squatted near him, considering what to do. I wanted to kill him, but in this latest chapter of my life, it turns out that I was the good guy. Murder was my hard line. Logan was in the air. If I was going to blackmail this guy, I wanted to wait for my brother to be at my side.

After a moment, he began coming around, coughing and moaning. Then he seized, twisting in the air, and a scream ripped from him.

I rolled my eyes and stood, grabbing his shoulder. "Stop whining." I left the cage, dragging him behind me. He bounced on the steps, and I let go when he hit the bottom so he landed with a good, hard thump. He looked around, then at me, blinking.

"Relax. I didn't go to town on your ass like you did on that kid."

He groaned, rolling over. He coughed up some blood. Nope. He looked at his fingers. It was just saliva.

Grabbing his ankle, I continued dragging him out the door.

"Wait! Wha—" He twisted around. "Is anyone here? Help? *Help!*"

I walked to the middle of the parking area and dropped his ankle.

He continued to look around, panicked. "He-help!" He coughed again. More saliva. "Help! *Help me!* He's going to kill me."

I squatted again. *What a shitshow.* "You're so fucking dramatic."

He just kept looking around.

"No one's here." I shook my head. "Or at least no one who'll help you. No one's coming, Moreaux. You're all fucking alone. Are you hearing me? Alone."

Wariness tightened over his face. He lifted himself to sit cross-legged, still coughing. "What do you want, Kade?"

I sighed. "That's what I keep asking myself." I studied him. *Maybe...* I tried a bluff. "We called you the night my brother and I crashed your kid's party. Remember that? We called all of those kids's parents, and we waited until each one showed up to pick up their child. Except you. You never showed. Since it was your house, your kid, there wasn't much more we could do, but then we tried your wife. The number your kid gave us was out of order, and the number Logan found in the kitchen didn't work either. But my point is, we were in your house." I tilted my head to the side. "We were *in* your *house.*"

I waited. I wanted to see what his reaction would be to that information.

His eyes narrowed.

Finally some reaction.

He was thinking. His mouth opened. "Wha..." He shook his head and blanched.

"Yeah. I hit you hard. I wouldn't make sudden movements with your head like that. If you're concussed, you don't want to make it worse."

"What?" He coughed again and moved slowly, lifting his feet so his knees were bent. He braced himself, hands curling around the front of his legs.

Smirking, I stood up, just to make him hurt more.

He cursed under his breath, paling. "Wh-what are you inferring? What about that party?"

"That we were in your house." I raised an eyebrow.

"Yeah. So?"

Fuck. He really didn't get it. Or there was nothing there he cared that we might've found. Still, I had to play my card. I wanted to see if there was something there. I lifted an eyebrow. "Do you think when we got to your house, we immediately went to where the kids were?"

"They would've been in the basement. Bell knows to only have his parties there. Everything else is off-limits..." He went rigid, his voice trailing off.

"We were in your house, Phillip. Me and my brother." I lowered myself to his eye level. I was nice like that. "You think this is the first time we've had enemies like you? Granted, high school enemies were a little different. It was simpler back then. Whoever beat the others up the worst was usually the winner. Then there was the guy who wanted to rape my girlfriend, so I set that fucker up. Got him sent to prison. We've had other enemies—took down a secret society and put it all on one guy. That worked out. Turned out he was a serial rapist. But here's the thing. My woman wanted me to change. We couldn't keep going the path we were going. That's what I did. I changed. Got a career. Grew up. Became an adult. I was a different person. I am a different person, but here I am, back in Fallen Crest. Back where I'm doing everything I can not to keep beating the shit out of you, even though that's the *only* thing I want to do."

The bloodlust was stirring. "I want to make you bleed, and I want you gone. You're a cancer. You're the kind that won't go away. You'll keep eating away until you've rotted everything that's good. That's what you're going to do to your kid. You're going to infect him until he's just like you."

Shit. The way he was glaring at me, if he'd had a gun on him, he would've already shot me. Point blank and right between the eyes.

My amusement died.

Just like my fucking dad.

"What do you want, Kade?" He gritted his teeth, blanching as he tried to move.

"I told you." I held him back in place, and he winced under my hold. "I want you to go away. Can't use my old ways. I have a feeling if you got set up or charged with something, it would't stick. You've got money. You've got lawyers. Still, though..." I eyed him. Now was the time to play my bluff. "We were in your house, Moreaux. We had access to *every* room. Open access. What do you think we did before we went downstairs?"

The alarmed look was back.

I wanted to see it grow. "Are you putting the pieces together? We got into your files."

His eyes were panicked, and then, bullseye. He lost all color in his face. There was something on the computer.

"What do you want?" he sputtered, trying to regroup. "I'll— I have money hidden. I have information on the other share-holders. I was using it to blackmail them, but I'll give it to you instead. You can do what you want with it. I'll give it all to you. Just..."

He was scared.

Fuck. What was in those files?

The roar of engines came from behind me. I looked, but the

sound hit me before the headlights peeked over the hill. Motorcycles. They were coming down the road, two by two. Twelve total.

"Oh shit." Phillip suddenly jerked forward. "Hide me. Quick. You can have my shares. I promise. I'll..." The motorcycles slowed, turning down the road toward us. "Please! They're going to kill me."

Well, fuck. They got closer and I could see who exactly was headed our way. The Red Demons. They ran the other fighting ring. Was this their turf?

"Mason, please."

I shook him off like he was a flea and stepped away. I didn't know what was about to happen, but I reached into my pocket. Unlocking my phone, I turned the volume up and made quick work so when I hit the call button, it should be going to Logan. This would be a second gift when he landed.

Their headlights had both of us in the spotlight. They would be watching everything now so I kept my hand in my pocket.

Their charter's president got off his bike first. "Mason."

I lifted my chin. "Ghost, right?"

His face was grim. Eyes were empty. Mouth was in a hard line. Taking off his gloves, he motioned to me. "Let's take a walk."

I got a weird sense of déjà vu from another time a guy wanted to go on a walk with me. I kept that to myself. We walked past the circle of Harleys toward Max's truck, the vehicle left behind so I could drive myself home.

"Got a call thirty minutes ago," Shane spoke casually, like it was a good day to go to the beach. He kept strolling along, and I heard a thud behind us. I glanced back, seeing one of the bikers had kicked Moreaux. They circled him.

"Focus here, Mason," Ghost said.

"We're on a first name basis? Should I call you Shane?"

More thuds were heard from behind us. My pulse spiked. If they killed him, I was a witness.

He clipped out, "Don't you want to know who called me? Or what the call was about?"

I tried to concentrate, but they were *really* laying into More-aux. And I *really* didn't want them to kill him when I was here. "Not particularly. I'm thinking the less I know of your business, the better. Also figure the only person who's got a right to ask those questions is your wife."

Ghost stopped in his tracks.

I tensed, waiting.

Then he laughed. His whole face transformed. *Jesus.* Now he looked like a Shane, like a regular kind of guy—just one who was capable of ordering murder. "That's funny, but no. My wife wouldn't ask that question unless it has something to do with someone she knows. All bets are off because she's fucking merciless sometimes. Who called me was a friend of yours."

I frowned. "What?"

All lightness melted from his tone. He stared at me. Hard. "How do you know Kai Bennett?"

I did a double-take. I'd heard him wrong. *"Who?"*

We had a conversation.

44

MASON

When I pulled into the courtyard, light shone through every window in my house. Everyone was awake. Sam had called and left a message when they were leaving the hospital, so I knew what I was walking into.

I also knew who was in there.

My conversation with Ghost hadn't been a long one, but it'd been packed with bombshells. Thinking on it now, another conversation came back to me.

"I thought he would've called."

I hated hearing the pain in Sam's voice. *"Your dad?"* I'd asked her.

"Garrett, yeah." She'd fought off tears. *"What's wrong with me? He doesn't want to know me... Why couldn't he have room for two daughters?"*

I hated this, all of this, but most importantly, I hated what I was about to do.

I parked Max's truck off to the side so Logan would be able to pull in when he got here. After this night, I was ready to skewer the rest of the shareholders, but my conversation with Ghost took precedence.

I thought back to it now,

"You're friendly with the head of the biggest criminal organization in the Northern Hemisphere?" he asked.

I was cautious, every cell in my body telling me I needed to wade through this conversation like I was skating on very thin ice with bombs set to detonate at the first crack. "What did you just say?"

"Kai Bennett. The head of the Bennett mafia family." Ghost had not been laughing. "He runs the entire Canadian mafia syndicate. How the fuck do you know Kai Bennett?"

He swiftly closed the distance between us, getting in my face. "I was under the impression when you paid for a night to let off steam that it was also your first connect with us. When I asked the reason for that, Stripes told me you might want information on the exact same fucking person who called me out of the blue tonight." His eyes had flashed. "I'm aware you've got a big name and that before that, you and your brother had a reputation around these parts. I don't give a fuck about any of that, because I live here now too. I've got family here. I've set down roots. My guys are here. We gutted the last charter. Every single one of my guys, I picked. I trust my brothers. And I get dangerous when it comes to protecting those I love. Are you understanding me?"

Jesus. Fuck. This guy. I gritted my teeth and clamped down on the rage that had built inside of me. "Same, Ghost. Fucking same here."

"Then why the fuck is Kai Bennett giving me a call on my personal phone?" he asked. "Not long ago, he was considered my enemy. You aware of that?"

I expelled a ragged breath. "Why the fuck would I know that? I'm not in your world."

"You're standing in front of me, ain't you?"

"I was told something about Kai Bennett that led me to

believe he was possibly an enemy of mine." I said it calmly. "He found out. He came to me."

"I'm listening."

"He told me it was a lie. That he wasn't my enemy," I continued. "He came personally to course correct me. I believed him. Should I not have?"

I kicked it back to him and waited, the pressure building in me as he stared at me. Long and hard. When he stepped back, I almost sagged with how that pressure lifted off me.

"Kai Bennett is not known to be a liar. If he came to you, I'd believe what he said. Were his brothers there?"

"Just him and guards."

"That's good. Tanner's a whole different trip. And the other..." He trailed off, staring into the distance.

I frowned. "The other one?"

"Nothing." He pulled out a piece of paper. "Here. He's the one who notified us about what was happening here tonight. We run the fighting rings in the area. Moreaux thought he could open his own ring based on the fact that we already have a relationship with him. He thought wrong. Any operation in this area goes through us. We either have a hand in it or we okay it. We didn't okay this."

"What business are you in with him?" Could I ask that? But he was giving me the information...

He gave me another long scrutiny. "We use some of his businesses to wash money for us. And you might be wondering why I told you that just now. All casual and easygoing like." His eyes had fallen to the piece of paper in my hand. "That's a message from Kai Bennett. He told me to write it down for you, word for word. For whatever fucking reason, Kai Bennett's taken an interest in you. He's got eyes here. We knew about this place, but we hadn't made a move. Timing wasn't right. He told us if we wanted to deal with our local problem, tonight was the right time. We didn't know what we were going to come up on when we rolled in, except that you'd have a hand in it and Moreaux would be here. At the end of our conversation, he said to give you that message. I don't have any idea what it means, and unless it has something to do with me and mine, I don't want to know." He lowered his head, eyes still pinned on mine. "With Bennett's interest in you, you're being read into this world. You need to have a better comprehension how me and mine operate. There's an agreement in place with some of your friends—Monroe, his people. We steer clear of Roussou and they do the same with Frisco. I'm thinking you're a new authority in your town so I'll offer you the same. You steer clear of our business, and we'll do the same for yours. No more fight nights at our place. We're not going to be friends."

"I'll tell Logan to stop making friendship bracelets."

"I'll be heartbroken."

I jerked my chin in the direction of Moreaux. "And him? He was beating the shit out of his son and his friends tonight. I have a feeling my wife is going to want to take his kid under her wing—"

"Done," he said.

I stopped, surprised.

"As long as you care for the kid, we'll keep Moreaux Senior away from you and your kind—all the way away. Consider his shares sold. If he lives in your neighborhood, he'll be moving. If he's on a board where you go to church, have kids in the school, whatever it is, he's gone. As long as you care for the kid."

Some more pressure eased in my chest. I wasn't about to be a witness to Moreaux's murder.

"Is the kid... Do you know his kid? I need to know if you do. I gotta know of any potential minefields in the future."

He shrugged. "It's nothing personal with the kid. I don't have a connection with him. I just really hate dads who think they can beat on their kids. The only minefield ahead is that kid's trauma." He clipped his head toward the road. "Get gone, Kade. It's time us bad guys be bad guys."

I hadn't read the paper until I was at a stoplight in town.

As soon as I did, I wished I hadn't. Now parked outside of my own house, I didn't want to go inside. I didn't want to do what I was about to do.

I was about to shatter Sam's world.

45

SAMANTHA

M ason came in and time stopped.

I didn't know what was wrong, but I knew something was wrong. I never questioned it. Every fiber in my body began panicking and I took one stuttering step toward him before I stopped just as abruptly. I was in the hallway, my arms full of bedding. I was taking it to some of the other rooms to get the beds changed for the guys.

Mason held my gaze just inside the door, and I... Pain sliced through me. I didn't know where it came from. I didn't know why it was there, but it was there. One look from the boy I'd fallen in love with, the man I married, had children with, and was my other half. He was devastated.

I just didn't know why.

"Mason," I choked out. The bedding fell from my hands. I still didn't move. "What is it?"

He continued to hold my gaze, and for a second, the absolute longing he let me see singed me. I'd never not remember that look from him. It was raw, deep, and it cut to the bone. Then he closed his eyes. Some of the contact was broken between us, but he only lifted his head, and drew in some air. His shoulders lifted, rolled back, and settled back down.

He was preparing himself.

For what? To do what?

"Mason." My voice was still so hoarse. "What is it?"

His eyes opened. They were so bleak.

I was gutted from seeing that look from him. It wasn't supposed to be there. Not him. Not anymore. We'd gone through our trials. We'd had so many battles, and none of them broke us. We persevered and we were better because of it, but that look wasn't supposed to come back on his face.

My heart began pounding.

"Mom?" Maddy came over from the living room. I'd been in view of their room where she had been, her and the others. Max came over next, rounding Maddy's side to step into the hall. He looked from myself to Mason, and as soon as he did, he snapped to attention. He drew in a sudden breath, before looking to me again.

Max, the dear boy—no. He was a man by now. A young man. He settled a hand on Maddy's arm and positioned himself so he was between her and us. I noticed the movement, but it wasn't to protect her from us. It was to protect her from what Mason was bringing with him, but as soon as he registered his own motion, his shoulders dropped just as abruptly because he knew, just as I did, that whatever Mason had to say, he was going to say no matter what.

Max couldn't stop it from happening. He couldn't stop it from hurting Maddy, and I watched as he came to that realization as well. A sudden look of defeat flared over his face before he folded his chin and stepped close to Maddy's side. He got as close as he could.

Sounds of movement came from behind them. The others came in.

Beltraine, Axel, and Steele. Cautious and confused expressions were on all three of them. Guarded too.

I tried to give them a reassuring smile, but I knew it fell flat.

"Mom?" Maddy asked, her voice dropping.

Her heart clenched because she'd resorted to the same voice she used when she was a little girl. She was scared. My little girl who was convinced she was some sort of sociopath. Her voice trembled in fear. "What's going on?"

Mason cleared his throat.

She looked his way. "Dad?"

There was a hallway that separated the others from where Mason stood, but he heard them approaching and I held his gaze. His nostrils flared. His eyes met mine, holding mine for a moment, before a wall slammed into place.

No... I ached at seeing that expression on his face.

It'd been so long since I saw it.

I hadn't realized till now that I never missed it. Not once. I wished I'd never have to see it again, but here it was.

My heart thumped hard in my chest, and with it, I reeled back in time to when I was Maddy's age. When being numb or rageful were the only two emotions that got me through life.

"What's going on?" Beltraine asked the question, stepping forward as their leader. His voice was also hoarse, but that was from all the vomiting he'd done before going to the hospital.

I ignored him. I ignored all of them, including my daughter and Max. A bitter laugh slipped from me as I addressed Mason. "I thought we were done with this?"

I had tunnel vision on my husband. Everything else was pushed to the back, including the gasp I heard from my daughter. She hadn't moved a muscle. Nor had I, but suddenly, she was a mile away.

The mask lifted from Mason's face, but only just barely. I got a hint of an apology, and that sealed everything inside of me.

I began shaking my head and took a step back. No.

No.

I wasn't going to deal with this. Not anymore. My ghosts were gone. My mother was dead. I had no other skeletons in the closet, but Mason continued to hold my stare.

Whatever *this* was, whatever he was bringing into the house, it had to do with me.

If it'd been him, he wouldn't be looking as if he'd rather cut out his own heart than deliver what news he had. If it'd been about the kids, he wouldn't still be in the doorway. Anyone else, he would've called or said it to me directly. There'd be none of this premonition heartbreak.

Maddy was speaking, but I couldn't pull myself out of this trance.

Mason continued to look only at me, and I did the same, and dammit, my eyes watered as tears slid down my face.

I was going to get my heart broken.

Mason saw the realization land with me and started for me. "Sam," he said.

I shook my head, holding up a hand. "No. Just—" My voice broke. I needed a second. A fucking second. I was a mother, goddammit. Pulling myself out of the trance, Maddy was at my side, tugging on my arm. "Mom! MOM!" She was yelling, in my face, trying to get my attention. "Mom?" she whimpered.

"Maddy," Max tried to soothe her, pulling her into his arms.

She evaded his hold, not moving an inch from my side.

I looked over our daughter's head and asked her father, "Does she need to be here?"

"What? Be here for what? She is me, right?" She was looking between us as Mason came closer. He could now see the other boys, who had drawn closer as well. A new hardness cemented over his face, but he softened it as he looked at Maddy. "It'd be better if she wasn't—" He glanced at Max, who'd been following everything with a keenness that belonged to someone twice his age.

He gave us both a brisk nod. "Maddy, let's go to your room."

"What?"

He began pulling her away.

She dug her heels in. "No!"

He took her hand.

She shook him off. "I'm not leaving. Something's going on with my parents, and I—" Her tone trembled, breaking. "I need to be here for them."

He was watching us over her head.

Mason gave him another nod.

He clipped his head down before he bent forward and tossed my daughter over his shoulder.

"Hey—HEY! No! What are you doing?"

He raised his eyebrows. "I'll keep her in her room as long as possible, but you both know you won't have long to do what you need to do. Also, make sure I'm breathing when she comes back down." He went up the stairs after that, my daughter struggling and yelling over his shoulder.

It was the three boys and us now.

All were quiet, all so on guard.

I waited, wondering if Mason would dismiss them, then deliver what news he needed to tell me, but as I waited, he didn't.

What...

I inhaled sharply as new comprehension settled into place. This—whatever he had to tell me—it had to do with them?

I continued to frown as Mason turned to them, facing them as he stood at my side, and I held my breath, not knowing what was about to happen next.

"Tell her who the fuck you are."

What?

Tell me?

The boys? But—I studied them. Each of them.

Beltraine's eyebrows were pulled together, his head cocked to the side. Confused.

Axel... He was pissed. Clenched jaw. Hands in fists at his side. His shoulders were so rigid.

"Tell her. Now." Mason was looking at him. Dominant authority came off him in waves. There was no room to move here. He *would* tell me or he would face the consequences of Mason, but my husband took another step forward.

He wasn't speaking to Axel.

My eyes trailed, finding who my husband was addressing, and there was a faint pitter patter in my chest. The last boy.

Steele... His last name wasn't coming to me right now, but *Steele.*

Unlike his two friends, there was no confusion on his face. He stood at his tallest height. His shoulders back. His head lifted. He wasn't even focused on Mason. There was no fear. His eyes were on me, directly on me, and they weren't wavering. A new light shone from them. A new resolve or was it something else? He was calm, but there was more. He was resigned to whatever was about to happen.

I blinked, though, and I took a step toward him.

I'd felt a pull toward him since I first saw him in the warehouse. I'd done a double-take because for a second, just a brief second, I thought I saw someone else in him. But I looked again, and it was gone. I only saw a boy in pain, someone I didn't know, but someone I wanted to help.

He continued to hold my gaze.

"Steele is a nickname, and Manning is from my mother's side. My actual name is—"

I gasped as I saw it.

It happened in a flash, so fast. All the pieces connected, but I'd been wondering in the back of my mind all evening myself. I'd been focused on other items, more prominent issues first, but since that double-take, there'd been something nagging at me, a whisper from the back of my mind that I knew this boy. I may never have met him, but I knew him.

His name wasn't Steele. Not his real name.

The truth rocked through me.

He started, "Stirling—"

"—Brickshire," I ended.

He was my brother.

46

MASON

"You're my brother." Sam said the words quietly, a slight hint of wonderment mixed in.

Beltraine fell back a few steps, his entire head rearing back. Axel had moved his hands up, grabbing onto two fistfuls of hair, but at Sam's statement, his mouth fell open at the same time his hands slid slowly down, landing with a thud against his legs. Their eyeballs were almost bulging out.

Steele chanced them a look, hesitating before his head hung down again. "Yeah," he said it almost as softly as Samantha. His eyes remained on her, a wall in place between them.

I watched in real time as my wife fell in love.

She'd reached out a hand to him, but seeing the distance he put between them, she blinked, her eyes shining with unshed tears, and let her hand fall. She swallowed tightly. "I—Steele?"

He blinked rapidly a few times, his own Adam's apple moving up and down. He drew in some air, readying himself. "It's my nickname. I—" His gaze swung to his friends, his mouth flattening before curving down. "They didn't know. I..." His eyebrows pulled together again, his gaze swinging my way. "You knew."

I raised my own eyebrow because this little prick had the balls to sound accusatory to me. "I know everything. You tell her the rest, *now*."

Sam drew in more air, her chest rising and holding. She was preparing herself for what was still to come.

Just then, we heard a crash upstairs, followed by a door opening. One set of feet pounded the hallway. A second set of feet pounded after, until—*thud. Thump.*

Maddy yelled, "Ow! Fucker."

Max grunted. "You need to give them time. Jesus, Mads."

Her voice went low, but we could still hear it. "If you don't let me go, I swear to God, Max, I'm going to do permanent damage to your dick."

Enough was enough. I went to the stairs and shouted, "Logan Malinda Kade."

They fell quiet. The sounds of their wrestling ceased.

"Dad, I—"

"We are figuring some shit out. Go to your room and wait."

Thunk.

Max groaned.

"Do not hurt Max's—*any* body part of his. Just go to your room."

"But, Dad—"

"We will read you in when we know everything ourselves. Until then, go to your room."

They were quiet again, until Maddy began whispering.

"What? No, Mads. Do what he said. I mean—"

She whispered again, more fervently.

Max fell quiet.

She raised her voice, "Okay, Dad! We're going to my room. We'll have the door closed so no worries about the loudness of your voices. We won't hear a thing." To Max, we could hear her hiss, "Come on! Let's go."

He groaned again, but their feet faded, going in the direction of Maddy's bedroom.

I met Sam's gaze and saw some dark amusement pooling in them. Some of the stress in me lifted, just slightly. She didn't know everything. When she did, that amusement would be gone and I didn't know when it would come back again, but I was grateful to my daughter for putting it there now. Only if it was going to be a short time.

Sam and I shared a look, on the same wavelength. Sam said, "You know she's going to—"

I nodded, already moving. "Go around to the back end of the house and sneak downstairs, where they can overhear us. Let's move this to the study."

I led the way.

The boys followed next with Sam bringing up the rear. She and Steele kept sneaking looks at the other.

Beltraine joked as we went inside, his voice strained, "You guys have a study? And I thought we were rich."

No one laughed.

He grimaced. "Tough crowd."

"It's not fucking funny, Traine. Shit. Are you listening to what's happening?" Axel exploded, his arm thrust out toward Steele. "Fucking Steele's been lying to us this whole time."

Beltraine grimaced again, but this time there was some guilt mixed in. His eyes shot to where Steele had braked.

Axel saw the look. His arm dropped dramatically and he squared up against his friend. "You knew? You fucking knew?"

Beltaine shared another look with Steele before opening his mouth, but nothing came out. He cringed, before closing it back up. He shrugged, admonishing, "I..."

Sam closed the door, but she didn't move far from it. Her back was to it, and she stood there as if she were barring anyone from leaving or entering. I tried to get a feel on what was going on with her, but she wasn't letting me. Her eyes were heavy, some sadness shone out, but that was it. She wasn't closed off, but she wasn't meeting my gaze either.

Steele interjected, raspy until he coughed to clear his voice, "He didn't know the specifics, but he just knew I wasn't being on the up and up for why I'm here."

"Why are you here?" Sam asked quickly. Clearly. Her gaze was only on her brother.

"I..." He trailed off, flinching before raking a hand through his hair.

There was a lot of that happening. A lot of people not finishing their statements. A lot of grimacing. A lot of fucking lies that needed to be out, and the sooner the better.

I growled, bringing all attention to me. "Drop the act. You come clean now, or I swear to God, kid, I'll do it for you. I've got a feeling you'll appreciate if you say the words first. You hear me?"

He paled, the first fucking time showing some fear.

Good.

This kid had no idea the shitstorm coming for him.

I jerked my head toward where the other part of my heart stood outside of my body. "She deserves the truth. You either deliver it, or I will."

He held my gaze for a moment before everything changed. The rigidness left. His shoulders slackened. The lines around his mouth softened. His eyes grew sad. "You're right. Fuck. You're right." He sank down, taking a seat.

Beltraine leaned against one of the walls in the far corner.

Axel sat on the same couch as Steele, but at the farthest end. He was there, watching his buddy.

Beltraine only had eyes for Steele as well.

Sam and I didn't move.

Steele waited a moment, maybe to gather himself, I didn't know, but then he started talking.

"Some of it, I don't know myself. Brinna—"

"Brinna?" Sam's voice was hoarse.

"My sister. That's what we call her. She, uh—"

"Your dad used to call her Seb."

My heart tightened, hearing that. 'Your dad.' No longer her dad. I hated that this was happening, that this had happened. God, Sam. I kept my eyes on her, as if I could block the pain that was happening in front of me, and how more of it was going to land on her as he would continue to unravel everything.

"Yeah." Steele shot her a slight grin before it faded, his face going flat again. "She informed everyone when she turned thirteen that she no longer wanted that name. She didn't like it, said it was too guy-like for her." He scoffed.

"Why are you here, Steele? Did you know who I was this whole time?"

He looked haunted, that slipped out before he locked it down, as quick as it showed. "Yeah. I—Brinna... God. This is all messed up." He shot to his feet, one of his hands in his hair, fisting it and he held onto it. He began to pace. His shoulders and back tightening. "There's things that I can't tell you because I don't fully know myself. I just—" He let loose a myriad of curses, swiftly and savagely.

Sam asked when he took a breath, "Where are your parents?"

He swung those heavy-lined eyes her way, stopping in his pacing. His hand lowered from his head. Some of the wall began to fall from his face, and soon, it completely collapsed. He stared at Sam, stricken. He couldn't look away. "They're in Europe. They were banned from being here since the last time he saw you."

Those words held a punch. It slammed into Sam. She fell back a step before righting herself. "What?"

"It was one of the conditions. He had to cease communication with you. He was having a hard time with it, or that's what I was told. I guess he kept reaching out and then finally they said he couldn't live in the country anymore. He and my mom have been in Europe most of my life. Since I was four, I think?"

Sam looked my way, a question in her depths if I knew this information.

I shook my head. This was new to me.

I knew about Steele. I knew about the sister and about what she did. We'd not gotten to that part.

"Where's your sister?" Sam was frowning to herself. "Maddy said..." Her head tilted up and to the side, her lips pursing together briefly. "She mentioned her. You're the friends she talked about, aren't you? The ones where the sister comes on the weekend, but she was told not to ask any question about where she goes to school. That's you guys. That's Sabrina, she's talking about. Not the other friends I thought she was referencing." She lifted her eyes to me again, and I got it. Noted it. Our daughter lied. That'd be added to the list for another discussion with her.

I gave her a brief nod back, letting her know I was with her.

Sam closed her eyes for a beat before focusing on her brother again. He hadn't answered. "Steele," she prompted.

"Yeah. I—I don't know. Maddy hangs out with us."

Axel spoke up, "There's another girl that she talks to in class. Lucia. But they don't hang out outside of school. That's us. She's been hanging out at Traine's house with us on the weekends. Her and Monroe."

"Dude," Beltraine hissed.

Axel shot him a dark look. "Get over it, Traine. Real shit's happening here."

He glared back. "Where's your fucking loyalty to Mads? She's our friend."

"And you think she's going to find out Steele's been lying, that you had an idea, and not go apeshit on both of you?" He gestured to the ceiling. "She's an animal. If you think she's going to protect you over her parents, you are delusional."

Beltraine continued to glower at him.

Axel scoffed, shaking his head. He leaned back on the couch, shoving his hands in his pockets. "Whatever, dude. She's not you. She has good parents. She's not like us in that vein."

"But I am," Sam spoke. She gestured to me. "So is he. *We're* like you guys." She lingered on Steele before adding, "I'm not sure about you. Are your parents..." She hesitated and began chewing on her bottom lip. "What are they like?"

Steele sat up and his head rose. His chest filled. "They're good parents. I swear to God, Sa—Mrs. Kad—I don't know what to call you."

"Sam," she said, huskily. "Sam or Samantha. I'm not Mrs. Kade to you."

He held her gaze before swallowing and nodding again. "Yeah. You're right. Sa... Sam. Samantha. My mom and dad are good parents. They really are. They didn't like what was happening and Dad, he—he tried to stop it. He really did. It's why he stopped talking to you. It was their condition. If they were going to leave you alone, then he had to as well. It's..." He stared at her, that stricken look returning. "He loves you. He does. It's why he left you. I swear it."

Sam and I shared another look. Both of us were confused.

"Who are you talking about? Who, Steele?" She moved away from the door.

He stiffened, his pupils dilating before he shook his head. As much as he'd opened before, the opposite happened now. He folded in on himself. If he could've balled up and disappeared, he would've. He croaked out, almost too quietly to hear, "I can't tell you about them. I'm not supposed to even know, but I do. I..." He was back to hesitating. "I can't be the one to tell you."

Beltraine ripped away from the wall, stalking to his friend.

He touched his shoulder, but turned so he was shielding him from us. "That's fucking enough. He told you what he could."

No. It wasn't enough.

I stalked forward, meeting the little shit's gaze. "He tells us everything—"

Beltraine jerked his chin up, drawing to his full height to stand against me. "Or what?" His eyes turned mean. Glittering from heat. "You going to make us do shuttle runs too? Beat us up? What are you going to do?"

This was a kid, going toe to toe with me.

I didn't want to like this kid, or respect him, but I did. It came in, grudgingly, but it was there. He was protecting his friend. I made sure to soften my voice, but he had to know the ramifications. "There's a whole side to his story that I didn't know about, but we will hear it all. You hear me? What he's withholding threatens my family. I get that you consider him your family. That's obvious, and trust me, I do get that, but he's saying there's someone out there that wanted to come after my wife. That's Maddy's mom. We have you in our home. She was making up beds for you so while it's cool you want to protect your friend, you need to think long term. My wife still hasn't heard all of it and I'd much rather she hear it from him, than me. He might be able to offer up some understanding for why he did what he did." I moved to the side as I spoke, my eyes falling on Steele as I said that last piece.

Blood drained from him. He grabbed onto the couch, just before his entire body wavered to the side.

Axel cursed, shifting over. He grabbed hold of Steele, keeping him from toppling over.

Beltraine whipped around too, also cursing. Both righted their friend simultaneously.

"Fuck this." Axel looked up.

"Axe," Beltraine warned.

"No. Fuck this, Traine." His gaze skirted between Sam and

me. "You need to call his sister. She's behind all of this. Whatever all of this is, it's her. Guaranteed. It's her."

Something shifted inside of me. He was giving me a new target. "What are you saying?"

"You want answers, you get them from her. Fuck. She'll probably gloat about it."

Beltraine and Steele didn't argue with what he was saying. Both remained quiet.

Axel added, almost as a curse, "She's the mastermind behind whatever this is."

I took out my phone and tossed it to him. "Call her."

47

MADDY

I. Was.
Going.
Insane.
I needed to know what was happening.
Anything could be happening.
Someone might be getting murdered.
Someone might be murdering.
I sucked in my breath because what then?
I had to be a part of it, of whatever *it* was happening.
I cursed under my breath, looking over at Max where he was sleeping on the couch.

I talked him into sneaking downstairs, but he didn't realize that we should've been able to overhear them except that when we got down here, we couldn't. They left. Slippery little parents.

And the guys. Traine, Axe, and Steele. They were my friends.
What was going on?
I wanted to pull my hair out, or my nails.
I had to move. I couldn't stay down here anymore.

Patting Max on his arm, I stood, whispering, "I'm sorry, my love."

Who knew Benadryl was so fast acting. The few times I took it, it usually took an hour. When I slipped it into Max's water, it hit him almost immediately.

Reaching for a blanket, I covered him up, and that was when the doorbell rang.

I perked up. Now we're talking. It was almost a party.

I was moving up the stairs when I heard my dad going to the door. He and Mom walked differently. I would recognize the sound of his footsteps for the rest of my life. They were quiet, but ominous at the same time. I rolled my eyes at that thought.

Ominous. My dad. Pfft.

Then I heard a voice I knew.

"Hello!" That was Brinna and she was sounding all bright and cheery, but it wasn't real. She was... I didn't like how she was sounding. "This has been a long time coming, don't you think? Brother-in-law."

I froze on the stairs. *Brother-in-law?*

Why was Steele's sister saying that to my dad?

I kinda regretted drugging Max now.

48

MASON

Sabrina Brickshire was a cocky little shit. Maybe there's a better way to describe her, but I don't care to expend that energy. I opened that door, took one look at her, and hated her on sight. She's got Sam's eyes, her chin, and her body type. And that is all. The rest of her is maniacal bullshit. I get why Axel said she was the mastermind. She was gloating when she got here.

This was always my dilemma.

I loathe when other girls messed with Sam because I couldn't punish them. You hurt us. We hurt you back tenfold, except I never knew what to do with the female gender.

It was the same problem now, except what I really wanted to do, Sam would not be down for that. I'd wait. I'd hear it all, make my decision, and proceed from there.

She was almost skipping when I led her to the study. There was a bounce to her stride and she kept looking at me, giving me a fucking coy smile.

I gave her nothing.

It didn't penetrate with her. If I hadn't already been operating with the assumption the girl had legit mental instability, I would've thought she was on something. Her laugh was high and coarse. She was flushed. Some beads of sweat on her forehead. But her eyes were the kicker. They were not here. She was off in some other universe in her head.

I held open the door, and she went in first.

After Axel called her on my phone—and it should be noted that she answered, and agreed to coming without once asking about her brother—the guys had a heated discussion. A heated fight was a better word because all three threw down for their opinions.

Steele wanted them gone. This was family business, literally.

Axel and Beltraine vehemently disagreed.

Beltraine flat-out said, "Fuck no, dude. Your sister is the most cunning and unstable bitch I've ever met. I'm not fucking leaving." He declared that and plopped down on a chair. Folding his arms over his chest, he gave Steele a pointed glare and smirked.

Steele's mouth hung open. "I—you never said any of this shit to me before."

Beltaine laughed before using his head to indicate the room. "And we've not heard any of this shit. You said you needed a place to stay and to tell people we're cousins because you had family drama back home."

"That's the truth."

Beltraine's eyes flicked upward. "You lied to me, but whatever, dude. I love you and I'm not leaving. Next." He jerked his chin toward Axel.

Steele cursed under his breath, his fingers dug into his temples before round two happened.

He started, "Axe—"

"No." Axel dropped back on the couch where he'd been sitting before.

I liked both their arguments, but I liked Beltraine's more.

And I really liked it now after having met Sam's little sister, but as we walked inside, I caught the look those two shared.

Neither were fans of Steele and Sam's sister.

Sam, though, I studied her and a metal cage fell down around me, locking me in, because I was watching my wife fall in love all over again. This time it was with her sister.

Her eyes softened. Warmed. "Sabrina." She started for her, her arms lifting for a hug when the girl in question started laughing.

Laughing.

And it was the same high-pitched unhinged laugh.

Sam stopped in her tracks.

Steele cursed. "Stop it, Brinna."

The laughter died, and a hollowness lingered in an echo after.

I would never describe this girl as beautiful, because she wasn't. On the outside, she might've passed for that description. She had wavy brown hair. It fell just past her shoulders. She was slender. I'm sure she was dressed as a normal college student would dress. Maybe one going to a party. A white crop-top. High-waisted jeans a lot of other girls wore. Sandals. Glowing, sun-kissed tan skin. Her face was what all the pretty girls looked like, but she couldn't hold a candle against someone like her sister.

Sam was beautiful on the outside and inside. She surpassed this girl. Hands fucking down. Sam was better in every way, always would be better. The girl had no chance, but my wife, with the good heart she had, wasn't thinking about any of that.

I knew what she was thinking.

She was thinking about the day she first held her sister in her arms.

She was remembering that day and remembering all the love she had for her, and after needing to suppress it for so long, it was flooding back to her. She wasn't seeing how her sister wasn't her sister anymore. She was an enemy. She was someone who wanted to hurt her.

I thought she could tell Sam, tell her what she did, how Steele had told Samantha who he was.

I was dead fucking wrong.

This girl was going to do it. She was, I saw that, but she was going to do it in the cruelest way she could. She wanted to inflict the worst kind of pain she could on Samantha.

I wasn't going to let that happen.

"What, little brother? Aren't you happy to see me?"

He didn't go to her. He didn't hug her. He just stood there, glared, and fisted his hands at his sides.

She'd been taking him in at the same time, because she let out a harsh laugh. "Are you kidding me?" Her head tilted. Her eyes narrowed, cold calculation smearing her face. Her lips twisted in a snarl. "You were supposed to make contact."

"I did," he bit out.

"You were supposed to become friends with their daughter."

"I did do that." He glanced at Sam, warily.

Her tone went mean. "You weren't supposed to start caring for her, you dipshit."

He flushed. "She's my sister, Brinna."

"So?" She taunted. "She's also the reason Uncle Seb went to prison."

Sam gasped, her eyes tearing my way, just as mine shot to hers. Shock and alarm branded me. "Uncle Seb?"

She went still, eerily still, before rotating to face me. The entire motion made my skin crawl, but the smile on her face wasn't right. She wasn't right. She continued with that mocking tone. "Yes. My godfather. I believe you knew him as Park Sebastian." She winked at her brother. "Why do you think I wanted a different nickname? Seb is his name. Not mine. We can't have the same nickname."

Uncle Seb. Park Sebastian. Holy shit.

I was rocked.

The ground could've fallen out from underneath me and I wouldn't have noticed.

Our past *had* come back to haunt us.

"He went to prison."

"Yes, he did. For what The Network pinned on him."

She knew about The Network.

She thought they set him up? For being a serial rapist? She had no idea what he'd done. No idea at all.

"The—" Beltraine asked, his face scrunched up. He cast Steele a look before saying, "Never mind."

"The Network." She sing-songed the name, clapping her hands. "I'm so excited for this moment. I've been waiting so long for this. Yes, Traine. The Network. It was a secret society that your new Mommy and Daddy destroyed."

Sam was so pale, shaking her head.

The list of shit he'd done to us, the worst was to her.

"Except they decided they didn't want to be a part of it so they took something that generations built and they burned it all down to the ground. Much like another building, am I correct, brother-in-law?"

She knew about the fraternity house. She knew about The Network.

I said, "You're still in contact with Park, aren't you?"

She began laughing, this time a genuine trickle of amusement coming from her. "Still in contact? I've never not been in contact with my godfather. Some might say I'm closer to him than my own father." Her lips curved up. "Those people would be correct. I know everything you've done to him—"

"I very much doubt that," Sam snapped.

There she was.

The shaken look was gone. The old Sam was back, mixed with the new one, and she was even stronger. More powerful.

This was the kickass Sam, and God, I loved her. Pride swelled in my chest, along with arousal and desire. My woman made me hard.

Sabrina frowned, and she faltered a step. This wasn't the sister she thought she'd be meeting.

"What—" she started to say something.

Steele cut off his own sister. "He's brainwashed her."

"Steele!" She slapped him.

Whoa.

Sam's eyes widened at how quick her reaction had been, and she wound up to do it again.

"I don't fucking think so." Beltraine was there, getting between her and her brother. "Step back, you bitch."

Sabrina inhaled sharply, but her target just switched. Her hand went back again. She was going to slap Beltraine instead.

"Fuck no." Axel got involved, shoving her backward. He followed her, stopping after a few feet, now blocking both Beltraine and Steele from her. "You ever touch your brother like that again and I don't give a fuck who you are, I will ruin your life."

I met Sam's gaze over their heads, both of us in shock. These kids were us. Me. Logan. Her. They were in the form of Beltraine, Axel, and Steele? This was a whole head trip that I didn't see coming.

Sabrina growled, "You're the one who called me to come here."

"Because your brother won't tell them about whatever sick secrets you've made him keep. He came clean that he's her sister, but that's it. You have to come clean about everything else. Tell them the truth. Enough with these fucking manipulations."

Her eyes grew uncentered, a wild gleam taking root in them. She tipped her head back, another chortling laugh rippling up and out of her throat. "Oh? It's like that. Is it? I come on command and what? Confess? Is that supposed to save my soul, Axel? My brother's soul?"

Axel switched, going from heated to a cold smirk in point zero seconds. But the transition made her uneasy. That only reinforced his smirk. "I don't give a fuck about your soul. I've listened to you rant enough to know you are gone. You've been brainwashed. There's no coming back for you."

Her face grew heated, reddening. She flung her hand out, pointing at Sam and me. "These people—you don't even know what they did."

"I don't care." He got right back in her face. "You want to know what these people did for me? For Beltraine? For your own brother? You wanna listen to that because I can tell you. It happened in real time. In front of me. It's not a story I've heard from someone else, who is so fucking obvious about his agenda, that you're batshit stupid to believe one fucking word of it."

"He's been there for me—"

"I've been there for you!" Steele roared, stalking around his friends and getting in his sister's face.

She blinked, and blinked again. He kept going at her, and she backtracked. They didn't stop until she hit against the wall and even then, Steele got all up in her space. He was taller than her so he leaned down, his voice chilling. "Do you know what Bell's dad was doing to us?"

Some of the fight faded. "Wha—what are you talking about?"

"Phillip Moreaux. We didn't know anyone here. You're the one who approached Moreaux. You're the one who put me in Bell's house, but I'm the one who got Bell to agree to lie for me. He just didn't know the truth. How'd you know to contact Phillip Moreaux?"

"What... What was he doing to you? What did he do to

you?" Her voice rose, becoming sharp again. The beginning of some panic was setting in.

Steele ignored her, speaking low, almost depressed. Some of his shoulders loosened again, becoming defeated. His voice become replete, empty. "It wasn't just once. We've been playing football for almost two months now. We started the end of August. Do you know... You have no idea, but they did. They stopped it."

"What did he do to you?"

Fuck. That voice. The unhinged tone was gone, and in that voice, she was stripped down to a sister. She fucking sounded like Samantha. The same voice. I did not want to hear that familiarity from her. Fuck no. I didn't want a reminder whose blood she shared, because in that voice, as Sam heard it too, I saw hope rekindle in my wife's heart.

Fuck, fuck, *fuck*.

The hope gave way to new determination. I knew, right then and there, that Sam was going to do what she needed to save this sister of hers.

Goddamn. *No*. No!

Steele didn't tell her. Axel didn't either. Beltraine did. And as he did, as we all heard what else his father had done to them and how many more times he'd had them go into that shed, more than I wanted to think about because he hadn't used the excuse of a lost football game to justify his need to abuse them, Sabrina was shaking by the end of it.

"I didn't know. I swear." All the blood was gone from her face. Her lips were trembling. "Steele, I swear. I didn't know."

"Yeah," he bit out. Rough. "But someone did. Who told you to contact him?"

"I didn't contact him. That's not how this happened. I was... We were introduced and we went from there."

"Who did the introductions?"

The answer was there, right on the tip of her tongue, but as she thought about answering, she looked at my wife. Just that, one look, and I could see all the brainwashing return back to her forefront. The raw vulnerability she had when hearing her little brother had been hurt was covered up by the cruel glee-fulness of whatever this creature was in front of me.

Park Sebastian did this. He did a masterful job of it. I had to give him that.

He took away someone Sam loved.

"Who do you think? Come on." She laughed again; the chortling was back. "You want to know everything? I mean, that *is* why I came here. I knew when Mom and Dad figured it out, then the gig was up. Or most of it is up, but don't worry. I'll tell you everything. I *want* to tell you everything. Are you ready?"

Sam stared back at her, but she had masked the earlier love I saw in her gaze as she watched her sister. An expressionless mask was in its place. She deadpanned, "Not in the least."

Sabrina didn't care. She began talking.

49

MADDY

I found them!

They were in the study, and who knew when Nova's snake went missing it ended up being a blessing because I knew about a vent that I could overhear *everything*. It'd been where Nova's snake was hiding. Natessia's the one who got it out. Max's little sister.

I didn't think I was scared of anything, but that's not true. I'm terrified of something happening to my family...and snakes. Nat, though. She *really* isn't scared of anything. Nolan used her gifts, like a honing beacon, led us to the study, and from there, Nat stuck her hand down, grabbed the snake and hauled that sucker out of there.

It was wrapped all around her arm, but it was awesome.

I didn't want to miss anything, but I made a detour through the kitchen to grab a snack. Uncle Logan instilled that in me from an early age. If there's drama, you grab popcorn. It's proper etiquette now. If someone else is watching, or in this case listening, with you, you share.

Also good etiquette.

I didn't have time to pop anything, but there was a bag

ready to go so I grabbed it, along with a soda and here I was, snuggled up on the other side of the vent. I had snacks. A drink. And a blanket I snatched on the way.

Getting comfortable, I was ready.

Okay. So the way I figure is that this entire showdown had three parts. The first part I missed because *Max*.

The second part, I could *not believe* what I was hearing.

Brinna was my mom's sister? Half sister?

I was a little fuzzy on some of the details, but holy shit, Brinna was a bitch. She was the definition of a HBOTC. Also, I wasn't liking how she was talking to my mom. Like she was taunting her or something.

Then, wham bam, I almost fell over ma'am when I heard about what Traine's dad was doing to them. I went all growly and had to stuff the blanket over my mouth to keep from alerting them to my spot. I was making a list of people that I could hurt and Traine's dad was on it. They had not shared that part with me when Max and I made our dramatic entrance or when we were at the hospital. I asked, but everyone was tense and Max kept telling me he'd tell me later.

Sometimes I liked playing that game with him. If he said he'd tell me something later, and if he didn't, then I'd get inventive in how I'd make him tell me. Because of the idea of that game, I didn't push on finding out the details.

I regret that now.

I kept listening.

Oooh. Some understanding was happening. She'd been brainwashed by this other guy, someone that Mom and Pop hurt. That made sense. I mean, that sucked, but it made a bit more sense how someone who was my mom's sister was such a cunty bitch.

Part three of the showdown was when Brinna explained the evilness of her evil plans.

Turns out, there used to be a secret society. Mom and Dad blew it up. Go 'rents.

They set up the Godfather Brainwashee Guy to take the fall, who was sent to prison because he was a serial rapist. The HBOTC was in denial of that fact, but it seemed legit to me. If someone's going to brainwash someone all their life, I mean, hello, that's just another form of grooming.

The big twist was that another secret society was erected.

Pause for laughter. I just said erected.

The new secret society was better, more elite, more powerful, and they changed some rules. They were all about blackmailing first and not holding information to blackmail later. That part didn't make sense, but I'm sure if someone was in that old secret society, that'd make sense to them. The bottom line was that a lot of blackmailing was happening. The new secret society was worse than the first.

If I was hearing that right? Most things are worse the second time around.

Oh. Whoa. They were behind why Grandpa Garrett couldn't see my mom. That made sense. He knew about them and when they wanted to hurt my mom and dad, Grandpa Garrett put his foot down. He said no, sirree. They countered with, 'Oh, so we can't hurt your daughter? *Fine.* Then you can't see her either.'

So not cool.

The new secret society sounded like assholes. Then again, anyone who was in a secret society would be an asshole. I'm sure it was a requirement.

That sucked for Mom. It bothered her that her bio dad never reached out. His heart seemed to be in the right place. If we took this new one down, Grandpa Garrett could come around again. Mom would be happy to see him.

The new secret society was added to my list.

PEOPLE, PLACES, OR THINGS FOR DESTRUCTION:

1. Traine's a-hole dad
2. HBOTC (new leader) Brinna
3. New secret society

That'd keep me busy the rest of high school, but they were still talking.

Aaannnddd, my fingers hit the bottom of the popcorn bag. I ran out of my snack. I might need to grab some more—

"Maddy."

Err. Screech. Say what?

All thoughts of going for more popcorn was abandoned because the HBOTC just said my name.

I turned around so I could press my ear to the vent to make sure I didn't miss anything. She was bringing me into this.

As far as I was concerned, that gave me permission to do anything and everything I was planning.

Thank you, HBOTC.

50

SAMANTHA

I couldn't process what this person was saying.

My sister.

My God. My brother.

They were both here.

I... How could I process this? But Sabrina wasn't mine. He'd gotten to her. He took her away from me. He turned her against me. I stood here and listened as Sabrina talked about this new secret society. How great it was. How powerful. How elite.

The punchline was her.

Park Sebastian wanted to hurt us and he won in the end. He was a part of the new secret society, even from prison. He orchestrated everything.

Jesus Christ. Did Garrett know how much in contact Sabrina had been with Park? I couldn't imagine he'd be okay with it. He knew what Park tried to do me, and my sister was telling me that Park wasn't a serial rapist. That we set him up.

She believed it. Everything he said. She believed every damn word.

No.

I made up my mind.

He didn't get to have her. I didn't care how long he spent grooming her, making her believe his bullshit. I wouldn't allow it.

"Where is he?"

My sister shut up. I tuned her out because everything she was saying was on repeat. There was nothing new. It was crazy rhetoric. Half was about how amazing the new secret society was, and the other half was how enraged she was on Uncle Seb's behalf for what the old secret society did to him. Round and fucking round.

"Who?"

"Park."

Her eyes got wide before more glee beamed from her. "He's still in prison. They got him convicted for being a serial rapist, remember? *Such* bullshit charges, but he has a new lawyer and there's a new judge in the secret society. They're going to get him out. It's a matter of time now. I can't wait." She rubbed her hands together.

Bullshit charges. I shook my head. They weren't bullshit charges. I looked over her head to Mason, saw the concern he had for me. He knew what Park tried to do to me.

But Garrett left, seemingly to protect me, and what? He left his daughter behind? How the hell had Sabrina been in contact with Park all her life? Why wasn't she in Europe with her parents?

I needed to talk to Garrett. I needed Sabrina to shut the fuck up. She was spouting nonsense. And I needed to talk to Steele. He'd been quiet since her arrival.

"You need—I need to talk to your father."

She stopped talking again, but then a wicked smile stretched over her face. "But you haven't asked me the best part. The big reveal, sister. Don't you want to know the real reason I'm here? Why I sent Steele to go to school here ahead of me? It's really good. I promise."

God.

I didn't want to know.

I didn't know if I could stomach it, whether it was real or bullshit.

I started to tell her just that, but she tilted her head to the side, softening her grin. "It has to do with Maddy."

I went still, hearing that.

My daughter.

What did my daughter have to do with whatever dark plans my sister had concocted? Steele too. I sent him a scathing look, but he was watching his sister with confusion.

"They changed the recruiting rule. You remember how it worked the last time, right?"

I did, remembering when Park himself explained it all to me.

The families were legacies. My grandfather. My father. It made sense why they tapped Sabrina to join the new one. Park's family started it all. They initiated my mother, except she was blacklisted. They tried to initiate me. They wanted Mason, Logan. They really wanted James Kade, though he was considered a special exception. The recruiting happened in college. They pulled people in through friendships and bonding, finding out their secrets and using that to keep them inside the society. It was a cult. If you left, all of your secrets were released and your life was ruined.

The power of The Network had been terrifying. If this new one was worse, that gave me chills.

My mouth was dry, feeling like I was scraping over bark as I asked, "How did they change it?"

"We can recruit in high school now."

Oh, God.

She sent Steele here. He was in the same school as Maddy.

Steele was cool. Popular. That was obvious to see. His group of friends seemed to be friends with my daughter.

I shared a horrified look with Mason, both of us realizing what she was trying to do. I rasped out, "You're trying to recruit my daughter?"

Her eyes were soulless. She tucked her hands behind her back and swung her shoulders from side to side. All demure-like and the devil incarnate. "That's the thing. Right? The dangerous part of secret societies. Cults. Once you get in someone's head, in their emotions, you can't get out. I'm in Maddy's head. The guys were nice enough to introduce us, to let us hang out at Beltraine's house on the weekend. Your daughter is real nice. She looks up to me. She likes me."

Axel's nose was wrinkled. His top lip curled up in disgust.

Steele's eyes were bulging out, as if he couldn't believe what he was hearing.

Beltraine shared the same, but there was an undercurrent with him. A darker feeling. He was plotting and the way he was staring at Sabrina, those thoughts were about her.

God.

Was it true? Did Sabrina already have a handle on Maddy? Was she so far in that we'd never be able to get Sabrina's influence out of her? We were seeing the real life product of this recruitment in person. My sister was proof of how powerful, how dangerous that type of recruitment could be.

I had no idea what kind of person my sister might've been because she was all Park Sebastian personified. She was his puppet.

No.

I shook my head, eyes closing. It couldn't be true, but I thought Maddy had been spending time with different friends. I met them. Thought they were great influences. I didn't know it had all been a lie, but Maddy had consistently been lying since James died.

James...

Oh—no, no, *no*.

No—I locked eyes with Mason, but...

He knew. He already knew.

He'd been waiting for me to get there.

The old secret society wanted James. Badly.

The new one... They were about revenge, apparently.

They hadn't come after me because of my father, but there would've been nothing to keep them away from James.

My stomach twisted. I covered my mouth as vomit churned up my throat.

Dear Lord. *No.*

My sister quieted as she watched me. As I pieced things together, her smile only grew.

Her face wasn't even human right now. If I'd been told a demon possessed her, I would've believed it. Her eyes were bone chilling. She was so eager. Her head inclined toward me, and she tucked some of her hair behind her ear. "Did you figure it out? Are you there yet?" She was so breathless from her excitement.

I couldn't voice it.

I couldn't put into words what I was thinking because it would've been a nightmare come to life. I couldn't do that to Mason. To Logan. He'd been their father. My children's grandfather. But he would've been vulnerable.

Analise died and he'd been lost, missing her.

"You're there, aren't you? You can tell me. Give me a hint. I don't want to jump ahead if you're not there yet. It's best if you got there on your own. More fulfilling that way." She took two steps my way, the exhilaration vibrating off her body. Her eyes were wild, gone, as if she were on drugs. "Give me a hint. Come on. Something."

I shook my head, taking a step away from her. Wrapping my arms around myself, I couldn't stomach being around her. She wanted to boast about it. She was begging for me to let her spill all the horrible details.

"Sam," Mason murmured, starting for me.

"Don't!" I held up a hand, stopping him. I bit out, "Don't. What they did—" I couldn't finish. My throat spasmed, choking me. "It was them, Mason. They did it."

"I know." His words were quiet.

This was what he was referring to when he said we hadn't learned it all. This was the rest.

I couldn't handle it if there was more.

I was going to snap. My sanity would shatter, and I'd be like my mother. It was genetic. I was predisposed. Just needed the right type of environment and I could follow in her footsteps.

"You're there. Aren't you? Come on." She was writhing, whining as if we were having sex and she was pleading for more, more, more. "I already told you about Maddy, but there's one more. Can you guess? I need you to guess. He told me I couldn't say anything until you brought it up. He said that'd be burying the lead, whatever that means. So. Come on. Puh-lease. Just say his name—"

I couldn't give her the satisfaction.

Holding Mason's gaze, seeing the sadness and yearning in him, he wasn't going to say his father's name either.

"Okay. I know. I'll give you a hint." She clapped and bounced. "Oh! This is so exciting. So, first hint is that we never thought we could get him to kill himself—"

"Shut up," Mason wrangled out in a menacing warning.

It was enough to silence Sabrina. Her face went blank. She blinked a few times before she tipped her head back and laughed. She laughed and laughed and no one could say anything to stop her.

What she just acknowledged was—I didn't have the words.

She took away a person's life.

"How?" I didn't recognize my own voice. It was animalistic. Wounded.

Her laughter dried up abruptly. She gave me a slow blink,

assessing me calmly before a pitying grin took over her face. "How did we get him to take his own life, you mean?"

I flinched, hearing it put into words again.

She migrated to me, one step. "I never thought he'd do it, not that quickly. We hoped. It'd been in the works, but then we heard the news that the great Mason Kade was retiring and his family was moving back to Fallen Crest. It was all lining up. The time was perfect. James was sixty-eight. Guess how many members from The Network killed themselves from the email you leaked?"

What?

She leaned into me, breathing on me as she whispered, "Sixty-eight. Sixty-eight people took their lives because of something you did. That's your destruction. One email got sixty-eight people killed. It was only fitting if we sent James the same type of email, right? Guess how many emails we needed to send him?" The ends of her mouth curved up in an impish grin. Her eyes were sparkling. She was loving this. "We sent him sixty-eight emails. Though, I don't know if he opened them all, but we felt it was symbolic. Sixty-eight people died. James was sixty-eight. Sixty-eight emails, all laying out how someone that terrified Mason's daddy was coming to hurt his family. Course, we made it about the company, but Park helped me with the wording. There was an undercurrent threat that Kai Bennett was coming to take his family away." She cast a look over her shoulder to him, her tone turning coy. Almost seductive. "It worked. We couldn't believe it."

My mind was spinning. Sixty-eight people killed themselves because of the email we leaked? That... Was that on me? The information on there had been their secrets, but it was leaked to the other members. We only wanted to have them turn on Park, which they did. We were told they did. Clearly they hadn't stopped there.

I tore from the room, going to the bathroom across the hallway.

I killed those people. Their lives were on me.

I landed on my knees in front of the toilet and I spewed.

I couldn't stop.

It kept coming up.

Self-disgust.

Self-loathing.

Self-hate.

I killed all of those people.

I was the reason James was dead.

This was all about me.

51

MASON

S am fled the room, shoving open the door.

"Go."

Beltraine was speaking to me. He nodded in the direction my wife just went before giving a bob toward Sabrina's direction. "We got her. She's not going anywhere. Go take care of your woman."

She was in the bathroom across the hallway, puking.

"Babe." I sank down next to her, pulling her hair back and ran a hand over her shoulders.

What did I say in this situation? Her sister was a psychopath. If it was true, then people died because of something we did. I knew Sam would carry that, no matter what I said.

I sighed.

I wished Logan was here.

"Those people are dead because of me." She stopped vomiting. She hiccupped, tears falling from her eyes.

"No," I growled. Bending forward, I hauled her up and moved her so she was on my lap, sitting sideways. She could completely rest against me. As she did, a shudder went through her body and I smoothed a hand over her hair, down her arm, her back, and I repeated. I'd repeat that forever if it made her feel better.

"People died," she whispered, burrowing into my chest.

"No. Fuck that. No."

She tensed. "Mason."

"No," I snapped.

She looked up, surprised.

I looked down, met her gaze and I hated that look in her eyes. That her sister, of all fucking people, put that defeated and self-loathing look there. Fuck Sabrina. Fuck Garrett. He let his daughter become open and vulnerable to fucking Park Sebastian.

He was in prison. We helped put him there.

Why the fuck was he able to resurrect himself to fuck with us again?

"All those assholes in The Network did shit that put them on that blackmail list. We leaked it, yes, but we didn't do whatever their secrets were. We didn't put ourselves in the position to become blackmailed by The Network in the first place. I don't care. I know you do and I want to be sensitive, but I don't give a fuck. They were trying to ruin our lives. They were trying to pull us in and they would've controlled us for the rest of our fucking lives. We fought back. That's what we did. We leaked their own shit to themselves and we did it from a piece of shit rapist. He tried to rape you. He tried to end my football career. He tried to get Logan expelled from college. Jesus Christ. Are you really feeling bad that other people did what they did for whatever reason? You don't know if it's true and you don't know the circumstances. None of it. Maybe it was shame? Or maybe someone else in The Network was going after them too? Who the fuck knows. That's not on you, that's all I know."

She let some of the tension go, settling more fully over me.

She rested her forehead against my chest. "My dad was on that list."

"And your dad is still around, isn't he?"

Unlike mine.

I didn't say the words but we both fell quiet, hearing them anyway.

She tensed all over again. "Mason..."

"Don't, Sam."

"But Mase—"

I shook my head. She tried to sit up, to look at me, but I kept her against my chest. I just wanted to hold her. I didn't want to hear her sympathies about what her sister helped put in motion.

"Your dad," she still tried.

"No, baby." I tipped her chin back, my eyes falling to hers. Brushing some of her hair behind her ears, I held her back for a moment. "This is all I want to say about my dad. He made the choice. He was helped in making that choice, but he did it. I will never know how much he was actually in fear for his life or if it was his excuse to go and be with Analise. He's gone. Your sister and Park capitalized on him, but he pulled the trigger."

"What are you saying?"

I didn't realize she'd been wearing makeup, but some of her mascara smudged from her vomiting session. Two lines traced down her face. What did it say about me that somehow, that made her even more beautiful? I smoothed the lines away, using my thumbs. I needed to grab a washcloth to wipe the rest away, but I was so far gone for this woman.

Every word I said in my wedding vows was true. I meant them then. I meant them now. I'd always mean them. She was it for me. There was no one else, there would be no one else, and if anything happened to her, I would burn the world down. Feeling all the love, the tenderness for her, remembering how she'd been there for me after James died, I would never be able to love her enough. I'd never be able to show her the magnitude of how much I loved her.

No words, no gestures, none could touch the depth of how my soul cherished this woman in my arms. I still tried, whispering, "It would break my heart if you let one word of what that deranged girl said into your soul. It's poison. Plain and simple. She's toxic. Park Sebastian got inside her head and he infected her. His sister turned her back on him. His mother. His father chose us over him. He has no one and somehow he was able to get his tentacles on her. That's not on you, and most certainly anything that comes from her mouth is tainted by him. You'd never believe a goddamn word if Sebastian himself were saying it, so why are you letting yourself take to heart what she said? She's a goddamn mouthpiece for him."

A sheen of tears swam over her eyes, pooling on her eyelids. The agony was there, so fresh, so real. Strong. She closed her eyes, clasping them tight as she whispered, "But what if it's true?"

I tightened my hold on her, as if that could keep out anymore of her self-blame. My voice was rough as I replied, "It's still not on you. We meant to hurt one person with what we did. If there was collateral, we'll look into it and we'll make what amends we can, but I will not let you shoulder that. It's not yours, Sam. It's not yours to carry."

"What? So you can carry it? Is that what you're saying instead?"

"Yes," I snapped.

Her eyes widened.

In this matter, yes. I would always carry what I could so she didn't. That was my job. That was my right as her husband. "I can carry it. It's not going to weigh me down, but you need to let me carry it. Okay? You carry all the love for our family. You let me have this." I caught her face in my hands, holding her with gentle care. My thumbs rubbed over her cheeks again, brushing the tears that slipped free. "The girl has hurt you, hurt my father, hurt me, and she's trying to hurt our daughter. You don't let her hurt you anymore, you got me? If you don't do it for me, for yourself, do it for Maddy. Push out what she said because if you don't, it'll infect you too. It's like letting him inside of you. *Don't.*"

I got through.

I saw the crack, and there was a peek of the old Sam looking back at me. She was doing it, battling to stop the poison from slipping any further inside of her. She was mostly doing it for Maddy, but it did the trick. She loved our kids more than anything.

Sabrina had no idea. Nor did Sebastian.

They would never win against a mother's love.

"What are you going to do?"

My arms tightened around her again. "About what?"

"She's the one who hurt your father. I know you, Mason. You have to avenge your dad, even if you're trying to tell me that you don't blame them completely. I still know you."

I closed my eyes, wishing I could close my heart just as easily. But I couldn't. Not to Sam. Not to my kids. Not to my brother. Not to anyone I consider family, but that was the joke of it all because Sabrina was Sam's sister.

"Are you asking me not to?" I guarded myself, waiting for her response.

Her hand rose to rest on my chest. She spread her fingers out, her palm splayed there. My heart knew it was there and tried pushing its way out of my chest, trying to get to her touch.

She dropped her voice. "She's been warped. She's his weapon. You hurt her; you're not hurting the right person."

I didn't want to talk anymore. I knew what Sam was saying. There was logic there, but Sabrina still made a choice. She did a whole lot to hurt my father and laid the groundwork to angle closer to Maddy.

"Mason?"

I shook my head, cupping her face and pulling it to my chest. "I don't know what I'm going to do."

She resisted, keeping some space so she could see me better. Her fingers laced with mine. "Promise me you'll talk to me before you do anything. I'm not saying she shouldn't face consequences, but I want a say in it. That's all I'm asking. I'm not forgetting that she wants to take Maddy from us." She held my gaze, studying me intently.

I didn't want to lie to her. Grazing a finger under her jawline, I felt her tremble under my touch. I murmured, "Once I know what I'm going to do, I'll talk to you about it."

Her relief was palpable.

I hated seeing that because while Sam was torn, I wasn't.

Sabrina was her sister.

She wasn't mine.

52

MADDY

I heard all the bullshit Brinna was spewing.

Her mind was all messed up. Kudos to that douchebag. Job well done if he wanted to fuck up lives. Goal accomplished. Brinna was never going to be a normal functioning person again.

Mom and Dad moved from commiserating in the bathroom with my mom going to their bedroom. My dad went to the kitchen where he was now getting answers from my friends.

"I want you to call Garrett." That was my dad talking to my uncle. *Snicker*. "Find out if he knew about this? Why the fuck he allowed it?"

"The secret society?" That was Steele.

"No. I know he's aware. It's why they're in Europe. Why didn't you two go with them?"

"We were. We did. We were there most of our lives, but Brinna wanted to go to college stateside. We weren't *always* over there. We have other family here on my mom's side that we visit, but the plan was that Brinna would be at a university for the next four years. Dad didn't like she was going to Cain, but it's where we're all going. It's a family tradition. I came because I wanted to be close to her."

"How the fuck did you end up *here*? Cain's three hours away. There's other high schools closer."

Steele didn't reply right away. I heard some scuffling sounds. "My dad doesn't know I'm here. Brinna enrolled me. She's dealing with the payments, and all she told me was to get close to Maddy. I'm not a total dumbass. Once I knew Maddy's last name, I figured out the connection early on. Brinna's always talked a certain way about our older sister, but I've never let that influence me. I wanted to see for myself, make up my own thoughts about our sister."

"Is my dad in this secret society thing?" That was Beltraine asking, his voice sounding strained.

"As far I know, no. He's not in, but I'm remembering a few things Brinna said. I think he's aware of the secret society and that he wants to be in. She mentioned a fake recruiting exception for him, but she laughed about it, said they were just using him. I didn't know what she was talking about. I hadn't met you and I thought he was being used for me, letting me stay here. Now I think he was letting me stay here as a way of getting initiated. Maybe. Or that's what he thought."

"You knew who Sam was?" My dad.

Another beat of silence. "I always knew who she was, but seeing her in person was... She's not how Brinna said. I don't— I'm not on board with *anything* my sister did. I knew she was going sideways, but I didn't realize the extent of it until we all heard what she said. She's messed up. She needs help."

"She tried turning you against Sam?"

There wasn't a response, and my heart hurt at that because of course she would. Brinna was cracked. If she were an egg, she'd been cooked the wrong way and her shell was all splintered up.

I listened to more, as Steele explained that once he met

Beltraine, they bonded within the first weekend. It was an easy friendship. How Beltraine and Axel had no idea what Steele was doing. They were told he needed to hide from some bad family members. They didn't push Steele for more, assuming he'd tell them what was going on when he felt comfortable to do that.

Grandpa Garrett had no idea what was going on, any of it. He had no idea Brinna was in communication with the guy in prison.

I barely remembered Grandpa Garrett myself.

The other bottom line is that they had no idea what to do with Brinna.

Which brought me back to where I was currently standing. Outside the study.

Brinna was inside. They were all in their kitchen meeting, deciding what to do with her.

I opened the door and walked inside.

Brinna straightened from where she was sitting in a corner chair. She unfolded her legs and brightened, the Brinna mask she wore when we hung out slid into place. Her smile seemed so genuine, like it always had.

"Maddy! Hi." She laughed, tossing some of her hair over her shoulder. She smoothed her hands over her legs. "You must be confused at seeing me here, huh?" She motioned behind me. "Steele called. Told me what happened. I wanted to be here for my brother."

So warm and caring. She was the picture of a doting big sister.

I shut the door, locking it.

She frowned at that, a slight flicker of worry showing before she hid it again. Her smile was back in its place. "It's late for you, right? Have you been sleeping this whole time?"

I didn't reply, only smiled at her.

That seemed to ease some of her worry. She relaxed back in

her seat, the lines around her mouth softening before she grew pensive. "I'm in some trouble, Mads."

I moved closer to her.

She looked away, and a hand reached up to rub at her forehead. "I—uh...I got a little out of hand and told Steele some things I'm now thinking I shouldn't have. I don't think he's happy with me." Her shoulders lifted up and went back down as she blew out some air. "Do you think... I shouldn't ask. Never mind."

I shifted closer to her. "What? Tell me."

Her eyes latched onto me, sharpening. A keenness showed. Her smile stretched. "Steele took my phone from me—"

Lie. My dad took her phone.

"There's a friend I need to contact. He'll know what to tell me to do. Plus, I kinda told some of his secrets and they weren't all mine to tell. You know? So stupid of me." She rolled her eyes at herself, her mouth curving up. Being wry.

"What do you need me to do?"

"Do you have your phone on you?" She leaned forward, her hands folded in her lap, but I saw how she was holding onto her pants. Tightly. Desperately.

I went over to the desk and pulled out some paper and a pen.

My eyes caught on something else inside the drawer.

I hadn't known what I was going to do when I came into this room, but there was something pulling on me. Calling to my darkness, asking to be let out. And Brinna, I lifted my eyes to her. She was watching me, but she wasn't worried about me.

She was thinking ahead, plotting. Thinking about her next move? How to get out of the trouble she was in?

I took the paper and pen to her. "I don't have my phone on me but write what you need to tell him and how to get in touch with him. I'll send your message. I'll do it right away. They won't know I was even in here talking to you."

She grew cautious, studying me.

I wasn't lying. I *would* get the message to the guy.

She must've read the truth on me because she took the paper. As she wrote, she told me, "This is his email. He has a phone available to him, but he can't always use it so send the email ASAP. He'll get to that first and he'll call when he can." She hesitated, her gaze darting to the door. She bit down on her lip. "I'm—I'm, huh, I'm not sure when I'll get my phone back." A sardonic chuckle spilled from her, pulling at the corner of her mouth. "Steele's really mad at me, but everything I've done is for him. I've protected my little brother all my life. You get that, right? You have a little brother and sister." Some darkness shone in her gaze.

"I get it. I do." I wasn't lying.

Her entire body relaxed and she went back to scribbling her instructions. "So here's his email. Write that out to him. If you give him your number, he'll call you." Her voice hitched, but I caught the excitement on her face.

I took the paper from her, sliding it into my pocket.

As I did, she let out a dramatic breath. "Thanks for this—" She choked, her eyes wide and alarmed. Shocked. She looked down at what was protruding from her body. When I put her message in my pocket, I grabbed the letter opener I took from my dad's desk.

It was easier than I thought. I put some force into my stab, making sure it slid inside of her. The far right side of her stomach, in the middle.

She went to reach for it, but my hand closed over it. "No, no. Can't do that. You pull that out and you might bleed to death."

She made another choking sound, her face going pale. She let go of it, falling back into her chair.

I grinned at her, inspecting it. Pride filled me. I did a good job. "I wanted to make sure to miss your organs. That way you may still live. You won't have permanent damage, but it'll be a bitch to heal. A lot of pain. A lot of time for you to think. Process." I laughed.

This was good.

I was enjoying this.

I felt almost drunk.

"Please—" She gasped.

I grinned at her, sinking into the chair across from her. "What? You think you're the only one capable of wearing a mask? Bitch, please." I got comfortable, sitting back. "The way I figure it is that you're a psychopath. I didn't just come in and *happen* to find you." Rolling my eyes, I laughed. "I heard everything."

"What—" She was holding onto the letter opener and tried to stand up.

I moved, shoving her back down. "*Stay*. Please. I wouldn't want to accidentally move that letter opener again. Maybe puncture something that couldn't get fixed, you know?" I winked.

She gaped at me, making a mewling sound.

"Oh, calm down. You'll live if you don't fuck it up. Now, sit a bit. Let someone else have a say, hmm?"

She swallowed, her hands shaking. Sweat began streaming down her face, or maybe that was tears. She looked a mess. I liked seeing that. That was my handiwork.

I drew in a breath. Where to start? Right. "Your first mistake was thinking you could brainwash me. So stupid of you. I'm not you. I'm not weak. *Weak* minds get brainwashed. That leads me to your other mistake. See. I've been going through this whole phoenix changing thing since we moved here. I kinda love it, but I'm hating how it happened. I used to think I was a sociopath, but now I just think I have sociopathic tendencies. I have emotions. For example, I *really* don't like that you hurt my mom." I dropped the smile and let her see the real Maddy, the one that I was scared to show anyone.

She gulped, shrinking in her seat. She was still holding onto that letter opener, which I didn't think was a good idea. But it was her body, I guess.

"Dad doesn't know what to do with you. You're a girl. He always has hang-ups about that. And you're Mom's sister so there's that. Even though you'd love to continue to emotionally torture my mom, the sad truth is that my mom loves you. She probably thinks you're some byproduct of that guy's revenge and how she won't let him have you." I snorted. That felt right to me. "Bet you anything she's determined to do whatever she needs to do to 'get her sister back.' I can already see it. She went to bed. Who knows if she's sleeping, but she'll come out with a plan. I'm sure that they'll probably call your dad. Let him know what's been going on, if he was actually in the unknown. Jury's out on that verdict. I'm not convinced he didn't know."

She was still shaking, still pale She gasped, "He didn't. My dad's not like that."

I grinned at that. "He's not sick in the head like you?" I bulged my eyes out for dramatic effect. "Like me? Thought it was from Grandma Analise. Maybe it's genetic on Grandpa Garrett's side? But yeah. I can see my mom calling him, maybe having him fly here to have a whole talk about everything. Get it all out in the open. You—" I sat forward, resting my elbows on my knees. My head tilted to the side. "You'll probably get sent to a facility. My mom's all for those facilities. They helped Grandma Analise. Years of therapy, you're looking at. That's if they don't decide to go another route. See if they can get you convicted for killing Grandpa James."

The blood drained from her face all over again.

I bit out an irritated sigh. I'd have to call for an ambulance soon, but dammit. I wanted to have some more fun. This was going too fast.

I narrowed my eyes on her. "I don't know what my mom is going to say about what you did to my grandpa, but you killed him. That's what I say and right now, in this room, what I say is the only judgment that matters. He was already hurting. Missing Grandma Analise. As far as I think, you put the bullet in the gun and you handed it to him. You told him to pull the trigger. You're the reason he's dead. You killed him. That's how I see it." I frowned, not understanding part of it. "What did you say to get him to do it?"

"What?" Some of the fight was draining from her.

Dammit. I really would need to call 911 soon.

"What did you say to him? To get my grandpa so scared to take his life. It must've been something big—"

"Kai Bennett."

I frowned. "Who?"

"He's—" She cursed, squirming in her seat. "Are you serious with this? Call the ambulance! You don't want me dead, then you gotta call for them. I think you punctured something serious."

I gave her a considering look, testing to see if I cared about that. I grinned. I didn't. "Tell me who Kai Bennett is and what about him got in my grandpa's head so much."

She cursed some more, glaring at me.

I liked seeing that look on her face.

"You're so... You're insane."

"Already covered that. So are you. Come on. Kai Bennett. Who is he? What is he?"

"He's—" She cursed some more, but I wasn't moving.

"I never would've been brainwashed. That was your plan, right? Brainwash me away from my parents. Make me hate them like you do?" So stupid. "You only achieved one of your goals. My grandpa. That's why you needed to get punished. Now, the severity of that punishment is up to you. Tell me what I want to know, and I'll call 911. Don't, and die. I don't care. I should care. My parents will be horrified I did this, but I did it for them. I'm letting my dad off the hook for vengeance against what you did to his dad. And I'm letting my mom off the hook of trying to save you. She's always going to be tormented about what you did to my family. Not me, though. Eye for an eye as far I see it. Pun not intended there. You killed my grandpa. I don't mind if you die. But that's up to you. You can still live. Just tell me what I'm asking—"

"I don't know who or *what* he is."

I scowled. "You're lying."

"I'm not. I swear. Uncle Seb told me to use that name. Said he was a threat to our group."

"Your group?"

"The System. That's the name of the society that replaced The Network. The old secret society."

"The one that my parents destroyed?"

"Yes," she hissed at me. "Uncle Seb said he wanted to see if two of his enemies would take each other out. And if they didn't, then at least one might eliminate the other. That was the goal. It worked. James Kade took his own life because the threat of Kai Bennett terrified him more. Whoever he is. I don't know who or what he is. That's all Uncle Seb said. That he was a threat to The System. I tried googling him, but there's almost nothing on him online. You want to know who he is? Ask your dad. I'm sure he knows all about him by now."

I growled, getting to my feet and stalking her. "You're lying. *Stop lying.*"

"I'm not!" she shouted before cringing, grasping onto the letter opener. She didn't pull it out. She was just holding onto it.

I shook my head. "I wouldn't do that. You're probably moving it, making it worse."

"Call 911," she demanded in another gasp. "*Please.*"

I considered her, considered what she said, considered what was said earlier. I was contemplating all of it and I sighed. "You made another mistake. For being this psychopath mastermind, you keep fucking up. You're not very good at it."

She snarled, the lines around her lips turned white. "What are you talking about?"

I smirked at her.

I knew that this would give my parents nightmares, what I was about to do, what I'd already done, but they didn't understand that I was doing this for them. Both of them couldn't hand out the punishment that Brinna deserved. I could shoulder it. It was helping me learn more about myself, but I also meant what I said to my mom. I would use my abilities for the good and doing this to someone who hurt my family was the right thing to do.

I leaned over her and smiled. "You already proved that you could hurt my family and you brought up Nolan and Nash. You didn't think I was aware of the underlying threat when you brought them up, but I'm better at this game than you are. You threatened my little sister and brother and I won't let you hurt them. Because of that, I'm willing to roll the dice and see where it lands. If you die, you die. If you don't..." I let that sentence hang between us and I reached forward, grasped the letter opener.

She tried fighting me off, but she was weak in body and mind.

It was almost too easy.

I tossed the dice and pulled out the letter opener.

53

MASON

We heard a blood-curdling scream and bolted. I got there first, finding the door locked.

I didn't have time to consider what I'd find on the other side. I reared back to kick the door down, but by that time, the others caught up. They saw what I was doing and all of them joined. I don't know if they all hit the door, but it worked.

The door landed, and I had the equivalent of a heart attack. An intense pressure pushed down on me, making me fold under the weight of it. My knees buckled before I readied myself, forcing myself to take in what every parent's nightmare is.

My child was standing in the middle of a giant pool of blood.

"Sabrina!" Steele's voice was wrangled, hoarse, as he slid to where her body was crumpled in the pool. A letter opener had fallen to the side.

The blood was hers.

I blinked a few times, to make sure I was seeing that correctly.

Rushing to Maddy, I ran my eyes over her before padding

her for any injuries. There was a haze in her eyes. She was here, but not totally here. I didn't know what that meant.

"Yeah. There's—uh, I don't know what happened. There's blood. A lot of blood. We need an ambulance."

Beltraine was on the phone, running a shaking hand through his hair. He looked like he'd lost the blood. Axel too. Steele, I couldn't see his face. He was holding onto his sister, his head bent over. He found the source of the blood, on the far right middle side of his sister's stomach.

I leaned in closer, cursing under my breath. Let's hope no organs were punctured.

I cupped Maddy's face and rested my forehead to hers. "Are you okay?"

"Yes." She spoke calmly, no infraction. No tremor. "She tried to hurt herself when I came in. I tried to get out, but she locked the door. Then she was saying something about a life taken. An eye for an eye. Something like that. I'm not sure what it meant."

My daughter was lying to me. Lying through her fucking teeth.

"What's your address?" Beltraine shoved his phone in my hand.

I took it, reciting it quickly to the 911 operator. I handed it back and said to Axel, who stood back, taking everything in. Everyone was rattled. That amount of blood was bad, so fucking bad. "Axe—you'll need to open the gate for them."

He jerked his head in a nod and ran out.

"The first gate," Steele choked out, lifting his head.

I reeled from the expression on his face. It wasn't too far off from the same look Sam had an hour ago. The similarities were a punch to my gut. And he was a kid. No kid should have that stricken and anguished look on their face. No kid.

I cursed, reaching for my phone.

It was then when a new voice spoke up from behind us, "What the fuck?"

I spun, fucking glad to hear that voice because my brother was here. Logan stood in the doorway, stunned at what he was seeing. Then he switched, raking over Maddy quickly before moving onto me and he held.

I grimaced. "Shit's gone down since we last talked."

"I'm seeing that," he said faintly, then zeroed in better on where Steele was holding his sister, who was now unconscious. That wasn't good. "What happened?"

"She hurt herself."

I waited a beat, then said over my daughter's words, "Knife wound to the stomach. Call Taylor."

Logan's eyes pinned on us both, lingering, before he took in the bloodied letter opener on the ground. On the other side of Brinna. "Uh. Okay. That wound needs to be stopped now or she'll bleed out before they get here." He had his phone out and was talking into it within a flash. "Taylor, how do I cauterize a knife wound?"

Steele froze in place, riveted by Logan. He tracked his every movement.

Beltraine was on the phone and ran out of the room.

Shit. The front gate.

But Maddy was speaking, murmuring into it, "...an ambulance is coming in. Yes. Please. Let them through. Thank you."

She was almost serene. Smooth. Acting perfect.

She ended the call and handed the phone back to me. "The front gate is taken care of. They'll get right in." I didn't take the phone. I knew what she'd done. There was no way Brinna took that letter opener and stabbed herself. That was the story, but I knew better. I knew my daughter and I knew how she looked when she lied.

She bit down on her bottom lip and put the phone in my pocket herself.

I didn't know if Sam had fallen asleep. She told me she was going to crawl in bed. I'd meant to check on her, but the talk with the boys took precedent. After that, I'd wanted to figure out what to do with Sabrina. Considering what just happened, I was praying with everything in me that Samantha had fallen asleep and would remain asleep.

I did not want her to walk in and see what I saw.

I said under my breath, "Show me your hands."

She blinked, the corners of her mouth curved down, but held them up. They were clean. Which meant she had taken the time to wipe them clean somewhere.

There was movement happening around us.

Logan was taking instructions on how to stop the bleeding now, not later. Steele was doing what he could to help without letting go of his sister. Beltraine was on the phone with the emergency responder. Axel had gone to open our initial gate leading to our house and wave down the ambulance.

And for myself, my daughter took priority.

I tugged her aside, speaking low, "Paramedics are going to come in here. They're going to survey the scene before they get her on the stretcher. They'll haul ass out of here with her, but the police will be called. What you're going to do is stay behind. Whatever you used to clean your hands, you'll find it and you'll burn it. You hear me?"

Another scream hurled through the air.

Logan was straddling her, pushing down a towel over her stomach. She came awake, violently, but he held my gaze. His eyes were dead serious.

He knew what happened. He might not know the specifics, but he knew me. He knew Maddy. He knew there'd only be one reason why I wasn't over there helping.

A flicker passed from me to him before he nodded, just slightly, and turned his attention back to the screaming girl. Maddy gave the initial story already. When the paramedics would ask what happened, they'd recite it. They wouldn't think to question it. My daughter was smart, too smart. It was eerie how smooth all of this had been for her, which meant we had a huge problem on our hands.

"What?" Sam stumbled in the doorway, a hand pressed to her stomach. "Oh my God. *Maddy!*"

She ran for us, ripping Maddy from my arms and into her arms. She rocked her, hugging her before continuing to take in the rest of the scene.

I held my breath, waiting to see Sam's reaction. There'd been another scene like this that she found by herself, when she was younger. I knew that'd been traumatizing to her and worried she'd be retraumatized.

Her forehead wrinkled and her eyebrows pulled down. She locked onto me. A darker question passing from her to me, asking me what the hell happened. I couldn't answer, but I let my gaze drop down to my daughter.

Sam slowed until she was standing still, holding our daughter. Her gaze fell, still going at the slow pace, to Maddy. She gazed at her daughter before continuing, her head moving so she could see the scene again.

The paramedics rushed into the room.

Logan was still in place over her, stopping the bleeding. "I wanted to cauterize it, but my wife said that could make it worse. An infection or something?"

"Okay. We'll load her up. You'll need to stay on her."

"No."

"Yes—"

Logan moved, and one of the paramedics cursed, taking his place.

Steele yelled, but the other paramedic began giving him orders. Steele followed them and soon they took her out of the house.

Steele went with them. So did Beltraine.

I followed until the ambulance was gone. Beltraine and Axel got in their car and trailed after them. Once the gate was closed again, Logan turned to me. All pretenses were gone. He demanded in a no-nonsense voice, "What the fuck happened?"

I grunted, moving past him. "What the fuck do you think?"

I motioned to him. "Check the security footage. We don't have cameras in the house, but double check nothing is on the ones we do have."

"And if I find something?"

"Wipe it." I glared at him. "What do you think?"

"Just making sure we're aware of what we're about to do." His face was grim. "We still have the shareholder meeting."

Fuck.

Fuck.

Everything had to happen on the same night.

I took a second. I needed to regroup. I needed to think of every fucking detail to make sure nothing slipped through when Sam spoke up from in the hallway, "Go."

Logan and I looked at her.

I asked, "Where's Maddy?"

"Showering." She held up a bag. Red splotches could be seen inside. Something metallic was also inside. "I'm going to burn this. Then we'll clean up. I called Heather. Channing's coming here to help. Heather's going to the hospital to cover us there. We got this."

"They're going to help cover up—"

She tipped her chin up, her mouth flattening. "It's *Maddy*, Mason. What do you think?" Her eyes flashed. "We're all in this *together*. We'll do what we have to do to protect our child and afterward, we'll do what we need to do to protect her from herself. If that means therapy, meds, I don't give a *fuck*. Right now, we're in crisis mode. Get to that meeting. Deal with it, then get to the hospital because when my sister wakes up, we need to figure out a way to have her corroborate Maddy's story."

Logan inhaled at the mention of Samantha's sister. That was right. He didn't know who she was. He'd just been rolling with us, following our lead when finding a girl bleeding out in my house. I had a few things to share with him on the way to the meeting.

"What about Max?"

Sam winced before stating, "She drugged him. Benadryl. He's zonked out on the couch in the basement."

A small relief that he was one less person pulled into this mess, but also, she drugged him.

"Jesus Christ," I said faintly.

I didn't know what else to say.

My daughter did all of this.

What else was she capable of?

54

MASON

Thirty minutes after Logan and I arrived at the shareholders's meeting, my phone buzzed with a notification. A signed contract was in my email from Phillip Moreaux and Holdings.

Shane King came through. Moreaux sold me his shares.

Before the events of this night, I'd been looking forward to the meeting. All that was gone. Any and all blackmail material that might've been revealed in the meeting wasn't shared. There was no big reveal. No emergency news to tell them except two items.

Right before we were about to end the meeting, I brought up the first item.

"Avoy," I called one of the shareholders. "If you open your fucking mouth one more time to tell your kid that Kade Enterprises is going under, that's the reason my father killed himself, and you're going to buy it and change the title to Avoy Enterprises, I will yank your shares so fast, so ruthlessly, that your head will spin and you won't be able to know what's up and what's down. Are you understanding me?"

He tried to bluster, but all he did was turn lobster red in the face and tug at the collar of his shirt so many times, he ripped some of the seams. "You can't do that—"

"I can and I will. Mouthing off about bullshit you have no understanding of is one thing, but spreading that false narrative to your kid, who spread it to *my* kid. I had a teenage daughter come to me, asking me if we're going to be poor and if that's the reason my father killed himself. You violated company ethics and because of that, you're banned from future meetings and social gatherings. I won't force you to sell what small amount of shares you do have, but it's so minuscule, you barely get a vote. I do have executive power to pull that vote you might've had in the future, which I'm enforcing because frankly, I don't ever want to see your fucking face. The claim you let your daughter spread wasn't just false, the thought that you'd be able to purchase enough shares in order to force a title change is beyond false. It's ludicrous."

The other members took note, sharing looks.

It was the first time they were witnessing this side of me.

Logan began snickering. "Slow clap for my brother, Mason Fucking Kade." He leered at them around the table. "We handle things differently than our father. Also, to catch you up on another change in this meeting and future meetings, you'll have noticed the absence of Phillip Moreaux. It seemed that between when he called for this meeting and now, he decided to sell his portion of shares to my brother."

That got a ripple of attention. More alarm.

Logan smirked, standing up. "Any future business deals you have with Moreaux, I'd advise you to close. Anyone associated with Kade Enterprises will not be associated with Phillip Moreaux. We don't do business with anyone that has mafia or cartel connections. That's just not good for business."

That also got their attention, and I had a strong feeling Moreaux would be losing partners and investors for *all* of his companies in the near future.

I shot Logan a look as we left. "Did you need to put it out there that blatantly? The connections you just shared are the very ones who helped us with Moreaux."

Logan shrugged, chuckling. "Red Demons aren't mafia or cartel. They're a group of guys who enjoy riding motorcycles together. A biker club." He winked. "Also, you had enough fun without me here tonight. I needed to have a little. We need to get to the hospital, but can we stop at the new coffee place? I was too worried about getting here and then too wired listening to what you sent to my phone. Now I've started to slack and we have one more showdown to tackle."

I could use the coffee myself.

We picked up a bunch.

The decision had been made to keep Maddy away from Sabrina so Max was woken up. When Channing took Max home, Maddy went with them. When we entered that hospital room, I knew that Sam and Heather would be waiting, but so would Steele, Beltraine, and Axel. And by proxy, Garrett and Sharon had been called and notified what happened.

They weren't able to leave immediately, but once they were able to take care of an item, they'd be on the first plane to California. Logan missed it. We didn't have just one showdown. We had two. One was just going to be on a later plane.

The first one, three teenage boys that had already gone toe to toe with me.

Logan was jumping on his toes to see what was going to happen. The excitement and restlessness was bouncing off him, ricocheting around the elevator as we took it up to the floor Sabrina was on.

He caught a look from me and asked, "What?"

I hid my grin. "It's nothing. Just forgot how much you used to live for these types of confrontations."

He shrugged, a genuine grin appearing. "I'm more excited about these kids. Things changed from the last time I dealt with them. That was when Maddy took two of them to an underground fight club. Now add in a mystery brother, and these two others and yeah, I'm riled up. This is the side of Fallen Crest I always loved."

I frowned at him, hearing a twinge of... Was that nostalgia? Mixed with something else? "What does that mean?"

He gave me another shoulder shrug, but the elevator stopped. The doors slid open and he smirked at me as he took the lead. "Not saying anything yet. I need to talk to the Missus before I do."

That had my eyebrows arched all the way up. "Wait. What?"

He laughed, ducking his head.

A few people in the hallway noticed us. Some workers, both women and men. One of the guys started to ask if he could help us, but Logan blasted him with a grin. "We're good. We know where we're going. We're family, after all."

55

MASON

I hadn't been sure what to prepare for, but Sabrina was asleep. She looked peaceful, unlike herself. They'd brought in extra chairs. Steele was sitting in the main visitor's seat by the bed, holding his sister's hand. Axel and Beltraine had pulled up some folding chairs so they were beside Steele.

Sam and Heather were also on folding chairs, but toward the wall.

Seeing us, Heather stood. Letting out a tired yawn, she pulled Sam in for a hug before coming over and grabbing one of the coffees from the holder Logan had in his hands. "Your arrival is my cue that I get to go home, and this coffee is my gift. Love you all. Good seeing you again, Logan. Let's do it again, but later. Much later. Think I'd like to sleep half the day, if only my children would let that happen." She gave a wave to the other boys. "See you, guys. Your sister will be just fine, I have a feeling. Don't be strangers."

Her eyes met mine, holding, and I got a message that there was something extra to her words. She flicked a look in Sam's direction and I gave her a small nod. I'd be checking in with my wife, finding out what happened before her arrival and ours.

But before I could say anything, Steele shoved up from his chair. Glowering at us, he said hotly, "We all need to fucking talk." He didn't let anyone respond, stalking out of the room.

Beltraine and Axel shared a look before following their friend.

"What happened?" I asked Sam.

She stood, moving at a slower pace. I felt a kick inside at seeing the sadness in her eyes. I didn't like seeing it there. And it was worse because I wouldn't be able to remove it, not anytime soon. She came over, giving Logan a hug first before moving to my chest. My arms came around her.

"Come on, my Threesome Fearsome Sister. We brought coffee for you. Isn't that like catnip for you?"

A grin tugged at her mouth, which warmed me a little.

I mouthed thank you to my brother over her head.

He only lifted one corner of his mouth up in response, his eyes in shadow.

Sam took one of the coffees offered but didn't move from my shelter.

The door was shoved open from the side.

Axel stood there, grimacing when he saw us. "Uh, Steele's going to lose his shit if we don't get on the same page."

Logan took point for us, advancing on him. "And what page would that be?"

Axel was eyeing him, giving him a quizzical look. He started to respond.

Logan cut him off, "Oh, by the way. I just saw your folks. It'd been on the agenda to let him know your mom's fucking your buddy's father, but then Moreaux didn't show up, so that news never came to light. You're welcome." He breezed past the kid, who gaped after him.

I almost felt sorry for the boy. Almost.

There was no surprise on Axel's face so he'd known, but Logan blasted him with that news that we also knew, and on this night, it would've felt like he'd been hit with a grounder from left field. I knew what Logan was doing.

He'd been briefed on the drive and that Sabrina was the opposition. In Logan's view, her brother and the two guys that stood shoulder to shoulder with him were also the opposition. He was knocking them off-balance, one by one. As we followed him, who was following behind Beltraine, who was walking at a slower pace to where Steele was waiting, I knew we'd witness something similar to each of the other two. I just wasn't sure what Logan was going to use as ammunition.

"Fucking finally," Steele snapped, going through a door that he'd held open for us. Beltraine got there first, holding it for Logan, who swept past him.

He blinked at him in surprise before his gaze jerked to us, and he nodded to himself. As if reminding himself that Logan was with us. I didn't blame him. The only one who really noticed Logan's presence at the house before the ambulance got there was Steele because Logan had been the one who helped stop the bleeding.

We entered the room, which I almost started laughing because it was a chapel.

Logan was fighting back a grin, which doubled at seeing my reaction.

I groaned. "Fuck's sakes."

"Now, now. None of that cursing, Mason. The Head Honcho wouldn't approve." Logan held up his finger at me.

I flicked him off. "Fuck off."

A genuine laugh came next from him.

Steele was at the altar, his back to it, and the glowering hadn't eased up. It seemed to have worsened. His hands were in fists again, pressed tight to his pants, as if he needed to hold himself back from... Doing something he didn't want to do.

Beltraine came in last, shutting the door.

"Lock it," Steele ordered.

Click.

"Done," Beltraine commented, coolly. He rounded around us, barely sparing us a look as he went to join his friends. "You got the floor, Steele."

He cocked his head up, skewering me. He lost some of the heat when his gaze went to Sam, then returned as he flicked Logan a wary look. "I want to know what the fuck happened in that room. And don't bullshit me. My sister would never hurt herself. I know what Maddy said, but I don't believe her."

Logan opened his mouth.

"No," Sam said to him. Her voice was sharp. "This is my brother, Logan. I'll handle this."

Logan's eyes met mine, but he gave a nod, stepping back.

Sam pulled away from me, going toward her brother. Her voice was soft, but strong. I hoped he was noting that. "What do you want me to say, Steele? You want me to put into words that my daughter might've harmed your sister?"

His head folded down. "My sister wouldn't have—"

Her head went with him, just a bit. But not her tone. She was strong as ever as she continued, "But she did. She harmed my husband's father. She harmed my daughter's grandfather. Your friend's grandfather. You heard her. If Maddy wasn't Maddy, your sister planned to try and take her away from us. If she'd been successful, in getting Maddy to want to join The System, you know what that would've done. Park Sebastian has only sought to hurt Mason and myself. Since the beginning. Your sister doesn't know the true history. She was one part of his revenge on us. He took away my father and in doing that, he also took away my sister." Now her voice softened. "I've wanted to know you for so long. I wanted to know my dad. Park Sebastian took you away from me. He took me away from you. Are you thinking of it that way?"

"Don't tell me how to think," he snarled. "It's my sister that he put all that fucked up shit in her head. But he's not the one who stabbed my sister and was standing there, in her blood, just watching it pool at her feet. Your daughter did that—"

"Dude," Beltraine barked. "That was Mads. Our friend. I get that it was your sister's blood on the floor but keep perspective. We didn't befriend Maddy because your sister told you to. You were the one who didn't want us hanging out with her. Remember? You said she was weird. Well, I like her weirdness. She's fucking cool."

Steele turned that skewer on his friend. Glowering.

"Bell, man." Axel nudged him.

"No. He needs a fucking wake-up call. I'm not vouching for your sister. She's fucked in the head. We know what Maddy really did, but the story should stand."

What... My eyes darted to Logan, who looked just as surprised. This was a turn I'd not expected.

"What are you saying?" Steele hissed at him. He jerked forward a step, but Sam was there. She held up a hand so he wouldn't knock into her, and at the contact, he made another hissing sound, wrenching away from her. He backed into the altar, making it shake and the two glass jars that'd been on top fell to the floor. They rolled over, stopping in front of Sam. She bent down to pick one up.

She said, so gently, "It's a candle. I think we should light it for James."

Her eyes met mine for a fleeting second.

My throat swelled up. "My dad would love that. You can do the other for—"

"My daughter."

Everyone looked in Logan's direction, taken off guard by his sudden hoarse exclamation. He cleared his throat, a brief apology crossing his face for Sam. "Sorry. I know you were going to say your mom, but I tend to avoid these places. Since I'm here... I think Taylor would appreciate it."

She picked up the other, handing it to Logan. "You're right.

We'll light the one for James and my mother. The second one for your daughter."

I moved to the back, content to be there and watch Sam and Logan do their thing. Part of this was legit. They really were lighting those candles for the ones we've lost, but they were also doing this as a wake-up call to get through to Steele. He was the one blocked by his rage. Seeing his sister bleeding out on the floor tore out a primal instinct to protect his loved one.

Welcome to the club.

I studied Beltraine and Axel, who were watching Sam and Logan as if they were new animals in a zoo. Both seemed mystified by this simple act of lighting a candle for lost family members. But, fuck. I got it then, what they were seeing that I didn't think Sam and Logan were even taking into account.

They were witnessing two adults, both parents, express love and kindness.

Was this really such a new thing to them? They must've witnessed other adults express... This was different. This was personal. This wasn't a show. This wasn't fake. There was genuine love being expressed from Sam and from Logan. And as they lit the candles, I watched the boys hold their breaths.

Beltraine blinked a few times, his eyes a little glassy.

Axel leaned against the wall, one of his hands in his pockets. He lifted the other to drape around Beltraine's shoulder. The closeness between the two was visibly evident. It seemed they'd adopted Steele into their group so he was just as close, so I wasn't surprised to see him glancing at them a few times.

When Logan placed the candle on the altar, Beltraine was enraptured. He let out a soft sigh, his head angling down so it rested against Axel's, who shifted to stand a little closer so they were more comfortable. Beltraine gave Steele a brief grin. He lifted up the corner of his mouth, letting it fall just as quick as it appeared. If it was meant to be reassuring, I didn't know, but whatever hold that'd been on Steele began to crumble.

His shoulders slumped down.

His head went further.

He raised his fists to press into his face, and as he hunched further over, his shoulders began to shake. We all heard a sob come from him.

Sam froze before glancing at me.

I gave her a nod, gesturing to her brother.

"Hey." She pulled him to her, and as if in slow motion, they began to sit down on the floor. Sam held out her hand, the one with the candle. Logan took it quickly, putting it on the altar next to the one for his daughter. By then, Steele was sobbing into Sam's shoulder.

We all stood and watched.

I didn't know the reasons Steele was crying, but the sounds he was making were gut-wrenching. He was letting himself be exposed in this room, raw in a way I'd only experienced with my family. His friends weren't holding back their tears. Both boys had tears streaming down their faces. They weren't ashamed of them or brushing them away. They were just letting them flow.

Seeing that, seeing how freely they felt for their friend and let it be seen, remembering what Beltaine just said for Maddy and remembering some of his past supportive comments about Maddy, I was beginning to change my mind about this group being friends with my daughter. Of course, in Maddy's case, it wasn't really about anyone being a bad influence on her, but why add to it? I'd been concerned after seeing the drugs at Beltraine's house but I also knew that Sam had every intention of bringing these three boys into the fold so the drugs would go anyway. She'd never stand for that, and knowing my wife, she'd schedule a K9 dog to come through the house for unexpected visits.

Logan migrated over to me. He gave me a look, and I grinned back, hooking an arm over his shoulder as Beltraine and Axel were standing. It felt good to stand like this with my brother. I'd missed him when he went to Boston. It felt right being back here, having him by my side.

He gave me a smartass grin. "Are we going to bump foreheads too?"

"Fuck no. That'd hurt my back."

"But Mason—"

"Shut up."

He laughed, but he stopped talking.

Steele grew quiet after a few minutes. He shifted so he was facing the rest of us. Sam moved so she wasn't hugging him, but she was still there. Right at his side.

He wiped the palms of his hands down his face, trying to wipe away the tears before he lifted his eyes to take the rest of us in. Whatever he saw had him cursing. "Shit's been stressful with my family."

Beltraine gave him a wicked grin. "Dude. We know. We've literally had a front row seat."

Axel asked, somber, "You okay, Steele?"

"Yeah. I..." His face closed off before he looked at Sam, then found me. "My dad told me to do whatever you and Sam said to do, but I don't think he'd agree with—"

"Stop, Steele," Axel clipped out. "I get what you don't want to do, but we're going to do it. She's going to wake up and say that she didn't try to hurt herself, that Maddy stabbed her. But we're going to all say that she's lying. Of course she doesn't want to admit that she tried to hurt herself and of course, she's going to try to blame it on Maddy, because it's going to be apparent how much your sister hates your other sister. But, we're all going to say the same thing. Your sister needs help, real serious help. So fucking what if this one thing is the truth she's saying. Everything else is twisted and fucked up and a lie. We're taking a page out of her playbook. That's it."

I spoke, my eyes on Steele, "It's either this or I'll involve the police. There's witnesses to what she said she did for her part in my father's death. Things are changing now. People are being charged with committing crimes if they maliciously and inten- tionally meant to cause harm. It's my father, Steele. I will throw everything I have at the district attorney to ensure he brings charges against your sister. She either needs to be locked up in a hospital of some sort or prison."

"Mason—"

I cut my eyes to Sam. "No. This was my father. Logan's father. I won't destroy her in the way I want to because she's your sister, but she will be punished. That's nonnegotiable."

"I know. I'm not arguing on her behalf. I was going to say that you're speaking for both of us. I'm with you. Always." She let out a soft sigh. "She wants to hurt my daughter. I'll never forget that."

I shouldn't have doubted her.

"I can't—" Steele shoved to his feet. "I know what you all are going to say. Cops said they'd come back when she was awake." He said to the rest of us, "They already took Traine and Axe's statements, and they backed up what Maddy said. Mrs. Monroe showed up when they started to ask for my statement, but she tossed 'em out. Said they needed to come back when parents were present. Course, that was bullshit, which they'll find out later, but I know. I get what you all are saying. And I get what you're saying, Mr. Kade, about picking your battles. Hospital or prison. I know which one I'd pick, but I made a promise to my sister. She used to get confused when we were little sometimes and I promised her that I'd never lie to her. I can't lie to her. I won't go back on that promise."

"Technically, you're not lying to her. You're lying for her. Just, whenever she confronts you, evade and then answer truth- fully in private."

Steele stared at Logan. "What?'

"You're lying for her, not to her. Just say it that way. She won't push you and you're still holding up your promise to her."

It was a thought Steele had never had before, apparently. He looked dumbfounded, but Axel was looking at Logan with stars in his eyes. That's when I knew everything was going to be okay.

This particular fight was over.

I wasn't worried for when Garrett and Sharon would arrive. They couldn't fight this.

The next morning a detective took Sabrina's statement. She said what we all knew she would, but afterward, Steele gave his statement.

Sam gave hers.

I gave mine.

Logan was next, adding what he saw when he got to the room.

The same detective came to our house that afternoon and took Maddy's statement. She kept to her story, and when the detective left, a myriad of mixed emotions battling over her face, Sam and I had another huge talk with Maddy.

No charges would be pressed against our daughter, but that didn't mean we were out of the storm. Maddy was her own storm, all by herself. These sociopathic tendencies would need to be addressed.

So we were going to do that. It didn't matter how long it would take, how hard it was going to be, we'd do it. That was always a nonnegotiable.

When it came to family, we were all in.

56

MASON

A few days later.

Three SUVs pulled to the side of the road beside me. And instead of not knowing who was inside like the last time similar SUVs circled me, this time I fully knew.

This time, I was the one who asked for this meeting.

I waited where I stood, on a long stretch of road, out in the middle of nowhere. There'd be no cameras. No witnesses who could risk overhearing or overseeing this meeting because what I was here to give Kai Bennett was something I never wanted to be tied to.

The front passenger door to the middle SUV opened. A guard got out of the vehicle, giving me a look before scanning the area. I knew the drill. He was a big tall motherfucker, dressed in a business suit, and all the side bulges under his coat were his weapons. He didn't check me over, except for the one look up and down before he must've been appeased.

He opened the back door, and Kai Bennett got out.

He'd been focused on his phone, only looking up when his door opened.

He handed it to the guard, before giving me the rest of his attention. Crossing the small stretch of space that separated us, he gave me a slight nod. "Mason."

The first names felt weird to me. I enjoyed using last names. It allowed distance between myself and that other person. If it was someone I didn't like, I didn't need to use their first name. That gave a sense of familiarity. But responding with his last name didn't feel right either. I ended with, "Kai."

He gave me another scrutiny, flicking over me before he cleared his throat. "You wanted a face to face. Insisted on it. Why am I here?"

I got it. He was a busy man. Busy. Powerful. Dangerous. All the reasons why I'd asked him, and knowing Kai Bennett was direct and appreciated the whole no-bullshit approach, I pulled out a thumb drive.

His eyes fell to it. "There are such things as a Dropbox online. You can put all sorts of information in there and can even password protect the thing."

"Call me old-fashioned. This is shit you don't want online where someone could hack it."

He held out his hand and I dropped it down. "You told me that you'd find who used your name to manipulate my father. That's giving you the real culprits."

"Culprits? I found the person who used my name. The same person who planted her brother in the same school as your daughter." He held up the thumb drive. "Why are you giving me this? I'm aware that someone put Sabrina Brickshire in the hospital. She's recovering from a stabbing, I believe? Nasty injury. An inch over and she would've nicked something vital." He stared at me, a blank wall that gave me nothing. "Pity."

"That's my wife's sister."

"Your wife's sister who plotted and was successful in manipulating your own father's suicide. There's no love lost. You can't tell me you'd rather the girl was dead."

He was a wall, but so was I. I stared at him, knowing he was looking for something inside of me. I gave him nothing. "My wife has a bleeding heart."

That got my first reaction from him. The end of his mouth twisted up. A hint of dark amusement showed before all of it was gone. "I'm sure."

Gritting my teeth, I kept with the business at hand. "A secret society that goes by the name of The System considers you a threat. One of the founding members is also a past enemy of mine. My wife and I had a hand in putting him in prison, along with destroying the secret society that preceded this new one. They're the ones who used your name against my father."

Maddy stabbed Sabrina only a few days ago. Garrett just arrived at Fallen Crest, being there to help in the future care for his second daughter. An agreement was made that we wouldn't go to the police as long as she would be committed to a certain deconditioning facility. We'd done our research. I'd gone to Zeke to ask for his assistance in verifying that this particular facility did what they said they did. That there was no secret abuse happening. That the reputation truly was stellar, which the facility broadcasted as their company line.

It was. Zeke validated everything.

After my meeting with Zeke, and after I needed to give him enough information about The System and why we needed Sabrina's treatment to be hush-hush, he'd taken the initiative to look into the secret society. The amount of information he unearthed on the members was astounding.

He handed it over to me, on that thumb drive, and told me to use it as collateral.

I'd asked him at the time, "Why are you giving me this?"

"It's my apology. To you. To your family. For bringing Kai

Bennett to you personally." A darker emotion flickered over his face. His mouth strained before he shoved it away. "It took me a while to understand why you tortured me, but I understand now."

"I wanted to make sure I got the real truth from you. If I'd just asked, I couldn't know if it was true or if you were telling me what I wanted to hear. You stalked me and my family. You crossed the line of normal boundaries and because we don't know you, it made us uneasy. We have a right to feel that way."

His entire face flinched before he shut that down. He spoke, monotone, "You tortured me to break me. You wanted to destroy the image I had of you." His jaw clenched. "It worked, but I don't think it worked in the way you wanted. I see the real you now. I see the darkness inside of you. So yeah. In a way, the torture achieved what you wanted, but it also didn't. I know now what you're capable of doing."

The way he was looking at me, I didn't think I'd need to worry anymore about stalking. I was choosing to focus on the matter at hand. "This is for Kai Bennett?"

He clipped his head in a nod. "Yes." So brisk.

He was business-oriented. Professional. My brother cared about the guy. I had to hurt him to push him back, but how he was currently treating me was how it should've been from the start. Where we were strangers because we didn't know each other.

We were starting on the first line again. Where we went from here, who knew but I felt that he'd proceed with caution. Just like I always fucking did.

I said to Kai now, "It's a gift from the hacker, and an apology for going where he shouldn't have gone."

I had a feeling I amused him, but there was no reaction from him. There was no reason to give me that feeling. None-theless, I still felt like I had.

He put the thumb drive in his pocket. "We'll go through it. I'm assuming you're hoping I'll go after whoever's on here in place of seeking retribution against your wife's little sister?"

The casual way he said all of that put me on edge. "They're the real threat. Not a brainwashed little girl."

A hint of a grin appeared again, but faded just as quick. "Don't insult my intelligence, Mason. I'm quite aware how dangerous that 'little girl' is, along with the other one you're really protecting."

My body went cold.

He studied me again. The wall he kept in place fell away, but it only showed a sense of curiosity more than anything else. "You didn't have to lie, say the thumb drive was an apology from your hacker. I'm assuming it was actually meant to be an apology to you, not me. He already sent an apology. If you speak to your hacker, you can tell him that my wife appreciated the information he sent our way. The people she worked with do good in this world. He helped them a great deal. Though, if your hacker *ever* invades any account that belongs to my family in the future, I might not kill him as quickly as I would've before, but I won't hesitate to send the FBI to his front doorstep. I don't think Mrs. Allen would appreciate that." He dipped his head to me. "With that said, have a good life, Mason. It seemed you had a good father. I am sorry for how he passed away."

I felt off-balance, learning that he knew Zeke's identity, but his guard opened the back door.

He dipped inside, and the three SUVs pulled away just as smooth as they arrived.

I wanted to destroy who helped take my father away. I was doing it how I could, with the options given to me.

I did that. I gave a criminal lord the information on who helped to hurt my family.

In a way, the gun they helped load and put in my father's

hands, I simply turned it around and gave it to a bigger monster than them.

I was okay with what I just did.

57

MADDY

A few days later. Again.

M ax was here.

There was no chill.

None. The chill had left the building, because I know he didn't think I saw him, but I did. An arm came down around my shoulders as a body pressed against my side where I was leaning against my locker. "What's up?"

I didn't look, already knowing it was Traine. I reached up, lacing my fingers with the hand that hung over my side. He squeezed me back. "Max is in the office."

He tensed. "Wait. What?"

I was breathless. I was so excited. "He's transferring here."

Angling his head so he could read my face better, he arched an eyebrow. "No shit?"

I was so happy. "No shit. He doesn't think I know today's the day he's transferring, but I do. I overhead the entire conversation he had with his parents and mine. Come Monday, he's an official Fallen Crest Academy student."

"Shit. We still have football. He should play. He kicks literal ass."

I wrinkled my nose at him. "He's mine first."

Beltraine relaxed back against my side, giving me a fond half-grin. "Maxie boy is always going be yours first, and the same the other way around. We're cool with that."

"Yo." Steele and Axel joined us.

Steele tipped his chin up while Axel gave us a half-hearted wave with his book.

The other students automatically moved for them. It was so ingrained in them and us, that I almost didn't even notice anymore. We got looks too. There were always others watching us. Other girls. Guys eyeing me. Guys eyeing the guys. We drew attention. It was just part of the deal now of going to school here. Max would be included in that soon, not that he wouldn't by himself because it was Max. Everyone was going to be as obsessed with him as I was.

Which, come to think of it, I wasn't okay with that.

The last bell just rang, but I'd snuck out of class early because I wanted to see Max going into the office. The plan had been to surprise me, but well; that was hard to do with me.

I had my ways.

He'd been pissed at me for drugging him, but *furious* because he hadn't been able to be there for me when I stuck my half-aunt in the tummy. There'd been an entire discussion about my behavior. My parents were alarmed. Like, hella alarmed. Max's parents were just as concerned, if not more because what were they going to do if they decided I couldn't see their son? Talk about waving a red flag in front of a bull. I would've declared war the size of a small country on Heather and Channing if they tried to take Max away. It'd be a different story if Max himself decided that was it. Drugging him was the final straw. I'd have to respect his wishes, but it would've killed a part of my soul.

I still would've done it.

I messed up. I got that. I really did. (With drugging Max, not with anything else.)

But even with the other stuff, it worked out.

Everyone rallied for me. I wasn't sure if they should've. I mean, I did stab a person, but she needed to be stopped. I'd done that. She was gone now. Her parents flew in. I officially re-met my grandfather. The whole re-meeting Grandpa Garrett again was weird. It'd been awkward. Nolan and Nash were confused as well, but Mom seemed happy to see him. That's all that was important.

They left the next morning to take Brinna to Switzerland. That's where the facility was located, the one that was supposed to help her.

I'd been giving my parents the side-eye lately because if they started getting ideas, I had a plan. So far, they'd not said anything about shipping me off. They were just the *ultra* heli-copter parents. Watching me. Telling me they loved me, but also, what was I doing? Where was I going? Like I didn't know they would increase the Parental Maddy Watch Program.

I even understood it.

But I'd been good. I really had. Course, it'd only been a week but I had no intentions to use my tendencies for bad. Only good. Protecting my loved ones, if I could do something that others couldn't, sign me up.

That included these three guys because all of them covered for me.

Even Steele, who was technically my uncle? Half-uncle?

I gave him a look, and he noticed. "What?"

I didn't answer.

Traine started laughing. "She's trying to figure out the family connection again."

"Oh." Steele cringed. "Let it go, Mads. We're related. Just leave it at that. We got our whole lives to deal with that shit."

That made me happy because he was right.

The office door opened, and I straightened away from the locker. My heart was thumping in my chest, so hard.

Max came out and stopped, seeing me. He gave me the cutest grin before shaking his head. "I should've just known you'd know."

I launched myself at him.

Max caught me, with ease and that was hot. One of his arms curved around my back, keeping me in place, and he held the other out behind me. "Hey, man." He was doing his fist-greeting thing he'd started with my friends. "Yo. Hey. How's it going?" I couldn't decipher who the last two were for, but it didn't matter.

I was just so happy.

This was part of the Parental Maddy Watch Program. They'd discussed if I should transfer to Fallen Crest Public, but the general consensus was that I would get in more trouble there considering the students were rougher? I probably would've loved going there, but Max agreed with coming here instead. The parentals also sat down with the three guys behind me.

Steele moved into the house. That'd been an automatic, but Beltraine and Axel were given the option if they wanted to also move into our house.

Both agreed immediately.

They were transfixed with my parents. Both of them, which I got too. My mom and dad both fought for them, each one of them. My parents had a special conversation with the twins, making sure both of them were okay with the guys living with us for a year. Though, we all knew it wouldn't be for just the year.

They'd go away to college, but when they came back, they'd come to our home. Thanksgiving. Christmas. Easter. Draft Day. All the major holidays, they'd be at our house.

I'd been concerned because I didn't know if I wanted them

in the house, not around Nolan and my little brother. But Nash was already the top guy in his class. I didn't need to be worried about him. It was more Nolan, but my little sister reassured me everything would be fine.

When she gave me *the look*, I knew not to question it. She knew in the special way she knew things. So if the twins were good, I was good.

We'd unofficially adopted three more kids.

"What's up, Stevie? How's it going."

I tensed, hearing Max greeting another girl. A deep possessive churning swirled in my chest.

Max was mine. He wasn't allowed to have female friends, or talk to other girls, or look at other girls.

Okay, okay. I needed to bring back the chill.

I eased down to the ground, and Max threw me a frown, but he let me go. Stevie stopped at her locker, which I forgot was in this area. She opened it, casting a wary glance at me and the others behind us. "Hey, Max. How's it going with you? You headed to Cieran's this weekend?"

Max stayed by my side, but he answered her. "The fighting shed got shut down."

"What?"

"Yeah. It burned down last weekend."

I could *feel* the looks the guys were giving each other behind me.

"You're kidding?"

"Nope."

Stevie stared at him, a blank expression on her face. She was caught off guard by the news. "That's horri—"

"What are *you* doing *here*?" Aurelia Avoy's snide question cut Stevie off, who immediately schooled her features. The momentary surprise was gone and her whole face was blank.

Aurelia put her hands on her hips, facing off against Stevie.

Her head angled to the side. "I asked you a question. Answer me."

Stevie didn't even blink. She just shut down. "Nothing." Her gaze met Max's and her eyebrows furrowed, but she shook her head. "It's nothing. Cool to see you again, Monroe. See you around."

Aurelia cast the guys a look, some mean shining from her eyes. Her mouth lifted up in a cocky smirk.

I was moving without thinking about it, but as Stevie shut her locker, she began to turn toward the parking lot. She put her foot forward, and Aurelia tossed her bag in her way. Stevie hit the bag, tripping, and she fell down.

Or she would've.

Aurelia tossed her bag, but two things happened before that happened.

I reached for Aurelia's hair and yanked her backward, and as she let her bag loose, Max plucked it out of the air. He swung it around before he got a better hold of it.

"Damn!" Beltraine whooped behind us.

A few others made sounds of surprise because everything happened so fast, so seamlessly, it was as if Max and I had been doing things like that all the time. Which, I guess we had.

Stevie braked abruptly, blinking a few times because her brain needed to catch up with her body. Nothing happened. She was still standing. She hadn't tripped. All was good.

"What the fuck?" Aurelia shrieked.

I let her go, but I only stepped in front of her. I was now face to face with Stevie.

I smiled.

She gave me another alarmed look.

That made me frown because I'd never done anything to her. "Hi."

"Uh, Maddy..." Max sidled to my side.

One of the guys snorted. Another one began snickering. Or the same one. I wasn't sure.

"Shut it, man." That was Beltraine.

He always stood up for me. I puffed my chest up, but I was here for a reason. I cleared my throat. That seemed to make Stevie even more alarmed.

I deflated. "Jesus. I'm not a monster."

More than one of the guys coughed behind me. I gave them a middle finger, which made them break out into laughter. Others were joining in. We were attracting an audience.

Max wasn't laughing. He was regarding me with caution.

I ignored him, instead saying to Stevie, "My parents are throwing a birthday party for me this weekend. It's at the house on Sunday. You should come."

Aurelia scoffed from the sidelines.

I cast her a warning. "You're *not* invited."

Her face twisted up, but she stormed away.

Stevie watched her go, unable to hide her worry.

"Look, whatever. Come if you want. It's a family thing and after last weekend, your uncle is basically family now."

"What happened last weekend?"

"Nothing," Max said quickly, inserting himself into the conversation. He put his arm around my shoulders, tugging me against him. "We're also having an unofficial birthday party for Mads at Bell's house."

"That's right. We're still using it for parties." Beltraine stepped up.

Steele joined beside Beltraine.

Axel was to Max's left. He flicked up two fingers to Stevie. "It'd be cool if you joined. It's after the football game. We'll be at the Sunday event too." He winked at her.

Stevie floundered, momentarily unable to say something back, but I'd extended the invitation. If she came, she came. If she didn't, then that was on her. As if we were all one being, the five of us began walking for the parking lot. Max's arm dropped from my shoulder, but he tucked his finger in the back of my pants, keeping me next to him.

Which I loved. I really loved.

Axel groaned. "We should've made a rule no dating within the group. Watching you two is going to get old."

Traine laughed. "Speak for yourself. This is like constant foreplay happening live and in person. I'm going to have so much sex watching them."

"Seriously, you guys!" Steele snapped. "Her mom is my sister."

A guy going the opposite direction overheard him and stopped in his tracks. "Her mom is your what?"

Steele cursed. "Nothing. We're just—we're cousins. Move along." He glared at the guy, who blanched and sped away. He looked over his shoulder a few times, but no one was going after him.

I grinned at Steele. "Cousins, huh?"

He rolled his eyes, but he didn't respond.

The others laughed, and I moved closer to Max, making our sides brush against each other.

His eyes darkened, watching me back.

I got all happy inside, all warm, all giddy.

I *loved* that we moved to Fallen Crest.

As we got to the door, it swung open. I frowned at seeing who was coming inside. "Uncle Mark?" Technically he was my mom's stepbrother, but for all intents and purposes, he was Uncle Mark.

Steele stiffened, throwing a dark look at him.

"Oh hey, Maddy." He saw Max and did a double-take. "Max. What are you doing here?"

"Transferred in. I'm going to school here now."

"What? When?"

"Just transferred. First day is Monday." Max was studying

the bouquet of roses my uncle was holding in his hand. "Got a study date?"

Mark was still frowning at Max, and at how close we were standing. At Max's question, his face cleared before he jerked the flowers up. "Oh. Right! I forgot. Uh. No. No study date, but a date. I'm here to see..." He caught himself, taking note of my sudden attention, his gaze sliding to a few other students how they stopped to eavesdrop. "Never mind. I'm just here getting to know someone. Not anyone for you to cyberstalk or tell your mother about." He rethought that, adding to Max, "Or your mother." Back to me. "Or my mother. Got that. Keep this between us."

Steele shook his head. "Yeah. That's one way to stop the gossip in its tracks. Good luck, dude."

I asked, "So you and Cass are really done, huh?"

Uncle Mark softened. "It's for the best. If we were supposed to be together, we would've made it work a long time ago. I, just, I got comfortable. It's all on me, but if you're attached to Cass, I don't think you should worry. Rumor has it that she's on a plane to Hawaii as I speak. I don't think she's going to be leaving the adult group chat any time soon, if you get what I mean." He pressed a quick kiss to my forehead. "Love you, Mads. Don't tell any of your mothers about this. Thanks. Gotta go."

Me, I couldn't move. He just dropped the bomb of all bombs on me. My mouth was on the floor. "There's an *adult group chat*?"

58

MASON

It was Maddy's birthday and the house was full.

Though Sam enjoyed having the house full. She used to not be like this, but I knew she wanted to surround herself and everyone else with as much love as possible. She was making our home the opposite of what she grew up with Analise.

We were in the backyard.

The dogs thought the party was for them. Their tails were wagging. Tongues hanging out of their mouths. Nolan took over caring for the dogs and petitioned hard for them to be allowed to run free with the festivities today. It was Maddy's birthday, but Maddy tended to be a pushover for whatever her siblings wanted so Maddy was okay with the dogs running loose. Each of the German Shepherds were giving their ball out to anyone who'd toss it for them. Nolan persuaded us to let her start fostering so we had a new dog darting around as well. Gus. He was smaller, golden fur, and he enjoyed herding people. Nolan thought it was the funniest thing. I knew Nash helped her with the dogs. The rest of us would help, but Nolan seemed to want to shoulder the responsibility for them. I was assuming she was gearing up for some big ask down the line, but until then, she was doing a great job. The newest foster dog kept getting distracted when he would run for his ball. If someone tossed it where he'd have to run past the pool, he would jump in.

Ball. Ball. Pool! What ball? Splash.

Nolan melted every time it happened, and seeing the soft smile on her face, I had a feeling that dog wasn't going to be a foster soon. Gus was going to be adopted.

By us.

The kids were in the pool, doing as many cannonballs as possible. They were good with Gus swimming around everyone. No one left the pool shrieking. Yet.

Maddy never went far from Max's side. She was a little clingier than normal, some part of her body was always touching his. I stared at them, long and hard, not sure if I should step in or not.

I wasn't the only one noticing.

Channing and Heather arrived a few hours ago. Heather headed inside where Sam was, but Channing grabbed a beer and joined Logan and I at the table.

"Cannonball!" Axel yelled out, launching in the air before he hit the middle of the pool. Some of the other girls squealed. Turned out that Maddy did have female friends. The girl Maddy originally introduced as her friend arrived with an entire entourage accompanying her. Lucia was her name, if I was remembering it correctly. I was confused who Maddy's real friends were. I knew the trio: Axel, Steele, and Beltraine were solid with her. Max seemed to be included in that group as well, not like anyone was going to tell Maddy that Max couldn't be there.

She seemed to be enjoying the new group of friends who arrived.

Sam stepped out to check on everyone, saw Lucia and the new arrivals, watched Maddy laugh with them, and she relaxed. A faint smile pulled at her mouth. She met my gaze, a message passing between the two of us. She was worried.

Fuck. So was I.

Was Maddy only friends with guys? I didn't know how that would work out for our daughter, but I was also learning the truth of the situation was that we didn't need to worry about Maddy getting hurt. We had an appointment scheduled next week to talk with a psychiatrist. We wouldn't be only talking to him. Sam was adamant we'd be shopping around. Psychologist. Counselor. Social worker. She wanted to talk to a whole bunch of people, even mentioning reaching out to some intuitive people as well. When I asked who those people were, she explained they were people with similar gifts as Nolan.

I had a feeling it'd be a while before we found the right person or persons who could help us with Maddy. Maybe a specialist who worked with sociopaths?

"Nate's here," Logan remarked, kicking out a chair as Nate was winding through the party, heading our way.

"Uncle Nate!" Maddy shouted from the pool. She had a hand on Max's shoulder and jumped up, right fucking in front of him, her other hand stretched in the air, waving.

I loved seeing the bright smile on her face, but fuck. Seriously. She was launching herself right in Max's face, wearing that bikini both her and Sam insisted was fine to wear. I grunted.

Channing wore a slight grimace too.

I cut him a look. We'd talked about the two of them as a couple, because it was obvious that's what they either already were, or would be soon. A part of me worried they'd be concerned their son was my daughter's point of obsession.

Shit. Situation reversed, and I'd be worried.

So far neither raised the topic of getting some distance between the two. If they did, and again, I couldn't blame them, we'd figure things out then. But I couldn't bring it up now because Nate was at our table.

Everyone stood up, greeting him.

Logan hugged him first, pounding on his back. "Good to fucking see you, man. Couldn't stay away, huh? Where's your turtle?"

"Fuck you. Harold is at the rescue shelter. Thankfully." Nate grinned, cupping the back of his neck before moving to return Channing's hug. "You expect me to stay away? After all the shit that happened last weekend? We love being near Quincey's family, but I have to admit that I started considering moving back for the first time in a while. Had some real FOMO. Hey, buddy." He clasped Channing's shoulder, then moved to me.

I pulled him close for a hug.

I'd called him the day after everything happened, and filled him in. He'd been concerned. We texted and called daily. That was our norm, but it was more this last week.

Logan. Channing. Nate. They were all there for me.

He stepped back, considered me. There was the same unspoken question in his gaze that he'd asked me every day. *Was I okay?* I gave him a nod, and he grinned before he moved to sit in the chair across from me. Channing was on one side. Logan on the other. Nate took the seat by Channing so he had a better view of the backyard.

"You want a beer?" I asked before sitting.

"Uh." He began to look around. "Sure. Yeah."

Logan pushed up from his seat. "I got it."

"Logan," I started to say.

He was already heading for the cooler, and waved me off, shooting me a small frown. "I'm good. Monroe? Beer?"

Channing had returned to watching Maddy and Max but raised his empty beer in the air. "Please." His eyes never left our kids.

Nate noticed, his eyes jumping to me as I took my seat

again. "How, uh," Nate started. "How's that going?"

It took a little bit before Channing realized the question wasn't for me.

He jerked his head to him, sitting up straighter. "Me?" He cast me a glance, rubbing a hand over his face. I saw the shadows there. He was concerned, more than he'd expressed to me.

I tipped my chin to him. "You can be honest. She is my kid, but I'm not blind."

He still hesitated before shrugging. "I don't think it matters what any of us think. Your kid shows her obsession more, but trust me, Max is just as fixated on Maddy."

I leaned forward, needing to know. "Chan."

He looked my way. Held my gaze.

"Do you want them to back off?"

He considered my question for a beat before saying anything. When he spoke, his forehead tipped forward a little. "Am I concerned about how tight they are at this age? Fuck yes. Am I getting alarms to the point where I think we need to move in and do something about it? Honestly, no."

Some of my tension eased in my chest.

"It'd be different if Max wasn't all in too. Though, I don't think Maddy would be as obsessed if he wasn't. It's both of them and if it came down to it, if we put our foot down and insisted they don't get as serious as they are, I think the problem wouldn't be your kid. It'd be Max. Maddy shows her heart on her sleeve. She's almost proud of it. Max keeps it contained inside of him. They counter each other out, and fuck, like I can talk about childhood sweethearts." He looked in the direction Heather and Sam were now coming from the house.

They weren't alone. Brett Broudou, his wife, and his niece were also in attendance.

"Stevie!" Maddy saw them at the same time, waving. She pushed off of Max, swam to the edge, and pulled herself up.

Steele was there, handing her a towel. When it wasn't big enough to completely cover her, he snatched it away with a scowl, and shoved a blanket at her instead. She laughed at him, but held the blanket wrapped around her. She made her way over to Stevie, smiling politely at Brett and his wife before tugging Stevie in the direction of the food and beverages.

"That's new," Logan noted, returning at that time with two beers. He handed one to Nate, one to Channing, and placed the other items in his hand on the table. Two glasses and a bottle of bourbon.

He winked at me before pouring one for me, one for him.

Brett found us by then.

Logan held up the bottle. "You want to join? Or do you want a beer?"

Brett hesitated, before his face cleared and he shook his head. "I'm good for now. I might grab a beer later."

I'd gone back to watching Maddy as she and Stevie were filling up their plates with food. Maddy looked to be talking her ear off. I couldn't tell how Brett's niece felt about that.

I indicated them. "Did she want to come today?"

He twisted in his seat so he could see them as well. "She did. She's the one who brought it up, said your kid extended an invite."

"What's your read on the situation?"

He shrugged. "Stevie's been through shit, a lot of shit. She's always going to be cautious, but her being here says a lot." His eyes flicked in Channing's direction. "She likes your kid. Says she trusts him. Stevie doesn't trust so I think that's also part of the reason she's here."

Channing smirked, lifting his beer for a drink. "Everyone trusts Max. Everyone loves Max. Only a few actually know him. It's how he wants it."

Nate met my gaze, frowning a little, but there was also amusement on his face too.

"We're moving back."

All eyes jerked to Logan. He puffed his chest up, raising his glass.

I already knew. He told me that he'd made the decision after he arrived on the night from hell but needed to talk it over with Taylor before saying anything. She agreed with the move, said it felt right to return. They wanted Sammy to grow up with his cousins, along with their new kid. Said they wanted Malinda to spoil their kids too so no favoritism happened.

He made the announcement over dinner last night to the family as well. The kids were over the moon, but especially Nash which had surprised me. I knew Logan and Maddy were close. She had his name, for fuck's sakes, but Nash blinked back tears before he moved to hug his uncle Logan. He came over to my side right after and leaned against me.

Nash and Nolan were quiet, well-behaved, but my kid was going to be something else. I could tell. He dressed for varsity on Friday and played most of the game, scoring two of the four touchdowns.

The crowd was enamored, but there were rumblings among the parents in the stands. Logan glared at every adult sitting around us as if silently challenging them if they had something to say, they were welcome to say it to our faces.

That fight would come, but it wasn't one I was concerned about.

I did ask Nash how the other guys on the team were handling his presence. He rolled his eyes, shrugged, and only said, "No one's going to say shit, Dad. Not with Traine, Axe, and Steele on the team. They're setting the tone, but I'd handle it if they didn't. Everyone's scared of Maddy too." He left it at that, but I could read into my kid.

Maddy wasn't the only kid of mine who could handle themselves. She was just the one who got caught.

I had a feeling my twins weren't the easygoing angels they

presented, not that I could say anything. I loved my kids. They had more good in them than I did.

They got it from their mother.

"Is that Mark? Who's that with him?"

Sam's stepbrother walked into the backyard, holding hands with a young woman.

Sam and Heather perked up and were at his side right away, but it was the kids who had the biggest reactions.

"No way!" one of the teenagers exclaimed. I had no idea their name. "Mrs. Kline?"

The young woman stiffened, a smile fixed on her face. "It's Ms. Kline, Clayton. And we don't need to stick with the last names out of school. You can call me Tatum today."

Beltraine remarked, "That must've been some study date."

Axel laughed. "Yeah. What happened to, 'don't tell your mothers'?"

They laughed. Maddy shot 'em a grin over her shoulder.

The other kid snorted. "I don't think your boyfriend's going to want all of us to start calling you Tatum. He already looks all territorial, Ms. Kline."

She tensed, but Mark pulled her to his side and pretended to growl. "That's right. As long as you know your place, kid." He winked at the group, who laughed.

One of those same kids walked by later, saying to his friend, "I cannot believe Maddy's uncle landed the hottest teacher from school. What's in their DNA, man? All of 'em just score, like literally. All the time."

I shared a look with the table because everyone heard.

Logan snickered. "Wait till my kids get here. Fallen Crest will never be the same."

I had to agree.

I was suddenly thankful we moved back.

It felt right.

We were home.

EPILOGUE
MASON

A month later.

My phone buzzed right as I walked into the bedroom.

Garrett: The most ironic chain of events happened today.

I paused but was already grinning because I saw the news.

Me: Oh yeah?

Garrett: Nearly every member of The System was either raided by the FBI, arrested by their local authorities, voted out of their company, or their company's stock plummeted. All of that happened today. Every single member, except for myself.

My grin widened. I'd enjoyed the news footage of the different members in handcuffs being led to police cruisers outside.

Me: That's quite a coincidence.

Garrett: Is it?

Sam came out of the bathroom, running her fingers

through her hair. She'd just taken a shower, and seeing the way her tank top clung to her body, and how those tiny sleep shorts of hers rode even higher than normal against her damp thighs, my dick was hard. All the way hard.

She paused, seeing me standing in the middle of the room on my phone. "Who is it?"

I didn't want to lose my hard on so I didn't mention it was her dad. That would make her remember her deranged sister, and then guilt would flash across her face. Her eyes would go sad, and the lines around her mouth would tighten.

"Just getting some news."

"Oh." She crossed the room, coming to me. She pressed a hand to my chest and reached up on her toes. She brushed a kiss to my lips. I wanted to chase those lips as she stepped back, but I wanted to finish this text conversation first. Get it out of the way. "Good news?" She went to check her own phone, frowning at it.

Me: Are you accusing me of something?

I said to her, "Karma's always good news."

Her head lifted back up. "What?"

Garrett: Did you do this?

"One second. Let me finish this up."

Me: No.

Garrett: Do you know who did this?

A different number flashed across my screen. I clicked on the new text.

Unknown: Channel 8. Now. Scrolling news.

I frowned but went to pick up our television's remote. Turning it on then clicking to the channel they said, I waited; it was the evening news.

Sam gasped, seeing it first. "What?" She stepped toward the television without thought. Her eyes were wide and her mouth parted.

Then I saw it and stilled.

The grandson of deceased business tycoon Gerald Sebastian was found dead in his cell where he was an inmate in the Potomahmen prison. Parker Sebastian sustained multiple stab wounds. Authorities are investigating. So far, no answers have been given from prison officials. This story is still developing.

"No." Sam swung her eyes my way, filled with wonder. Shock. "How'd you know?" Her gaze fell to my phone and understanding clicked. She straightened upright. "Who just texted you?"

I showed her the phone. "I don't know."

She read the text, then clicked out of the message and saw her dad's name just underneath the unknown number. She tapped on his name and read through those texts. As a different sort of tension filled the room, she didn't say a word. Not for a few seconds. Then she powered down my phone and put it aside.

She held my gaze.

A deeper understanding was there.

Sam knew I did something.

I told her that her father was in the clear to come to us, to collect her sister, to continue to be in contact with Samantha. I never told her what I did, and Sam never asked.

Then she did. "Do I need to know?"

She reached for the remote and turned the television off, returning the remote to the bedside stand. She stepped close to me, so close I could feel the heat from her shower still coming off of her skin. Her hand moved to my chest and stayed, her fingers splayed out.

I looked down, seeing the butterfly tattoo on her hand. She had the color retouched recently.

I took her hand, slid my fingers through hers, and gazed where my black and white butterfly tattoo lined up with hers. I tugged her into me, catching her behind her back. "I gave

someone some information. What they did with the information is on them. That's all you need to know."

"Am I going to regret not pushing to know everything?"

I bent before I straightened again, picking her up as I did.

There was no squeak from surprise. Sam knew my move
and her eyes darkened, knowing I was going to do it before I
did. Her hands went to my shoulders. She kept her body loose,
relaxed, and as I picked her up, her legs parted to wind around
my waist. She ran her fingers through my hair, a half scoff
coming from her mouth when I walked her right back into the
bathroom. "I just showered."

"That's nice." I nuzzled her neck, finding her pulse and
lingering there. I fucking loved leaving my mark on my woman.
My phone was out there, so was hers. I had nothing else on me,
so after I turned the water back on and since it didn't take long
to reheat, I simply walked us both inside the shower.

My mouth found hers and I was hot and demanding.

I needed to fuck my wife.

I needed it five minutes ago, yesterday, a month ago. I
needed it now. "You're not going to regret not knowing everything." I lifted my head, needing her to know the truth of that.
My eyes held hers. "I promise."

She held my gaze before her eyes fell to my mouth. She
jerked her head in a nod. "Okay."

"I love you." My forehead fell to hers, jerking back so it
rested against her softly.

She breathed me in, her body molding against mine on her
exhale. "Me too."

"So goddamn much."

Her hand tightened around mine. "So goddamn much."

Months later.

MY PHONE WOKE US FIRST.

Sam's was right after.

We both tensed but rolled to answer them.

I got to mine first. "What?"

It was Logan on the other end, half shouting, all the way frantic. "Taylor's in labor! You need to get to the hospital. Bring —fuck. I don't know. Bring everything. Her water already broke and we're going to have our kid in point-zero-too-fucks-early!"

I heard Sam yelp behind me.

We were both scrambling out of bed.

It was three in the morning. Sam ran for the closet. I heard her saying, "Okay. We'll be in the car soon. We'll come over and get everything you need. I'll call Malinda myself. Do you have Sammy with you?"

I pulled on my sweats and grabbed an Orcas's hoodie, tugging it over my head. I asked in the phone, "What do you—"

He snapped, "I don't fucking know! I was a mess when Sammy was born, and fuck, Mase. I'm a mess this time too. Taylor's on the phone with someone and she sounds as if she's planning the agenda for the next PTA meeting. Are you coming to the hospital? You're coming to the hospital, right?"

"Of course. And she's on the phone with Sam."

"What? We *both* called you guys?"

"Yeah."

He cursed. "We both don't need to be calling you."

I waited, but he didn't end the call. "Logan, what do you need?"

He sighed. "I have no idea. I don't know what I'm doing, brother."

Brother.

The word made me feel happy, but also gave me a tinge of worry. My little brother was losing it.

"Hey," I said, low and calm.

"Hey back?" He laughed at himself.

I grinned, but spoke in the same tone, low, reassuring. "Sam and I will handle anything you need. Okay? She's on the phone with Malinda. I can hear her in the closet. She's calling Malinda to come over and watch Sammy. You moved in next door. That was a smart move on your part, renting that place while your other house is built. She'll be there by the time you get off this call. She'll help put together whatever you need. We had things packed and ready to go by the door when Maddy was born. Did you do that this time?"

"Fuck." He was so quiet, breathless, and panicky. "Yeah. Yeah, we did. Taylor did. Taylor?" He said to me, "I gotta go. I need to find my wife."

"Okay. You got this. Find your woman. Knowing Taylor, she's probably already let Malinda inside and is in your car waiting for you."

I heard sounds from his end, different voices talking.

He half laughed to me. "Malinda's here. I need to go."

"Do you have clothes on?"

"What?"

"Look down. Are you clothed? Can you go to the hospital in what you're wearing?"

He cursed under his breath. "I need pants. My fucking dick's out, all shriveled up too. Imagine me walking into the hospital like that? Even my own kid would've laughed at me." He sounded a little calmer now. Good.

"I doubt Taylor would've let you out of the house like that, but I'm sure Malinda's thankful not to see your dick."

He bit out another laugh. "I gotta go. Taylor's calling me. Totally useless here. Been on the phone with you while she called in the troops."

"Yeah. Calling in Malinda is sorta the same thing. You good now?"

"I'm good. Thank you. Love you."

"Love you."

"Oh, hey!"

"Yeah?"

"I'm having a kid."

My smile stretched, along with that pride for my brother. "I'm having another nephew or niece."

He laughed again before saying, "See you at the hospital."

The call ended and I lifted my head. Sam was waiting for me in the doorway, all ready to go and with our own bag packed for whatever she thought Taylor and Logan would need and that they forgot to pack themselves. She grinned at me. "Ready? I woke Maddy up. She'll stay to watch the twins. The boys are all still asleep, but I left a note in the kitchen."

My little brother was having another kid. I tossed her the keys. "You're driving. I'm going to enjoy waking everyone up."

And I did.

Nate.

Channing and Heather.

Matteo.

Even Zeke.

An hour later, the door opened and in walked all three of the kids, along with Steele, Beltraine, and Axel. Max came in with them, even though his parents arrived earlier. Either he went to them at our place or they went to him. Whichever way, seeing the four of them together wasn't a surprise anymore. They were a unit.

TEN MINUTES LATER, my goddaughter was born.

Maya Maysen Kade.

ANOTHER EPILOGUE
MADDY

A year and months later.

I t's World Domination Day.

Or, as more common people would say, move-in day at Cain University.

I studied the other girls on my floor when we arrived. They were excited, but nervous. The dorm advisor met with us, going through all the information I needed to know. My key. My roommate's information. A map of the university. Where to go for registration. There was freshman orientation, but as soon as my parents were gone, I already knew I was going to skip.

Max drove separately to help me move in, and the guys were coming over to help as well. Steele, Axel, and Beltraine. They were sophomores this year so they were living in the house my parents owned. I didn't know if they were renting, but I was sure my parents were giving them a deal. Not that they needed one. Each of those three guys were wealthy. I told my dad he should double his price. He just laughed at me.

"Hi." A girl was in the doorway, carrying a box. She entered the room and held her hand out to me. "I'm Havana. I think you're my roommate. Are you Logan Kade?"

Max snorted, unloading one of my boxes on my desk.

She looked his way, frowning, but then did a double take when she caught a better look at his face. Interest lit up her eyes, and her lips parted as she gave him a onceover. I couldn't blame her. He looked particularly edible, wearing his ragged and well-worn jeans and a black band shirt. With some added tattoos, one on his neck and another vine winding down around his arm, Max was looking beyond tasty.

I understood her attraction, but I didn't have to like it.

I moved to block her view, giving her a forced smile. "Logan's my first name, but I generally go by my middle name. Maddy. I used to spell it with a *y*, then decided to change it up and made everyone spell it with ie at the end. Since then, I've returned to my earlier years when I spell it M-A-D-D-Y." No one needed to hear any of my explanation, but I enjoyed giving it.

Max was laughing again. "Jesus, Mads. Give the girl a break."

I threw him a scowl over my shoulder before focusing on her again. "I took the left side of the room. I hope that's okay?" My dad jerked his head up and seeing the motion, I remembered what he offered earlier. "Or my dad can put the beds up in bunks so we can have more room? I don't care. This is my mom and dad."

I didn't introduce Max. He was mine.

"Oh. Uh." She was taking in everyone in the room.

The guys hadn't shown up yet, but they texted. They were on their way. Until then, it was my parents and Max. Nolan and Nash stayed behind, wanting to be with their friends. They were becoming normal, and were doing normal things like hanging out with friends.

Or that's how they were acting. I knew my brother and sister. There was nothing normal about us.

"That'd be great. Thanks." She gestured over her shoulder. "My dads are bringing up the rest of my stuff, but they mentioned something similar. About putting the beds all the way at the top?"

Voices were heard coming down the hallway, and I recognized them.

Beltraine appeared first, stopping behind Havana, who was staring up at him, slack-jawed.

He barely gave her a glance before stepping past, a lazy grin on his face. "Yo!" He tossed me a smirk and head-lift but headed for my parents first.

I got it. I wasn't insulted.

We had the rest of the night to hang out, but since the guys moved in with us, they had this thing with my parents. Adoration. They cared about my mom and dad, and it was reciprocated.

"Traine." My mom got to him first, hugging him. She would gush over him for a little bit. He and the others. Then they'd move to give my dad a hug, who would ask how they're doing. Do they need anything? Etc. My parents would take us to dinner before they would head back, but they hadn't just made the trip to bring me here. They came up to also check in with these guys. When everything was getting close to being done with my room, my mom was going to slip away and check out the house. She'd probably fill the place with food and check on their laundry. She enjoyed being a mom to them, and the guys preened under her attention. Steele had the most normal parents growing up, and his were hiding from a secret society cult so go figure. That said a lot for Axel and Traine.

Axel appeared next. Steele was right after him.

My roommate's jaw was officially on the floor.

More greetings were shared as everything happened that I

knew was going to happen, complete with some extra hugs Steele got from my mom. He got all flushed, but he loved it.

Havana was frowning, watching the exchange.

I motioned to them. "That's his big sister. Don't pay him any attention. He's been starved of attention from not having a normal big sister role model. His other one got stabbed—"

"Maddy!" Four different people shouted my name, with different varied emotions on each of their faces. Horror. Apprehension. Nervousness. My dad's eyes narrowed with that same concerned look he got when he thought I was going to let one of my sociopathic tendencies show.

It'd been way over a year and it'd been all-hands-on-deck with my "situation." I was doing a lot better and gave them all a cocky grin. "I was just going to say she's been overseas since she was assaulted." Different breaths of tension left each of them. I said to Havana, "I'm hoping she stays, but these two hope she'll heal and get better. To each their own."

She was blinking at me in confusion. "Wait." Her eyes narrowed, skirting between my mom and Steele. The question was forming, if my mom was his sister that would mean Steele was my—but at that moment, two guys showed in the doorway and stopped in their tracks.

They were big and burly. Tan. Tattoos. Both had their arms full of boxes and totes.

One dropped his items and his mouth fell open with it, his eyes bulging out at my dad. "You're–you–you," he sputtered out, slapping the guy next to him. "Honey, it's Mason Fucking Kade."

Another guy yelped down the hallway, probably another dad. "*What?*"

It was happening. News started to spread that the Kades arrived. Of course, the news was camouflaged first as to who my dad was. NFL Hall of Famer. Mason Kade. My dad had fans all over so I knew it'd hit social media. My mom had her own fans, and since we were at Cain University, I knew my uncle was well known. Or well feared, depending on who recognized his name. He wasn't exactly a wallflower.

It was my turn now. I was looking forward to everyone learning my name.

I was Maddy Fucking Kade.

Cain University was about to become my playground.

Thank you for reading Kade!
If you enjoyed, please leave a review.
They *really* do help a lot.

Join my newsletter here to keep updated,
www.tijansbooks.com

I fully never intended to write second generation books, but when I wrote this book, Maddy had so much to say that I'm unable to *not* write more of her story.
Her story will continue.
Stay tuned for the Cain University Series.

ACKNOWLEDGMENTS

I want to thank my agent! It was her idea for me to write Kade and title it as Kade. The idea was when all the paperbacks are together, Mason is at the front and Kade is at the end. Love it!

Thank you to all the readers who have continuously loved this world. I always thank you guys, but it's so very true. I would not be writing if it weren't for all your support.

Thank you to my editor, my beta readers, and my proofreaders.

Thank you to Crystal, Kelly, and Tami for all the help the three of you have given me behind the scenes. It's truly made a difference.

I truly hope that Kade was enjoyed. I know that I enjoyed writing everyone. I really loved writing Maddy, which surprised me. I never intended to write books for the children as they're older, but Maddy bowled me over with that decision. Her voice just kept chirping at me and once I began writing her POVs in the book, her voice just kept getting louder and louder. So thank you to Maddy herself as well!

And as always, thank you to my eleven-year-old pup Bailey. He's my constant.

ALSO BY TIJAN

Kess (short story)

Frisco (standalone)

Hot Biker Neighbor (novella)

If you wanted to read more about the Red Demon's history mentioned, check out:

The Boy I Grew Up With

Crew Princess

Always Crew

Series:

Broken and Screwed Series (YA/NA)

Jaded Series (YA/NA suspense)

Davy Harwood Series (paranormal)

Carter Reed Series (mafia)

The Insiders

Mafia Standalones:

Cole

Bennett Mafia

Jonah Bennett

Canary

Paranormal Standalones and Series:

Evil

Micaela's Big Bad

The Tracker

Davy Harwood Series (paranormal)

Young Adult Standalones:

Ryan's Bed

A Whole New Crowd

Brady Remington Landed Me in Jail

College Standalones:

Antistepbrother

Kian

Enemies

Contemporary Romances:

Bad Boy Brody

Home Tears

Fighter

Rockstar Romance Standalone:

Sustain

Christmas novellas:

A Kade Christmas

A Christmas Song (Ryan's Bed holiday novella)

More books to come!

PINE RIVER
CHAPTER ONE

C *reak!*

I opened my eyes to the sound of someone sneaking into the house.

I rolled over and checked the clock. Seven twenty-eight in the morning.

I knew who was sneaking in. It usually wasn't the parent creeping in at this time of day. I sighed and sat up. My mom was coming home from a double shift at Pine River Nursing Center. She was being the adult, doing all sorts of adult things the way she always did. She'd made the hard decision that what we'd had back in Cedra Valley was dunzo, and since we were in a situation where we needed family, off we went to Pine River. The population here was barely three thousand, which was the opposite of everything we were used to. My last school had that number of people just in my grade.

I got up, not fighting a yawn, and headed to the bathroom.

Washing. Putting on makeup—the whole ordeal.

Then came choosing my clothes, and since it was my first day at Pine River High School, I knew I needed to be smart about it. Clothes were important. Clothes made the first impression, and I didn't want too flashy. That was another lesson learned from this last year: Don't be flashy. Don't stick out. Don't be a target. But I wasn't a wallflower either. I wasn't a pushover.

Hmmm...

I went with tight black jeans, a textured gray short-sleeve tank that tied in the front with a red flannel shirt over it to cover my arms. My light gray high tops rounded out the outfit—oh, and long, black feather earrings.

There.

I was preppy, edgy, and cutesy, but also nothing on me stood out to put me in the pretty-girl clique. I was pushing toward fashionable tomboy, and that was more me than I'd ever been back in Cedra Valley.

It felt good.

It felt right.

I could pull this uniform off for a year—my last year, then it was off to college and WTFK (who the fuck knew).

I sighed and took one last look in the mirror.

I had dark brown hair, but my highlights gave me a tawny brown look. I kept it shoulder length so I could sweep it back and not worry about it.

Not that I had to since it never got flat. It never got frizzy. There was always a slight curl to it, and when it dried, it looked healthy and shiny. I had fan-fucking-tastic hair. That also meant I stayed away from product. I wasn't a dummy. I splurged with what money I had and bought the good stuff for shampoo. No conditioner. That was it. I kept it simple, but it worked for me.

I had almond-shaped dark eyes and a heart-shaped face—symmetrical. I'd been told that meant it was appealing to the eye. No bullshit, I had a face I could do almost anything with. Being confident in my looks wasn't my problem. I was confident, but not arrogant. There was a difference. My mama taught me to love my body, love my mind, and love my soul. I did all three, but that didn't mean everyone else did. Because of that, I was on a mission for no drama, no fighting, no targeting, no jealousy. *Blend* but not let anyone target me either.

Okay. My pep talk done, I nabbed my backpack and headed to the kitchen.

"Hey, sweetie," my mom called.

I left my bag in the hallway and rounded the corner. She was at the toaster, and I stopped for a moment and took her in. She was tired. She had the same hair as me, but she'd put hers up into a clip. She also didn't believe in makeup because, what was the purpose anymore? Her scrubs were baggy on her because she'd gone to the thrift store for those. She had good sneakers, though. She needed them since she was on her feet for sixteen hour shifts.

"Morning. Did you eat?" I asked as I helped myself to the coffee, knowing she'd brewed this pot for me.

"I did on my last break." She set my toast on a plate and put it on the counter.

After grabbing some creamer, I went over and sat, but I didn't stop eyeing my mom.

We were in an odd situation.

We had money, or we were supposed to have money. My dad's family was fighting for what he'd left us, so what money we had, we might just lose to the lawyers. Mom and I understood that, while we might have some nice things from our previous life, those could be the only nice things we'd have for the foreseeable future.

My mom had gotten an education, but she had never used her degree. She married my dad and did whatever housewives did. Back in Cedra Valley, that was a lot of volunteering, a lot of luncheons, a lot of shindig parties in the evening, and a lot of gossiping. To Mom's credit, she didn't partake in the gossip, but she was friends with those ladies because usually the bigger the gossip, the bigger the purse. My mom cared about giving back, so being friends with those types was a requirement.

Sucks that they turned on her after my dad died, but not only had my mom taught me to love my body, mind, and spirit but also she taught me to believe in karma. One day those hypocritical, self-righteous bitches would be ousted when their husbands wanted an upgrade that came in the form of a newer and younger version of them.

"Ramsay, are you ready for your first day?" Mom leaned back against the counter.

I had to grin. She was more nervous than I was. I took a bite of my toast and gestured to her. "You can chill, Mom. I'll be fine."

She let out a sigh. "A part of me knows you'll be fine. Your cousins are there, but the other part of me . . ." She gave me a sad smile. "You know I worry, honey."

Yeah. Because the last year almost took the life out of us.

I got real and lowered the mask a little. "I'll be fine, Mom. I mean it."

She eyed me for a moment and then nodded. I could see the relief come over her. Her head lifted, and the worry lines eased. They were replaced by exhausted lines instead, but one small victory at a time. Reassuring my mom so she could get some much-needed sleep? That was a victory I'd carry with me all day. Score one for myself.

She crossed the room. "Okay, sweetie." Cupping the back of my head, she pressed a kiss to my forehead. "I love you very much. Don't let Clint get you in trouble today, and I'll see you after school. Want me to pick you up?"

I shook my head, giving her a hug. "I'll be good, Mom. I promise. I might bike, give the car a rest."

She frowned, taking in my coffee and the piece of toast I still had left. "You're going to bike and carry your coffee?"

"I'm super talented. I can do many things at once."

She groaned, but chuckled. "I have no doubt. Just . . . be okay, okay?"

Be okay. The other mission I had for this year.

"I will." The words slipped out on a whisper. I hadn't meant for that to happen, but she looked even more relieved.

"Safe and smart." That was my motto.

Biking in Cedra Valley wouldn't have been safe and smart—too many interstates and bad neighborhoods. But Pine River? Totally safe. I'd visited my cousins so many times and they'd driven me through the town. If there were a bad part of town, it was isolated to one or two blocks. For the most part, this town seemed like the quintessential small town—everyone knew everyone. Everyone looked out for everyone.

Right?

I'd have to wait and see. I only knew my cousins here.

After pouring my coffee into a to-go cup, I finished my last slice of toast in four bites and took it with me. My mom was already upstairs, and she'd be out within a few minutes, or so I hoped. I locked the door behind me, making sure my phone was in my bag.

I grabbed my bike and headed out.

Keep reading Pine River here.